The Junior Classics

A · LIBRARY · FOR BOYS · AND · GIRLS

P. F. Collier & Son Company
New York

THE
JUNIOR CLASSICS

SELECTED AND ARRANGED BY
WILLIAM PATTEN
MANAGING EDITOR OF THE HARVARD CLASSICS

INTRODUCTION BY
CHARLES W. ELIOT, LL. D.
PRESIDENT EMERITUS OF HARVARD UNIVERSITY

WITH A READING GUIDE BY
WILLIAM ALLAN NEILSON, Ph. D.
PROFESSOR OF ENGLISH, HARVARD UNIVERSITY
PRESIDENT SMITH COLLEGE, NORTHAMPTON, MASS., SINCE 1917

VOLUME TWO

Folk Tales and Myths

P. F. COLLIER & SON COMPANY
NEW YORK

The Collier Press, New York
Electrotyped, Printed, and Bound by
P. F. COLLIER & SON COMPANY

AH, NAUGHTY PANDORA!   —page 351
From the painting by Maxfield Parrish

CONTENTS

CONTENTS

ILLUSTRATIONS

NOTE

The character of the contents of volumes 1, 2 and 3 is so closely related that they may be said to constitute three volumes under one general title. There are myths of Greece and Rome in this volume as well as in volume 3, and there are more animal myths in volume 1, particularly of the Hindoos and of the North American Indians.

What gives the volume a special character is the large group of stories from the Sagas or Epic Songs of the Northmen, including the story of Brunhilda and Siegfried, and a particularly attractive version of Lohengrin, condensed, but not rewritten, from the story by Miss Maud.

These stories belong to us, in a very particular sense, since the blood that flows in the veins of English and American boys is largely the blood of the fair-faced, fair-haired Northmen (or Scandinavians, or Danes, or whatever we call them) who invaded England in the ninth and tenth centuries. Their strong bodies and strong wills have worked wonders in the world and have made the world a pleasanter place to live in. It was the Northman blood that sent Robinson Crusoe a-wandering, and helped Christian defeat the Giant in Doubting Castle.
—W. P.

THE NORTHMEN'S STORY OF HOW ALL THINGS BEGAN

By E. M. Wilmot-Buxton

ONCE upon a time, before ever this world was made, there was neither earth nor sea, nor air, nor light, but only a great yawning gulf, full of twilight.

To the north of this gulf lay the Home of Mist, a dark and dreary land, out of which flowed a river of water from a spring that never ran dry. As the water in its onward course met the bitter blasts of wind from the yawning gulf, it hardened into great blocks of ice, which rolled far down into the abyss with a thunderous roar and piled themselves one on another until they formed mountains of glistening ice.

South of this gulf lay the Home of Fire, a land of burning heat, guarded by a giant with a flaming sword, which, as he flashed it to and fro before the entrance, sent forth showers of sparks. And these sparks fell upon the ice-blocks and partly melted them, so that they sent up clouds of steam; and these again were frozen into hoar-frost, which filled all the space that was left in the midst of the mountains of ice.

Then one day, when the gulf was full to the very top, this great mass of frosty rime, warmed by the flames from the Home of Fire and frozen by the

9

cold airs from the Home of Mist, came to life and became the Giant Ymir, with a living, moving body and cruel heart of ice.

Now there was as yet no tree, nor grass, nor anything that would serve for food, in this gloomy abyss. But when the Giant Ymir began to grope around for something to satisfy his hunger, he heard a sound as of some animal chewing the cud; and there among the ice-hills he saw a gigantic cow, from whose udder flowed four great streams of milk, and with this his craving was easily stilled.

But the cow was hungry also, and began to lick the salt off the blocks of ice by which she was surrounded. And presently, as she went on licking with her strong, rough tongue, a head of hair pushed itself through the melting ice. Still the cow went on licking, until she had at last melted all the icy covering and there stood fully revealed the frame of a mighty man.

Ymir looked with eyes of hatred at this being, born of snow and ice, for somehow he knew that his heart was warm and kind, and that he and his sons would always be the enemies of the evil race of the Frost Giants.

So, indeed, it came to pass. For from the sons of Ymir came a race of giants whose pleasure was to work evil on the earth; and from the Sons of the Iceman sprang the race of the gods, chief of whom was Odin, Father of All Things that ever were made; and Odin and his brothers began at once to war against the wicked Frost Giants, and most of all against the cold-hearted Ymir.

Now when, after a hard fight, the Giant Ymir

was slain, such a river of blood flowed forth from his wounds that it drowned all the rest of the Frost Giants save one, who escaped in a boat, with only his wife on board, and sailed away to the edge of the world. And from him sprang all the new race of Frost Giants, who at every opportunity issued from their land of twilight and desolation to harm the gods in their abode of bliss.

When the giants had been thus driven out, All-Father Odin set to work with his brothers to make the earth, the sea, and the sky; and these they fashioned out of the great body of the Giant Ymir.

Out of his flesh they formed Midgard, the earth, which lay in the centre of the gulf; and all round it they planted his eyebrows to make a high fence which should defend it from the race of giants.

With his bones they made the lofty hills, with his teeth the cliffs, and his thick curly hair took root and became trees, bushes, and the green grass.

With his blood they made the ocean, and his great skull, poised aloft, became the arching sky. Just below this they scattered his brains, and made of them the heavy grey clouds that lie between earth and heaven.

The sky itself was held in place by four strong dwarfs, who support it on their broad shoulders as they stand east and west and south and north.

Tne next thing was to give light to the new-made world. So the gods caught sparks from the Home of Fire and set them in the sky for stars; and they took the living flame and made of it the sun and moon, which they placed in chariots of gold, and harnessed to them beautiful horses, with flowing manes of gold and silver. Before the horses of the sun they placed a mighty shield to protect them from its hot rays; but the swift moon steeds needed no such protection from its gentle heat.

And now all was ready save that there was no one to drive the horses of the sun and moon. This task was given to Mani and Sol, the beautiful son and daughter of a giant; and these fair charioteers drive their fleet steeds along the paths marked out by the gods, and not only give light to the earth but mark out months and days for the sons of men.

Then All-Father Odin called forth Night, the gloomy daughter of the cold-hearted giant folk, and set her to drive the dark chariot drawn by the black horse, Frosty-Mane, from whose long wavy hair the drops of dew and hoar-frost fall upon the earth below. After her drove her radiant son, Day, with his white steed Shining-Mane, from whom the bright beams of daylight shine forth to gladden the hearts of men.

But the wicked giants were very angry when they saw all these good things; and they set in the sky two hungry wolves, that the fierce, grey creatures might forever pursue the sun and moon, and devour them, and so bring all things to an end. Sometimes, indeed, or so say the men of the North, the grey wolves almost succeed in swallowing sun or moon; and then the earth children make such an uproar that the fierce beasts drop their prey in fear. And the sun and moon flee more rapidly than before, still pursued by the hungry monsters.

One day, so runs the tale, as Mani, the Man in the Moon, was hastening on his course, he gazed upon the earth and saw two beautiful little children, a boy and a girl, carrying between them a pail of water. They looked very tired and sleepy, and indeed they were, for a cruel giant made them fetch and carry water all night long, when they should have been in bed. So Mani put out a long, long arm and snatched up the children and set them in the moon, pail and all; and there you can see them on any moonlight night for yourself.

But that happened a long time after the beginning of things; for as yet there was no man or woman or child upon the earth.

And now that this pleasant Midgard was made, the gods determined to satisfy their desire for a home where they might rest and enjoy themselves in their hours of ease.

They chose a suitable place far above the earth, on the other side of the great river which flowed from the Home of Mist where the giants dwelt, and here they made for their abode Asgard, wherein they dwelt in peace and happiness, and from whence they could look down upon the sons of men.

From Asgard to Midgard they built a beautiful bridge of many colors, to which men gave the name of Rainbow Bridge, and up and down which the gods could pass on their journeys to and from the earth.

Here in Asgard stood the mighty forge where the gods fashioned their weapons wherewith they fought the giants, and the tools wherewith they built their palaces of gold and silver.

Meantime, no human creature lived upon the

earth, and the giants dared not cross its borders
for fear of the gods. But one of them, clad in
eagles' plumes, always sat at the north side of
Midgard, and, whenever he raised his arms and let
them fall again, an icy blast rushed forth from the
Mist Home and nipped all the pleasant things of
earth with its cruel breath. In due time the earth
brought forth thousands of tiny creatures, which
crawled about and showed signs of great intelligence. And when the gods examined these little
people closely, they found that they were of two
kinds.

Some were ugly, misshapen, and cunning-faced,
with great heads, small bodies, long arms and feet.
These they called Trolls or Dwarfs or Gnomes,
and sent them to live underground, threatening to
turn them into stone should they appear in the
daytime. And this is why the trolls spend all
their time in the hidden parts of the earth, digging
for gold and silver and precious stones, and hiding
their spoil away in secret holes and corners. Sometimes they blow their tiny fires and set to work to
make all kinds of wonderful things from this buried
treasure; and that is what they are doing when, if
one listens very hard on the mountains and hills of
the Northland, a sound of tap-tap-tapping is heard
far underneath the ground.

The other small earth creatures were very fair
and light and slender, kindly of heart and full of
goodwill. These the gods called Fairies or Elves,
and gave to them a charming place called Elfland
in which to dwell. Elfland lies between Asgard
and Midgard, and since all fairies have wings they

can easily flit down to the earth to play with the butterflies, teach the young birds to sing, water the flowers, or dance in the moonlight round a fairy ring.

Last of all, the gods made a man and woman to dwell in fair Midgard; and this is the manner of their creation.

All-Father Odin was walking with his brothers in Midgard where, by the seashore, they found growing two trees, an ash and an elm. Odin took these trees and breathed on them, whereupon a wonderful transformation took place. Where the trees had stood, there were a living man and woman, but they were stupid, pale, and speechless, until Hœnir, the god of Light, touched their foreheads and gave them sense and wisdom; and Loki, the Fire-god, smoothed their faces, giving them bright color and warm blood, and the power to speak and see and hear

It only remained that they should be named, and they were called Ask and Embla, the names of the trees from which they had been formed. From these two people sprang all the race of men which lives upon this earth.

And now All-Father Odin completed his work by planting the Tree of Life.

This immense tree had its roots in Asgard and Midgard and the Mist Land; and it grew to such a marvellous height that the highest bough, the Bough of Peace, hung over the Hall of Odin on the heights of Asgard; and the other branches overshadowed both Midgard and the Mist Land. On the top of the Peace Bough was perched a mighty eagle, and ever a falcon sat between his eyes, and kept watch on all that happened in the world below, that he might tell to Odin what he saw.

Heidrun, the goat of Odin, who supplied the heavenly mead, browsed on the leaves of this wonderful tree, and from them fed also the four mighty stags from whose horns honey-dew dropped on to the earth beneath and supplied water for all the rivers of Midgard.

The leaves of the Tree of Life were ever green and fair, despite the dragon which, aided by countless serpents, gnawed perpetually at its roots, in order that they might kill the Tree of Life and thus bring about the destruction of the gods.

Up and down the branches of the tree scampered the squirrel, Ratatosk, a malicious little creature, whose one amusement it was to make mischief by repeating to the eagle the rude remarks of the dragon, and to the dragon those of the eagle, in the hope that one day he might see them in actual conflict.

Near the roots of the Tree of Life is a sacred well of sweet water from which the three Weird Sisters, who know all that shall come to pass, sprinkle the tree and keep it fresh and green. And the water, as it trickles down from the leaves, falls as drops of honey on the earth, and the bees take it for their food.

Close to this sacred well is the Council Hall of the gods, to which every morning they rode, over the Rainbow Bridge, to hold converse together.

And this is the end of the tale of How All Things began.

HOW THE QUEEN OF THE SKY GAVE GIFTS TO MEN

By E. M. Wilmot-Buxton

BY the side of All-Father Odin, upon his high seat in Asgard, sat Frigga, his wife, the Queen of the Asas. Sometimes she would be dressed in snow-white garments, bound at the waist by a golden girdle, from which hung a great bunch of golden keys. And the earth-dwellers, gazing into the sky, would admire the great white clouds as they floated across the blue, not perceiving that these clouds were really the folds of Frigga's flowing white robe, as it waved in the wind.

At other times she would wear dark grey or purple garments; and then the earth-dwellers made haste into their houses, for they said, "the sky is lowering to-day, and a storm is nigh at hand."

Frigga had a palace of her own called Fensalir, or the Hall of Mists, where she spent much of her time at her wheel, spinning golden thread, or weaving web after web of many-colored clouds. All night long she sat at this golden wheel, and if you look at the sky on a starry night you may chance to see it set up where the men of the South show a constellation called the Girdle of Orion.

Husbands and wives who had dwelt lovingly together upon earth were invited by Frigga to her hall when they died, so they might be forever united within its hospitable walls.

Frigga was especially interested in all good housewives, and she herself set them an excellent

17

example in Fensalir. When the snowflakes fell, the earth-dwellers knew it was Frigga shaking her great feather bed, and when it rained they said it was her washing day. It was she who first gave to them the gift of flax that the women upon earth might spin, and weave, and bleach their linen as white as the clouds of her own white robe.

And this is how it came about.

There once was a shepherd who lived among the mountains with his wife and children; and so very poor was he that he often found it hard to give his family enough to satisfy their hunger. But he did not grumble; he only worked the harder; and his wife, though she had scarcely any furniture, and never a chance of a new dress, kept the house so clean, and the old clothes so well mended, that, all unknown to herself, she rose high in the favor of the all-seeing Frigga.

Now one day, when the shepherd had driven his few poor sheep up the mountain to pasture, a fine reindeer sprang from the rocks above him and began to leap upward along the steep slope. The shepherd snatched up his crossbow and pursued the animal, thinking to himself: "Now we shall have a better meal than we have had for many a long day."

Up and up leaped the reindeer, always just out of reach, and at length disappeared behind a great boulder just as the shepherd, breathless and weary, reached the spot. No sign of the reindeer was to be seen, but, on looking round, the shepherd saw that he was among the snowy heights of the moun-tains, and almost at the top of a great glacier.

Presently, as he pursued his vain search for the animal, he saw to his amazement an open door, leading apparently into the heart of the glacier. He was a fearless man, and so, without hesitation, he passed boldly through the doorway and found himself standing in a marvellous cavern, lit up by blazing torches which gleamed upon rich jewels hanging from the roof and walls. And in the midst stood a woman, most fair to behold, clad in snow-white robes and surrounded by a group of lovely maidens.

The shepherd's boldness gave way at this awe-some sight, and he sank to his knees before the Asa, Frigga, for she it was. But Frigga bade him be of good cheer, and said: "Choose now whatsoever you will to carry away with you as a remembrance of this place."

The shepherd's eyes wandered over the glittering jewels on the walls and roof, but they came back to a little bunch of blue flowers which Frigga held in her hand. They alone looked homelike to him; the rest were hard and cold; so he asked timidly that he might be given the little nosegay.

Then Frigga smiled kindly upon him.

"Most wise has been your choice," said she. "Take with the flowers this measure of seed and sow it in your field, and you shall grow flowers of your own. They shall bring prosperity to you and yours."

So the shepherd took the flowers and the seed, and scarcely had he done so when a mighty peal of thunder, followed by the shock of an earthquake, rent the cavern, and when he had collected his senses he found himself once more upon the mountain side.

When he reached home and had told his tale, his wife scolded him roundly for not bringing home a jewel which would have made them rich forever. But when she would have thrown the flowers away he prevented her. Next day he sowed the seed in his field, and was surprised to find how far it went.

Very soon after this the field was thick with tiny green shoots; and though his wife reproached him for wasting good ground upon useless flowers, he watched and waited in hope until the field was blue with the starry flax blooms.

Then one night, when the flowers had withered and the seed was ripe, Frigga, in the disguise of an old woman, visited the lowly hut and showed the shepherd and his astonished wife how to use the flax stalks; how to spin them into thread, and how to weave the thread into linen.

It was not long before all the dwellers in that part of the earth had heard of the wonderful material, and were hurrying to the shepherd's hut to buy bleached linen or the seed from which it was obtained. And so the shepherd and his family were soon among the richest people in the land; and the promise of Frigga was amply fulfilled.

THE DWARFS AND THE FAIRIES

By A. and E. Keary

"THE earth is very beautiful," said Odin, from the top of his throne, "very beautiful in every part, even to the shores of the dark North Sea; but, alas! the men of the earth are puny and fearful. At this moment I see a three-headed giant striding out of Jötunheim. He throws a shepherd-boy into the sea, and puts the whole of the flock into his pocket. Now he takes them out again one by one, and cracks their bones as if they were hazel-nuts, whilst, all the time, men look on, and do nothing."

"Father," cried Thor in a rage, "last night I forged for myself a belt, a glove, and a hammer, with which three things I will go forth alone to Jötunheim."

Thor went, and Odin looked again.

"The men of the earth are idle and stupid," said Odin. "There are dwarfs and elves, who live amongst them, and play tricks which they cannot understand, and do not know how to prevent. At this moment I see a husbandman sowing grains of wheat in the furrows, while a dwarf runs after him, and changes them into stones. Again, I see two hideous little beings, who are holding under water the head of one, the wisest of men, until he dies; they mix his blood with honey; they have put it into three stone jars, and hidden it away."

Then Odin was very angry with the dwarfs, for he saw that they were bent on mischief; so he called

21

to him Hermod, his Flying Word, and despatched him with a message to the dwarfs and light elves, to say that Odin sent his compliments, and would be glad to speak with them, in his palace of Gladsheim, upon a matter of some importance.

When they received Hermod's summons the dwarfs and light elves were very much surprised, not quite knowing whether to feel honored or afraid. However, they put on their pertest manners, and went clustering after Hermod like a swarm of ladybirds.

When they were arrived in the great city they found Odin descended from his throne, and sitting with the rest of the Æsir in the Judgment Hall of Gladsheim. Hermod flew in, saluted his master, and pointed to the dwarfs and elves hanging like a cloud in the doorway to show that he had fulfilled his mission. Then Odin beckoned the little people to come forward. Cowering and whispering they peeped over one another's shoulders; now running on a little way into the hall, now back again, half curious, half afraid; and it was not until Odin had beckoned three times that they finally reached his footstool.

Then Odin spoke to them in calm, low, serious tones about the wickedness of their mischievous propensities. Some, the very worst of them, only laughed in a forward, hardened manner; but a great many looked up surprised and a little pleased at the novelty of serious words; while the light elves all wept, for they were tenderhearted little things. At length Odin spoke to the two dwarfs by name whom he had seen drowning the wise man. "Whose blood was it," he asked, "that you mixed with honey and put into jars?"

"Oh," said the dwarfs, jumping up into the air, and clapping their hands, "that was Kvasir's blood. Don't you know who Kvasir was? He sprang up out of the peace made between the Vanir and yourselves, and has been wandering about these seven years or more; so wise he was that men thought he must be a god. Well, just now we found him lying in a meadow drowned in his own wisdom; so we mixed his blood with honey, and put it into three great jars to keep. Was not that well done, Odin?"

"Well done!" answered Odin. "Well done! You cruel, cowardly, lying dwarfs! I myself saw you kill him. For shame! for shame!" and then Odin proceeded to pass sentence upon them all. Those who had been the most wicked, he said, were to live, henceforth, a long way underground, and were to spend their time in throwing fuel upon the great earth's central fire; while those who had only been mischievous were to work in the gold and diamond mines, fashioning precious stones and metals. They might all come up at night, Odin said; but must vanish at the dawn. Then he waved his hand, and the dwarfs turned round, shrilly chattering, scampered down the palace-steps, out of the city, over the green fields, to their unknown, deep-buried earth-homes. But the light elves still lingered, with upturned, tearful, smiling faces, like sunshiny morning dew.

"And you," said Odin, looking them through and through with his serious eyes, "and you——"

"Oh! indeed, Odin," interrupted they, speaking

all together in quick, uncertain tones; "Oh! indeed, Odin, we are not so very wicked. We have never done anybody any harm."

"Have you ever done anybody any good?" asked Odin.

"Oh! no, indeed," answered the light elves, we have never done anything at all."

"You may go, then," said Odin, "to live among the flowers, and play with the wild bees and summer insects. You must, however, find something to do, or you will get to be mischievous like the dwarfs."

"If only we had any one to teach us," said the light elves, "for we are such foolish little people."

Odin looked round inquiringly upon the Æsir; but among them there was no teacher found for the silly little elves. Then he turned to Niörd, who nodded his head good-naturedly, and said, "Yes, yes, I will see about it;" and then he strode out of the Judgment Hall, right away through the city gates, and sat down upon the mountain's edge.

After awhile he began to whistle in a most alarming manner, louder and louder, in strong wild gusts, now advancing, now retreating; then he dropped his voice a little, lower and lower, until it became a bird-like whistle—low, soft, enticing music, like a spirit's call; and far away from the south a little fluttering answer came, sweet as the invitation itself, nearer and nearer until the two sounds dropped into one another. Then through the clear sky two forms came floating, wonderfully fair—a brother and sister—their beautiful arms twined round one another, their golden hair bathed in sunlight, and supported by the wind.

"My son and daughter," said Niörd, proudly, to the surrounding Æsir, "Frey and Freya, Summer and Beauty, hand in hand."

When Frey and Freya dropped upon the hill Niörd took his son by the hand, led him gracefully to the foot of the throne, and said, "Look here, dear brother Lord, what a fair young instructor I have brought for your pretty little elves."

Odin was very much pleased with the appearance of Frey; but, before constituting him king and schoolmaster of the light elves, he desired to know what his accomplishments were, and what he considered himself competent to teach.

"I am the genius of clouds and sunshine," answered Frey; and as he spoke, the essences of a hundred perfumes were exhaled from his breath. "I am the genius of clouds and sunshine, and if the light elves will have me for their king I can teach them how to burst the folded buds, to set the blossoms, to pour sweetness into the swelling fruit, to lead the bees through the honey-passages of the flowers, to make the single ear a stalk of wheat, to hatch birds' eggs, and teach the little ones to sing— all this, and much more," said Frey, "I know, and will teach them."

Then answered Odin, "It is well;" and Frey took his scholars away with him to Alfheim, which is in every beautiful place under the sun.

HOW THOR WENT TO JÖTUNHEIM

By A. and E. Keary

ONCE on a time, Asa Thor and Loki set out on a journey from Asgard to Jötunheim. They travelled in Thor's chariot, drawn by two milk-white goats. It was a somewhat cumbrous iron chariot, and the wheels made a rumbling noise as it moved, which sometimes startled the ladies of Asgard, and made them tremble; but Thor liked it, thought the noise sweeter than any music, and was never so happy as when he was journeying in it from one place to another.

They travelled all day, and in the evening they came to a countryman's house. It was a poor, lonely place; but Thor descended from his chariot, and determined to pass the night there. The countryman, however, had no food in his house to give these travellers; and Thor, who liked to feast himself and make every one feast with him, was obliged to kill his own two goats and serve them up for supper. He invited the countryman and his wife and children to sup with him; but before they began to eat he made one request of them.

"Do not, on any account," he said, "break or throw away any of the bones of the goats you are going to eat for supper."

"I wonder why," said the peasant's son, Thialfi, to his sister Roska. Roska could not think of any reason, and by-and-bye Thialfi happened to have a very nice little bone given him with some marrow in it. "Certainly there can be no harm in my break-

26

ing just this one," he said to himself; "it would be such a pity to lose the marrow;" and as Asa Thor's head was turned another way, he slyly broke the bone in two, sucked the marrow, and then threw the pieces into the goat's skins, where Thor had desired that all the bones might be placed. I do not know whether Thialfi was uneasy during the night about what he had done; but in the morning he found out the reason of Asa Thor's command, and received a lesson on "wondering why," which he never forgot all his life after.

As soon as Asa Thor rose in the morning he took his hammer, Miölnir, in his hand, and held it over the goat-skins as they lay on the floor, whispering runes the while. They were dead skins with dry bones on them when he began to speak; but as he said the last word, Thialfi, who was looking curiously on, saw two live goats spring up and walk toward the chariot, as fresh and well as when they brought the chariot up to the door Thialfi hoped. But no; one of the goats limped a little with his hind leg, and Asa Thor saw it. His brow grew dark as he looked, and for a minute Thialfi thought he would run far, far into the forest, and never come back again; but one look more at Asa Thor's face, angry as it was, made him change his mind. He thought of a better thing to do than running away. He came forward, threw himself at the Asa's feet, and, confessing what he had done, begged pardon for his disobedience. Thor listened, and the displeased look passed away from his face.

"You have done wrong, Thialfi," he said, raising him up; "but as you have confessed your fault so bravely, instead of punishing you, I will take you with me on my journey, and teach you myself the lesson of obedience to the Æsir which is, I see, wanted.

Roska chose to go with her brother, and from that day Thor had two faithful servants, who followed him wherever he went.

The chariot and goats were now left behind; but, with Loki and his two new followers, Thor journeyed on to the end of Manheim, over the sea, and then on, on, on in the strange, barren, misty land of Jötunheim. Sometimes they crossed great mountains; sometimes they had to make their way among torn and rugged rocks, which often, through the mist, appeared to them to wear the forms of men, and once for a whole day they traversed a thick and tangled forest.

In the evening of that day, being very much tired, they saw with pleasure that they had come upon a spacious hall, of which the door, as broad as the house itself, stood wide open.

"Here we may very comfortably lodge for the night," said Thor; and they went in and looked about them.

The house appeared to be perfectly empty; there was a wide hall, and five smaller rooms opening into it. They were, however, too tired to examine it carefully, and as no inhabitants made their appearance, they ate their supper in the hall, and lay down to sleep. But they had not rested long before they were disturbed by strange noises, groanings, mutterings, and snortings, louder than any animal that they had ever seen in their lives could make.

By-and-bye the house began to shake from side to side, and it seemed as if the very earth trembled. Thor sprang up in haste, and ran to the open door; but, though he looked earnestly into the starlit forest, there was no enemy to be seen anywhere. Loki and Thialfi, after groping about for a time, found a sheltered chamber to the right, where they thought they could finish their night's rest in safety; but Thor, with Miölnir in his hand, watched at the door of the house all night. As soon as the day dawned he went out into the forest, and there, stretched on the ground close by the house, he saw a strange, uncouth, gigantic shape of a man, out of whose nostrils came a breath which swayed the trees to their very tops. There was no need to wonder any longer what the disturbing noises had been.

Thor fearlessly walked up to this strange monster to have a better look at him; but at the sound of his footsteps the giant-shape rose slowly, stood up an immense height, and looked down upon Thor with two great misty eyes, like blue mountain-lakes.

"Who are you?" said Thor, standing on tiptoe, and stretching his neck to look up; "and why do you make such a noise as to prevent your neighbors from sleeping?"

"My name is Skrymir," said the giant sternly; "I need not ask yours. You are the little Asa Thor of Asgard; but pray, now, what have you done with my glove?"

As he spoke he stooped down, and picked up the hall where Thor and his companions had passed the night, and which, in truth, was nothing more than his glove, the room where Loki and Thialfi had slept being the thumb.

Thor rubbed his eyes, and felt as if he must be dreaming. Rousing himself, however, he raised Miölnir in his hand, and, trying to keep his eyes fixed on the giant's face, which seemed to be always changing, he said: "It is time that you should know, Skrymir, that I am come to Jötunheim to fight and conquer such evil giants as you are, and, little as you think me, I am ready to try my strength against yours."

"Try it, then," said the giant.

And Thor, without another word, threw Miölnir at his head.

"Ah! Ah!" said the giant; "did a leaf touch me?"

Again Thor seized Miölnir, which always returned to his hand, however far he cast it from him, and threw it with all his force.

The giant put up his hand to his forehead. "I think," he said, "that an acorn must have fallen on my head."

A third time Thor struck a blow, the heaviest that ever fell from the hand of an Asa; but this time the giant laughed out loud.

"There is surely a bird on that tree," he said, "who has let a feather fall on my face."

Then, without taking any further notice of Thor, he swung an immense wallet over his shoulder, and, turning his back upon him, struck into a path that led from the forest. When he had gone a little way he looked round, his immense face appearing less like a human countenance than some strange, uncouthly-shaped stone toppling on a mountain precipice.

"Ving-Thor," he said, "let me give you a piece of good advice before I go. When you get to Utgard don't make much of yourself. You think me a tall man, but you have taller still to see; and you yourself are a very little mannikin. Turn back home whence you came, and be satisfied to have learned something of yourself by your journey to Jötunheim."

"Mannikin or not, *that* will I never do," shouted Asa Thor after the giant. "We will meet again, and something more will we learn, or teach each other."

The giant, however, did not turn back to answer, and Thor and his companions, after looking for some time after him, resumed their journey. Before the sun was quite high in the heavens they came out of the forest, and at noon they found themselves on a vast barren plain, where stood a great city, whose walls of dark, rough stone were so high, that Thor had to bend his head quite far back to see the top of them. When they approached the entrance of this city they found that the gates were closed and barred; but the space between the bars was so large that Thor passed through easily, and his companions followed him. The streets of the city were gloomy and still. They walked on for some time without meeting any one; but at length they came to a very high building, of which the gates stood open.

¹ Ving-Thor—Winged-Thor.

"Let us go in and see what is going on here," said Thor; and they went.

After crossing the threshold they found themselves in an immense banqueting hall. A table stretched from one end to the other of it; stone thrones stood round the table, and on every throne sat a giant, each one, as Thor glanced round, appearing more grim, and cold, and stony than the rest. One among them sat on a raised seat, and appeared to be the chief; so to him Thor approached and paid his greetings.

The giant chief just glanced at him, and, without rising, said, in a somewhat careless manner: "It is, I think, a foolish custom to tease tired travellers with questions about their journey. I know without asking that you, little fellow, are Asa Thor. Perhaps, however, you may be in reality taller than you appear; and as it is a rule here that no one shall sit down to table till he has performed some wonderful feat, let us hear what you and your followers are famed for, and in what way you choose to prove yourselves worthy to sit down in the company of giants."

At this speech, Loki, who had entered the hall cautiously behind Thor, pushed himself forward.

"The feat for which I am most famed," he said, "is eating, and it is one which I am just now inclined to perform with right good will. Put food before me, and let me see if any of your followers can dispatch it as quickly as I can."

"The feat you speak of is one by no means to be despised," said the Utgard king, "and there is one here who would be glad to try his powers against yours. Let Logi," he said to one of his followers, "be summoned to the hall."

At this, a tall, thin, yellow-faced man approached, and a large trough of meat having been placed in the middle of the hall, Loki sat to work at one end, and Logi at the other, and they began to eat. I hope *I* shall never see any one eat as they ate; but the giants all turned their slow-moving eyes to watch them, and in a few minutes they met in the middle of the trough. It seemed, at first, as if they had both eaten exactly the same quantity; but, when the thing came to be examined into it was found that Loki had, indeed, eaten up all the meat, but that Logi had also eaten the bones and the trough. Then the giants nodded their huge heads, and determined that Loki was conquered. King Utgard now turned to Thialfi, and asked what he could do.

"I was thought swift of foot among the youth of my own country," answered Thialfi; "and I will, if you please, try to run a race with any one here."

"You have chosen a noble sport, indeed," said the king; "but you must be a good runner if you could beat him with whom I shall match you."

Then he called a slender lad, Hugi by name, and the whole company left the hall, and, going out by an opposite gate to that by which Thor had entered, they came out to an open space, which made a noble race-ground. There the goal was fixed, and Thialfi and Hugi started off together.

Thialfi ran fast—fast as the reindeer which hears the wolves howling behind; but Hugi ran so much faster that, passing the goal, he turned round, and met Thialfi half-way in the course.

"Try again, Thialfi," cried the king; and Thialfi, once more taking his place, flew along the course with feet scarcely touching the ground— swiftly as an eagle when, from his mountain-crag, he swoops on his prey in the valley; but with all his running he was still a good bow-shot from the goal when Hugi reached it.

"You are certainly a good runner," said the king; "but if you mean to win you must do a little better still than this; but perhaps you wish to surprise us all the more this third time."

The third time, however, Thialfi was wearied, and though he did his best, Hugi, having reached the goal, turned and met him not far from the starting-point.

The giants again looked at each other, and declared that there was no need of further trial, for that Thialfi was conquered.

It was now Asa Thor's turn, and all the company looked eagerly at him, while the Utgard king asked by what wonderful feat he chose to distinguish himself.

"I will try a drinking-match with any of you," Thor said, shortly; for, to tell the truth, he cared not to perform anything very worthy in the company in which he found himself.

King Utgard appeared pleased with this choice, and when the giants had resumed their seats in the hall, he ordered one of his servants to bring in his drinking-cup, called the "cup of penance," which it was his custom to make his guests drain at

₁ draught, if they had broken any of the ancient
rules of the society.

"There!" he said, handing it to Thor, "we call
it well drunk if a person empties it at a single
draught. Some, indeed, take two to it; but the
very puniest can manage it in three."

Thor looked into the cup; it appeared to him
long, but not so very large after all, and being
thirsty he put it to his lips, and thought to make
short work of it, and empty it at one good, hearty
pull. He drank, and put the cup down again;
but, instead of being empty, it was now just so
full that it could be moved without danger of
spilling.

"Ha! ha! You are keeping all your strength
for the second pull I see," said Utgard, looking
in. Without answering, Thor lifted the cup again,
and drank with all his might till his breath failed;
but, when he put down the cup, the liquor had only
sunk down a little from the brim.

"If you mean to take three draughts to it," said
Utgard, "you are really leaving yourself a very
unfair share for the last time. Look to yourself,
Ving-Thor; for, if you do not acquit yourself better
in other feats, we shall not think so much of you
here as they say the Æsir do in Asgard."

At this speech Thor felt angry, and, seizing the
cup again, he drank a third time, deeper and longer
than he had yet done; but, when he looked into
the cup, he saw that a very small part only of its
contents had disappeared. Wearied and disappointed he put the cup down, and said he would
try no more to empty it.

"It is pretty plain," said the king, looking round on the company, "that Asa Thor is by no means the kind of man we always supposed him to be."

"Nay," said Thor, "I am willing to try another feat, and you yourselves shall choose what it shall be."

"Well," said the king, "there is a game at which our children are used to play. A short time ago I dare not have named it to Asa Thor; but now I am curious to see how he will acquit himself in it. It is merely to lift my cat from the ground—a childish amusement truly."

As he spoke a large, grey cat sprang into the hall, and Thor, stooping forward, put his hand under it to lift it up. He tried gently at first; but by degrees he put forth all his strength, tugging and straining as he had never done before; but the utmost he could do was to raise one of the cat's paws a little way from the ground.

"It is just as I thought," said King Utgard, looking round with a smile; "but we all are will-ing to allow that the cat *is* large, and Thor but a little fellow."

"Little as you think me," cried Thor, "who is there who will dare to wrestle with me in my anger?"

"In truth," said the king, "I don't think there is any one here who would choose to wrestle with you; but, if wrestle you must, I will call in that old crone Elli. She has, in her time, laid low many a better man than Asa Thor has shown himself to be."

The crone came. She was old, withered, and

toothless, and Thor shrank from the thought of wrestling with her; but he had no choice. She threw her arms round him, and drew him toward the ground, and the harder he tried to free himself, the tighter grew her grasp. They struggled long. Thor strove bravely, but a strange feeling of weakness and weariness came over him, and at length he tottered and fell down on one knee before her. At this sight all the giants laughed aloud, and Utgard coming up, desired the old woman to leave the hall, and proclaimed that the trials were over. No one of his followers would *now* contend with Asa Thor, he said, and night was approaching. He then invited Thor and his companions to sit down at the table, and spend the night with him as his guests. Thor, though feeling somewhat perplexed and mortified, accepted his invitation courteously, and showed, by his agreeable behavior during the evening, that he knew how to bear being conquered with a good grace.

In the morning, when Thor and his companions were leaving the city, the king himself accompanied them without the gates; and Thor, looking steadily at him when he turned to bid him farewell, perceived, for the first time, that he was the very same Giant Skrymir with whom he had met in the forest. "Come, now, Asa Thor," said the giant with a strange sort of smile on his face, "tell me truly, before you go, how you think your journey has turned out, and whether or not I was right in saying that you would meet with better men than yourself in Jötunheim."

"I confess freely," answered Asa Thor, looking

up without any false shame on his face, "that I have acquitted myself but humbly, and it grieves me; for I know that in Jötunheim henceforward it will be said that I am a man of little worth."

"By my troth! no," cried the giant, heartily. "Never should you have come into my city if I had known what a mighty man of valor you really are; and now that you are safely out of it, I will, for once, tell the truth to you, Thor. All this time I have been deceiving you by my enchantments. When yóu met me in the forest, and hurled Miölnir at my head, I should have been crushed by the weight of your blows had I not skilfully placed a mountain between myself and you, on which the strokes of your hammer fell, and where you cleft three deep ravines, which shall henceforth become verdant valleys. In the same manner I deceived you about the contests in which you engaged last night. When Loki and Logi sat down before the trough, Loki, indeed, ate like hunger itself; but Logi is fire, who, with eager, consuming tongue, licked up both bones and trough. Thialfi is the swiftest of mortal runners; but the slender lad, Hugi, was my thought; and what speed can ever equal his? So it was in your own trials. When you took such deep draughts from the horn, you little knew what a wonderful feat you were performing. The other end of that horn reached the ocean, and when you come to the shore you will see how far its waters have fallen away, and how much the deep sea itself has been diminished by your draught. Hereafter, men watching the going

THOR

out of the tide will call it the ebb, or draught of Thor.

"Scarcely less wonderful was the prowess you displayed in the second trial. What appeared to you to be a cat, was, in reality, the Midgard serpent, which encircles the world. When we saw you succeed in moving it we trembled lest the very foundations of earth and sea should be shaken by your strength. Nor need you be ashamed of having been overthrown by the old woman Elli, for she is old age; and there never has, and never will be, one whom she has not the power to lay low. We must now part, and you had better not come here again, or attempt anything further against my city; for I shall always defend it by fresh enchantments, and you will never be able to do anything against me."

At these words Thor raised Miölnir, and was about to challenge the giant to a fresh trial of strength; but, before he could speak, Utgard vanished from his sight; and, turning round to look for the city, he found that it, too, had disappeared, and that he was standing alone on a smooth, green, empty plain.

"What a fool I have been," said Asa Thor, aloud, "to allow myself to be deceived by a mountain giant!"

"Ah!" answered a voice from above, "I told you, you would learn to know yourself better by your journey to Jötunheim. It is the great use of travelling."

Thor turned quickly round again, thinking to see Skrymir behind him; but, after looking on every side, he could perceive nothing, but that a high, cloud-capped mountain, which he had noticed on the horizon, appeared to have advanced to the edge of the plain.

HOW THOR'S HAMMER WAS LOST AND FOUND

By E. M. Wilmot-Buxton

MOST precious in the eyes of Thor was his magic hammer, Miölnir, of which even the mighty Frost Giants stood in dread.

Always he laid it by his side when he went to rest, and always it was the first thing for which his hand was outstretched when he awoke. Judge then of his horror and dismay when, on opening his eyes one morning, the hammer was nowhere to be seen.

Starting up with a roar of rage, Thor commenced to search everywhere for the missing weapon. Up and down his wonderful palace, built of the thunder clouds, he tramped, with a noise that shook the whole city of Asgard. But the hammer was not to be found.

Then he called upon golden-haired Sif, his wife, and bade her help in the search; and still the hammer was nowhere to be seen. It was clear that someone must have stolen it, and, when he realized this, Thor's wrath broke all bounds. His bristling red hair and beard stood up on end, and from them flew a whole volley of fiery sparks.

Presently, as the angry Asa was shaking the

palace with his thunderous voice, Red Loki came along to inquire into the trouble. He was not likely to sympathize with Thor, but, always brimful of curiosity, he loved to have a part in everything that happened.

"What's the matter, Asa Thor?" said he; and Thor replied, lowering his voice as he spoke, for he did not want his loss to be too widely known:

"Now listen to what I tell thee, Loki—'tis a thing which is known neither on earth below nor in heaven above. My hammer's gone."

This news was most interesting to Loki, who had long owed Thor a grudge, which he was afraid to pay openly. "Ho, ho!" said he. "Then shall we soon have the giants turning us out of Asgard, brother Thor."

"Not if you use your wits as you know how," growled Thor, still in a very bad temper. "Come, you call yourself a clever fellow. Find out for me who has robbed me of my thunderbolt, my hammer, my Miölnir."

Then Loki gave a grin and a wink, and promised to do what he could—not because he cared for Thor, but because he loved to be of importance, and was, moreover, really frightened as to what might happen to Asgard if the magic hammer was not at hand.

It was not long before he noticed that an extraordinary kind of tempest was raging in the regions below—not an orderly kind of tempest, with first some thunder, and then some rain, and then a gust of wind or two, such as Thor was wont to arrange, but a mixture of hail and wind and thunder and lightning and rain and snow, all raging together in a tremendous muddle, so that the earth folk thought the end of the world was come.

This gave Loki a hint, and he began to peer about between the clouds, until at length he saw that the trouble was coming from a certain hill which stood in the centre of Giantland.

Now on the top of this hill lived a certain Thrym, prince of the Frost Giants, who for a long time past had been very envious of the might of Thor. He had, indeed, done his best to imitate him as far as he could, and had managed to get up a very good imitation of lightning and hail and rain; but he had not been able to manage the thunderbolts, for they could only be made by means of Thor's hammer, Miölnir.

All this was well known to Red Loki, and he was therefore not at all surprised to find that, somehow or other, Thrym must have got hold of the magic weapon; for here were thunderbolts crashing about the earth and sky at a terrible rate.

When informed of the discovery, Thor flew into a still more tremendous rage, and wanted to rush off at once to try conclusions with the giant. But Loki, who loved rather to get a thing by trickery and deceit, persuaded him that violence would never do.

"Remember," said he, "that Thrym *with* the hammer is much stronger than Thor without it. This is a matter which must be managed by clever wit and craft, not by force and loud talking. Leave therefore the whole matter to me."

To this Thor very reluctantly agreed.

THOR'S HAMMER

Then Loki bethought him of some disguise wherein he might visit Giantland in safety, for he was not at all anxious to risk his life. He betook himself to the House of Maidens, over which ruled Freya, fairest of all in Asgard, she who was wont to shake the spring flowers from her golden locks as she passed over the frozen uplands, leaving behind her a region of green and smiling beauty. Loki found the goddess, and begged the loan of her magic falcon plumes, in which she was wont to flit to and fro over the earth; and when she learnt for what purpose he needed them she gladly assented.

Then Loki took the appearance of a great brown bird, and spreading his wings he flew away toward Giantland.

It was a long journey, as he already knew, and, although the tempest had now ceased to rage, he found the country of the giants darker and colder and drearier than ever.

The longest journey comes to an end, and at length Loki reached a mountain where sat the Giant Thrym, his huge legs dangling to the ground, playing with a puppy as large as an elephant.

Perching as near as he dared, Loki gazed at the giant with his bright, round eyes, and was wondering how to begin, when Thrym, who, at a glance, had seen completely through his disguise, said calmly, in a voice as much as possible like Thor's thunderous roar: "Oh, ho! Loki, what are you doing so far from Asgard? Are you not afraid, little fellow as you are, to venture alone into our country?"

Then Loki, thinking to win his way by flattery, replied: "Sad indeed is it in Asgard, now that Miölnir has vanished. Clever was that one who spirited it away from the very side of Thor. Methinks none but you could have done it, O mighty Thrym!"

Pleased with the compliment to his cleverness the giant chuckled before admitting: "Ay, Loki, the hammer is mine, 'tis very true; and now men will know who really is the Thunderer."

"Ah well!" sighed cunning Loki, "some men are strong by reason of their weapons, and some are just as strong without. Small need have you, O mighty Thrym, for hammers, but Thor is naught without it. Yet, since all the world knows that you are his master, let him have his plaything back, that we may cease to be troubled by his peevish outcry."

But though Thrym was as stupid as he was big, he was not to be caught thus.

"No, no, my little Loki," he said. "Mine is the hammer, and deep have I buried it beneath the bottom of the sea. Go, tell this to your Asa folk, and say to them that I will give it back on one condition only—and that is, that they send me Freya, that fairest of maidens, to be my wife."

At this suggestion Loki could scarcely keep from laughing, for the idea of sending the beautiful Freya, the joy and delight of Asgard, to be the wife of this ill-favored Frost Giant was too absurd for words.

It was not much to him, however, what happened to anyone except himself, so he hastened to reply: "Be sure, O Thrym, that everything I can do to further the matter shall be done. And if Freya is of the same mind as I you will soon be welcoming that most sweet maiden to Giantland—farewell!"

So saying, he spread his brown wings and flew back to Asgard, delighted to think of the mischief he could now set brewing.

First of all he visited Thor, and told him of what had passed. And the Thunderer, when he heard of Thrym's boastful words, was filled with wild wrath and wanted to start off, then and there, and wrest the hammer from the depths of the sea. But Loki pointed out the difficulties that stood in the way and, leaving the Asa to ponder over his words, he hurried off to Freya and informed her of Thrym's proposal.

The beautiful Freya was walking in her garden, and round her neck she wore her famous necklet of stars. When she heard Loki's suggestion that she should wed a hideous giant she fell into such a rage that she broke her necklet, and all the stars went falling through the sky, so that men cried:

"See how the stars are shooting!"

Meantime the Asa folk had met together to consider all that had happened, and, having calmed the fury of Thor, they pointed out to him that Asgard stood in the gravest danger of an attack which would find them quite unprotected. When they had said this several times over, Thor began to weary of the subject, and he replied with great surliness: "Very well, then. Let Freya go to Thrym

as his wife, and then shall we be as before, with
Miölnir to defend us."

When Freya heard this, her rage turned to tears
and lamentations, and she declared that it would
be death to her to send her to the gloomy halls of
Giantland, whence she could never hope to revisit
the flowery meads and grassy slopes of Asgard.
And the Asas, unable to bear the sight of her grief,
with one voice declared that they would never spare
her from the Home of Bliss.

Then there stepped forward Heimdall, the
watchman who sits on guard over the Rainbow
Bridge by night and day.

Now Heimdall had the gift of seeing into the
future, and the Asas were always ready to hear
his words, well knowing them to be wise.

"My plan is this," said he. "Let Thor borrow
the clothes of Freya and put a thick veil over his
face; and let him go thus to Thrym's castle and
pass for his bride. And if he cannot by some
means manage to get hold of the hammer when
he is there—why, he must give it up altogether."

At this suggestion the Asas clapped their hands
with approval—all, indeed, save Thor, who looked
most glum, and was extremely unwilling to agree
to the plan.

"Dress me as a bride!" he grumbled. "A pretty
maiden I shall make. Ready enough am I to fight,
but I will not make myself a laughing-stock if I
know it."

But the Asas besought him to give way, while
Loki twitted him with cowardice. Fair Freya, too,
appealed with tearful eyes; and so at length, with

great reluctance, the Thunderer agreed to do what they wished.

Fortunately the maiden Freya was very tall, but even so it was with some difficulty that they managed to cover the burly form of Thor with her robes.

He insisted, moreover, upon wearing his own shirt of mail and his girdle of strength; and these took much drapery to hide. Great was the laughter in the halls of Asgard that night as the Battle Maidens brushed and curled Thor's long yellow hair, and set a jewelled headdress upon it; and finally, when the maidens proceeded to cover up his thick beard and angry eyes with a silken veil, the mirth of the Asas was unrestrained. To complete the disguise the maidens hung round his neck the famous necklet, which had now been re-strung, and finally Frigga, the wife of All-Father Odin, secured at his girdle the great bunch of keys proper to brides at a wedding in the Northland.

While this was being done, Loki, more than all, had been convulsed with merriment at the success of his mischief-making. The very sight of Thor's disgusted looks, and of his great hands clenched with rage under the delicate veil, nearly killed him with laughter; and when all was ready he declared himself unable to lose an atom of the fun in store.

"Let me go with you," he implored. "See, I will dress myself as your handmaiden. Ah, you had better agree, for without me to prompt you, you will never play your part."

So Loki was dressed as a waiting-maid, and took his seat very demurely by the side of Thor in the goat-car. Loud was the laughter in Asgard as the Asas watched the two drive off together and heard the roar of the Thunderer's voice issuing from the folds of a meek maiden's veil as he urged his goats upon their course. Long and stormy was that ride to Giantland, for Thor was still in the worst of tempers, and drove his chariot so furiously that

> "The mountains crashed
> The earth stood in flames,"

as the hoofs of the goats clattered over mountains and waters, striking sparks wherever they touched a rock.

Thrym was much overjoyed when he heard that a chariot containing the two maidens was approaching his door. Away ran his servants in different directions, some with orders to make ready a grand banquet, some to prepare the chamber of the bride, some to receive her at the door.

The giant himself assisted them to alight, and looked with admiration at the stately figure of his bride; but he made no attempt to see her face, since it is the custom in the Northland for the bride to remain veiled until the marriage has been completed.

"A bride worthy of a giant!" murmured his servants, as he led her to a lofty seat beside his own great throne of gold; and they looked with approval also on the buxom form of the waiting-maid, who stood, closely veiled, behind her mistress's chair.

Now the journey had been long and cold, and it was with joy that the new-comers noticed that the preparations for the banquet were complete, for they were exceedingly hungry.

The giants are huge eaters, and they gathered round the board whereon were displayed an enormous ox roasted whole, a vast dish of salmon and various other dainties. But because the bride was a woman, and modest withal, they brought her tiny morsels on a dainty golden plate.

This was too much for Thor, who had always possessed a most healthy appetite, and was now more than usually ready for his supper. Gradually drawing nearer to the table, while the others were busy with the meal, he managed to get hold of the dish of roasted ox, and within a few minutes the whole of the animal had disappeared.

Then he put out his hand to the platter of salmon, and in eight mouthfuls disposed of eight of the great fish. After this he noticed a large plate full of cakes and sweetmeats, which was set apart for the ladies of the party. Of these, too, he made short work.

Finally, feeling thirsty after his huge meal, he took up two barrels of mead, and tossed them off, one after another, down his capacious throat. Then he sat back on his chair with a sigh of deep content.

These proceedings had been watched by Loki with uneasiness, but by Thrym with open-mouthed dismay. Was this the usual appetite of this dainty maiden, who had eaten more than the company of giants? But Loki bent toward him and whispered in his ear that the thought of marrying had so excited Freya that she had eaten nothing for eight days, and had therefore been on the point of starvation.

This reassured the giant, and being now himself filled with mead he drew nearer and, lifting a corner of the veil, tried to kiss the cheek of his future bride.

But Thor, who was longing to be at close grips with him, threw him such a fiery glance that he drew quickly back, saying: "Why does fair Freya's eye burn like a spark from a furnace?" "Pooh!" whispered Loki again, "that is nothing but her love for you, which for eight days has raged like a flaming fire."

This news was still more pleasant to hear, and Thrym, in high good humor, cried: "Bring in the hammer, my wedding gift, wherewith to plight the maid. For when I have laid it on her lap she will be my own forever, and together we will work dire evil against the Asa folk, whom I hate with all my heart."

What was that unmaidenly sound that issued from under the silken veil at these words? But though Loki turned pale to hear it, Thrym, busy sending for the hammer, did not pay any heed.

Back came the giant's servants at length, bending under the weight of Miölnir. And as they bowed before the silent maiden, sitting with meekly bent head upon the throne, Thrym cried with a merry jest: "See, here is little Thor's tiny plaything—a pretty toy truly for his feeble hands. Take it, fair Freya, as my wedding gift."

"And take *that* as mine!" roared Thor, in a voice of thunder, as he flung off the veil and rose to his full height. And with the words he swung the hammer once—and ere the eye could follow its

movement, it had crashed through Thrym's skull,
and had knocked over a round dozen of his guests.
Yet again did it swing in the Asa's hand, and this
time it left not a giant standing in the hall.

A third time it was swung, and on this occasion
the roof and walls of the palace came tumbling on
every side, and only Thor and Loki were left alive
amid the ruins.

"Ha! ha!" laughed Red Loki, "that was neatly
done, fair Freya."

Thor, who was now busily tearing off the hated
robes and veil, stayed to look threateningly at his
companion. "No more of that, Loki," said he, "the
thing had to be done, 'tis true, but talk not to me
again of this woman's work. We will remember
only that I am the Thunderer, and that my hammer
that was lost is found."

So they drove back peacefully to Asgard.

And this is the end of the tale of How Thor's
Hammer was lost and found.

IDUNA'S APPLES OF YOUTH

By A. and E. Keary

I. REFLECTIONS IN THE WATER

OF all the groves and gardens round the city of
Asgard—and they were many and beautiful
—there was none so beautiful as the one where
Iduna, the wife of Bragi, lived. It stood on the
south side of the hill, not far from Gladsheim, and

it was called "Always Young," because nothing that grew there could ever decay, or become the least bit older than it was on the day when Iduna entered it. The trees wore always a tender, light green color, as the hedges do in spring. The flowers were mostly half-opened, and every blade of grass bore always a trembling, glittering drop of early dew. Brisk little winds wandered about the grove, making the leaves dance from morning till night and swaying backwards and forwards the heads of the flowers.

"Blow away!" said the leaves to the wind, "for we shall never be tired."

"And you will never be old," said the winds in answer. And then the birds took up the chorus and sang:

"Never tired and never old."

Iduna, the mistress of the grove, was fit to live among young birds, and tender leaves, and spring flowers. She was so fair that when she bent over the river to entice her swans to come to her, even the stupid fish stood still in the water, afraid to destroy so beautiful an image by swimming over it; and when she held out her hand with bread for the swans to eat, you would not have known it from a water-lily—it was so wonderfully white.

Iduna never left her grove even to pay a visit to her nearest neighbor, and yet she did not lead by any means a dull life; for, besides having the company of her husband, Bragi, who must have been an entertaining person to live with; (for he is said to have known a story which never came to an end, and yet which never grew wearisome), all the

heroes of Asgard made a point of coming to call
upon her every day. It was natural enough that they
should like to visit so beautiful a grove and so fair a
lady; and yet, to confess the truth, it was not quite
to see either the grove or Iduna that they came.

Iduna herself was well aware of this, and when
her visitors had chatted a short time with her, she
never failed to bring out from the innermost recess
of her bower a certain golden casket, and to request
as a favor, that her guests would not think of going
away till they had tasted her apples, which, she
flattered herself, had a better flavor than any other
fruit in the world.

It would have been quite unlike a hero of Asgard
to have refused such courtesy; and, besides, Iduna
was not as far wrong about her apples as hostesses
generally are, when they boast of the good things
on their tables.

There is no doubt her apples *had* a peculiar
flavor; and if any one of the heroes happened to be
a little tired, or a little out of spirits, or a little cross,
when they came into the bower, it always followed
that, as soon as he had eaten one apple, he found
himself as fresh, and vigorous, and happy as he
had ever been in his life.

So fond were the heroes of these apples, and
so necessary did they think them to their daily comfort, that they never went on a journey without
requesting Iduna to give them one or two, to fortify
them against the fatigues of the way.

Iduna had no difficulty in complying with this
request; she had no fear of her store ever failing,
for as surely as she took an apple from her casket

another fell in; but where it came from Iduna could never discover. She never saw it till it was close to the bottom of the casket; but she always heard the sweet tinkling sound it made when it touched the golden rim. It was as good as play to stand by her casket, taking the apples out, and watching the fresh rosy ones come tumbling in, without knowing who threw them.

One spring morning Iduna was very busy taking apples out of her casket; for several of the heroes were taking advantage of the fine weather to journey out into the world. Bragi was going from home for a time; perhaps he was tired of telling his story only to Iduna, and perhaps she was beginning to know it by heart; and Odin, Loki, and Hœnir had agreed to take a little tour in the direction of Jötunheim, just to see if any entertaining adventure would befall them. When they had all received their apples, and taken a tender farewell of Iduna, the grove—green and fair as it was—looked, perhaps, a little solitary.

Iduna stood by her fountain, watching the bright water as it danced up into the air and quivered, and turned, and fell back, making a hundred little flashing circles in the river; and then she grew tired, for once, of the light and the noise, and wandered down to a still place, where the river was shaded by low bushes on each side, and reflected clearly the blue sky overhead.

Iduna sat down and looked into the deep water. Besides her own fair face there were little, wandering, white clouds to be seen reflected there. She counted them as they sailed past. At length a

strange form was reflected up to her from the water
—large, dark, lowering wings, pointed claws, a
head with fierce eyes—looking at her.

Iduna started and raised her head. It was above
as well as below; the same wings—the same eyes
—the same head—looking down from the blue sky,
as well as up from the water. Such a sight had
never been seen near Asgard before; and, while
Iduna looked, the thing waved its wings, and went
up, up, up, till it lessened to a dark spot in the
clouds, and on the river.

It was no longer terrible to look at; but, as it
shook its wings a number of little black feathers
fell from them, and flew down toward the grove.
As they neared the trees, they no longer looked
like feathers—each had two independent wings and
a head of its own; they were, in fact, a swarm of
Nervous Apprehensions; troublesome little insects
enough, and well known elsewhere, but which now,
for the first time, found their way into the grove.

Iduna ran away from them; she shook them off;
she fought quite bravely against them; but they
are by no means easy to get rid of; and when, at
last, one crept within the folds of her dress, and
twisted itself down to her heart, a new, strange
feeling thrilled there—a feeling never yet known to
any dweller in Asgard. Iduna did not know what
to make of it.

II. THE WINGED-GIANT

In the meantime Odin, Loki, and Hœnir proceeded on their journey. They were not bound
on any particular quest. They strayed hither and

thither that Odin might see that things were going on well in the world, and his subjects comporting themselves in a becoming manner. Every now and then they halted while Odin inspected the thatching of a barn, or stood at the smithy to see how the smith wielded his hammer, or in a furrow to observe if the ploughman guided his plough-share evenly through the soil. "Well done," he said if the workman was working with all his might; and he turned away, leaving something behind him, a straw in the barn, a piece of old iron at the forge-door, a grain in the furrow—nothing to look at; but ever after the barn was always full, the forge-fire never went out, the field yielded bountifully.

Toward noon the Æsir reached a shady valley, and, feeling tired and hungry, Odin proposed to sit down under a tree, and while he rested and studied a book of runes which he had with him, he requested Loki and Hœnir to prepare some dinner.

"I will undertake the meat and the fire," said Hœnir; "you, Loki, will like nothing better than foraging about for what good things you can pick up."

"That is precisely what I mean to do," said Loki. "There is a farm-house near here, from which I can perceive a savory smell. It will be strange, with my cunning, if I do not contrive to have the best of all the dishes under this tree before your fire is burnt up."

As Loki spoke he turned a stone in his hand, and immediately he assumed the shape of a large black cat.

In this form he stole in at the kitchen-window

of a farm-house, where a busy housewife was intent on taking pies and cakes from a deep oven, and ranging them on a dresser under the window. Loki watched his opportunity, and whenever the mistress's back was turned he whisked a cake or a pie out of the window.

"One, two, three. Why, there are fewer every time I bring a fresh one from the oven!" cried the bewildered housewife. "It's that thieving cat. I see the end of her tail on the window-sill." Out of the window leant the housewife to throw a stone at the cat, but she could see nothing but a thin cow trespassing in her garden; and when she ran out with a stick to drive away the cow, it, too, had vanished, and an old raven, with six young ones, was flying over the garden-hedge.

The raven was Loki, the little ones were the pies; and when he reached the valley, and changed himself and them into their proper shapes, he had a hearty laugh at his own cleverness, and at the old woman's dismay.

"Well done, Loki, king of thieves," said a chorus of foxes, who peeped out of their holes to see the only one of the Æsir whose conduct they could appreciate; but Odin, when he heard of it, was very far from thinking it well done. He was extremely displeased with Loki for having disgraced himself by such mean tricks.

"It is true," he said, "that my subjects may well be glad to furnish me with all I require, but it should be done knowingly. Return to the farm-house, and place these three black stones on the table from whence you stole the provisions."

Loki—unwilling as he was to do anything he believed likely to bring good to others—was obliged to obey. He made himself into the shape of a white owl, flew once more through the window, and dropped the stones out of his beak; they sank deep into the table, and looked like three black stains on the white deal-board.

From that time the housewife led an easy life; there was no need for her to grind corn, or mix dough, or prepare meat. Let her enter her kitchen at what time of day she would, stores of provisions stood smoking hot on the table. She kept her own counsel about it, and enjoyed the reputation of being the most economical housekeeper in the whole country-side; but one thing disturbed her mind, and prevented her thoroughly enjoying the envy and wonder of the neighboring wives. All the rubbing, and brushing, and cleaning in the world would not remove the three black stains from her kitchen table, and as she had no cooking to do, she spent the greater part of her time in looking at them.

"If they were but gone," she said, a hundred times every day, "I should be content; but how is one to enjoy one's life when one cannot rub the stains off one's own table?"

Perhaps Loki foresaw how the good wife would use her gift; for he came back from the farm-house in the best spirits. "We will now, with Father Odin's permission, sit down to dinner," he said; "for surely, brother Hœnir, while I have been making so many journeys to and fro, you have been doing something with that fire which I see blazing so fiercely, and with that old iron pot smoking over it."

"The meat will be by this time ready, no doubt," said Hœnir. "I killed a wild ox while you were away, and part of it has been now for some time stewing in the pot."

The Æsir now seated themselves near the fire, and Hœnir lifted up the lid of the pot. A thick steam rose up from it; but when he took out the meat it was as red and uncooked as when he first put it into the pot.

"Patience," said Hœnir; and Odin again took out his book of runes. Another hour passed, and Hœnir again took off the lid, and looked at the meat; but it was in precisely the same state as before. This happened several times, and even the cunning Loki was puzzled; when, suddenly, a strange noise was heard coming from a tree near, and, looking up, they saw an enormous human-headed eagle seated on one of the branches, and looking at them with two fierce eyes. While they looked it spoke.

"Give me my share of the feast," it said, "and the meat shall presently be done."

"Come down and take it—it lies before you," said Loki, while Odin looked on with thoughtful eyes; for he saw plainly that it was no mortal bird who had the boldness to claim a share in the Æsir's food.

Undaunted by Odin's majestic looks, the eagle flew down, and, seizing a large piece of meat, was going to fly away with it, when Loki, thinking he had now got the bird in his power, took up a stick

that lay near, and struck a hard blow on the eagle's
back. The stick made a ringing sound as it fell;
but when Loki tried to draw it back, he found that
it stuck with extraordinary force to the eagle's
back; neither could he withdraw his own hands
from the other end.

Something like a laugh came from the creature's
half-human, half-bird-like mouth; and then it
spread its dark wings and rose up into the air, drag-
ging Loki after.

"It is as I thought," said Odin, as he saw the
eagle's enormous bulk brought out against the sky;
"it is Thiassi, the strongest giant in Jötunheim,
who has presumed to show himself in our presence.
Loki has only received the reward of his treachery,
and it would ill-become us to interfere in his behalf;
but, as the monster is near, it will be well for us to
return to Asgard, lest any misfortune should befall
the city in our absence."

While Odin spoke, the winged creature had risen
up so high as to be invisible even to the eyes of the
Æsir; and, during their return to Asgard, he did
not again appear before them; but, as they approached the gates of the city, they were surprised
to see Loki coming to meet them. He had a crest-
fallen and bewildered look; and when they questioned him as to what had happened to him since
they parted in such a strange way, he declared
himself to be quite unable to give any further account of his adventures than that he had been carried rapidly through the air by the giant, and, at
last, thrown down from a great height near the
place where the Æsir met him.

Odin looked steadfastly at him as he spoke, but he forbore to question him further: for he knew well that there was no hope of hearing the truth from Loki, and he kept within his own mind the conviction he felt that some disastrous result must follow a meeting between two such evil-doers as Loki and the giant Thiassi.

That evening, when the Æsir were all feasting and telling stories to each other in the great hall of Valhalla, Loki stole out from Gladsheim, and went alone to visit Iduna in her grove. It was a still, bright evening. The leaves of the trees moved softly up and down, whispering sweet words to each other; the flowers, with half-shut eyes, nodded sleepily to their own reflections in the water, and Iduna sat by the fountain, with her head resting in one hand, thinking of pleasant things.

"It is all very well," thought Loki; "but I am not the happier because people can here live such pleasant lives. It does not do me any good, or cure the pain I have had so long in my heart."

Loki's long shadow—for the sun was setting—fell on the water as he approached, and made Iduna start. She remembered the sight that had disturbed her so much in the morning; but when she saw only Loki, she looked up and smiled kindly; for he had often accompanied the other Æsir in their visits to her grove.

"I am wearied with a long journey," said Loki abruptly, "and I would eat one of your apples to refresh me after my fatigue." The casket stood by Iduna's side, and she immediately put in her hand and gave Loki an apple. To her surprise, instead of thanking her warmly, or beginning to eat it, he turned it round and round in his hand with a contemptuous air.

"It is true then," he said, after looking intently at the apple for some time, "your apples are but small and withered in comparison. I was unwilling to believe it at first, but now I can doubt no longer."

"Small and withered!" said Iduna, rising hastily. Nay, Asa Odin himself, who has traversed the whole world, assures me that he has never seen any to be compared to them."

"That will never be said again," returned Loki; "for this very afternoon I have discovered a tree, in a grove not far from Asgard, on which grow apples so beautiful that no one who has seen them will ever care again for yours."

"I do not wish to see or hear of them," said Iduna, trying to turn away with an indifferent air; but Loki followed her, and continued to speak more and more strongly of the beauty of this new fruit, hinting that Iduna would be sorry that she had refused to listen when she found all her guests deserting her for the new grove, and when even Bragi began to think lightly of her and of her gifts. At this Iduna sighed, and Loki came up close to her, and whispered in her ear:

"It is but a short way from Asgard, and the sun has not yet set. Come out with me, and, before any one else has seen the apples, you shall gather them, and put them in your casket, and no woman shall ever have it in her power to boast that she can feast the Æsir more sumptuously than Iduna."

Now Iduna had often been cautioned by her husband never to let anything tempt her to leave the grove, and she had always been so happy here, that she thought there was no use in his telling her the same thing so often over; but now her mind was so full of the wonderfully beautiful fruit, and she felt such a burning wish to get it for herself, that she quite forgot her husband's commands.

"It is only a little way," she said to herself; "there can be no harm in going out just this once;" and, as Loki went on urging her, she took up her basket from the ground hastily, and begged him to show her the way to this other grove. Loki walked very quickly, and Iduna had not time to collect her thoughts before she found herself at the entrance of Always Young. At the gate she would gladly have stopped a minute to take breath; but Loki took hold of her hand, and forced her to pass through, though, at the very moment of passing, she half drew back; for it seemed to her as if all the trees in the grove suddenly called out in alarm, "Come back, come back, Oh, come back, Iduna!" She half drew back her hand, but it was too late; the gate fell behind her, and she and Loki stood together without the grove.

The trees rose up between them and the setting sun, and cast a deep shadow on the place where they stood; a cold, night air blew on Iduna's cheek, and made her shiver.

"Let us hasten on," she said to Loki; "let us hasten on, and soon come back again."

But Loki was not looking on, he was looking up. Iduna raised her eyes in the direction of his, and her heart died within her; for there, high up over her head, just as she had seen it in the morning, hung the lowering, dark wings—the sharp talons—the fierce head, looking at her. For one moment it stood still above her head, and then lower, lower, lower, the huge shadow fell; and, before Iduna found breath to speak, the dark wings were folded round her, and she was borne high up in the air, northwards, towards the grey mist that hangs over Jötunheim. Loki watched till she was out of sight, and then returned to Asgard. The presence of the giant was no wonder to him; for he had, in truth, purchased his own release by promising to deliver up Iduna and her casket into his power; but, as he returned alone through the grove, a foreboding fear pressed on his mind.

"If it should be true," he thought, "that Iduna's apples have the wonderful power Odin attributes to them! if I among the rest should suffer from the loss!"

Occupied with these thoughts, he passed quickly among the trees, keeping his eyes resolutely fixed on the ground. He dare not trust himself to look around; for once, when he had raised his head, he fancied that, gliding through the brushwood, he had seen the dark robes and pale face of his daughter Hela.

III. HELA

WHEN it was known that Iduna had disappeared from her grove, there were many sorrowful faces in Asgard, and anxious voices were heard inquiring for her. Loki walked about with as grave a face, and asked as many questions, as any one else; but he had a secret fear that became stronger every day, that now, at last, the consequence of his evil ways would find him out.

Days passed on, and the looks of care, instead of wearing away, deepened on the faces of the Æsir.

They met, and looked at each other, and turned away sighing; each saw that some strange change was creeping over all the others, and none liked to be the first to speak of it. It came on very gradually—a little change every day, and no day ever passing without the change. The leaves of the trees in Iduna's grove deepened in color. They first became a sombre green, then a glowing red, and, at last, a pale brown; and when the brisk winds came and blew them about, they moved every day more languidly.

"Let us alone," they said at length. "We are tired, tired, tired."

The winds, surprised, carried the new sound to Gladsheim, and whispered it all round the banquet-hall where the Æsir sat, and then they rushed back again, and blew all through the grove.

"We are tired," said the leaves again; "we are tired, we are old; we are going to die;" and at the word they broke from the trees one by one, and fluttered to the ground, glad to rest anywhere; and the winds, having nothing else to do, went back to Gladsheim with the last strange word they had learned.

The Æsir were all assembled in Valhalla; but there were no stories told, and no songs sung. No one spoke much but Loki, and he was that day in a talking humor. He moved from one to another, whispering an unwelcome word in every ear.

"Have you noticed your mother Frigga?" he said to Baldur. "Do you see how white her hair is growing, and what a number of deep lines are printed on her face?"

Then he turned to Frey. "Look at your sister Freya and your friend Baldur," he said, "as they sit opposite to us. What a change has come over them lately! Who would think that that pale man and that faded woman were Baldur the beautiful and Freya the fair?"

"You are tired—you are old—you are going to die,"—moaned the winds, wandering all round the great halls, and coming in and out of the hundred doorways, and all the Æsir looked up at the sad sound. Then they saw, for the first time, that a new guest had seated herself that day at the table of the Æsir. There could be no question of her fitness on the score of royalty, for a crown rested on her brow, and in her hand she held a sceptre; but the fingers that grasped the sceptre were white and fleshless, and under the crown looked the threatening face of Hela, half corpse, half queen.

A great fear fell on all the Æsir as they looked, and only Odin found voice to speak to her. "Dreadful daughter of Loki!" he said, "by what warrant do you dare to leave the kingdom where I permit you to reign, and come to take your place among the Æsir, who are no mates for such as you?"

Then Hela raised her bony finger, and pointed, one by one, to the guests that sat round. "White hair," she said, "wrinkled faces, weary limbs, dull eyes—these are the warrants which have summoned me from the land of shadows to sit among the Æsir. I have come to claim you, by these signs, as my future guests, and to tell you that I am preparing a place for you in my kingdom."

At every word she spoke a gust of icy wind came from her mouth and froze the blood in the listeners' veins. If she had stayed a moment longer they would have stiffened into stone; but when she had spoken thus, she rose and left the hall, and the sighing winds went out with her.

Then, after a long silence, Bragi stood up and spoke. "Æsir," he said, "we are to blame. It is now many months since Iduna was carried away from us; we have mourned for her, but we have not yet avenged her loss. Since she left us a strange weariness and despair have come over us, and we sit looking on each other as if we had ceased to be warriors and Æsir. It is plain that, unless Iduna returns, we are lost. Let two of us journey to the Urda fount, which we have so long neglected to visit, and enquire of her from the Norns—for they know all things—and then, when we have learnt where she is, we will fight for her liberty, if need be, till we die; for that will be an end more fitting for us than to sit here and wither away under the breath of Hela."

At these words of Bragi the Æsir felt a revival of their old strength and courage. Odin approved of Bragi's proposal, and decreed that he and Baldur should undertake the journey to the dwelling-place of the Norns. That very evening they set forth;

for Hela's visit showed them that they had no time
to lose.

It was a weary time to the dwellers in Asgard
while they were absent. Two new citizens had
taken up their abode in the city, Age and Pain.
They walked the streets hand-in-hand, and there
was no use in shutting the doors against them; for
however closely the entrance was barred, the
dwellers in the houses felt them as they passed.

IV. THROUGH FLOOD AND FIRE

At length, Baldur and Bragi returned with the
answer of the Norns, couched in mystic words,
which Odin alone could understand. It revealed
Loki's treacherous conduct to the Æsir, and declared that Iduna could only be brought back by
Loki, who must go in search of her, clothed in
Freya's garments of falcon feathers.

Loki was very unwilling to venture on such a
search; but Thor threatened him with instant death
if he refused to obey Odin's commands, or failed
to bring back Iduna; and, for his own safety he
was obliged to allow Freya to fasten the falcon
wings to his shoulders, and set off towards Thiassi's
castle in Jötunheim, where he well knew that Iduna
was imprisoned.

It was called a castle; but it was, in reality, a
hollow in a dark rock; the sea broke against two
sides of it; and, above, the sea-birds clamored day
and night.

There the giant had taken Iduna on the night on
which she had left her grove; and, fearing lest Odin

should spy her from Air Throne, he had shut her up
in a gloomy chamber, and strictly forbidden her
ever to come out. It was hard to be shut up from
the fresh air and sunshine; and yet, perhaps, it was
safer for Iduna than if she had been allowed to
wander about Jötunheim and see the monstrous
sights that would have met her there.

She saw nothing but Thiassi himself and his servants, whom he had commanded to attend upon her;
and they, being curious to see a stranger from a distant land, came in and out many times every day.

They were fair, Iduna saw—fair and smiling;
and, at first, it relieved her to see such pleasant
faces round her, when she had expected something
horrible.

"Pity me!" she used to say to them; "pity me! I
have been torn away from my home and my husband, and I see no hope of ever getting back."
And she looked earnestly at them; but their pleasant faces never changed, and there was always—
however bitterly Iduna might be weeping—the same
smile on their lips.

At length Iduna, looking more narrowly at them,
saw, when they turned their backs to her, that they
were hollow behind; they were, in truth, Ellewomen, who have no hearts, and can never pity
any one.

After Iduna saw this she looked no more at their
smiling faces, but turned away her head and wept
silently. It is very sad to live among Ellewomen
when one is in trouble.

Every day the giant came and thundered at
Iduna's door. "Have you made up your mind yet,"

he used to say, "to give me the apples? Something dreadful will happen to you if you take much longer to think of it." Iduna trembled very much every day, but still she had strength to say, "No;" for she knew that the *most* dreadful thing would be for her to give to a wicked giant the gifts that had been entrusted to her for the use of the Æsir. The giant would have taken the apples by force if he could; but, whenever he put his hand into the casket, the fruit slipped from beneath his fingers, shrivelled into the size of a pea, and hid itself in crevices of the casket where his great fingers could not come—only when Iduna's little white hand touched it, it swelled again to its own size, and this she would never do while the giant was with her. So the days passed on, and Iduna would have died of grief among the smiling Ellewomen if it had not been for the moaning sound of the sea and the wild cry of the birds; "for, however others may smile, these pity me," she used to say, and it was like music to her.

One morning when she knew that the giant had gone out, and when the Ellewomen had left her alone, she stood for a long time at her window by the sea, watching the mermaids floating up and down on the waves, and looking at heaven with their sad blue eyes. She knew that they were mourning because they had no souls, and she thought within herself that even in prison it was better to belong to the Æsir than to be a mermaid or an Ellewoman, were they ever so free or happy. While she was still occupied with these thoughts she heard her name spoken, and a bird with large wings flew in at the window, and, smoothing its feathers, stood upright before her. It was Loki in Freya's garment of feathers, and he made her understand in a moment that he had come to set her free, and that there was no time to lose. He told her to conceal her casket carefully in her bosom, and then he said a few words over her, and she found herself changed into a sparrow, with the casket fastened among the feathers of her breast.

Then Loki spread his wings once more, and flew out of the window, and Iduna followed him. The sea-wind blew cold and rough, and her little wings fluttered with fear; but she struck them bravely out into the air and flew like an arrow over the water.

"This way lies Asgard," cried Loki, and the word gave her strength. But they had not gone far when a sound was heard above the sea, and the wind, and the call of the sea-birds. Thiassi had put on his eagle plumage, and was flying after them. For five days and five nights the three flew over the water that divides Jötunheim from Asgard, and, at the end of every day, they were closer together, for the giant was gaining on the other two.

All the five days the dwellers in Asgard stood on the walls of the city watching. On the sixth evening they saw a falcon and a sparrow, closely pursued by an eagle, flying towards Asgard.

"There will not be time," said Bragi, who had been calculating the speed at which they flew. "The eagle will reach them before they can get into the city."

But Odin desired a fire to be lighted upon the walls; and Thor and Tyr, with what strength remained to them, tore up the trees from the groves and gardens, and made a rampart of fire all round the city. The light of the fire showed Iduna, her husband and her friends waiting for her. She made one last effort, and, rising high up in the air above the flames and smoke, she passed the walls, and dropped down safely at the foot of Odin's throne. The giant tried to follow; but, wearied with his long flight, he was unable to raise his enormous bulk sufficiently high in the air. The flames scorched his wings as he flew through them, and he fell among the flaming piles of wood and was burnt to death.

How Iduna feasted the Æsir on her apples, how they grew young and beautiful again, and how spring, and green leaves, and music came back to the grove, I must leave you to imagine, for I have made my story long enough already; and if I say any more you will fancy that it is Bragi who has come among you, and that he has entered on his endless story.

HOW THE FENRIS WOLF WAS CHAINED

By E. M. Wilmot-Buxton

FAIR as were the meads of Asgard, we have seen that the Asa folk were fond of wandering far afield in other regions. Most restless of all was Red Loki, that cunning fellow who was always bringing trouble upon himself or upon his kindred. And because he loved evil, he would often betake himself to the gloomy halls of Giantland and mingle with the wicked folk of that region.

Now one day he met a hideous giantess named 'Angur-Boda. This creature had a heart of ice, and because he loved ugliness and evil she had a great attraction for him, and in the end he married her, and they lived together in a horrible cave in Giantland.

Three children were born to Loki and Angur-Boda in this dread abode, and they were even more terrible in appearance than their mother. The first was an immense wolf called Fenris, with a huge mouth filled with long white teeth, which he was constantly gnashing together.

The second was a wicked-looking serpent with a fiery-red tongue lolling from its mouth.

The third was a hideous giantess, partly blue and partly flesh-colour, whose name was Hela.

No sooner were these three terrible children born than all the wise men of the earth began to foretell the misery they would bring upon the Asa folk.

In vain did Loki try to keep them hidden within the cave wherein their mother dwelt. They soon grew so immense in size that no dwelling would contain them, and all the world began to talk of their frightful appearance.

It was not long, of course, before All-Father Odin, from his high seat in Asgard, heard of the children of Loki. So he sent for some of the Asas, and said:

"Much evil will come upon us, O my children.

from this giant brood, if we defend not ourselves against them. For their mother will teach them wickedness, and still more quickly will they learn the cunning wiles of their father. Fetch me them here, therefore, that I may deal with them forthwith."

So, after somewhat of a struggle, the Asas captured the three giant-children and brought them before Odin's judgment-seat.

Then Odin looked first at Hela, and when he saw her gloomy eyes, full of misery and despair, he was sorry, and dealt kindly with her, saying: "Thou art the bringer of Pain to man, and Asgard is no place for such as thou. But I will make thee ruler of the Mist Home, and there shalt thou rule over that unlighted world, the Region of the Dead."

Forthwith he sent her away over rough roads to the cold, dark region of the North called the Mist Home. And there did Hela rule over a grim crew, for all those who had done wickedness in the world above were imprisoned by her in those gloomy regions. To her came also all those who had died, not on the battlefield, but of old age or disease. And though these were treated kindly enough, theirs was a joyless life in comparison with that of the dead warriors who were feasting and fighting in the halls of Valhalla, under the kindly rule of All-Father Odin.

Having thus disposed of Hela, Odin next turned his attention to the serpent. And when he saw his evil tongue and cunning, wicked eyes, he said:

"Thou art he who bringest Sin into the world of

men; therefore the ocean shall be thy home for ever."

Then he threw that horrid serpent into the deep sea which surrounds all lands, and there the creature grew so fast that when he stretched himself one day he encircled all the earth, and held his own tail fast in his mouth. And sometimes he grew angry to think that he, the son of a god, had thus been cast out; and at those times he would writhe with his huge body and lash his tail till the sea spouted up to the sky. And when that happened the men of the North said that a great tempest was raging. But it was only the Serpent-son of Loki writhing in his wrath.

Then Odin turned to the third child. And behold! the Fenris Wolf was so appalling to look upon that Odin feared to cast him forth, and he decided to endeavour to tame him by kindness so that he should not wish them ill.

But when he bade them carry food to the Fenris Wolf, not one of the Asas would do so, for they feared a snap from his great jaws. Only the brave Tyr had courage enough to feed him, and the wolf ate so much and so fast that the business took him all his time. Meantime, too, the Fenris grew so rapidly, and became so fierce, that the gods were compelled to take counsel and consider how they should get rid of him. They remembered that it would make their peaceful halls unholy if they were to slay him, and so they resolved instead to bind him fast, that he should be unable to do them harm.

So those of the Asa folk who were clever smiths set to work and made a very strong, thick chain;

and when it was finished they carried it out to the yard where the wolf dwelt, and said to him, as though in jest:

"Here is a fine proof of thy boasted strength, O Fenris. Let us bind this about thee, that we may see if thou canst break it asunder."

Then the wolf gave a great grin with his wide jaws, and came and stood still that they might bind the chain about him; for he knew what he could do. And it came to pass that directly they had fastened the chain, and had slipped aside from him, the great beast gave himself a shake, and the chain fell about him in little bits.

At this the Asas were much annoyed, but they tried not to show it, and praised him for his strength.

Then they set to work again upon a chain much stronger than the last, and brought it to the Fenris Wolf, saying:

"Great will be thy renown, O Fenris, if thou canst break this chain as thou didst the last."

But the wolf looked at them askance, for the chain they brought was very much thicker than the one he had already broken. He reflected, how-ever, that since that time he himself had grown stronger and bigger, and moreover, that one must risk something in order to win renown.

So he let them put the chain upon him, and when the Asas said that all was ready, he gave a good shake and stretched himself a few times, and again the fetters lay in fragments on the ground.

Then the gods began to fear that they would never hold the wolf in bonds; and it was All-Father

Odin who persuaded them to make one more attempt.

So they sent a messenger to Dwarfland bidding him ask the Little Men to make a chain which nothing could possibly destroy.

Setting at once to work, the clever little smiths soon fashioned a slender silken rope, and gave it to the messenger, saying that no strength could break it, and that the more it was strained the stronger it would become.

It was made of the most mysterious things—the sound of a cat's footsteps, the roots of a mountain, the sinews of a bear, the breath of fishes, and other such strange materials, which only the dwarfs knew how to use.

With this chain the messenger hastened back over the Rainbow Bridge to Asgard.

By this time the Fenris Wolf had grown too big for his yard, so he lived on a rocky island in the middle of the lake that lies in the midst of Asgard.

And here the Asas now betook themselves with their chain, and began to play their part with wily words.

"See," they cried, "O Fenris! Here is a cord so soft and thin that none would think of it binding such strength as thine."

And they laughed great laughs, and handed it to one another, and tried its strength by pulling at it with all their might, but it did not break.

Then they came nearer and used more wiles, saying:

"*We* cannot break the cord, though 'tis stronger

than it looks, but thou, O mighty one, will be able to snap it in a moment."

But the wolf tossed his head in scorn, and said:

"Small renown would there be to me, O Asa folk, if I were to break yon slender string. Save, therefore, your breath, and leave me now alone."

"Aha!" cried the Asas. "Thou fearest the might of the silken cord, thou false one, and that is why thou wilt not let us bind thee!"

"Not I," said the Fenris Wolf, growing rather suspicious, "but if it is made with craft and guile it shall never come near my feet."

"But," said the Asas, "thou wilt surely be able to break this silken cord with ease, since thou hast already broken the great iron fetters."

To this the wolf made no answer, pretending not to hear.

"Come!" said the Asas again, "why shouldst thou fear? For even if thou couldst not break the cord we would immediately let thee free again. To refuse is a coward's piece of work."

Then the wolf gnashed his teeth at them in anger, and said:

"Well I know you Asas! For if you bind me so fast that I cannot get loose you will skulk away, and it will be long before I get any help from you; and therefore am I loth to let this band be laid upon me."

But still the Asas continued to persuade him and to twit him with cowardice, until at length the Fenris Wolf said, with a sullen growl:

"Have it your own way then. But, as a pledge that this is done without deceit, let one of you lay his hand in my mouth while you are binding me, and afterwards while I try to break the bonds."

Then the Asa folk looked at one another in dismay, for they knew very well what this would mean.

And while they consulted together the wolf stood gnashing his teeth at them with a horrid grin.

At length Tyr the Brave hesitated no longer. Boldly he stalked up to the wolf and thrust his arm into his enormous mouth, bidding the Asas bind fast the beast. Scarce had they done so when the wolf began to strain and pull, but the more he did so the tighter and stiffer the rope became.

The gods shouted and laughed with glee when they saw how all his efforts were in vain. But Tyr did not join in their mirth, for the wolf in his rage snapped his great teeth together and bit off his hand at the wrist.

Now when the Asas discovered that the animal was fast bound, they took the chain which was fixed to the rope and drew it through a huge rock, and fastened this rock deep down in the earth, so that it could never be moved. And this they fastened to another great rock which was driven still deeper into the ground.

When the Fenris Wolf found that he had been thus secured he opened his mouth terribly wide, and twisted himself right and left, and tried his best to bite the Asa folk. He uttered, moreover, such terrible howls that at length the gods could bear it no longer. So they took a sword and thrust it into his mouth, so that the hilt rested on his lower, and the point against his upper, jaw. And

there he was doomed to remain until the End of
All Things shall come, when he

> "Freed from the Chain
> Shall range the Earth."

THE STORY OF BALDER THE BEAUTIFUL

By E. M. Wilmot-Buxton

FAIR beyond all the sons of Odin was Balder
the Beautiful, Balder of the snow-white brow
and golden locks, and he was well beloved not
only by the Asa folk, but also by the men of the
earth below.

> "Of all the twelve round Odin's throne,
> Balder the Beautiful, alone,
> The Sun god, good and pure and bright,
> Was loved by all, as all love light."

Balder had a twin-brother named Hoder, who
was born blind. Gloomy and silent was he, but
none the less he loved his bright sun-brother best
of all in heaven or earth.

The home of Balder was a place with silver roof
and pillars of gold, and nothing unclean or impure
was allowed to come inside its doors.

Very wise in all magic charms was this radiant
young god; and for all others save himself he could
read the future; but "to keep his own life safe and
see the sun" was not granted to him.

Now there came a time when Balder's bright

face grew sad and downcast; and when his father Odin and his mother Frigga perceived this they implored him to tell them the cause of his grief. Then Balder told them that he had been troubled by strange dreams; and, since in those days men believed that dreams were sent as a warning of what was about to happen, he had gone heavily since these visions had come to him.

First he had dreamt that a dark cloud had arisen which came before the sun and shut out all brightness from the land.

The next night he dreamt again that Asgard lay in darkness, and that her bright flowers and radiant trees were withered and lifeless, and that the Asa folk, dull and withered also, were sorrowing as though from some great calamity.

The third night he dreamt yet again that Asgard was dark and lifeless and that from out of the gloom one sad voice cried:

"Woe! Woe! Woe! For Balder the Beautiful is dead—is dead!"

Odin listened to the recital of this story with heavy heart, and at its conclusion he mounted his coal-black horse and rode over many a hard and toilsome road till he came to the dark abode of Hela. And there he saw, to his surprise, that a great banquet was being prepared in the gloomy hall. Dishes of gold were set upon the table and all the couches were covered with the richest silken tapestry, as though some honoured guest were expected. But a throne that stood at the head of the table was empty.

Very thoughtfully Odin rode on through those

dim halls till he came to one where dwelt an ancient prophetess, whose voice no man had heard for many a long year.

Silent he stood before her, until she asked in a voice that sounded as though it came from far away: "Who art thou, and from whence dost thou come to trouble my long rest?"

Now Odin was fearful that she would not answer him did he give his real name, so he told her that he was the son of Valtam, and asked anxiously for whom the grim goddess of Death was preparing her banquet.

Then, to his great grief, the hollow voice of the prophetess replied that Balder was the expected guest, and that he would shortly be sent thither, slain by the hand of Hoder, the blind god of Darkness.

"Who then," asked Odin, in sorrowful tones, "shall avenge the death of Balder?"

And she answered that the son of the Earth-goddess, Vali by name, should neither

> "Comb his raven hair
> Nor wash his visage in the stream,
> Nor see the sun's departing beam,
> Till he on Hoder's corse shall smile
> Flaming on the funeral pile."

And learning thus of the fate of his two favourite sons, All-Father Odin went sadly back to Asgard.

Meantime Mother Frigga had not been idle. Filled with anxiety for her darling son, she decided to send her servants throughout the earth, bidding them exact a promise from all things—not only living creatures, but plants, stones, and metals, fire, water, trees and diseases of all kinds—that they would do harm in no way to Balder the Beautiful.

Theirs was an easy task, for all things loved the bright Sun-god, and readily agreed to give the pledge. Nothing was overlooked save only the mistletoe, growing upon the oak-tree that shaded the entrance to Valhalla. It seemed so insignificant that no one thought it worth while to ask this plant to take the oath.

The servants returned to Frigga with all the vows and compacts that had been made; and the Mother of Gods and Men went back with heart at ease to her spinning-wheel.

The Asa folk, too, were reassured, and, casting aside the burden of care that had fallen upon them, they resumed their favourite game upon the plains of Idavold, where they were wont to contend with one another in the throwing of golden disks.

And when it became known among them that nothing would hurt Balder the Beautiful they invented a new game.

Placing the young Sun-god in their midst, they would throw stones at him, or thrust at him with their knives, or strike with their wooden staves; and the wood or the knife or the stone would glance off from Balder and leave him quite unhurt.

This new game delighted both Balder and the Asa folk, and so loud was their laughter that Loki,

who was some distance away pursuing one of his
schemes in the disguise of an old woman, shook
with rage at the sound. For Loki was jealous of
Balder and, as is usual with people who make themselves disliked, nothing gave him such displeasure
as to see a group of the Asas on such happy terms
with each other.

Presently, in his wanderings, Loki passed by the
house of Fensalir, in the doorway of which sat
Frigga, at her spinning-wheel. She did not rec-
ognize Red Loki, but greeted him kindly and
asked:

"Old woman, dost thou know why the gods are
so merry this evening?"

And Loki answered: "They are casting stones
and throwing sharp knives and great clubs at
Balder the Beautiful, who stands smiling in their
midst, daring them to hurt him."

Then Frigga smiled tranquilly and turned again
to her wheel, saying:

"Let them play on, for no harm will come to him
whom all things in heaven and earth have sworn
not to hurt."

"Art thou sure, good mother, that *all* things in
heaven and earth have taken this vow?"

"Ay, indeed," replied Frigga, "all save a harmless little plant, the mistletoe, which grows on the
oak by Valhalla, and this is far too small and weak
to be feared."

And to this Loki replied in musing voice, nodding his head as he spoke: "Yea, thou art right,
great Mother of Gods and Men."

But the wicked Asa had learnt what he desired

to know. The instrument by which he might bring harm to Balder the Beautiful was now awaiting him, and he determined to use it, to the dire sorrow of Asgard.

Hastening to the western gate of Valhalla, he pulled a clump of the mistletoe from the oak, and fashioned therefrom a little wand, or stick, and with this in his hand he returned to the plain of Idavold. He was far too cunning, however, to attempt to carry out his wicked design himself. His malicious heart was too well known to the Asa folk. But he soon found an innocent tool. Leaning against a tree, and taking no part in the game, was Hoder, the blind god, the twin brother of Balder, and to him he began:

"Hark to the Asas—how they laugh! Do you take no share in the game, good Hoder?"

"Not I," said Hoder gloomily, "for I am blind, and know not where to throw."

"I could show you that," said Loki, assuming a pleasant tone; "'tis no hard matter, Hoder, and methinks the Asas will call you proud and haughty if you take no share in the fun."

"But I have nothing to throw," said poor blind Hoder.

Then Loki said: "Here, at least, is a small shaft, 'twill serve your purpose," and leading innocent Hoder into the ring he cunningly guided his aim. Hoder, well pleased to be able to share in a game with his beloved brother, boldly sped the shaft, expecting to hear the usual shout of joyous laughter which greeted all such attempts. There fell instead dead silence on his ear, and immediately on this followed a wail of bitter agony. For Balder the Beautiful had fallen dead without a groan, his heart transfixed by the little dart of mistletoe.

> "So on the floor lay Balder dead; and round
>   Lay thickly strewn swords, axes, darts, and spears,
>   Which all the Gods in sport had idly thrown
>   At Balder, whom no weapon pierced or clove;
>   But in his breast stood fixed the fatal bough
>   Of mistletoe, which Loki the Accuser gave
>   To Hoder, and unwitting Hoder threw—
>   'Gainst that alone had Balder's life no charm."

Dreading he knew not what, Hoder stood in doubt for some moments. But soon the meaning of that bitter wail was borne in upon him, piercing the cloud of darkness in which he always moved. He opened wide his arms as though to clasp the beloved form, and then with: "I have slain thee, my brother," despair seized him and he fell prostrate in utter grief.

Meantime, the Asa folk crowded round the silent form of Balder, weeping and wailing; but, alas! their moans and tears could not bring Balder back. At length, All-Father Odin, whose grief was too deep for lamentations, bade them be silent and prepare to bear the body of the dead Asa to the seashore.

The unhappy Hoder, unable to take part in these last offices, made his way sadly through Asgard, beyond the walls and along the seashore, until he came to the house Fensalir.

Frigga was seated upon her seat of honour before the fire against the inner wall, and standing before her, with bent head and woeful, sightless gaze,

BALDER THE BEAUTIFUL

Hoder told her of the dread mishap that had befallen.

"Tell me, O mother," he cried in ending, and his voice sounded like the wail of the wind on stormy nights, "tell me, is there aught I can do to bring my brother back? Or can I make agreement with the dread mother of the Underworld, giving my life in exchange for his?"

Woe crowded upon woe in the heart of Frigga as she listened to the story. The doom was wrought that she had tried so vainly to avert, and not even her mother's love had availed to safeguard the son so dearly cherished.

"On Balder Death hath laid her hand, not thee, my son," she said, "yet though we fail in the end, there is much that may be tried before all hope is lost."

Then she told Hoder of a road by which the abode of Hela could be reached, one which had been travelled by none living save Odin himself.

"Who goes that way must take no other horse
To ride, but Sleipnir, Odin's horse, alone.
Nor must he choose that common path of gods
Which every day they come and go in heaven,
O'er the bridge Bifrost, where is Heimdall's watch.

"But he must tread a dark untravelled road
Which branches from the north of heaven, and ride
Nine days, nine nights, toward the northern ice,
Through valleys deep engulfed, with roaring streams.
And he will reach on the tenth morn a bridge
Which spans with golden arches Giöll's stream.
Then he will journey through no lighted land,
Nor see the sun arise, nor see it set;

And he must fare across the dismal ice
Northward, until he meets a stretching wall
Barring his way, and in the wall a grate,
But then he must dismount and on the ice
Tighten the girths of Sleipnir, Odin's horse,
And make him leap the grate, and come within."

There in that cheerless abode dead Balder was enthroned, but, said Frigga, he who braves that dread journey must take no heed of him, nor of the sad ghosts flitting to and fro, like eddying leaves. First he must accost their gloomy queen and entreat her with prayers:

"Telling her all that grief they have in heaven
For Balder, whom she holds by right below."

A bitter groan of anguish escaped from Hoder when Frigga had finished her recital of the trials which must be undergone:

"Mother, a dreadful way is this thou showest;
No journey for a sightless god to go."

And she replied:

". . . Thyself thou shalt not go, my son;
But he whom first thou meetest when thou com'st
To Asgard and declar'st this hidden way,
Shall go; and I will be his guide unseen."

Meantime the Asa folk had felled trees and had carried to the seashore outside the walls of Asgard a great pile of fuel, which they laid upon the deck of Balder's great ship, *Ringhorn,* as it lay stranded high up on the beach.

BALDER THE BEAUTIFUL

"Seventy ells and four extended
On the grass the vessel's keel;
High above it, gilt and splendid,
Rose the figurehead ferocious
With its crest of steel."

Then they adorned the funeral pyre with garlands of flowers, with golden vessels and rings, with finely wrought weapons and rich necklets and armlets; and when this was done they carried out the fair body of Balder the Beautiful, and bearing it reverently upon their shields they laid it upon the pyre.

Then they tried to launch the good ship, but so heavily laden was she that they could not stir her an inch.

The Mountain-Giants, from their heights afar, had watched the tragedy with eyes that were not unpitying, for even they had no ill-will for Balder, and they sent and told of a giantess called Hyrroken, who was so strong that she could launch any vessel whatever its weight might be.

So the Asas sent to fetch her from Giantland, and she soon came, riding a wolf for steed and twisted serpents for reins.

When she alighted, Odin ordered four of his mightiest warriors to hold the wolf, but he was so strong that they could do nothing until the giantess had thrown him down and bound him fast.

Then with a few enormous strides, Hyrroken reached the great vessel, and set her shoulder against the prow, sending the ship rolling into the deep.

BALDER THE BEAUTIFUL

The earth shook with the force of the movement as though with an earthquake, and the Asa
folk collided with one another like pine-trees during
a storm. The ship, too, with its precious weight,
was well-nigh lost. At this Thor was wroth and,
seizing his hammer, would have slain the giantess
had not the other Asas held him back, bidding him
not forget the last duty to the dead god. So Thor
hallowed the pyre with a touch of his sacred hammer and kindled it with a thorn twig, which is the
emblem of sleep.

Last of all, before the pyre blazed up, All-Father
Odin added to the pile of offerings his magic ring,
from which fell eight new rings every ninth night,
and bending he whispered in Balder's ear.

But none to this day know the words that Odin
spake thus in the ear of his dead son.

Then the flames from the pyre rose high and
the great ship drifted out to sea, and the wind
caught the sails and fanned the flames till it
seemed as though sky and sea were wrapped in
golden flame.

> "And while they gazed, the sun went lurid down
> Into the smoke-wrapt sea, and night came on.
> But through the dark they watched the burning ship
> Still carried o'er the distant waters. . . .
> But fainter, as the stars rose high, it flared;
> And as, in a decaying winter fire,
> A charr'd log, falling, makes a shower of sparks—
> So, with a shower of sparks, the pile fell in,
> Reddening the sea around; and all was dark."

And thus did Balder the Beautiful pass from the
peaceful steads of Asgard, as passes the sun when

he paints the evening clouds with the glory of his setting.

Note.—Most of the poetical extracts throughout this chapter are taken from Matthew Arnold's "Balder Dead."

THE WONDERFUL QUERN STONES

By Julia Goddard

ONCE upon a time there was a king of Denmark, or Gotland, as it was then called, whose name was Frothi. He was a great-grandson of the god Thor, and a very mighty king, and wherever the Danish language was spoken there was Frothi's name honored and respected.

Among his treasures were two quern stones; nothing much to look at, simply two common millstones in appearance, and no one who did not know what they could do would think of taking any notice of them. Nevertheless these quern stones were of more worth than anything that King Frothi had, for they could produce anything that the grinder of the quern or hand-mill wished for. They would bring gold, silver, precious stones, anything and everything; and besides this they could grind love, joy, peace; therefore it is not too much to say that these stones were worth more than all the treasures of the king put together.

At least they would have been if he could have made use of them, but they were so heavy that few could be found to turn the quern, and just at the time of which I am speaking there was no one at

91

all in the land of Gotland able to work away at the quern handle.

Now the more King Frothi pondered over his wonderful quern stones, the greater became his desire to use them, and he sought throughout the land from north to south, from east to west, if perchance he might find someone strong enough to help him in his need. But all to no purpose, and he was utterly in despair when, by good luck he happened to go on a visit to Fiölnir, King of Sweden, and to hear of two slave-women of great size and strength. Surely, thought Frothi, these are just the women to grind at my quern Grotti (for so it was called), and he asked King Fiölnir to be allowed to see them.

So King Fiölnir ordered the slaves to be brought before Frothi, and when Frothi saw them his spirits rose, for certainly Menia and Fenia were strong-looking women. They were eight feet in height, and broader across the shoulders than any of Frothi's warriors, and the muscles of their arms stood out like cords. And they lifted heavy weights, threw heavy javelins, and did so many feats of strength that Frothi felt quite sure that they would be able to turn the quern handle.

"I will buy these slaves," said he, "and take them with me to Gotland."

Menia and Fenia stood with their arms folded and their proud heads bowed down, whilst Frothi counted out the gold to the seller. They were slaves; with money had they been bought, with money were they sold again. What cared Frothi who was their father, or how they had come into the land of Sweden?

And he took them home with him and bade them grind at the quern. Now he should be able to test the power of the wonderful stones.

"Grind, grind, Menia and Fenia, let me see whether you have strength for the work."

So spake the King Frothi, and the huge women lifted the heavy stones as though they had been pebbles.

"What shall we grind?" asked the slaves.

"Gold, gold, peace and wealth for Frothi."

Gold! gold! the land was filled with riches. Treasure in the king's palace, treasure in the coffers of his subjects—gold! gold! There were no poor in the land, no beggars in the streets, no children crying for bread. All honor to the quern stones!

Peace! peace! no more war in the land. Frothi is at peace with everyone. And more than that, there was peace in all countries where Frothi's name was known, even to the far south; and everyone talked of Frothi's peace. Praise be to the quern stones! Wealth! yes, everything went well. Not one of the counsels of King Frothi failed. There was not a green field that did not yield a rich crop; not a tree but bent beneath its weight of fruit; not a stream that ran dry; not a vessel that sailed from the harbors of Gotland that came not back, after a fair voyage, in safety to its haven. There was good luck everywhere.

"Grind on, grind on, Menia and Fenia! good fortune is mine," said King Frothi.

And the slaves ground on.

"When shall we rest, when may we rest, King Frothi? It is weary work toiling day and night."

"No longer than whilst the cuckoo is silent in the spring."

"Never ceasing is the cry of the cuckoo in the groves; may we not rest longer?"

"Not longer," answered King Frothi, "than whilst the verse of a song is sung."

"That is but little!" sighed Menia and Fenia, and they toiled on. Their arms were weary and their eyes heavy; they would fain have slept, but Frothi would not let them have any sleep. They were but slaves who must obey their master, so they toiled on, still grinding peace and wealth to Frothi:

> "To Frothi and his queen
> Joy and peace—
> May plenty in the land
> Still increase.
> Frothi and his queen
> From dangers keep;
> May they on beds of down
> Sweetly sleep.
> No sword be drawn
> In Gotland old,
> By murderer bold.
> No harm befall
> The high or low—
> To none be woe,
> Good luck to all,
> Good luck to all,
> We grind, we grind,
> No rest we find,
> For rest we call."

Thus sang the two giant women; then they begged again: "Give us rest, O Frothi!"

But still Frothi answered: "Rest whilst the verse

of a song is sung, or as long as the cuckoo is silent in the spring."

No longer would the king give them.

Yet Frothi was deemed a good king, but gold and good luck were hardening his heart.

Menia and Fenia went on grinding, and their wrath grew deeper and deeper, and thus at last they spoke.

First said Fenia: "Thou wert not wise, O Frothi. Thou didst buy us because like giants we towered above the other slaves, because we were strong and hardy and could lift heavy burdens."

And Menia took up the wail: "Are we not the race of the mountain giants? Are not our kind greater than thine, O Frothi? The quern had never left the gray fell but for the giants' daughters. Never, never should we have ground as we have done had it not been that we remembered from what race we sprang."

Then answered Menia: "Nine long winters saw us training to feats of strength, nine long winters of wearisome labor. Deep down in the earth we toiled and toiled until we could move the high mountain from its foundations. We are weird women, O Frothi. We can see far into the future. Our eyes have looked upon the quern before. In the giants' house we whirled it until the earth shook, and hoarse thunder resounded through the caverns. Thou art not wise, O Frothi! O Frothi; thou art not wise!"

But Frothi heard them not; he was sleeping the sweet sleep that the quern stones had ground for him.

"Strong are we indeed," laughed Fenia sorrowfully, "strong to contend with the puny men,—we whose pastime in Sweden was to tame the fiercest bears, so that they ate from our hands; we who fought with mighty warriors and came off conquerors; we who helped one prince and put down another. Well we fought, and many were the wounds we received from sharp spears and flashing swords. Frothi knows not our power or he would scarce have brought us to his palace to treat us thus. Here no one has compassion upon us. Cold are the skies above us, and the pitiless wind beats on our breasts. Cold is the ground on which we stand, and the keen frost bites our feet. Ah, there are none to pity us. No one cares for the slaves. We grind forever an enemy's quern, and he gives us no rest. Grind, grind; I am weary of grinding; I must have rest."

"Nay," returned Menia, "talk not of rest until Frothi is content with what we bring him."

Then Fenia started: "If he gives us no rest, let us take it ourselves. Why should we any longer grind good for him who only gives us evil? We can grind what we please. Let us revenge ourselves."

Then Menia turned the handle quicker than ever, and in a wild voice she sang:

> "I see a ship comes sailing
> With warriors bold aboard,
> There's many a one that in Danish blood
> Would be glad to dip his sword.
> Say, shall we grind them hither?
> Say, shall they land to-night?
> Say, shall they set the palace afire?
> Say, shall they win the fight?"

Then called Fenia in a voice of thunder through the midnight air: "Frothi, Frothi, awake, awake! Wilt thou not listen to us? Have mercy and let us rest our weary limbs." But all was still, and Frothi gave no answer to the cry.

"Nay," answered Menia, "he will not hearken. Little he cares for the worn-out slaves. Revenge, revenge!"

And Frothi slept, not dreaming of the evil that was coming upon him.

And again Fenia shouted: "Frothi, Frothi, awake! The beacon is blazing. Danger is nigh. Wilt thou not spare?"

But Frothi gave no answer, and the giant women toiled on.

"O Frothi, Frothi, we cannot bear our weariness." And still no answer came.

"Frothi, Frothi, danger is nigh thee. Well-manned ships are gliding over the sea. It is Mysingr who comes; his white sail flutters in the wind; his flag is unfurled. Frothi, Frothi, awake, awake! thou shalt be king no longer."

And as the giant women ground, the words they spake came to pass,—they were grinding revenge for themselves and brought the enemy nearer and nearer.

"Ho! hearken to the herald! Frothi, Frothi, the town is on fire. The palaces will soon be ruined heaps. Grind, Menia, ever more swiftly, until we grind death to Frothi."

And Menia and Fenia ground and ground till Mysingr and his followers landed from the ships. They ground until they had reached the palace.

"To arms, to arms!" shouted the warder, but it was too late. The Gotlanders armed themselves; but who could stand against the army that the slave women were grinding against them?

Not long did the struggle last. Frothi and his Gotlanders fought bravely, but the sea-king and his allies were mightier, for the giantesses were in giant mood, and turned the handle faster and faster, until down fell the quern stones. Then sank Frothi pierced with wounds, and the fight was over. The army that Menia and Fenia had ground to help Mysingr vanished; and Mysingr and his men alone were left conquerors on the bloody field.

They loaded their ships with treasure, and Mysingr took with him Menia, Fenia, and the quern stones.

But, alas! Mysingr was no wiser than King Frothi had been.

Gold, however, was not his first thought; he had enough of that, but he wanted something else that just then was more to him than gold.

There was no salt on board the sea-king's vessels; so he said: "Grind salt."

And Menia and Fenia ground salt for Mysingr.

At midnight they asked if they had ground enough.

And Mysingr bade them grind on.

And so they ground and ground until the ship was so heavy with salt that it sank, and the sea-king and all his men were drowned.

Where the quern stones went down there is to this day a great whirlpool, and the waters of the sea have been salt ever since.

THEY WOULD SWOOP DOWN AND BEAR HIS
LIFELESS BODY TO VALHALLA

—page 100

From the painting by K. Dielitz

BRUNHILDA AND THE MAGIC SWORD

By Constance Maud

O N the summit of a rocky mountain peak a beautiful maiden lay sleeping. On every side rose the tall dark pine trees, like huge giants on guard. A circle of magic fire formed a glowing wall around her rocky couch.

The sun rose and set, night succeeded day, winter and summer came and went, but the maiden slept on still.

From head to foot she was encased in shining armor. On her breast lay a shield, on her head glistened a warrior's helmet, and at her side a spear. For on a day long past it had been decreed that thus this maiden should sleep, till awakened by the kiss of one who would dare the flames for her sake, and claim her as bride.

Many a knight, hearing of the beautiful sleeper, had thought to win his way to her; but no sooner did he see the angry fire darting out on all sides, and feel the scorching heat of the great flames, than the bravest fell back discouraged.

Time was when this fair warrior had dwelt with the gods and goddesses in Valhalla, for she was none other than Brunhilda, favorite daughter of Wotan the king. She had eight sisters, each one beautiful as the dawn, and knowing neither fear nor weakness; but among them all Brunhilda was fairest, bravest, and strongest. These nine maidens were known as the Valkyrie, and each was a warrior perfect in the art of war. Chief among their duties was to attend all battles on earth. Riding on their winged horses, they would hover over the battlefield, and, when a hero fell, swoop down and bear his lifeless body to Valhalla, where he would awaken to live among the gods, and be from henceforth one of the chosen bodyguard of Wotan.

Now it happened on a day in these times long past that Wotan called to him Brunhilda, and charged her that she should defend Siegmund the Volsung in a deadly combat he was about to engage in with the grim and savage Hunding.

Wotan had reasons for wishing to grant Siegmund a special favor. The Father of the Gods had once struck a mighty sword into the heart of an ancient ash tree, decreeing that it should belong to him alone who could pluck it out. Many a valiant knight had tried to win the sword; but all in vain. Buried deep in the ash-stem it remained till Siegmund came and with one powerful wrench drew forth the weapon. Then Wotan rejoiced that a man had been found strong enough to win his sword, and he loved Siegmund the Volsung greatly.

But Wotan hated Hunding, for he was a tyrant and a bully. With all his strength and bluster, he had never been able to pluck out the sword, though many a time had he tried, grinding his teeth savagely over his failure.

Now the cause of strife between Hunding and Siegmund was this—Hunding had a beautiful wife, Sieglinda by name, whom he had married sorely against her will. With her whole soul she loathed and hated the cruel Hunding, and only longed to escape from him. So it befell one day she fled with Siegmund the Volsung; for the first moment they met, these two loved one another, and Sieglinda said to herself: "It were better far to die with Siegmund than to live with Hunding."

When Hunding discovered their flight, he set forth to pursue the lovers, uttering loud threats of vengeance, which echoed through the forest for miles round.

He called on Fricka, Queen of Valhalla, to help him, for he knew this goddess to be most stern in her view of the duties of wives.

"O mighty goddess," cried Hunding, "grant me thine aid! May thy justice and my righteous vengeance speedily overtake the miscreants! Let not the scoundrel Volsung turn the power of Wotan's sword to his own advantage, for then would all men surely say that the god's favor rests on faithless wives!"

Fricka promised him her warm support, and also that of Wotan, whom she knew she could bend to her all-powerful will, however opposed he might feel. Scarcely had Brunhilda left the presence of her father when the goddess Fricka drove up in a car drawn by two fierce fleet-footed rams.

With stern majesty she demanded that Siegmund should be given up to justice, and the magic sword he had won be broken against the spear of Wotan himself. It was for the honor of the gods and Valhalla, cried Fricka, that Hunding's prayer for vengeance on his faithless wife and her lover be answered.

In vain did Wotan plead every excuse he could devise for his favorite Siegmund. Not until he had solemnly sworn on oath to cast off Siegmund, and recall the order given to Brunhilda, did the stern goddess take her leave. Wotan sank on the nearest rock, a picture of utter dejection. In this sad state Brunhilda found him shortly after. She listened in dismay, when in gloomy tones he said to her:

"Thou shalt fight to-day as Fricka desires, and thou shalt vanquish utterly Siegmund the Volsung! Heed well my words—my former order I now recall."

Brunhilda could scarcely believe she heard aright. "Nay, but thou lovest Siegmund," she cried in sore perplexity, "and Hunding dost thou hate! Ah," she continued, as a new thought came to her, "this second decree is not given with thy heart! Rather will I abide by the first!"

Brunhilda spoke with good intent, but these were unlucky words. In many respects the mighty Wotan was not unlike a mortal man.

"How, froward child! Dost dare dispute my word?" he cried. "Thou who are nought but the blind tool used by my hand! Wake not my wrath, but heed well my command—Siegmund dies in the fight with Hunding. I have spoken—go!"

In sorrowful amaze the warrior-maiden took up her weapons and departed. She found the ill-starred lovers resting awhile in their wanderings through the trackless forest. Sieglinda's strength was utterly spent, and she had fallen into a deep swoon.

"Siegmund the Volsung," spoke Brunhilda in solemn tones, "I come to call thee hence!"

"Who art thou, so fair and stern?" he asked.

"Only those already doomed to death may look upon my face," she answered. "I am she who bears the fallen warrior to Valhalla."

"And will this my love come also to Valhalla?" asked Siegmund, gazing tenderly at the pale face of the sleeping Sieglinda.

"Nay," replied Brundhilda, "such is not the will of Wotan; Sieglinda must remain upon the earth. But thou shalt be with heroes, and the daughters of Wotan shall wait upon thee."

"If my love may not be there, I will have none of Valhalla's delights! I follow thee not!" answered Siegmund fixedly.

"Thou hast looked on the face of the Valkyrie —thou hast no choice but to follow her," said Brunhilda.

"By what warrior's hand must I fall?" asked Siegmund.

"Hunding will fell thee in the fight to-day," answered the Valkyrie.

But Siegmund laughed this prophecy to scorn. "Seest thou this sword?" he said, drawing forth the weapon of Wotan. "It was made by one in whose name I am sure of victory."

"He who bestowed that sword now withdraws the charm, and himself dooms thee to death!" cried Brunhilda in terrible ringing tones.

"Hush! or thou wilt awaken my love," said Siegmund, bending tenderly over Sieglinda. "If what thou sayest be true, woe and shame be to him who bestowed such a sword! If I must perish and desert her," he continued bitterly, "never will I pass to the Valhalla of Wotan."

"What!" cried Brunhilda in horror. "Thou wouldst forego the glory of Valhalla for the sake of this poor feeble woman?"

"If thou canst feel no pity, and canst give no help in my sore distress, then leave me at least in peace. Speak not of Valhalla's empty joys."

How help this heroic lover without disobeying the order of Wotan her father? "Confide thy beloved to my care—I will protect her, noble Siegmund," she said earnestly.

"I thank thee," replied Siegmund, "but none save I alone can protect my love. And if this sword, which a traitor fashioned, is to prove false in the fight, better it should take our two lives with one fell stroke." So saying, he drew his sword and held it over Sieglinda. But Brunhilda seized his arm.

"Stay thy hand, reckless man! Thou shalt not die, but live. Thou shalt not leave Sieglinda. Sooner will I, Brunhilda, cancel the death-lot. Doubt me not, my promise is spoken. Take up thy sword, it shall prevail, for I will aid thee. Speed now to meet thy foe. Hark to the sound of Hunding's horn! Farewell, Siegmund!"

With these words Brunhilda sprang on her winged horse, and soon vanished through the clouds.

Siegmund gazed after her with grateful eyes;

then, stooping, kissed Sieglinda, saying softly:
"Slumber in peace, my beloved, till the fight is
over and peril past." The horn of Hunding
sounded loudly in the distance, and Siegmund
hastened away to meet him, leaving Sieglinda still
asleep.

A terrible thunderstorm now broke over the
forest, thunderclouds rolled and clashed together.
All was dark as night, no light save from the
forked flashes which darted here and there in fiery
streaks, like the gleaming swords of an unseen
enemy fighting in the clouds.

Louder and louder called the hunting-horns of
Hunding and his followers. Presently a terrific
thunderclap awoke Sieglinda. She started up in
wildest terror. Siegmund was no longer by her
side, a dense darkness surrounded her, while near
at hand rang the voice of Hunding crying in tones
of wrath: "Ha, thou scoundrel Volsung! come out
and fight, or my hounds shall hunt thee down!"

The voices now seemed to come from a rock over
Sieglinda's head. She listened in eager anxiety as
they continued to shout to one another. Suddenly
a flash of lightning showed them fighting desper-
ately on a ridge of the rock.

Sieglinda rushed forward, forgetting all fears for
herself in an agony for Siegmund's safety.
Another blinding flash made her stagger backwards, dazed and giddy. For one instant the whole
mountain-peak was lit up, and she saw, hovering
over Siegmund in the air, a woman on a winged
horse, covering him with a shield as he fought.

"Now is the moment, Siegmund the Volsung,"

cried a clear voice from above. "Slay him with thy magic sword!"

But as Siegmund aimed his deadly stroke at the heart of Hunding, a dreadful disaster befell. Wotan, standing unseen at Hunding's side, put forth his spear and received the thrust of Siegmund's sword. "Back before my spear! Be splintered, thou sword!" roared the voice of the god in tones of thunder.

With a sharp sound like a cry the sword of Siegmund snapped and flew to pieces.

Brunhilda fell back in dismay as the gleaming eye of Wotan met her own; and instantly Hunding plunged his sword into the heart of his defenceless foe. Sieglinda fell senseless to the ground. Brunhilda, gathering up the fragments of the sword, hurried to her side, and, lifting her to the saddle, rode off at lightning speed through the clouds.

Siegmund's lifeless body lay at the feet of Wotan. Remorsefully he gazed upon the brave young warrior he would fain have spared. The sight of Hunding was more than he could bear. With a backward wave of his hand Wotan cried fiercely: "Go, knave! Kneel before Fricka and tell her how well Wotan avenged her slight!"

And at these words Hunding staggered and fell lifeless to the ground; for no mortal man could stand before the scornful wave of Wotan's hand, unless he were of the race of Heroes who know not fear.

So Hunding died; but there was no Valkyrie to bear him to Valhalla. All his life he had been a tyrant and a bully, and such men, were they the best fighters in the world, could find no favor with the warrior-maidens.

"Now for Brunhilda!" cried Wotan, his voice causing the very trees to quake and shiver. "She who has dared to defy and disobey me! Terrible shall be her punishment, though she be my best-loved child."

He sprang on his war-horse and followed where the parted clouds showed Brunhilda's recent track.

BRUNHILDA'S SLEEP GUARDED BY LOKI'S FIERY ARM

By Constance Maud

ON the summit of a lofty mountain the Valkyrie sisters met after the day's toil, to await their father Wotan, and present him with the heroes they had gathered from the battlefields on earth.

One by one they alighted on their winged steeds, shouting the Valkyries' war-cry as greeting to each other, "Hei-a-ha! Hei-a-hei! Hoyoto-ho!"

From the north came Helmwiga and Gerhilda well-laden; the fierce Norsemen never failed to supply fresh recruits for Wotan's bodyguard. From east and west and every quarter came some tribute to Wotan, borne on the Valkyries' saddle-bows.

"Where tarries our sister Brunhilda?" asked several eagerly. "She is late to-night. Ah, see, in the distance, who is that speeding hither like a cloud driven before the storm? Surely not so rides our queenly Brunhilda!"

With the fainting Sieglinda in her arms, it was indeed Brunhilda who came in sight at last, flying on the wings of the wind.

"Faster! oh, faster, Grani my steed!" she cried to the panting horse.

And Grani, his strong head downward bent, with his winged feet cleft the rolling clouds till they hissed like water meeting fire, while his breath came in great snorting gasps, and the foam flew from his mouth in big flakes like snow. Never before in his long service with his noble mistress had Grani been urged to flight, and he knew that dire indeed must be the danger which Brunhilda dare not stand and face.

"Well striven, good Grani, faithful steed!" cried Brunhilda, as the horse alighted on the mountain and dropped exhausted to the ground. Lifting Sieglinda, now fully conscious, from the saddle, Brunhilda hastened toward her sisters.

"She brings no hero! It is nought but a maiden!" they exclaimed in wonder and disappointment.

"Help me, O sisters! Shield me and this poor woman, I beseech you!" implored Brunhilda breathlessly.

"Why this furious haste? From whom fliest thou?" asked the Valkyries, crowding round her in amazement.

"I fly from our father! In terrible wrath he hunts me down!"

"Thou fliest from our father?" cried all the

sisters, horror-struck. "What hast thou done that thou shouldest fly from him?"

Brunhilda poured out her tale in eager haste. From one to another she looked for pity or sympathy but in vain. Sternly the Valkyries eyed her as she knelt and implored them to shelter her and the unfortunate Sieglinda from the wrath of Wotan.

"Woe to thee, most unworthy sister! How durst thou disobey the sacred command of Wotan our father? Nought but disaster can follow!"

And now, from the north, raging storm-clouds came sweeping toward them. One of the Valkyries mounted to the topmost peak, and, looking across the sky, called out:

"He comes! Wotan the wrathful father! flying furiously in the storm-clouds on his snorting steed!"

"Who will lend me a horse? Grani is spent,— see, he cannot even stand! Rossvisa, my sister, have pity, lend me thy racer!" Brunhilda implored, turning to a stately Valkyrie whose magnificent steed was at her side.

"My racer never yet fled our father in fear, and never shall!" replied Rossvisa coldly. To each one Brunhilda went, beseeching a horse.

"We stand by our father!" the Valkyries all answered her. Brunhilda was in despair.

Then Sieglinda, who had watched the scene in gloomy silence, came forward and spoke. "Sorrow not for me, noble maiden. Oh, why didst thou not leave me to die with Siegmund? If thou hast indeed pity on me, stretch forth thy sword and pierce me now to the heart."

"Nay, that must not be," answered Brunhilda. "Thou must live still, Sieglinda, for thou shalt have a son, who will one day be the greatest hero in the world. Heed now what I say. To the eastward there lies a mighty forest; there Wotan will not pursue thee, for he abhors the spot. It is the dwelling of Fafnir the dragon, his mortal foe. Thither haste thee. I will remain here to face the god's wrath, and hinder him till thou hast escaped far on thy journey."

"Fly, then, Sieglinda!" cried Brunhilda; "speed to the east! Faint not and fear not, whatever betide. Live for thy son, and call him by this name from me—Siegfried the Victor! Give him these shattered pieces of his father's sword—from the field of death I took them. One day he shall weld them into a mighty weapon. Farewell, Sieglinda!" It was none too soon. Another minute, and with a crash the angry god descended in the midst of the dismayed Valkyries.

"Where is Brunhilda, the rebel?" he roared in tones of fury. "Let her come forth! Dare any to shelter her, they shall share the same doom."

The Valkyrie sisters had closed round Brunhilda in the vain hope of hiding her; but at these words she came out from their midst, her face pale and set. "Here am I, my father, to suffer my sentence," she said firmly.

Wotan was not prepared for such calm fearlessness. "I sentence thee not," he answered. "'Tis thine own misdeed condemns thee!" Then, with

gathering wrath, he continued, "I made thee a
Valkyrie, highest in honor and favor. Thou hast
forsworn thy noble calling, and played traitor to
thy father. No longer mayst thou dwell in Valhalla as my child. . Never more will I send thee
for my dead heroes. Never again shalt thou fill
my cup at the feast! Degraded and exiled art thou
forever!"

Brunhilda stood as though turned to stone.

The Valkyries burst into loud lamentations.
"Woe! woe! Alas, our unhappy sister!"

Then Brunhilda cried aloud in great agony of
mind, "O father, disown me not! Take not from
me all thy gifts! Leave me not to utter desolation!"

But Wotan was not to be appeased, and the
worst part of the sentence was yet to come. "Thou
thyself hast called down my curse, and here where
we now stand it shall strike thee!" he answered.
"A deep, dreamless sleep shall overpower thee, and
to that man who first awakens thee shalt thou
belong from henceforth!"

At this grim sentence all the Valkyries lifted
their voices in a wail of horror and dismay, crying:
"Oh, terrible father, recall thy curse! Let not our
sister be degraded to such a shameful fate. Each
one of us shares in her disgrace."

Brunhilda's woe was too great for any cry.

"I have spoken once—my words abide forever!"
retorted Wotan. "Thy treacherous sister," he
continued, "no longer belongs to the glorious troop
of Valkyries. Her godhood is forfeit! The doom
she has earned is now to wed a mortal man."

At this picture of her future, poor Brunhilda sank with a deep groan to the earth.

Wotan turned to the eight sisters, who looked on in deep distress. "If ye desire not a like doom, forbear to pity the outcast. Away now, begone, every one of ye! Haste, lest I hurl the same woe on your heads!" The earth quaked and trembled as Wotan passionately stamped his foot, and fiery gleams shot from his eyes.

With a last despairing look at Brunhilda and a wild cry of woe, the Valkyries sprang on their horses and fled in hot haste. They knew if their stern father spared not his favorite Brunhilda, still less would he spare them.

The storm had now ceased. Brunhilda lay prostrate on the ground. Wotan stood motionless in silent gloom. His rage seemed spent, like that of the storm. Then Brunhilda rose slowly from the ground, and spoke in deep sorrowful tones. "Was my deed verily so shameful that such shame should fall upon me? Was it so base an act to fulfil thy *first* command? Speak, O my father, and soften thy wrath toward me."

"Thou didst wilfully disobey my sacred order. The *first* command I recalled," replied Wotan bitterly.

"But not of thine own will. 'Twas Fricka who made thee false to thy nobler self; and because I held in my heart thy true wish, I dared to slight thy second order."

The mention of Fricka brought an angry flash from the eyes of Wotan. "For that rebellious act the curse now falls on thee," he answered.

"But I knew how well thou lovedst Siegmund," pleaded Brunhilda; "and when I found him in the forest and told him of thy death decree, he revealed to me a wondrous thing I never before had known. For in his strong courage and his undying devotion to Sieglinda, I learned what love could be. And I resolved, whether victory or death came of it, to serve one so noble. In acting thus, O father, I was faithful to thee, even though disobeying thereby thy command."

Wotan groaned. "Thou knowest nought of what compelled my action. Dark clouds are gathering on every side—the day of doom threatens Valhalla! I dared not follow what my heart desired. But all this woe I kept from thee, that thy life might be happy and free from care. And thou, my favorite, my beloved child, hast turned thy hand against me and proved false to my trust. Never again may I behold thy face! Since love proved thy undoing, follow now that man whom thou perforce must love."

"If indeed I am banished forever, at least," she pleaded, "grant me one parting boon, O stern father. If I must wed a mortal man, let not thy Valkyrie fall a victim to some worthless poltroon, when fetters of sleep bind her fast. In this one thing, O father, hear my prayer—at thy command let magical fire spring up in a glowing wall around my couch, that the flames may scare and scorch the timid, and none save a hero stout of heart may dare' to approach me."

Wotan, stern and unbending though he was, could not refuse this one last petition. "Farewell,"

he said, "thou who wert once the light of my eyes.
I grant thee this last parting boon—tongues of
flame will I set round this place; with their terrible
fury shall they scare the faint-hearted. Only one
shall awaken the bride, he whose strength and freedom is greater than that of Wotan."

With a cry of grateful joy Brunhilda threw
herself into her father's arms. Tenderly he looked
at her, and slowly kissed her on both eyes. A
profound slumber instantly fell on Brunhilda, and
Wotan, taking her in his arms, laid her on a mossy
mound overshadowed by a great fir tree.

"Farewell forever, my beloved beautiful child,"
he murmured sadly, as he closed her helmet visor
and covered her with the long steel shield of the
Valkyries.

Then, going to a rock near by, he struck it three
times with the point of his spear, commanding in a
loud voice: "Loki! Fire-spirit, come forth. Spread
me thy flames around this fell. Here keep thou
guard as I decree. Loki, appear!"

And at his word, out sprang from the rock a
long tongue of flame, which quickly spread to a
mighty river of fire circling round and round the
mountain where Brunhilda lay sleeping.

Then Wotan, holding aloft his spear, cried in
ringing tones: "Only he whose spirit quaileth not
before the spear of Wotan shall pass this fiery bar!"
With these words he vanished into the clouds, and
the night fell.

Such was the story of Brunhilda's long sleep.

HOW SIEGFRIED KILLED THE DRAGON

By Constance Maud

WHEN Sieglinda fled from the wrath of Wotan, she went eastward, as Brunhilda directed. For long days and nights she journeyed, and came at length to the country of the Nibelungs, where dwelt the great dragon Fafnir.

Now the Nibelungs were a race of ugly dwarfs, who lived underground, burrowing in the depths of the earth for gold and treasure. They cared nothing for the free forest life, the sunshine, trees, and flowers, or pleasures of the chase. Like prisoners in a dungeon, they chose rather to pass their lives digging and toiling in the dark for gold, and hoarding it up with anxious care.

A vast heap of this treasure, including a magic Ring, stolen from the Mermaids of the Rhine, and a Wishing Cap of strange powers called the Tarnhelm, had fallen into the hands of Fafnir the giant, who, in order the better to guard these precious possessions, transformed himself into a huge dragon, the terror of all the country round.

Sieglinda lived a sad, lonely life in the forest. She avoided the caves where Fafnir dwelt, and as the dwarfs seldom came above ground, she saw nothing of them.

There was one, however, whom it was fated she should meet. His name was Mimi, and of all the dwarfs of the Nibelung race he was the ugliest and the meanest. Notwithstanding this, he was a

115

very skilful blacksmith, and could also do fine work in gold, silver, and steel. Like all the Nibelungs, he had a great dislike to fresh air, so he built his forge in a cave half sunk underground, with a great chimney in the roof.

Mimi was working at his anvil one day, when he heard a deep groan outside the cave. On going out, he saw a woman with a baby in her arms lying on the ground. She was dying, and Mimi had only found her in time to hear her last words.

"Have pity!" cried poor Sieglinda (for it was she). "Thy goodness shall be rewarded. I am dying. Take this my son and bring him up. Call his name Siegfried, for one day he will be the greatest hero in the world. Keep for him this broken sword—it was Siegmund his father's—'Needful,' he called it!"

Now Mimi was not a kind-hearted person, and nothing would have induced him to take care of a strange baby out of pity. But when Sieglinda said that her child was the son of the famous hero Siegmund the Volsung, and would one day himself be the greatest hero in the world, then a grand idea struck Mimi. He would bring up the boy as his own son, and when Siegfried was full-grown, he should be sent forth to kill Fafnir and win for his foster-father all the dragon's treasure!

So Mimi answered Sieglinda in a cracked voice, which he tried to make pleasant:

"Be comforted, poor woman. I will take the child out of the kindness of my heart, and do my best for him."

Sieglinda died with a blessing on her lips, and

Mimi took the little Siegfried to dwell with him in his cave.

But the dwarf soon found he had no easy task in bringing up this son of a hero. Never was such a daring, fearless, mischievous infant. Many a time would Mimi have turned him adrift, or put an end to him with a blow from his smith's hammer, but for the thought that this bold young imp was just the sort to delight in slaying a dragon, and pay no heed as to who took the treasure.

As soon as he could walk, the boy would escape into the forest, and there run wild all day; chasing the bears and foxes, feeling no fear of any living creature. He grew so fast that in a few years he was bigger and stronger than Mimi, whom from the first he disliked, perceiving the dwarf to be false and cowardly in all his actions.

Mimi always told the boy he was his father, and this was a great trouble to Siegfried. How he would have loved a father who was noble, fearless, and brave! But Mimi feared everything. He trembled and turned pale did a wolf but howl, or the thunder roll. He feared not only giants, but ordinary huntsmen and woodcutters, and always hid when they came in sight. He feared even Siegfried, so the boy soon became his master, and led him a sorry life. But creatures too small and weak to excite his fear Mimi would cruelly oppress and kill; and this, more than anything else, made Siegfried hate the very sight of him.

Time went on, and Siegfried grew into a tall strong youth, with fair locks shining in the sun like burnished gold, and fearless blue eyes, which

laughed danger in the face. At last the day came
when Mimi hoped to be repaid for all his trouble
with "the good-for-nothing cub," as he called the
boy. Siegfried had ordered him in a lordly way to
make a sword fit for his use—"one that does not
snap in two at the first stroke," he said, and strode
off to the forest for his day's hunt.

Mimi had undertaken the task more than once
lately, for he was anxious on his own account that
a sword should be fashioned strong and tough
enough to slay the dragon. But as yet every
weapon he welded had snapped in two at the first
trial of its strength by Siegfried.

With mighty effort Mimi hammered and
wrought at his anvil all that day. "A stouter sword
I never shaped! It would defy a giant," he said
at last, looking on his day's work. "Yet I sorely
fear, when grasped by that fiery youth, it will twist
up like a straw!"

Mimi sat down exhausted and despairing. "Ah
me! What is to be done?" he sighed. "If only
Siegmund's splintered sword could be welded together again! But no power on earth can do that!
Never saw I such mighty steel—all my craft is pow-
erless to melt it—the thing is magic!"

"Oho! Come on, friend Bruin!" cried a voice
from without, and Siegfried burst into the cave,
driving a great grisly bear, which he held in tow
with a rope.

Mimi started up in terror, and hid behind the
forge shrieking: "Take away the fearsome brute!"

Siegfried burst into peals of laughter at Mimi's
fear. "Mr. Bruin is a friend of mine. He has

come to ask for the sword—is it not finished yet?"

"Yes, it is finished. There it lies yonder. Take away the beast!" panted Mimi.

Siegfried seized the sword eagerly. "Go now, friend Bruin," he said, loosing the rope, and the bear gladly escaped.

"See how nice and bright is the sword," said Mimi, creeping out of his hiding-place.

"To what purpose is a sword bright if it is not hard?" asked Siegfried, with scorn. He struck it on the anvil, and the sword instantly flew to pieces. "What silly toy hast thou palmed off on me here?" he cried, flinging it away in disgust. "Dost call that a sword? Why talk to me of battles, and giants, and deeds of daring, if thou canst shape me no better weapon than that? Right well dost thou deserve that I break it on thy crazy old head!"

"Ungrateful boy! Think of all my goodness to thee! When a wretched, troublesome cub, who was it warmed, clothed, and fed thee? Who patiently taught thee all thou knowest? And what is my reward? nought but abuse and hate!" Mimi pretended to wipe away a tear, as though overcome by grief; but he had done this once too often.

"No doubt thou hast taught me much, and told me many lies," answered Siegfried, who was in no mood for polite speeches. "But there is one thing," he continued, "thou hast never taught me, and which I am now determined to know—Who and from whence are my father and mother? Long have I felt thou art no kin of mine. I see in the forest all the young resemble their parents; but thou and I are no more like than a toad and a bright shining fish!"

Mimi did not like the comparison. His eyes gleamed with hate.

"Tell me the truth, or I will shake it out of thee!" cried Siegfried, seizing him by the throat.

"Let loose, or thou wilt murder me, wretched boy!" screamed the dwarf in terror. "I will tell thee all!" Then, trembling and quaking, he told Siegfried all he knew of his unhappy parents, with many comments on his own exceeding kindness, to which Siegfried listened impatiently. Finally, in proof of his tale (which, for a wonder, was true), Mimi produced the two pieces of splintered sword, saying dolefully—"Behold, as reward for all my toil and trouble, this had I from thy mother!—a broken sword thy father died while wielding— 'Needful,' they called it—a foolish name, since it failed in time of need!"

Siegfried rejoiced at learning that he sprang from a noble race. He thought with tenderness of his unfortunate parents, and wished he could have brought some comfort to his poor brave mother. Eagerly he seized the broken pieces of his father's sword. "To me it shall be well named 'Needful'," he cried. "If thou hast any craft, show it now, Mimi. Up and forge me these fragments! My father's sword I will wield to-day, and with it go forth into the world." So saying, he went out of the cave, leaving Mimi looking disconsolately at the broken sword.

"No furnace can melt this hard steel. No

hammer can bend it. Yet this is the sword which alone can slay Fafnir!"

When Siegfried returned Mimi had still done nothing. He seemed to have just awakened from some bad dream.

"Ho, lazy fellow! Hast finished the sword?" he shouted.

Mimi crept up slowly from behind the anvil, looking round cautiously, lest Siegfried had brought some wild beast with him. "The sword?" he exclaimed in dismal tones. "How can I mend such steel? But, hark ye, boy;" and Mimi came close up, peering into his face; "hast ever known Fear?"

"Whom meanest thou by Fear? Never have I heard of him!" Siegfried answered impatiently.

"Alone in the forest on a dark night, near some gloomy spot, when a sudden rustle or roar startled thee close at hand, hast never felt grisly shudderings, thy heart beating and bursting in thy breast?"

The little dwarf's description of this unknown feeling interested Siegfried greatly. He even forgot to be angry about the sword. "Right strange and wondrous must that be," he cried. "My heart is ever firm and steady—how I long to feel sensations so new and curious—this shivering and shaking and beating and bursting! Tell me then, Mimi, how can I learn to know Fear?"

"I will tell thee!" said Mimi, delighted. "There is one I know of who will not fail to teach thee. A monstrous dragon he is, Fafnir by name. I will guide thee to his hole."

"Where is it? Let us be gone at once. Give me the sword, I will mend it myself. Verily thou art but a bungling smith." Heaping a mass of wood on the fire, Siegfried blew it up till the flames roared like hungry lions. Then, fixing the sword-splinters in a vice, he proceeded to file them to powder.

Mimi watched in wonder and envy. Now and then he timidly offered his advice, to which Siegfried paid as much heed as though it were the squeaking of a mouse.

Working away with a will, Siegfried performed the mightiest feats of strength with no more exertion than if he were shaping a toy for a child. When the sword was all in powder, he put it in a pot on the forge. Then, blowing up the flames afresh, he sang in a voice strong as a clarion a joyful song of freedom and victory.

The steel sword of his father seemed to understand the song, for it bubbled and spluttered all liquid in the pot, as though it would leap out for very joy.

Mimi listened, too, but he did not enjoy the song. His wily brain was hard at work planning his own ends. That Siegfried should remake the sword was very well, for without it Fafnir could not be slain—but supposing he took the Ring, the gold, and all? —what then would become of poor Mimi? So he prepared a wonderful draught of such powerful poisons, that one drop was enough to make a giant fall senseless to the ground. "When he comes home weary from his fight with the dragon, I will give him this refreshing cup," said Mimi, with a malicious chuckle.

Meanwhile Siegfried poured the molten steel into

a mould, which he forthwith plunged hissing into a tank of cold water. "Ha, ha, Mimi!" he cried. "So you have turned cook, and brew sauces while I brew swords! Methinks," he added to himself, "I would rather taste of my cooking than his!"

The dwarf's sharp little eyes glistened with hate as he stirred the potion, and crooned low his song of hope and vengeance. "So the pupil puts the craftsman to shame, does he? Only let him wait till this draught is duly prepared!"

"Now, Needful, come forth, and see what the hammer can do for thee!" cried Siegfried.

He took the sword hard and cold from the water, and thrust it in the red-hot coals till it glowed like a sword of flame. Then with a huge smith's hammer, he beat it out on the anvil. The sparks flew right and left like fireflies, and Siegfried sang again:

"Ha, Needful! So do I tame thy spirit! At my command thou glowest fiery red—then in the water I cool thine anger till thy sides gleam steely blue! Now with stalwart strokes I beat thee out, Needful, my famous sword—so does my spirit enter thee! Soon thy cold blade shall glow red again with the blood of traitors! Dead didst thou lie, but I, Siegfried, give thee life once more. Needful, come forth!"

Brandishing the sword, Siegfried brought down a mighty stroke across the anvil. With a crash it split from top to bottom, giving Mimi such a shock he nearly upset his precious pot.

So the sword was remade, and Siegfried forthwith started out, guided by Mimi, to find the dragon. Darkness had fallen, but Siegfried was too impatient for his first lesson in fear to wait till morning. All night they tramped through the forest. At every rustle of the branches, every snapping of a twig, Mimi started as though he were shot. Siegfried watched him with scorn; his mocking laughter reëchoed through the stillness.

And the dwarf's hatred grew more bitter with every step. Many a time he longed then and there to force down Siegfried's throat the draught he carried so carefully under his cloak.

On they went, Siegfried scarcely heeding the way, so high bounded his heart with thoughts of adventure. To fight and conquer giants and dragons—to go out into the wide world and be free as air—free from the false, cowardly Mimi—free to choose brave and noble companions whom he could honor and love! What unknown joys might not life be waiting to give him who dared to win them!

Day was dawning when at length they reached some rocky caverns at the foot of a mountainous chain. "This is the spot," said Mimi in a trembling whisper. "See'st thou yonder dark, yawning hole? Inside lies Fafnir. Day and night he guards his treasure—the gold, the Ring, and the Tarnhelm."

"So he is the master who will teach me Fear?" cried Siegfried joyfully. "Thou canst leave me now, Mimi—I need thee no more."

"Ungrateful boy!" sighed the dwarf. "But I will not go far. My heart will be torn with anxiety for thy safety. Fafnir is no common foe— with a single snap he could swallow thee whole!"

Siegfried laughed. "I shall be careful not to thrust myself down such a wide throat!"

"Eh, but his very breath is potent poison," continued Mimi, "and the foam of his mouth, if it but touch thee, will shrivel up both flesh and bones on the spot. While as to his tail, 'tis like a huge snake, which, once thou art in its coils, will grind thy limbs as though they were powdered glass!"

Mimi hastened away, muttering to himself, "Would that the dragon and the boy might slay one another!"

Siegfried threw himself down under the trees to wait for Fafnir. A bird began to sing in the branches overhead. Siegfried listened, and wished he could understand the bird's language. "Perchance if I but knew it, he sings to me of my mother, and of all I wish to know!"

Siegfried gazed up between the leaves at the bird, which paused for a moment, and fixed on him a pair of little black eyes; then started afresh, gurgling forth his liquid notes and trills.

"The language of the birds may be learned, so I have heard tell!" cried Siegfried, and springing up, he went down to the stream and cut a reed with his sword. With much trouble he fashioned a pipe, and returning to his friend in the tree, tried to imitate his music. The bird stopped to listen, much surprised. But it was a sorry performance, and though this bird was too polite to laugh, Siegfried distinctly heard a tittering and fluttering from other listeners. Much disheartened, he flung away the reed.

"It is no use!" he cried. "I alone in all the

world have no friend, no companion with whom I can speak. Well, at least, I will try if there is anyone will understand *this* language." He took the silver horn slung round his neck and blew a ringing challenge. It was answered in a moment by a low roar from the distant cave, followed soon by slow, crashing steps and deep-drawn snorts coming nearer and nearer.

Presently Siegfried beheld an enormous wriggling mass of shining scales advancing toward him. "So my call has awakened this lovely creature," he laughed, as the hideous monster came full in view.

"What is that?" asked a thick, guttural voice, and the dragon paused to gaze in wonder and contempt at the youth who faced him with such bold laughing eyes.

"So thou hast the gift of speech, Mr. Dragon? That is well!" remarked Siegfried lightly. "I have come to learn from thee, what is Fear."

"Overbold art thou," growled the voice, while from enormous jaws issued a volume of fire and smoke, filling the air with a noisome vapor.

"Bold or overbold, here am I to learn my lesson—so teach me without delay!" answered Siegfried. Fafnir opened his yawning jaws and showed two rows of jagged, pointed teeth, enormous in size.

"Verily thou hast a fine row of grinders, Mr. Dragon!" laughed Siegfried. "A most dainty little mouth!"

"I open not my jaw for senseless gabble, but for food!" growled Fafnir, and gave his tail a sudden switch round, which would certainly have caught

Siegfried in its toils, had he not sprung alertly to one side.

"Ho, ho! so that is the game, is it? Come on then, Mr. Dragon!" and Siegfried drew Needful sharply from the scabbard.

"Bah! Come on, thou boasting young cub! I will give the lesson thou cravest!"

Fafnir drew himself together and sent forth from his nostrils a venomous steam. Whatever it touched, whether trees or grass, shrivelled up instantly, as though scorched by fire. But again Siegfried was too quick for him, and Fafnir, who hoped to see a burnt-up body on the ground, was enraged to hear a cheerful voice behind him—"Look out, old growler! the 'boaster' is upon thee."

Then Fafnir set to work in good earnest, and Siegfried found that after all it was no child's play to fight a dragon. But though blinded and well-nigh choked with the poisonous smoke and steam, Siegfried fought on, nothing daunted. The only vital spot was, he knew, the dragon's heart, the back and sides of his huge carcass being entirely covered with scaly armor.

Nearer and nearer they closed on one another, till at last Fafnir, with a sudden twist, caught Siegfried in his serpentine tail. But before the coils had time to tighten round him, Siegfried had pierced Needful through a joint of the scaly tail. Fafnir sent up a howl of rage and pain, and for a moment relaxed his grip. With a bound Siegfried leapt on the back of his foe. Fafnir instantly prepared to roll over on one side and so crush Siegfried with his mountainous weight; but in turning, his breast for a brief moment was exposed, and in the twinkling of an eye down swept the sword of Siegfried, burying itself up to the hilt in the dragon's heart.

With a terrific groan Fafnir rolled over, while Siegfried sprang lightly to one side, crying: "Lie there, old growler, with Needful in thy heart!" In great puffs of smoke and fire, like an overturned steam-engine, came Fafnir's dying breath. His eyes rolled horribly; fixing them at last on Siegfried, he gasped, "Who art thou, clear-eyed youth?"

"In truth," replied Siegfried, "I know but little of myself or of my kin."

"A strange fate is mine!" groaned the dragon. "I, the great giant Fafnir, to die by the hand of a youth unknown even to himself! Young hero, heed well the dying words of him whom thou hast slain. The treasure I guarded is accursed. Death it brought to my brother, and now to me. If thou touch ought of it, the curse rests also on thee. Heed what I say!"

"Oh, tell me more, wise monster!" Siegfried entreated. "Tell me of my parents, and the race from which they sprang. Siegfried is my name!"

Fafnir heaved himself upwards in a last effort to speak. "Siegfried!"—he began, gasped for breath and then with a deep groan fell back dead.

As he rolled over on his side, Siegfried drew the sword out of his breast. He felt sorry the giant was dead, and had now quite a kindly feeling for him. Those last words had shown him to be a wise and thoughtful monster. But still, Siegfried was not sure he would take his advice. In drawing out the sword, some of the dragon's blood chanced to touch Siegfried's hand. It burnt like a red-hot coal, and he put it quickly to his mouth. As he did so, the song of the bird again fell on his ear. He listened in amazement—for now every note was a word which he understood!

This was what the bird sang in his sweet piping voice: "Hey, Siegfried! Siegfried the Victor has slain the dragon! Now to him belongs the gold, the Ring, and the Tarnhelm. With these he can conquer the world if he will."

"Thanks, little feathered friend, for thy good news—I will go and seek for these treasures!" and, nodding to the bird, Siegfried descended into Fafnir's dark cave.

Mimi, from a safe hiding-place in the trees, had watched the fight between Fafnir and Siegfried. He now crept out, and anxiously peeped after Siegfried as he disappeared into the dragon's hole. "Grant, O ye gods, that he take only the gold, and leave the Ring and the Cap for me!" prayed Mimi fervently.

Little did he guess how the singing bird had told Siegfried all he desired to keep most secret. He thought, "The bright, glittering gold will be sure to attract the youth more than a plain simple ring and a small cap of wrought chain." Presently Siegfried came out of the cave. Mimi crawled stealthily back to his hiding-place and peered out through the leaves.

"A curse on him!" he muttered, grinding his

teeth with rage. "The Ring is on his finger, and the Cap hangs from his belt!"

Siegfried looked round for his piping friend; perched on the branch of a lime tree the bird awaited him.

"Hey! Siegfried has now both Ring and Cap! Siegfried the Victor! But oh, he must beware of the treacherous dwarf! The dragon's blood will reveal to him the hidden meaning of all words— both true and false. His *thoughts* shall Siegfried hear when the dwarf Mimi speaks."

Carefully carrying his poisonous draught, Mimi now approached.

"Thou art tired after thy mighty conflict. See what I bring to restore thee! Take but a sip, and all I have worked and waited for will be mine— sword, treasure, and all." Mimi thought he was saying something very pleasant. He smiled and cringed as he offered the drinking-horn. But these were his thoughts as Siegfried heard them, in virtue of his newly gained power.

"So thou wouldst rob me of everything, even of life?" asked Siegfried sternly.

"How falsely dost thou distort my kind words!" replied Mimi in an injured tone. "Yet I give myself much trouble to disguise my true thoughts. Dear heart, thee and thy kin have I ever hated." (Mimi here looked lovingly at Siegfried.) "All these years I fostered thee, that thou mightest win for me the dragon's hoard. Come, now, take the draught; thou wert ever easy to fool."

Siegfried looked at the little dwarf and smiled ominously. "I should be right glad of a goodly

TENDERLY HE LOOKED AT HER, AND SLOWLY
KISSED HER ON BOTH EYES

—page 114

From the painting by K. Dielitz

draught," he said. "Of what didst thou make this?"

"Only drink and see, dear sonnie. Trust to my skill. Soon wilt thou be lying in a deathly swoon at my feet. Then, with thine own brave sword, off goes thy head! And Mimi will rest in peace with the hoard."

"So—I am to be murdered in my sleep?" asked Siegfried.

"What folly dost thou talk! Who spoke of murder? All I thought of doing was just to chop off thy head when thou liest insensible. A small return for the shameful treatment I have so long suffered at thy hands. Come, drink and die, thou hateful Volsung cub;" and Mimi, still smiling and leering, thrust the drinking-horn near Siegfried's lips.

"Taste thou my sword, false snake!" cried Siegfried. With a sudden movement of disgust and fury he struck at the dwarf with his sword. The next instant Mimi lay dead on the ground. Siegfried threw his body inside the dragon's cave, crying: "Lie there with the gold thou so lovest. I make thee a parting gift of it. And here is a famous watch-dog to scare away all thieves." With this Siegfried dragged the body of the dragon to the mouth of the cave, thereby entirely blocking up the entrance.

Then he turned away from the spot with a sigh of relief, and went back to the lime tree, where first the bird had sung to him. Throwing himself down under the shady branches, he called to his little friend: "Come, sing to me, happy bird. Alone am I in all the world. Never have I known a comrade save the hateful dwarf yonder. Tell me, O wise little prophet, where shall I find one I can love?"

All was stillness in the forest. The sun was now at its height. Only the soft, low hum of insect life filled the drowsy air.

Suddenly a flutter of wings overhead, and the clear note of the wood-bird piped out once more: "Hey, Siegfried the Victor! He has slain the treacherous dwarf. Now a glorious bride awaits him. But he must go through the flames to win and to wake her, for Brunhilda sleeps fast, guarded by Loki's fiery arm."

Siegfried started to his feet.

"Oh, sweetest song! How it fills my heart with joy and longing! Say, dear bird, how shall I find this bride, and break through the fire?"

Then the bird sang again: "Only he who knows not Fear can awaken and win the sleeping bride."

At this Siegfried laughed aloud with delight; for had not even Fafnir failed to teach him fear? "Perchance, from Brunhilda shall I learn to know what is Fear," he cried gaily. "Fly on before, sweet bird; point thou the road; I follow thee!"

The bird fluttered his wings joyfully and flew on ahead, Siegfried following with bounding step.

HOW SIEGFRIED FINDS BRUNHILDA

By Constance Maud

FOR many a day Siegfried journeyed, keeping the bird always in sight. At night he slept under a tree, and the bird rested in a branch above, but with the first whisper of dawn Siegfried would start up, impatient to be off again.

Over mountain and valley, across river and lake, Siegfried followed as though his feet were shod with invisible wings, never flagging, never weary. He came at length one evening to a narrow pass in the mountains. The way seemed to lead upwards, but daylight was fading, and Siegfried could see nothing clearly. All at once the bird circled rapidly over his head, sang a few sweet half-plaintive notes, and then, soaring upwards, vanished out of sight.

In the same moment a deep voice spoke close at hand: "Halt! What seekest thou here?"

Siegfried went forward, and standing in the narrow way he saw a tall dark form. "I seek for the fire-girt mountain where the beautiful maiden sleeps," answered Siegfried fearlessly. "Canst thou tell me the way?"

"Who told thee of such a maiden?" demanded the stranger sternly.

"A singing bird gave me the good news," said Siegfried. "By tasting the blood of a dragon I learned the language of the birds, and I know my bird spake true." He was getting impatient at so many questions and anxious to go on his way.

"So! thou hast slain old Fafnir. And with what weapon didst strike the death-blow, bold youth?" The stranger was in no hurry, evidently.

"With my father's splintered sword, which I welded together again," said Siegfried, with pride.

"But who first shaped that mighty sword?" asked the stranger.

"That I neither know nor care. 'Twas a mighty useless weapon till I took it in hand, that I know," answered Siegfried. "If thou canst not direct me on the road I seek, hold thy peace and let me pass on my way."

"Softly, young sir! Thou dost not know with whom thou speakest."

"I know that this path leads onwards to my lady, for thither pointed the bird before he left me. So make way and let me pass," returned Siegfried angrily.

"The bird fled to save its life. The way it pointed thou shalt never pass, presumptuous youth."

"Ha, ha! And who art *thou* to arrest my steps?" laughed Siegfried scornfully.

"I am the Guardian of yon mountain, where sleeps the maiden Brunhilda! A wall of flame encircles her, which even to approach would scorch thee to death. Begone then, rash fool, for to win thy way one step farther, thou must first overcome the mountain's Guardian."

Placing himself in the middle of the road, the stranger loomed above Siegfried gigantic and immovable as the rock itself.

But Siegfried remained unawed. "Begone thy-

134

self, old boaster!" he cried irreverently. "Think
not to scare me with such tales. I love the fire's
blaze! So out of my way, for I haste to where
Brunhilda sleeps."

"Thou fearest not the fire?" retorted the stranger.
"Then fear this my Spear, for it shall bar thy way
—this Spear, which once already has shattered thy
father's sword."

The sky had now become lurid; a terrific tempest was gathering. At the stranger's words, Siegfried sprang forward, and, drawing Needful from
the scabbard, shouted exultingly: "Have I then
found my father's foe? Thanks be to the gods for
letting me avenge his death!"

Then, falling on the powerful form that barred
his way, he hewed with long, swift strokes at the
Spear, which, had he hesitated one moment, or
made one false step, would have struck him dead.

There was a rushing sound of wings in the storm-
clouds overhead. Anxious faces peered down on
the scene. The warrior maidens, hovering above on
their war-horses, trembled and paled as they beheld
the Spear which once had been the terror of the
world hewn to pieces, while their father, recoiling
at last before the fiery youth, cried half triumphantly, in spite of his defeat: "Advance! I cannot
bar thy way." For Wotan's heart never failed to
rejoice in a real hero, even though he fought against
him.

A terrific clap of thunder followed, and a dark
cloud swept over the fighters. When it rolled
away, Siegfried looked in vain for his mysterious
foe. He had vanished. "Now through the fire to

win my bride!" cried Siegfried joyously, and leapt up the mountain side.

A ruddy glow soon told him he was nearing the fiery wall, and gusts of hot air swept across his face. Taking his silver horn, Siegfried blew a call which echoed far and near. "To greet my sleeping love!" he cried.

And now the fire was all about him, bursting up under his feet, pouring down from the skies, rushing round on every side. "Aha! This is glorious!" shouted Siegfried, plunging eagerly onwards, and laughing. The fierce flames which had scared so many nearly to death did not scorch even a hair of Siegfried's head. For the magic fire injured only those who retreated—he who dashed fearlessly onward remained unharmed.

Higher and higher up the mountain went Siegfried. Emerging at last from the flames, he found himself on the summit of a rocky peak, clad with tall dark pine trees.

He looked around him, and rejoiced for very joy to be alive in such a fair world. The stillness was wonderful. Not a sound could be heard, for the wood-bird will not build his home so near the sky, and the fire had kept out all wingless intruders.

Presently Siegfried saw, standing motionless under the trees, a stately horse. On going nearer, he was astonished to find that on his feet were wings. His eyes were closed in profound sleep. Siegfried stroked his flowing mane. "Awake good steed! The sun has arisen. This is no time for sleeping." His voice rang out clear as his silver horn, and with a start, Grani awoke.

But Siegfried looked around in vain for the bride —Brunhilda. Suddenly the rising sun struck with its glittering light on an object under a distant pine. Siegfried hastened forward, and with wonder beheld a sleeping form clad from head to foot in shining armour. "Here is some warrior, for sure," cried Siegfried. "This heavy helmet must press sorely on his head; I will loosen it for him."

He stooped, lifted the shield, and then carefully unfastened the helmet. As he removed it, the sleeper's hair rolled out in long curling locks of burnished gold. Siegfried started. Never had he seen anything so fair as that calm proud young face, framed in the wavy shining curls.

So still lay the sleeping warrior, so motionless, Siegfried bent down and listened anxiously for the deep slow breathing. "This coat of mail must weigh heavily on him; I will open it," he said. But in vain he sought to find a fastening: everywhere the iron rings closed tightly round. To Siegfried, who had never seen a soldier, and knew of no weapon save a sword, this iron garment seemed a terrible inconvenience, almost as cumbersome as old Fafnir's scales. He determined to free the young warrior, that he might at least sleep in comfort.

So, taking out his sword, he carefully cut through the rings of mail down each side, and then lifted off the corselet and greaves. As he did so, great was his astonishment to see lying before him a maiden in soft flowing garments.

He started back. His heart beat wildly. This must be none other than the maiden Brunhilda! Then he who had never known fear—who laughed in the face of the terrible dragon,—quailed not before Wotan the mighty god, and dashed fearlessly through fire—sank down trembling and afraid before the sleeping maiden.

"What is this feeling? Can *this* be Fear?" he cried.

"Awake! awake, O beautiful maid!" he cried, kneeling at her side.

Still she did not stir.

Bending over Brunhilda, Siegfried pressed his lips to hers.

Slowly she opened her eyes. Siegfried started back. She sat up dazed and wondering. Then her eyes rested on him. For a moment neither moved. But the silence between them said more than words, and though only a few brief instants went by, much happened in the time. For Siegfried passed from boyhood to manhood, and Brunhilda passed from the land of dreams and shadows back to the warm living earth.

At last she spoke. "Hail, thou sunshine, and light, and lovely daytime! Long has been my sleep!" Then, fixing shining eyes on Siegfried, "And who art *thou,*" she asked, "who hast awakened me out of my sleep?"

"I am Siegfried. Through the flames I won my way to thee. My sword it has cut through thy armour, O most glorious maiden!"

Brunhilda gazed at him in wonder and delight. "Siegfried! So thou art indeed Siegfried who hast awakened me? Siegfried, of whom in times long past I dreamed! My sun art thou, awakening me out of night and darkness!"

These words made Siegfried happier than ever. Never had his highest hopes or wildest dreams pictured one so fair and noble as this goddess-maid. For her sake what would he not do or dare?

But Brunhilda was now gazing sadly at her cast-off armour and shield on the ground. Slowly the words of her father's curse were coming back to her. Never more to ride free through the heavens —to be a mortal woman wedded to a mortal man!

Gently and sadly she pushed Siegfried from her side, and tried to turn his thoughts from herself. "See there my faithful steed," she said, pointing to Grani. "He also has been awakened by Siegfried the sun-god. Once he bore me through the heavens, and shared my life among the gods of Valhalla. With me also he slept. See how joyfully he has come back to life!"

"Alas!" cried Brunhilda, growing ever more melancholy. "Siegfried my hero, it is through you I forfeit my glorious estate! Brunhilda the Valkyrie is no more,—she is dead indeed."

Siegfried saw that a harder task yet remained to him than dashing through fire or cutting through steel, but he went on undaunted, for he felt his new-found love strong and great enough to carry him through all difficulties.

"Thou sleepest still, my beloved. I have but opened thy glorious eyes. Oh, wake, and rejoice that thou livest."

So spake Siegfried, and his passionate pleading turned at last, as a magic key, the locked door of Brunhilda's proud heart, which to no god or man had yielded before. She turned to him and as Siegfried clasped her to his heart, Brunhilda renounced for ever all she had counted most dear—all longings for the old free Valkyrie life, all dreams of bygone glory with the gods in Valhalla.

Now that her heart was won, Brunhilda gave it all, once and for ever; and a great and noble gift it was, worth any hero's winning, at any cost.

THE PLOT AGAINST THE BEAUTIFUL ELSA OF BRABANT

By Constance Maud

ONCE upon a time there lived, in the ancient city of Antwerp, a beautiful maiden called Elsa.

She dwelt in a grand old palace: the walls were thick as any fortress, and the towers looked proudly down on the town.

Elsa's father was the Duke of Brabant, a noble prince, who for long years had faithfully served his liege lord, the King of Germany, and had won much honor to Brabant.

Elsa had an only brother, the young Prince Godfrey; and these two loved each other more than any other brother and sister in the world.

One day the duke was taken ill, so ill that he could no longer attend to the affairs of state; and a few days later all Brabant knew that their beloved duke lay dying.

As their mother had been dead many years, and they had no near relatives, the duke then sent for his kinsman, Count Telramund. This man was imperious and hot-tempered, with manners uncouth as a bear; but he was brave as a lion, and the duke had full confidence in his good heart and knightly honor.

The count hastened to obey the royal summons.

"My trusted friend and kinsman, Frederick of Telramund," said the duke, "I am dying. With my last breath I confide to thy care my beloved children, Elsa and Godfrey. Watch over them, protect them from all ill till Godfrey be of an age to reign, and Elsa is married to a husband she loves. Until then, I appoint thee as Regent and Protector in Brabant."

Count Telramund knelt by the side of the dying duke, and swore solemnly to fulfil the trust, and, if needs be, to lay down his life for the young prince and princess.

"Thank Heaven!" murmured the duke. "And now, my cousin, is there aught that I can do for thee, in return for so great a service?" he asked.

"Oh, most noble prince, there is one boon I would ask, were it not so great a gift I scarce dare even to name it!" answered the count.

"Whatever thy wish, cousin, it is granted, if it be in my power to bestow," said the duke readily. "What is thy request?"

"Most gracious sovereign," stammered the count, growing red to the roots of his tawny beard, "I love the Princess Elsa—wilt thou give her to me to be my wife?"

Elsa started. Without stirring, and her face deadly pale, she listened breathlessly for her father's reply.

"Gladly would I give my child to thy safe keeping, noble cousin. But in this matter I must leave the maiden free to choose for herself. If she accept thy hand, thou hast my full consent and blessing. More than this I cannot say."

The count knelt and pressed his lips to the hand of the dying duke, who, blessing Telramund, sank back exhausted and bade him farewell.

Shortly after, the good prince died, at peace with all.

Elsa, heartbroken at her father's death, found her only consolation in her young brother Godfrey. For a long time she refused to see anyone else.

Count Telramund often sought opportunity to speak with her, but she avoided him with dread.

Then Telramund changed his tone, and demanded her hand as his right, the dying bequest of her father the duke.

"My father left me free," answered Elsa, indignant. "Never would he wish me to give my hand where I could not give my heart also, sir count."

No woman, and very few men, had ever dared to contradict his wishes; sooner or later, he vowed, she should be his.

Now there was a wicked lady, of a tall, commanding figure, dark and handsome—Ortruda by name. She was very learned, and had studied all manner of sorceries, which enabled her to exert the magic power of a witch. Her forefathers had once been mighty princes, who reigned over Brabant and all the countries round. She regarded Elsa and Godfrey as usurpers, holding what rightfully belonged to her; and she hated them with a bitter hatred. Also, there was another and a deeper cause for her hatred towards Elsa; and that was,

that she herself had long wished to marry Count
Telramund.

One day Telramund came to Ortruda and told
her how Elsa had dared to despise his love, and
reject his hand. That he should confide in her
pleased Ortruda well; also that Elsa should refuse
the count, though she loved her none the more for
doing so.

"The impertinent minx, to take on such airs!"

Telramund found comfort in Ortruda's indignation. His heart was set on marrying Elsa, and he
was willing to wait long if only he might win her
in the end.

When Ortruda saw this, she laid a deep plot, by
means of which she hoped to turn his love from
Elsa. In the depths of the forest was a lonely
tower. Here Ortruda was wont to retire and study
sorcery, for long days and nights together. She
became at last so practised, that she could by enchantments change people into different birds and
beasts.

One day, Elsa and Godfrey were roaming together alone in the forest. Ortruda, always on the
watch, followed them, unseen, at a distance. After
a while they sat down to rest by the side of a pool,
whose still depths, it was said, no one had ever
fathomed.

Presently, Elsa and Godfrey were startled by
hearing a piercing, pitiful cry, like that of some
animal caught in a trap. Godfrey started up, crying: "I must go and free that poor beast! Rest
here a while, Elsa; I will return shortly."

He sprang lightly through the thickly growing

bushes and trees, and was soon hidden from sight.

Elsa waited by the pool, thinking of all the happy plans she and Godfrey had been making for the future, when he would reign as duke. The trees overhead rustled strangely, and Elsa, looking up, saw a great white swan circling round, and waving his wings wildly as though in distress. Then with a sad cry, he flew away.

Elsa grew uneasy. Surely an hour must have passed, yet Godfrey had not returned! She called aloud: "Godfrey, Godfrey! where art thou?" But there was no answer save the echo of her own voice, which rang through the wood as though mocking her anxious cry.

Then, in deadly fear, she started up and tried to trace his steps, but the dense thicket left no track. Pale and trembling, Elsa returned at last to the palace, and told how Godfrey had mysteriously disappeared.

That night the forest was searched from end to end with torches and lanterns, and all the following day the search continued, but not a trace of the missing boy could be found.

Two days after Godfrey's disappearance, Ortruda came to Telramund. She appeared in deep distress, saying she had something to reveal, and dared no longer keep silence. "Alas!" replied Ortruda, "what I know is well-nigh too terrible to be spoken. Who will credit my dark tale? Listen," she continued; "thy search for Godfrey is useless."

"Two days ago I sat alone meditating in my tower in the forest, when I espied Elsa and Godfrey sitting together by the pool—that awful pool where, 'tis said, a drowning man may sink for a thousand years, yet never touch the bottom. On a sudden I heard a cry, and looking, saw Elsa, aided by a stranger, whose face was turned to me, push her young brother backward into the dread pool."

"Horrible! most horrible!" cried Telramund. "Thou sawest this with thine own eyes?"

"I saw it with these same eyes, that will I swear, though it were with my last breath!" replied Ortruda.

"Who could dream that such black sin dwelt in one so young and fair!"

"Ay," said Ortruda, eyeing him askance; "and knowing that thou lovedst her, I would have kept silence. But when thine enemies whispered that thou, being next of kin, might thyself have caused the lad's disappearance, then my love for thee made me bold to speak the dread secret."

"I thank thee, Ortruda. Thou hast ever shown thyself my faithful friend," said Telramund. "It were better had I given my love to thee, instead of wasting it on one so unworthy."

"My father's house once ruled in this land, and, in justice, should be ruling still. Ah! were poor Ortruda queen, with what joy would she lay her kingdom at thy feet, noblest and bravest of men!"

"Thou art worthy to be a queen!" cried Telramund, "and that shalt thou be, noble and wise Ortruda! For here do I swear to make thee my wife, instead of her in whom I have been so woefully deceived. As for the murderess, her cruel deed shall be brought to light. She shall be tried by our king, Henry of Germany, and both she and her base lover will assuredly be condemned to death."

In obedience to Telramund's orders, Elsa was then put under arrest, and placed in a dark prison-cell, to await her trial before the king. She was kept a close prisoner, no one save the followers of Telramund and Ortruda being allowed to come near her. In her grief and despair she knelt one night and prayed, one long bitter cry for help. And all at once her prayer seemed taken up, as though on angels' wings; above the narrow prison-cell—up, up, till it pierced the utmost heights of the sky above. Elsa listened till she heard the faint echo fade away far overhead. And, as she wondered what it might mean, a gentle sleep closed her eyes. She dreamt; and in her dream she saw a noble knight in shining silver armour. Swiftly through the air he came, and, descending to her prison-cell, stood by her side. No word did he speak, but with looks and signs he bade her banish all fear and sorrow, and trust in him, for he was sent by Heaven in answer to her cry.

When Elsa woke, the bitterness of her grief had passed. The vision had departed, but she felt assured her prayer was heard, and that, sooner or later, the Heaven-sent knight of her dream would come and bring her deliverance.

THE KNIGHTS OF THE HOLY GRAIL

By Constance Maud

FAR away, in the mountains of Spain, there dwelt a holy band of knights, vowed to the service of all those in distress or need.

The famous Knight Parsifal was at this time king of the Order, and under his reign the Knights of the Holy Grail were unsurpassed for valour and truth. When any cry of distress went up to Heaven, the great bells of the Grail temple would commence to swing slowly to and fro, and at this sign the knights assembled in their temple, whatever the hour, day or night: there the Holy Grail would reveal to them, in letters of fire, what service was required.

The same night on which Elsa knelt in her prison-cell, far away in Antwerp, the mighty bells of Mount Salvat suddenly broke the stillness of the peaceful night. With Parsifal at their head, the brothers of the Holy Grail hastened to the temple. Among them was one Lohengrin, a young knight of most noble fame, son of Parsifal, the king.

Round the altar knelt the knights; while the king mounted the steps and took from a golden shrine the miraculous crystal Cup, known as the Holy Grail. A dazzling ray of light instantly streamed down from the dome above the altar, lighting up the Cup, which then began to glow with letters of fire written round the brim. Parsifal held the Cup aloft, that all might read the message: "There is one falsely accused, in sore

148

need and trouble—the Princess Elsa of Brabant."
So ran the writing on the Holy Grail. The glowing letters slowly faded and vanished.

But while the knights discussed among themselves which of them should at once depart for
Brabant, the Cup again glowed with another message: "Let Lohengrin, the son of Parsifal, make
ready and depart. He it is, appointed to be her
champion."

Lohengrin rejoiced greatly at being chosen.
Kneeling before his father, he craved a blessing
before setting out on his journey. Then, buckling
on his armour and his sword, a golden horn slung
round his neck, he mounted his black charger, and
rode off into the silent forest.

On he rode. The tall, dark pine trees met over
his head; the silver moon peeped between the
branches, lighting him on his way. All the forest
slept. At length he came to the river which marked
the boundary of the Grail dominions. He was
about to ford the stream, when, to his amazement,
he beheld a boat, drawn by a snow-white swan,
evidently awaiting him.

Lohengrin dismounted, and recognized the swan
as a bird which had not long since appeared among
them, and taken up his abode with the knights. As
a white swan had always been held in good omen
by the knights, the bird received a hearty welcome.
And the more so when, shortly after his arrival, the
Grail revealed that the bird was none other than
a youth of noble birth, the innocent victim of a
wicked enchantment. Round the swan's neck was
a fine gold chain of curious workmanship, with

neither clasp nor fastening, so that no man could remove it without injury to the bird. From the day he appeared, the swan attached himself specially to Lohengrin. He would follow him about like a dog, and often gazed into his face as though he longed to speak with him.

Seeing this faithful bird awaiting him, Lohengrin asked him: "Wilt thou that I go with thee, dear swan?" The bird instantly bent his graceful head, and spread wide his white wings, as though impatient to start. Lohengrin then dismissed his horse, bidding him return to Mount Salvat, stepped into the boat, and the swan sailed away joyfully with him. Down the river they floated swiftly. The swan seemed quite sure of his way. Even when they came at last to the sea, he never paused, but steered a steady course right out of the bay, and away across the wide ocean.

LOHENGRIN THE CHAMPION OF ELSA OF BRABANT

By Constance Maud

IN the city of Antwerp great preparations were going forward.

King Henry of Germany had arrived in state, and had summoned all the ministers and chief nobles of Brabant to appear before him.

Elsa, in her prison-cell, was wakened early with the news that she would be tried this day before the king, in face of all the people.

She heard as though it scarce concerned her. Since the vision of the knight in shining armour, she no longer seemed to dwell in the dark prison. Her thoughts were far away, and she cared nothing for what took place around her.

It was noon when the king, with his heralds, outriders, and a numerous retinue, proceeded in solemn state to the Judgment Oak. Mid the cheers and blessings of the people, he ascended a gorgeous throne prepared for him.

Count Telramund bowed low before the king. Then, in a clear ringing voice, told his story, and made his accusation against Elsa, Princess of Brabant, of whose horrible crime he said he had, alas, convincing proof. He then claimed the kingdom of Brabant for himself, as next of kin to the late duke, and also in right of his noble wife Ortruda, whose fathers once ruled in that land.

"Now, O most noble king, thou hast heard me fully," he concluded. "Naught have I spoken but the truth—my oath upon it. Be thou our judge."

The crowd shuddered with horror at the story of Elsa's crime. Their own princess, so gentle and fair, the cruel murderess of her brother! Impossible! Yet who dare dispute it, since Count Telramund, whose honor no man could doubt, himself swore to the fact.

"What terrible accusation dost thou bring? Bid the accused appear!" cried the king. "The trial shall forthwith begin."

The herald blew his trumpet, and proclaimed the king's order. There was a stir in the crowd. All eyes turned towards her as Elsa appeared, followed by her ladies. Slowly she walked to the foot of the throne, gazing before her like one in a dream.

"Art thou Elsa of Brabant?" asked the king. Elsa bowed her head.

"Dost thou know the charge that is brought against thee?" he demanded sternly.

Again Elsa assented, drooping her head sadly, but without speaking.

"What answer canst thou make? Dost admit thy guilt?" the king inquired.

She gazed around her with a bewildered air, as though trying to remember something long forgotten.

"Alas," she sighed, "my poor brother!"

The people murmured: " 'Tis marvellous! What can it mean?"

"Speak, Elsa!" urged the king, wondering at her strange behavior. "Dost thou not trust in thy king?"

Then Elsa spoke in a low gentle voice, as to herself when alone in the prison: "In my misery I knelt one night and besought God's aid. My woeful cry seemed all at once caught up to the highest heaven. I listened wondering, then peace fell on my spirit, and a gentle sleep came over me."

The King thought Elsa's mind was certainly affected, whether from brooding on her crime, or on her innocence and the injustice of her imprisonment, he could not tell. "Come, Elsa," he said, in a rousing tone, "defend thyself now before the judge."

But Elsa appeared neither to hear nor understand, and continued her dream with a look of rapture: "Borne through the air he came—a knight of such perfection and nobility never yet I saw! Clothed in glittering armour,—in his hand a sword —slung round his neck a golden horn! No word he spake, but gazed on me tenderly. Peace and comfort came to me with his look. That knight will be my champion and deliverer!"

The king was sorely perplexed. This dreamy maiden hardly seemed like a criminal. Looking at the sad, fair face of the prisoner, he could not find it in his heart to believe her guilty. Yet he held the count, as a true and honorable knight, incapable of falsehood; one who had, besides, risked his life for king and country.

Turning to the count, he then asked solemnly: "Frederick of Telramund, wilt thou in mortal combat let Heaven's ordeal decide thine accusation as true or false?"

"Yea, that will I, O king," answered Telramund, with proud confidence.

"And thee also, I ask, Elsa of Brabant, wilt thou abide by Heaven's decree in the mortal combat that shall be fought for thy cause?"

Elsa's eyes were fixed on the far distance. "Yea, that will I," she replied slowly.

"What champion shall defend thee?" asked the king.

"That knight whom Heaven sent me! He and none other shall be my champion," replied Elsa. "And this is the reward I offer. He shall wear my father's crown, and high honor I shall deem it to give to him my land, my wealth, and my hand."

"A prize worth fighting for!" murmured the

people. Their hearts beat true to their princess, in spite of appearances against her.

"Let the summons go forth!" cried the king.

The heralds and trumpeters then marched to the outposts and proclaimed the challenge, so that all might hear it, far and near: "Let him who will fight in mortal combat for Elsa of Brabant now appear!" There was a long pause, and breathless silence followed. The echo of the trumpet's blast died away into the distance. But no one appeared in answer to the call. Elsa listened, looking round on all sides with anxious, expectant gaze. "O gracious king," implored Elsa, "I beseech thee let the call go forth once again to summon my knight. He dwells so far he has not heard."

"Let the summons go forth yet once more," he ordered. Again the heralds proclaimed the challenge.

There followed a longer pause and a longer silence. No one stirred. The people scarcely seemed to breathe, so great was the suspense and expectation.

Elsa fell on her knees, while her maidens closed round as though to protect her. "O Lord," she cried, "send my knight speedily, I beseech thee. Once, at Thy command, he came to me. Oh, send him now again. Tell him of my sore need," she implored in despair. Her women knelt also, weeping and praying.

Suddenly a cry went up from the people standing near the river-bank: "See! A wondrous sight! A swan! a swan drawing a boat! And, standing in the prow, behold a knight in shining armour. Lo, he comes with utmost speed!" All rushed forward eagerly to see.

The king from his throne looked towards the river and beheld the amazing sight. Elsa, on her knees, listened spellbound, in a transport of joy. Frederick of Telramund, struck dumb with awe and astonishment, looked at Ortruda. Her face had turned to an ashen hue. Her glittering eyes were dull, as though the light within had suddenly gone out. She gazed at the swan with greater terror than had he been a dragon.

" 'Tis a miracle! A miracle of Heaven!" exclaimed the men.

The women, on their knees, cried joyfully: "Oh, God be thanked, who hast heard our prayer! Hail to the Heaven-sent one who comes to save the guiltless!"

The boat had now reached the bank. Lohengrin stepped lightly to land, and then turned lovingly to the swan: "My thanks to thee, beloved swan," he said. "Return now o'er the waters to the blessed land from whence we came. Faithfully hast thou fulfilled thy task. Farewell, beloved swan."

He gazed sadly after his faithful companion, as the swan slowly turned and swam away.

The crowd made way for him eagerly, as Lohengrin advanced to the king's throne and bowed low. As he raised his head, Elsa turned, and uttered a cry of joy at beholding no other than the knight of her vision.

"Hail, royal Henry! May the blessing of Heaven ever rest on thee!" said Lohengrin.

"Welcome, sir knight!" replied the king graciously. "Surely by a miracle divine thou art come to this land?"

"I have been sent, O king, to fight for the honor of an innocent maiden, in sore need and distress," answered Lohengrin. Then, going before Elsa, he asked her: "Wilt thou trust thy cause to me, O Elsa of Brabant? Wilt thou take me for thy champion without doubt or fear?"

Elsa raised her eyes to his. "My deliverer, my knight—with my whole heart do I trust thee!" she answered. Lohengrin knelt and, taking her hand in his, asked: "And if, with Heaven's help, I win this fight for thee, wilt thou consent to be my bride?"

"I am thine—thine only, my knight. All I have I give thee gladly!" said Elsa, with shining eyes.

"One promise wilt thou give me?"

"To thee will I promise anything," Elsa answered readily.

"Then if thou desirest, as I, that nothing part us ever,—that thy people and thy country become from henceforth my people and my country,— never shalt thou ask of me my name and race, or whence I come," said Lohengrin earnestly.

"Never will I seek to know thy secret. Thy love is enough for me—nought else do I desire!"

"But Elsa, think well what it is I ask," urged Lohengrin. "Never must thou desire this knowledge, and never must this secret between us cause thee sadness."

Elsa was troubled that Lohengrin repeated his request. There was nothing in the world she would not gladly grant to him—her champion, her deliverer. "Thou hast never doubted my innocence," she answered. "Dost thou not trust in me? And shall not I also trust in thee, my knight, whate'er thou askest of me?"

Then Lohengrin stood forth, and, in a ringing voice that all might hear, proclaimed: "Hear now, all ye people, and ye nobles of Brabant! I hereby declare, before Heaven and before all men, by my honor as a knight, that free from every shadow of guilt is the maiden Elsa, Princess of Brabant. False and unfounded is thy black charge, Frederick of Telramund, and that will I prove by Heaven's ordeal!"

Telramund advanced with angry mien and flashing eyes: "What magic brought thee here, sir stranger, I know not. Thy talk is bold enough! But my answer is not in words. This, my good sword, shall defend mine honor. May victory be to right and truth, say I!"

Lohengrin turned towards the throne: "We await thy command, O king, to commence the combat."

The king ordered the fighting-ring to be measured; and this being done, he then besought Heaven that in this fight victory might be, not as in other fights, to skill and strength, but to the one on whose side was right. And all the people fervently echoed the good king's prayer.

Scarce a breath could be heard. Every eye was fixed on the gleaming swords, as they cut the air like flashes of lightning, and clashed with sharp, ringing strokes.

A few intense moments, which seemed to Elsa's beating heart a very eternity; then a crash of falling armour, a wild shout from the people, and the fight was over.

Telramund had fallen; over him, like an angel of judgment, stood Lohengrin. "Through Heaven's victory, thy life is mine!" he cried. "I give it thee again, that thou mayest use it for repentance."

"Victory, victory! Hail to the hero!" shouted a thousand glad voices.

"The victory I owe to thy innocence alone," said Lohengrin to Elsa. "All that thou hast suffered shall now be atoned to thee." Then Lohengrin and Elsa were lifted on the shields of the nobles, and all the people marched round them in a triumphal procession, shouting a hymn of joyful thanksgiving, in which the good King Henry himself joined lustily.

Only Ortruda and the defeated Telramund stood sullenly apart. "Woe is me! Mine honor and fame are undone," muttered the count. "It would seem indeed that Heaven is against me."

Ortruda, with clenched hands, asked herself in dismay: "Who can this be? Before whom even I feel my powers weaken! Who? and from whence?"

ORTRUDA PLOTS FOR REVENGE

By Constance Maud

THE stars came out in the deep blue sky of night, waiting for the summer moon.

The stately walls of the royal palace of Antwerp threw mysterious shadows all around. And in the darkness of these shadows crept two figures stealthily. They seated themselves at length under a tree which faced the windows of the Princess Elsa's apartments.

Looking up, they saw a light still burning.

Then they talked together earnestly in muffled tones.

By and by the moon arose, and cast her silvery light about, shifting the shadows according to her royal pleasure.

The two dark figures, a man and a woman, moved with the shadows, still keeping close to the palace. They took no thought of rest or sleep that night.

The man looked at the woman, and shuddered.

The woman turned to the man, a scornful light in her eyes. She was for action, and despised useless regrets and groans.

"Frederick of Telramund, why dost thou mistrust me?" she asked quietly.

"Why?" he cried wrathfully. "Was it not on thy false word that I accused the guiltless, and condemned an innocent maid? Thou who didst swear that thine own eyes beheld her murder the youthful Godfrey!"

"Dost thou know who is this mysterious hero, drawn hither across the sea by a wild swan?" she asked.

"Nay, I know not," he answered.

"Hearken now to me," said Ortruda. "It is forbidden him to reveal either his name or country. That, his own words allowed. The reason I will tell thee. Should he do so, all his magic power instantly vanishes. There is but one person who can tear his secret from him—she whom he so strictly forbade to ask him."

"Ha! Elsa! She must be made to do this!" cried Telramund eagerly. Ortruda looked at him and smiled. Her smile was very terrible. "If thou wilt be but silent and watchful, thou shalt taste the sweets of revenge. But—hist!"

The window opposite opened softly. Ortruda and Telramund drew back farther into the shadow. A white-robed figure came out on the balcony.

Ortruda whispered in Telramund's ear: "Go thou, and leave her alone with me," and Frederick withdrew.

"Elsa!" cried a wailing, miserable voice.

Elsa started. "Who calls me?"

"Is my voice so strange to thee?" answered Ortruda piteously. "Wilt thou repulse one in sore distress?"

"Ortruda! Thou! What doest thou here, and at this hour, unhappy woman?" asked Elsa, in surprise.

"Ah, woe is me!" moaned Ortruda. "What have I done, that such dark trouble should fall on me? How different thy fate! After a brief time of trouble, every cloud has vanished, and life smiles gloriously before thee."

"Most unworthy should I be of my great happiness, could I spurn one in misery such as thine, Ortruda. Come! I myself will open the door to you."

"Ortruda, where art thou?" called the gentle voice of Elsa, opening the door.

"Here at thy feet!" replied Ortruda, throwing herself down before the white-robed figure.

ORTRUDA

"Kneel not to me, I beseech thee, Ortruda," cried Elsa, much distressed. "Thou, whom I have always beheld in pride and magnificence! Freely I forgive thee. And if in aught thou hast suffered through my fault, I pray thee pardon me in like manner."

"How can I thank thee for such gracious favor?" returned Ortruda, in tones of great humility. "And for thy husband Telramund," continued Elsa, "I will beseech my noble bridegroom on the morrow, that he show him grace and pardon. So let me see thee once more restored to happiness. Arrayed in thy robe of state, come thou with me to the minister, where our marriage will to-morrow be celebrated before God and all men."

"Thou loadest me with chains of gratitude," said Ortruda. "Only one way is there in which I may perhaps repay thee—by my knowledge of the hidden arts I may be able to protect thy life, and warn thee should grave danger arise."

"What meanest thou?" asked Elsa, in astonishment.

"Trust not thy happiness too blindly," replied Ortruda darkly, "lest some evil entrap thee unawares." Ortruda drew closer, and lowered her voice: "Dost know by what magic art *he* came to thee?"

THE DEPARTURE OF LOHENGRIN

By Constance Maud

IT was the Princess Elsa's wedding-day.

The sober old city of Antwerp had blossomed out in colors gay as a spring garden, with banners, ribbons, garlands of flowers, and triumphal arches.

Not a burgher or a prentice but kept holiday.

Royal weddings were not an everyday sight, more especially when the bride was a princess of such beauty and virtue, and the bridegroom a knight who had risked his life for her sake.

Every maid in Antwerp would gladly have gone through fire and water just for a sight of the knight in silver armour. Greatly were those envied who had seen him arrive, drawn by the snow-white swan.

The bells of the old cathedral rang out a joyful chime. From every quarter came a stream of people, all hurrying to secure the best places from which to see the bridal procession. Guarding the entrance of the cathedral, on either side, were stationed knights and nobles in full court dress, ablaze with medals and decorations, helmets and waving plumes.

"She comes! She comes! Make way for the bride," sang a chorus of voices. And Elsa appeared, more beautiful than a spring morning. Little children, clad in white, strewed her path with flowers. Maidens of high degree followed, bearing her bridal train. Never had a fairer, happier maid passed through the ancient doorway to become a bride.

Smiling and bowing graciously, Elsa ascended the cathedral steps, when suddenly her way was barred by a tall commanding figure, who pushed through the astonished crowd and stood before her. It was Ortruda.

"Back, I say!" she cried wrathfully. "Thinkest thou that I am going to follow thee, like a serving-maid! No longer will I suffer it! The time has come when thou shalt bow before me!"

The attendants and courtiers stood aghast. "The woman must be mad!" they exclaimed to one another.

Elsa could scarce believe that this was the same Ortruda who, a few hours before, had knelt in the dust at her feet.

Pale and trembling she cried:

"Ortruda! Is it possible? What has happened to change thee thus terribly?"

Ortruda gave a mocking laugh.

"Thinkest thou," she answered, "that because I foolishly forgot my high position and my worth for one short hour, I must forever after approach thee crawling? My lord was first in all the land! Not a foe but feared his sword, not a tongue but spake his praise. But thy hero! No man ever heard of him! Thou thyself canst not even give him a name."

The people murmured indignantly:

"Will no man silence this slanderous woman?"

But all trembled, remembering her reputation as a witch, and not daring to brave her wrath.

Fortunately at this moment appeared the king's outriders, followed by the royal bodyguard, and

King Henry himself, riding side by side with the bridegroom.

"What! Ho!" cried the king, looking at the threatening figure standing across the bride's path. "Who dares to make strife on a wedding morn?"

Lohengrin hastened to Elsa's side. "What do I see? Why is this terrible woman near thee?" he asked.

"Oh, my deliverer, protect me from her! Pardon me, that I forgot thy warning. Seeing her in misery at my door last night, I took her in. Behold now how she turns on me, and mocks me for my trust in thee!"

Lohengrin stood between Ortruda and the trembling Elsa. "Begone, thou fearful woman!" he cried. "Carry elsewhere thy poison. Here is no soil in which it can take root."

"Hold there!" cried a loud harsh voice. "O king, hearken, I pray. Greatly hast thou been deceived. The combat was no Heaven's ordeal, for, by the evil power of magic, justice was turned aside. Here, before all men, I challenge him, the impostor, to declare his name and race, and from where he came, drawn hither by that unholy bird. If he dare not say, methinks it looks bad for his knightly truth and honor! I appeal to thee, illustrious prince! Demand thou a reply from this unknown hero. He will scarcely dare to call thee unworthy of his answer."

Lohengrin confronted the wrathful Telramund: "All honor would I ever show to his most illustrious majesty; but there is one only to whom I am bound to reveal my secret—that one is Elsa, my bride."

Lohengrin feared for one dread moment that the wicked Ortruda's poison had, after all, begun to work. One moment only; then, to his joy, Elsa raised her head, and shaking off all doubt, she cried: "What he keeps secret, that he does in wisdom. She whom he has saved, shall she not trust him?"

And the king added heartily: "My hero, pay no regard to evil-speakers. Thou art too far above them for such to tarnish thy spotless fame."

The nobles then pressed round Lohengrin, assuring him of their trust and devotion, even though he should never see fit to reveal his name; and the wedding procession entered the cathedral in solemn state.

When the wedding-feast was over and the wedding-guests had gone, Elsa and Lohengrin sat at the window, looking out on the star-lit night.

Elsa sighed. A tiny cloud crept over her heart at the thought that she knew no name by which to call her love.

Lohengrin noticed it and strove to turn her thoughts from the dangerous subject. But Elsa continued, as though forced to return to it: "Ah, show thou thinkest me worthy of thy trust! Now that we are alone, tell me thy secret and let it be buried in my heart, safe, where never the world can reach it."

"Have I not shown thee highest trust?" answered Lohengrin. "I have trusted in thy promise. Now my greatest joy is in thy love. It is the only reward

I ask for all I have left behind. For not out of
night and sorrow did I come to thee, but out of
light and glory."

"Alas!" cried Elsa. "Then art thou farther
removed, and I yet more unworthy, than e'er I
dreamt! Any day may rob me of thee! Ere long
thou wilt surely regret thy humble choice, and long
after thy departed glory." Tears blinded her eyes.
Lohengrin saw, too late, that what he had told her
but increased her doubt and unhappiness. She
longed now more than ever to be trusted with his
secret.

"The fear lest thou depart will haunt me day
and night! Who is this unknown one? Whence
comes he?" No peace now for Elsa, day or night,
until she can answer.

"Alas!" she cried, "it was by a miracle thou
camest here! Thy path is hidden, like thyself, in
mystery. Thy life is divided from mine by a cloud."

"Ah, look!" she cried, clutching wildly Lohengrin's arm. "See the swan? He comes! There—
down the river! He brings the boat! Thou hast
called him!"

"Oh, Elsa, cease this madness!" cried Lohengrin,
in despair.

"Nothing can give me peace again, till I know,
even though it cost me my life—Who thou art, and
whence thou comest."

"Alas!" groaned Lohengrin, covering his face
with his hands.

So absorbed were they both, that they did not
hear the stealthy tread upon the stair, nor the low,
muffled voices outside the door.

DEPARTURE OF LOHENGRIN

Suddenly there was a crash. The door was broken open, and a group of dark figures, cloaked and masked, barred the passage, while one of the number rushed towards Lohengrin, drawing his naked sword.

It was the work of an instant. Lohengrin had but time to seize his sword, when the stalwart figure closed with him.

In the flickering torchlight, he parried the foe's first deadly thrust, and before he had time for a second, the trusty sword of Lohengrin had pierced to his traitorous heart. With a deep groan he fell back, and Elsa beheld, as she suspected, the face of Frederick of Telramund.

Hearing the noise, Elsa's attendants and guards now crowded into the room. The dark masked figures had fled on seeing their master fall.

Lohengrin turned to the guards, and bade them bear the body of Telramund before the king's judgment-seat.

Then to Elsa's attendants, who supported their fainting mistress, he said sadly: "Make her ready to appear before the king. There I will meet her, and answer her question—Who I am, and from whence I come?"

At noon next day, King Henry held a review of his troops.

Before leaving Antwerp, the king desired to collect forces for a war against the savage Drohns, who were threatening the peace of Germany. The king counted greatly on Lohengrin's help, for never had he seen one more fitted to command and lead his troops.

DEPARTURE OF LOHENGRIN

But now the appointed hour had come, and still the king waited for the arrival of the knight.

Presently all were startled by the appearance of a solemn procession, bearing in their midst the body of a dead man. "Make way!" whispered the crowd, awestruck. "These are the followers of Telramund."

Close on them followed Elsa and her ladies. Alas, how changed from the happy bride of yesterday!

"Ah, here he comes! Our hero!" cried the people, as Lohengrin at length appeared. "Welcome, sir knight," said the king. "We look to thee to lead these brave troops on to victory."

"Alas, my lord the king!" answered Lohengrin, "it is not possible for me now to lead thy soldiers, as I hoped."

"Heaven help us! What means this?" cried the king, dismayed, not only at Lohengrin's words, but by his sad, solemn bearing.

"First, I ask thy righteous judgment, before all the people, concerning this man." He pointed to the body of Telramund. "In the middle of the night, he fell on me unawares. Was I right in that I slew him?"

"Thy hand was but the instrument of a just Heaven in so slaying him!" replied the king, sternly regarding the dead traitor.

"Ye heard all how she, my bride, gave me her promise, that never would she ask who I am or from whence I came. Now, alas! she has broken that promise—she has listened to traitorous counsel! Now hear, all ye people, whether my secret is

168

one to be ashamed of before king, nobles, and the world!" Lohengrin raised his voice till it rang on all sides like a clarion.

"In the distant land, far from hence, is a mountain named Mount Salvat. In the midst stands a temple; none on earth can compare with its magnificence. Therein is guarded a sacred treasure, brought thither years ago by an angel-host. It is the Holy Grail. The knight who serves the Grail derives divine strength from the power of its might. Before him evil flies, and death itself is vanquished. Even when far away in distant lands, so long as the knight remains unknown, the Grail still renews his strength. But the working of the Holy Grail must ever remain veiled. Once the source of mystery is revealed, the blessings granted must be withdrawn—such is the Grail's command. I was hither sent to you by order of the Grail. My father is Parsifal, the king—I am his warrior, Lohengrin!"

Elsa listened like one hearing her death-sentence. Had not her ladies supported her, she must have fallen.

"Oh, Elsa," he cried mournfully, "why didst thou tear my secret from me? Now, alas, we are parted forever!"

"The swan! The swan!" cried a chorus of voices near the bank of the river.

Elsa turned to look, and there, sailing swiftly towards them, came the snow-white swan, drawing the small boat in which the shining knight had arrived.

"Oh, my Elsa," he said, "the Grail has sent for

me—I dare not tarry. One year only, and I might have had the joy of seeing thee again united to thy long-lost brother. For he is not dead, and by the might of the Grail he was then to be restored to thee. Now hearken. Should he return, give him these—my sword and horn and ring. The sword will bring him victory in battle, the horn will bring him help in time of need, and the ring he shall wear in memory of me. Farewell, my beloved bride; farewell forever!"

THE WOOING OF THE DAUGHTER OF THE KING OF IRELAND

From the Gudrun Lay

WHEN Hettel, the young King of Denmark, but newly crowned, was minded to take him a wife, he sent and gathered together his high vassals and lieges to his palace in Hegelingen to give him counsel.

And Morung of Nifland said to the king: "There is one maiden that for comeliness surpasseth all others in the world: that is Hilda, daughter of wild Hagen, King of Ireland; and she is peerless."

"That may be so," answered the king, "but Hagen is waxed so proud that there is no dealing with him by fair words; and many kings and yarls which sought to carry her off by strength of arm now sleep the sword-sleep because of her."

Then spake the sweet-voiced Horant: "Full well I know the maiden. She is radiant as the soft new snow beneath the dawn. Stern is her father, and cruel as the north wind that tears the clouds and breaks the sea, and shakes the pines in his fists. Wherefore if the king must send a messenger, let him not choose me." Frute spake also: "Neither am I fain to go upon this errand. But let the king send and summon Yarl Wate of Sturmen; he is more reckless than any man, and heedeth no living thing."

But when Yarl Wate was come before the king, and understood what was required of him, he was but ill-pleased, and said: "I ween Horant and Frute to have counseled thee in this, and to have done in no friendly wise toward me. Howbeit I am not the man to pick an enterprise that hath no peril in it. I will go. But since Horant and Frute esteem my life so lightly, they shall go likewise."

Then Yrolt of Ortland and Morung said: "It is well spoken; and inasmuch as it behooveth none to hang back when brave men take their lives in their hands, we also will go with them."

So the king made ready a great ship of cypress wood, in fashion like a dragon. It was all aglow with golden scales; the anchor was of silver, and the steering paddle overlaid with gold. Within he furnished it abundantly with victual for the voyage, with armor and raiment, and presents of great price.

Then Yarl Wate and Morung, Horant and Frute and Yrolt, entered into the ship with seven hundred of their men. They drew aloft the embroidered sail; a fair wind arose and bore them out of harbor. For many days they tilled the barren sea-fields, until weary of sea toil they saw the welcome land, and steered in for Castle Balian, where Hagen the king kept court.

Being come to shore, Horant and Yrolt took precious jewels in their hands worth many thousand marks, and leaving their men hidden in the ship, came to King Hagen, saying: "Behold we have voyaged from a far country where we have heard of thy fame, and we pray thee take these presents at our hands." Hagen looked at the jewels and marvelled at their great worth. He said; "What kings are ye, and whence have you come with all this treasure?"

Horant answered, saying: "Banished folk are we. Hast thou not heard of Hettel, who is king in Hegelingen, and of his might and majesty, of the battles he has fought and the riches he has gathered together? He despiseth such as we, and being well befriended careth nothing for his men. Wherefore a few of us, weary of his overbearing ways, have left him seeking service." Then said Hagen: "Ye shall abide with me;" and he commanded to make ready lodgings for them in the city.

But Horant and Yrolt gave gold away so lavishly to all within the city that the people said, "Of a truth these must be the richest kings of the earth."

And the fair Hilda hearing of it desired greatly to see these strangers; wherefore her father bade them to a feast.

The Danish knights came at his bidding, arrayed most sumptuously. And the feast being over, and the wine outpoured, the queen and Hilda left the table, desiring that the guests might be brought to them in the inner chamber. First Yarl Wate went in, a huge and burly man, with a great rough beard and brawny hands. But when the queen bade him sit between her and the princess he blushed and stammered, and then blundered shamefaced to the seat. "Thou art strangely ill at ease in company of ladies," said the queen. "Aye, mistress," said Yarl Wate, "I am not over smooth of tongue. I am not skilled to lisp about the weather. What shall I say? This seat is soft enough. I never mind me to have sat so soft before, nor to have wrought so hard in doing it. By my life, good ladies!" he cried upstarting, "a good day's battle with a brisk enemy never wearied me so much, or made me deem myself so great a fool." Hilda and her mother laughed pleasantly at his bluff behavior, and sought to put him at his ease; but Wate would have no more; he strode off to the hall among the king and his men, and in an hour or so became himself again. For the king won on him. Hagen's big voice, his battle knowledge, and his love of fight, opened Yarl Wate's heart, and the two were soon made friends. But for the women, there was none in their esteem like the sweet-voiced Horant. He was fair to look upon as a woman, yet had no lack of courage in the battle time. His wit was quick; and when he talked his face was in a glow at sight of the strange pictures in his mind, whereby he likened things to one another in curious sort, so that all which heard him wondered and were glad.

Now Hagen spake much with Wate concerning sword play, and the mystery thereof. So presently Yarl Wate besought the king to appoint him a master of fence to teach him a little of it, because fencing after their manner was a thing in which he was little learned. Then King Hagen sent for the best fence master that he had, and set him to teach Yarl Wate the rules of sword play. But quickly losing patience at the long list of early rules which the fence master laid down, Hagen caught the foil from out his hands crying: "Away with you! Why all this stuff? In four strokes I will teach this man to use a sword."

So the king fell to with Wate, whom, however, he very soon found an exceeding skilful master of fence. Thereat being somewhat angry, he struck in fiercely; and they both carried on the sport till the buttons flew off the foils; yet neither gat the better of the other. Then Hagen throwing down his foil cried: "In sooth, never saw I youth learn so quickly." And Yrolt said: "There is very little wherein the serving men of our lord's country are not already learned."

So as Yarl Wate and his fellows abode continually at the king's court and feasted with him every day, it befell once on a time, when night was past and the day had begun to dawn, that Horant arose and tuned his voice to a song. The birds, waking in the hedges, had begun to sing, but hearing music sweeter than theirs, they held their peace. Ever higher and sweeter Horant lifted his song till it rang about the palace; and all the sleepers dreamed of Baldur and his home in Ganzblick in the sky.

Soon they woke; nor were they sorry to lose their dreams at hearing Horant's song. Hagen heard it and rose up from his bed. Hilda and her maidens heard it, and arose. Men and women came thronging to thank the singer; but when they came the song was done. Yet none the more would the birds begin their lays; they had lost their notes from wonder.

Then Hilda besought her father that by any means he should constrain Horant to sing again. And Hagen being no less crazed with the song, recked not for aught else, and he promised the singer a thousand pounds of gold by weight if he would sing again at eve.

At evening Horant sang. The people filled the hall and flocked about the castle for a great space. The sick came thither and remembered their pains no more.

The beasts in the forest and the cattle in the fields left their food; the worms forgat to go in the grass, and the fishes left swimming in the sea. And when the song was done and the folk went their ways, they heard the minster choirs and the chiming of the bells, but took no more pleasure in them.

Hilda sent twelve purses of gold to Horant, entreating him to come and sing to her in her chamber. The singer came and sang the song of Amile, the like whereof no man had ever heard save on the wild flute. No gold was ever so good. The maiden laid her hand within the singer's and bade him choose whatever he listed for a song-gift. He said: "I pray thee give me but the girdle from thy waist, that I may take it to my master." She asked: "Who is thy master?" He answered: "No banished men are we, but servants of Hettel, King of Denmark, come to woo thee for his bride." Then Hilda said: "So thou couldst always sing to me at morn and eve, I would not care whose bride I were." Horant said: "Lady, within my master's courts abide twelve minstrels, better far than I; and yet with all the sweetness of their singing my lord sings best of all." And Hilda said: "If that be so, I fain would follow thee and be King Hettel's bride. But I know not how. My father will give me to no suitor with his goodwill. I would go but I durst not." Horant answered her: "Since thou wouldst, be it ours to dare. We ask no more."

Then Horant and his comrades got ready their ship for sea, and afterward they came to Hagen, saying: "The time for our departure draweth nigh, and we must sail to other lands. But before we go, we pray you bring the queen and your fair daughter, that they may see the treasures which we have within the ship." So on the next day, after mass, King Hagen came down to the beach, with his queen, and the fair Hilda and her maids; with them went a thousand good knights of Ireland. The ship was swung to a single cable, the anchor aboard, the sail tackle free. Upon the sands were spread the Danish treasure chests, filled with costly raiment embroidered with gold and jewels. There was a crowding round the chests to see; Yarl Wate was there, and Frute, and Horant; and in the crowding Hilda was parted from her mother. Hagen and his knights saw nothing for the crowd, and the queen forgot her daughter at beholding the glories of the raiment. But suddenly they heard a shout, and looking up beheld Yarl Wate leap on the bulwarks with fair Hilda in his arms; the next moment Horant and Frute sprang on board with two other maidens. Yrolt smote at the cable with his axe; it parted. The sail was hauled aloft, and twenty oars shot out from either side to lift the ship along. Hagen and his

knights ran quickly down into the sea; but the
rowers rowed hard, and armed men in the ship
arose, seven hundred strong, and laid about them.
Short was the fight, and soon the vessel reached
deep water. Loud laughed the Danes to see on
the fading shore the angry crowd, the weeping
queen, and Hagen raging like a madman, up to
his waist in the sea.

Fast sped the ship and the wind was fair. The
Danes made Hegelingen in ten days, and Hettel
was wed to Hilda with great joy.

But while they yet sat at the marriage feast
Hagen's war-ship bore down upon their coast.
Quickly the Danes rose from the tables, put their
armor on, and ran down to the shore. Hagen
drave his ship upon the sand, and leaped into the
water with his men. A shower of arrows thick as
hail was his greeting. Hettel rushed foremost to
withstand him. There was fierce fighting between
the two for a little space; then Hettel fell, sore
wounded; and over his body Hagen and his
knights pressed on and hewed their way to land.
Fast fell the men, both Danes and Irelanders. Then
Yarl Wate encountered Hagen; and the battle
anger fell on both the men; they fought like wild
beasts of the wood, till, Wate being wounded on
the head, Hagen's war-pike brake at the next blow
he struck. Meantime the battle raged furiously.
The Irelanders kept their footing, but could not
drive back the Danish men; the numbers slain on
either hand were equal, man for man. Then Hettel's wounds being bound up, the Danish king cried
out to Hagen: "Of what avail shall it be to you

or me to fight this battle out? For every man of mine that falls a man of thine goes down. When it is done there will be an end to Danes and Irelanders alike. But if thou must needs prolong the fight, I will now meet thee, and if Hilda weeps for a dead husband she shall mourn a dead father too." Then Hagen cast down his sword, and called off his men. And he said to Hettel: "Give me thy hand; for in sooth my child has married a brave man; and had I half a score more daughters they should all come to Hegelingen." So the kings made peace together. And the marriage feast was all begun again, and kept for twelve days in King Hettel's palace. Moreover a wise woman brought forth herbs and roots, and healed the warriors of their wounds. And after the feasting, Hagen and his men were loaded with gifts, and they entered into their ship and departed to Ireland.

THE LADY OF KYNAST

By Xavier B. Saintine

THE LADY OF KYNAST owned a large domain, and on this domain a ruined old tower which stood on the summit of a steep, high rock, surrounded on all sides by a deep abyss.

Rich, young and beautiful, eagerly sought for by a number of admirers, The Lady of Kynast did not think, in her desire to keep them from becoming too pressing, of undertaking an endless piece of embroidery, like Penelope. She did not embroider; in fact she looked with contempt, and almost with disgust, upon every kind of work that was done by women. She told her admirers that she was betrothed to Kynast—this was the name of the old tower—and that aryone who thought of winning her good graces would first have to compete with her betrothed. To do this nothing was required but to climb up the rock and the tower, and having reached the battlements, to make a complete round, not on foot, however, or assisted by the hands and knees, but on horseback, without other assistance than the bridle.

The flock of lovers took flight instantly; only two remained, two brothers who had completely lost their heads.

After having cast lots, the first one attempted the task and seemed on the point of being successful. But that was all. He had no sooner reached the crenelated top of the old tower than he was seized with vertigo and instantly fell into the abyss.

The second brother, in his turn, climbed to the top and actually succeeded in riding some distance along the battlements; but soon his horse, feeling the stones slipping from under its hoofs, and the whole tower rocking under the weight, refused to go on. Determined to carry through the undertaking he encouraged his horse with his voice and with his spurs, but the poor animal remained immovable, apparently wedged in between the large stones of the tower. In the morning both horse and rider had disappeared.

For quite a while no other claimants appeared to woo the fair lady, when suddenly one day a third lover presented himself and asked leave to attempt the trial.

She did not know who it was, and this surprised her; for how could he have fallen in love with her? He might possibly have seen her on her balcony, or at some royal feast; perhaps he was only allured by her great reputation. However, there was nothing to lose by accepting the offer.

For some days a thick, heavy fog had shrouded the castle and the old tavern from top to bottom, so as to make the ascent impossible. The simple laws of hospitality required, therefore, that the lady should offer her castle to the newly arrived knight.

He proved to be a handsome man with a fine commanding figure, and the large number of his servants bespoke his high rank and large fortune. During three days he spent almost all his time with the young lady, but as yet he had not dared say a word of his love. On her side, however, the young lady felt herself gradually conquered by a feeling which had, until now, been unknown to her heart.

When the dense veil of mist was at length torn aside and the Kynast shone forth in its full splendor, she was on the point of telling the knight that she would not insist on the trial in his case.

When the moment came the Lady of Kynast felt her heart fail her. She shut herself in, she wept and she cried, and prayed that he might be successful. Loud clamors were heard below, and as she thought the spectators were bewailing the death of her last lover, she fainted away.

Cries of joy and of triumph roused her again; the knight had successfully accomplished the task. Overcome, she rushes to meet him, and in her excitement she forgets that all eyes are upon her, and breathlessly cries out: "My hand is yours." But he draws himself up to his full height, and haughtily and harshly he replies, with a proud smile:

"Have I ever asked you for your hand? I only came to avenge my two brothers, whom you have killed, and I have done it, for I do not, could not, love you, and yet you love me. Farewell!"

That same evening the wretched lady had herself conducted up to the top of the tower, from whence she wished, she said, to watch the setting sun. She was never seen alive again.

THE GUARDIAN ANGEL

By Xavier B. Saintine

A WHITE figure appeared before the young girl as she awoke. "I am your Guardian Angel!"

"Then you will grant me the wishes which I shall mention?"

"I shall carry them to God's throne. You may count upon my assistance. What are your wishes?"

"O White Angel, I am tired of continually turning the spindle and my fingers are getting to be so hard by constant work that yesterday, at the dance, my partner might have imagined he was holding a wooden hand."

"Your partner was that fine-looking gentleman from Hesse? Did he not tell you that he adored blue eyes and fair hair, and that he would make you a baroness, if you would go home with him, if you would wickedly run away?"

"White Angel, make me a baroness!"

The evening of that day a young peasant came and asked Louisa's mother for her daughter's hand. The mother said, Yes.

"White Angel, deliver me from this poor man. I want to be a baroness!"

The mother, who was a sensible woman, and a widow, had good sense enough and energy enough for two. The White Angel did not appear again, and Louisa married the peasant—and she kept on turning the spindle.

One day her husband, who was a hard-working

183

man, had over-exerted himself and was taken ill. In the meanwhile Louisa had seen her handsome gentleman again.

"White Angel," she said, "he loves me still. He has sworn he would marry me if I were a widow." She dared not say more. The husband recovered from his illness. The White Angel still turned a deaf ear to her wishes. She lost all hope of ever becoming a baroness.

Later her husband became more successful, so that his work alone supplied all their wants. Two beautiful children had come to gladden their lives, and now, when Louisa worked at the spindle, it felt quite soft in her fingers.

One evening, when she was only half asleep, the white figure appeared once more, and a gentle voice whispered in her ear this story:

"A little fish was merrily swimming about in the water and looking seriously at a pretty blackcap which first circled around and around in the air, and then alighted on a branch of a willow which grew close to the bank of the river.

" 'Oh,' said the little fish, 'how happy that bird is! It can rise up to the heavens and go high up to the sun to warm itself in its rays. Why cannot I do the same?'

"The blackcap, who was looking down at the fish, thought to himself:

" 'Oh! how happy that fish is! The element in which it lives furnishes it at the same time with food; it has nothing to do but to glide along. How I should like to sport in the fresh, transparent water!' "

THE GIANT WHO LAUGHED

"At that moment a kite pounced upon the poor little fish, while a scamp of a schoolboy threw a stone at the bird; the blackcap fell into the water—the fresh, transparent water—and for a moment struggled in it before it died, while the little fish, carried aloft, could go up on high to the sun and warm itself in its rays. Their wishes had been granted."

THE GIANT WHO LAUGHED AT A DWARF

By Xavier B. Saintine

AN old duke of Bavaria had at his court a dwarf named Ephesim, and a giant named Grommelund. The giant laughed at the dwarf, and the dwarf threatened to box his ears. Grommelund laughed a big hoarse laugh that seemed to come up from his toes, and dared Ephesim to go ahead. The dwarf accepted the challenge at once, and the duke, having been a witness of the scene, ordered that a field for a single combat should be gotten ready.

Everybody expected to do as the giant had done, and laugh at the pigmy, as the poor little fellow was hardly two feet high and would have had to climb a long way before reaching the giant's ears. The dwarf began by walking all around the giant, as if to take his measure. The good-natured giant, standing up immovable, looks down upon him and quietly laughs till his sides shake; but while he is holding his hands to his sides, the dwarf unties his shoestrings and then worries him by kicking and pinching his calves.

Grommelund laughs more loudly than ever, thanks to the tickling; takes a few strides, steps on his loose shoestrings, nearly stumbles, and at last, with thoughtful presence of mind, stoops down to tie the strings.

Ephesim was watching for this. He quickly slapped the giant's cheek so vigorous and sounding a smack that the duke and all the lords of the court looked up in astonishment.

The poor giant was so shamed and humiliated that he hurriedly shambled off the field and sought refuge in the mountains, where, it is said, he hid himself and refused to come out.

THE LEGEND OF SAINT CHRISTOPHER

By Lillian M. Gask

THERE was once a man named Offero, so tall and strong that he stood among his fellows as a sturdy oak in a grove of saplings. His eyes were keen and clear as some great eagle's, his lips spoke nothing but gentle words, and his heart was as pure and tender as a little child's. His spirit was brave and fearless, and while he was yet in the prime of his strength he resolved to devote it to some good purpose.

"My friends," he said, when he had called together his companions, "I must leave you now, for something within me whispers that I was born to serve a king so great that fear is unknown to him; a king to whom all men bow."

Then he strode away into the forest, and was seen by them no more.

For many a day he traversed valley and mountain, inquiring of all he met who was the greatest king. At last he came to a splendid country, where reigned a monarch of high renown. His armies were vast and powerful, and his fleet of warships was like a flock of birds bearing death on their grim brown wings.

When he was told that Offero desired to serve him, he welcomed him gladly, and liked the young man so well that he soon made him his trusted counsellor and friend.

It was Offero's pride to see how all men trembled at his master's frown, and he could not believe that there lived a monarch greater than he.

One day, however, when the king was present, a courtier made some remark about "the Evil One;" his Majesty's august brow grew pale, and Offero could have sworn he saw his stern lips quiver. Pained and surprised, he humbly asked the king why he was troubled.

"I am afraid of the Devil," said that monarch, "although I fear no mortal man. He is the King of Hades, and more powerful even than I."

"Then I must leave you, O king!" cried Offero with haste, "since I have vowed to serve none other than the most powerful monarch in existence." And sorrowfully he turned away.

"Where is the Devil?" he asked the first man he met.

"He is everywhere," returned the traveller, looking round uneasily; and this was the usual answer that Offero received to his inquiry. Wherever he went men looked uneasy at the Devil's name, but would not say where Offero was most likely to meet with him.

He found him at last among a group of idle men and maidens on the village green, and hailed him as his master. The Devil was glad to have so strong a follower, and amused himself by showing the astonished giant his power over rich and poor. There seemed to be no limit to his might; he swayed the nobles in their velvet robes, and the peasants in their tattered garments.

"He is indeed master of the world," sighed Offero, and though he liked not the Devil's ways, he stifled his distaste that he might keep his word.

One day his master led him through the outskirts of the town into the open country.

"We are going to visit a hermit," he said with a burst of laughter. "He has left the town to be quit of me, but he will find me in his cave!"

Before Offero could ask him what he meant to do with the good hermit, they came to a turn where four roads met. A rough wind swayed the branches of the trees, and a peal of thunder echoed among the lofty hills. It was neither wind nor thunder, however, that made the Devil tremble, but the sight of a wooden cross which some pious folk had erected here. With gaunt arms pointing east and west it stood immovable; the rain beat down on it mercilessly, as if to cleanse it from the roadside dust; and turning his head away that he might not see it, the Devil hastened past. Not until it was far behind them had Offero an opportunity of asking why he had trembled.

"I was afraid," answered his grim companion, with another shudder.

"Afraid?" repeated Offero in puzzled tones. "Why, what was there to be afraid of?"

"Did you not see the crucifix?" cried the Devil impatiently. "The figure on it is that of the Christ, and this is why I trembled."

The giant had never heard that Holy Name before, and felt more perplexed than ever as he demanded: "Who is this Christ whom you so fear?"

"He is the King of Heaven," was the reluctant reply.

"Is he more powerful, then, than you?" persisted Offero, planting himself in the center of the pathway so that his master could not pass on.

"He is more powerful even than I!" admitted the Devil, his eyes becoming points of fire.

"Then I shall serve Him, and Him only," the giant cried, and, turning on his heel, he left the Devil to go on his way alone.

When Offero reached the cross once more, a man was kneeling before it in prayer. As he rose from his knees, Offero asked him the way to Heaven.

"I cannot tell you," said the man. "The way is long, and hard to find. 'Tis well that Christ is merciful."

Offero met with like answers from many wayfarers whom he questioned, but at last came one who advised him to consult the hermit.

"He is a holy man," he assured him earnestly, "and has retired from the world that he may give his time to prayer and fasting. He thinks he can serve Christ this way better than any other."

So Offero sought the hermit, and learnt from him many things. He heard of the grandeur and goodness of Christ, and of the greatness of His Kingdom. All that he said made Offero more eager to serve Him than ever, and when the hermit explained that no one could enter the Heavenly Kingdom until he was summoned there by Christ Himself, he bowed his head in disappointment.

"How then can I serve this new Master," he said, "unless I can see Him and hear His commands?"

"Do as I do," replied the hermit. "Give up the world, and fast and pray."

"If I were to fast," said Offero shrewdly, "I should lose my strength, and then, when He called me to work for Him, I should be useless." And although the hermit tried to persuade him, he would not stay, but set off again on his journey, determined to find the way to Heaven.

Presently he met a company of pilgrims. They were dusty and travel-stained, and very footsore, but their faces shone with joy. There were men and women and little children; some came from distant lands, and some from near, but one and all they were filled with a deep content.

"Who are you, and whence do you travel?" Offero asked them wonderingly.

"We are the servants of Christ," they answered, "and we are marching towards Heaven. The path is rough, and the way is long, but His many mansions await us."

"I will come with you, and be His servant too!" said Offero, and they welcomed him gladly.

The way was long, as they had said, but to the giant the days passed quickly. He was learning so much that he could scarcely sleep for the wonder of it, and his face also shone with happiness. He grew very grave when he heard of the swift-flowing river that all must cross before they could hope to reach the Kingdom of Heaven.

"There is no bridge to span it," said an aged pilgrim, whose tottering limbs were now so feeble that but for Offero's support they would hardly have borne him along. "The trembling woman, the little child, must cross it alone in the gloom and darkness, for though they call, no friendly boatman appears in sight. When Christ has need of us, His messenger will appear; he is clothed in raiment white as snow, and although his voice is always gentle, it is as clearly heard in the rush and roar of the tempest as on a summer's day."

At length the pilgrims came to the river-bank, and as the giant gazed at the foaming current, and saw the waves dashing against the shore, he marvelled greatly at what he had been told. Surely, he thought, no feeble woman or little child could breast its waters and reach the other side.

Even as he mused on this the white-robed messenger called to an ailing girl who was almost too weak to move. Her Master had need of her, he said, and in the fair courts of Heaven she would be strong again.

What joy was hers when she heard His voice! But alas! when she crept to the edge of the bank, and saw the river that swept beneath it, her heart grew sick with fear. She quivered and shook from head to foot, and moaned that she dare not venture. An exceeding pity moved Offero to go to her help.

"Do not weep," he said, "but trust to me." And taking her tenderly in his arms, he lifted her on to his shoulder, and bore her tenderly across. In spite of all his strength, the pitiless current nearly swept him off his feet, and he fought with the icy waters as he had fought no mortal foe. The girl tried in vain to thank him as he placed her on the bank in safety; he would not let her speak.

"Tell Christ," he said, "that I am His servant, and that until He shall summon me to His side I will help His pilgrims to cross the River of Death."

From henceforth this was his work. He had no time to wonder when his own call would come, for day and night there arrived at the banks of the river pilgrims from every clime, and, since few had courage to face the dark waters alone, he crossed and recrossed it continually. In order that he might be always at hand, he built himself a rough log-hut by the waterside, and here he made his home.

One night when the waves rolled fiercely and the wind blew high, Offero laid him down to sleep. Surely, he thought, no one would dare to cross in such a storm. His eyes had scarcely closed, however, when he heard a knocking at the door.

"Who are you?" he cried as he threw it open. There was no answer, and by the light of his lantern he saw a wistful child on the river-bank. He was staring down at the rushing waters with piteous dread, but the tone of his voice was clear and firm as he turned and spoke to Offero.

"I must cross to-night," he said. Offero looked at him with deep compassion.

"Poor child!" he murmured, "I am glad I heard you. With a tide like this it will be difficult even for me, giant as I am, but you would be swept away."

With gentle hands he placed the boy on his shoulder, and bidding him not to fear, set out for the opposite shore.

SAINT CHRISTOPHER

He had not over-estimated the difficulties he had to face. Time after time he was beaten backward, and the icy waters nearly engulfed them both. It took all his strength to bear up against them, and the weight of the child seemed greater than that of the heaviest man he had ever borne. When at last he climbed the steep, high bank, he was bruised as well as breathless, for the hidden rocks had worked him grievous harm.

"Tell Christ——" he panted. And then he saw that the figure beside him was not that of a little child, but of a radiant Being of kingly mien, with a crown of glory on His brow. The giant knelt before Him, and the Vision smiled.

"I am the Christ," He said, "whom thou hast served so long. This night thou hast borne Me across the River of Death.... Thou didst find Me a heavy burden, for I bore the sins of the world."

Then He named Giant Offero "Christopher," meaning "He who has carried Christ," and took him to dwell with Him in His Heavenly Kingdom.

PRINCE IVAN AND THE GRAY WOLF

By Lillian M. Gask

IN a far-off land surrounded by snow-capped
mountains, and watered by rivers that flowed
swiftly down to the sea, dwelt a mighty tsar. His
people loved as well as feared him, for the glance of
his eagle eye was very kind, and he was ever ready
to listen to their pleas for help or justice. When he
rode abroad on the great white horse that was shod
with gold, they flocked to bless him, and throughout
the whole of his wide dominion there was not one
discontented man, woman, or child. He had no foes
to trouble him, since rival monarchs knew full well
that their troops would be dispersed like mist in
sunlight before the charge of his victorious army,
and his three sons, Dimitri, Vasili, and Ivan, were
all that a father could desire. Yet the good tsar's
brow was clouded as he walked in his garden, and
from time to time he uttered a deep sigh.

This garden was his greatest pride. In days gone
by the forests had been rifled of their most splendid
trees that they might spread their shade over the
rare and lovely flowers that travelers brought him
from every part of the globe. The perfume of his
million rose trees was carried on the wind for fifty
miles beyond the palace, and so wonderful were
their colors that the eyes of those who beheld them
were dazzled by so much brilliance. There were the

 Jun. Cl-2-7

gorgeous orchids which, in order that the garden of their beloved tsar might be the most beautiful in the world, men had risked their lives to obtain, and every imaginable kind of fruit hung in tempting clusters from the drooping boughs of the trees. To look at them was to make one's mouth water, and the sick folk in his kingdom shared with the tsar the pleasures of taste and touch.

The tree that gave him most pleasure bore nothing but golden apples. When spring came round, and tender buds appeared upon the whispering branches, the tsar caused a net of fine white seed-pearls to be spread around it, so that the sweet-voiced choristers who filled his groves with music should not come near them. They might feast at will on every other tree in his garden, he said, but the golden apples they must leave for him; and as if in gratitude for his many kindnesses, even when the net of pearls was taken away, and the apples gleamed like fairy gold amid the emerald-green of their shapely leaves, not one of the birds approached them. When cares of state pressed heavily upon him, the tsar sought rest beneath the loaded branches, and forgot his troubles in watching the sunlight play on the golden balls.

Now all was changed, and the tsar's deep sigh betokened feelings of deep annoyance. Morning after morning he found the apple tree stripped of its golden treasures, and its emerald leaves strewn on the ground.

This was the work of the Magic Bird, who once upon a time had lived in the great cloud castles that gather in the West, but was now the slave of a distant king. The feathers of the Magic Bird were as radiant as the sun-god's plumes, and her eyes as clear as crystal. When she had wrought her will on the apple trees, she would fly blithely home to the garden of her own master, and, try as they would, not one of the tsar's head gardeners could even catch sight of her.

The good tsar meditated much upon the matter, and one windy morning in autumn he called his three sons to him.

"My children," he said, "the source of my grief is known to you, and now I entreat your help. Will you each in turn forego your sleep, that you may watch in my garden for the Magic Bird? To him who shall capture her, I will give the half of my kingdom, and when I am called thence he shall reign in my stead."

"Willingly, O my father," answered each of his three sons; and Prince Dimitri, as the eldest, claimed the right to the first watch.

The garden was flooded with moonlight as the prince threw himself down on a moss-grown bank that faced the tree, and the fragrance of the roses soon worked its drowsy spell. From a grove of myrtles came the song of a sweet-voiced nightingale: *"Glück—glück—glück,"* she trilled, and in listening to her the prince fell fast asleep. When he awoke it was light again. The tree had been once more despoiled, and the Magic Bird had flown.

The same thing occurred when Prince Vasili took his turn in watching. It is only fair to him to say that he did not fall asleep until the night was far spent, but as the east began to quiver with light, he

too became overpowered with slumber. The Magic
Bird was watching her opportunity, and yet again
she robbed the tree. When questioned by the tsar,
both princes solemnly assured him that no strange
bird had visited the garden during the night, but
though he fain would have believed them, he could
not doubt the evidence of his eyes.

It was now Prince Ivan's turn to watch. He
was not nearly so good-looking as his brothers, but
he had a stout heart and a cool head, and he made
up his mind to keep awake at any cost. Instead of
reclining on the ground, he perched himself in the
boughs of the tree, and when the song of the
nightingale threatened to lull him to sleep, as it had
done the elder princes, he put his fingers into his
ears that he might not hear it.

An hour passed slowly; a second, and then a
third. Suddenly the whole garden was lit up as if
with a burst of sunshine, and with rays of light
flashing from every shaft of her golden feathers the
Magic Bird flew down and began to peck at the
shining apples. Prince Ivan, scarcely daring to
breathe, stretched out his hand and caught as much
of her tail as he could grasp. With a startled cry
the Magic Bird spread her beautiful wings and
wrenched herself free, leaving behind one glittering
feather, which the prince held firmly. At break of
day he took this to his father, humbly apologizing
for his ill success in not having caught the Magic
Bird herself.

"Nevertheless, you have done well, my son," said
the tsar gratefully, and he placed the feather, which
shone so brightly that at dusk it illuminated the

whole room, in a cabinet of cedar and mother-of-pearl.

The Magic Bird came no more to the palace garden, and the precious tree was never again despoiled of its golden apples. But the tsar was not content. He sighed to possess the bird that had robbed him, and once more he summoned his three sons.

"My children," he said, "I am sick with longing for the Magic Bird. Seek her, I pray you, and bring her to me. What I have promised already shall then be yours."

The princes assented gladly, each anxious to find the Magic Bird. Prince Ivan alone wished to please his father; his brothers were only thinking of the riches and honors they would gain for themselves. So dear was this youngest son to the monarch's heart that he was loath to part with him when the time came, but the youth insisted.

"It will not be for long, dear father," he cried. "I shall soon return with the Magic Bird you sigh for." So the tsar blessed him, and let him go.

Prince Ivan took the fleetest horse in the imperial stables, and rode on and on for many days. At last he came to a bare field set in the midst of fair green meadows, and in the center of this stood a block of rough gray stone. Inscribed upon the stone in crimson letters was a strange verse:

"Hungry and cold shall that man be
Who rides in pride straight up to me.
To ride from the left means death and sorrow,
Though his horse shall live for many a morrow.
He who rides from the right shall have good things all,
But ere three days pass his horse shall fall!"

Prince Ivan was greatly troubled at the thought of losing his horse, but to ride from the right seemed the wisest course for him to pursue. Accordingly he did so, and so swift was his horse's flight that he had soon left the gray stone far behind. On the third day, as he was passing the borders of a gloomy forest, a big Gray Wolf sprang out from a thicket, and, flying at his horse's throat, threw him on the ground and killed him in spite of Ivan's gallant attempt to beat him off. Ivan would now have run the Gray Wolf through with the jeweled dagger his father had given him as a parting present, but before he could rise from the spot where he had been thrown, the creature spoke.

"Spare me, wise prince," he entreated humbly. "I have but done as I was commanded. My death will not give you back your horse, while if you spare my life I will be your friend forever, and will carry you over the world."

Prince Ivan saw that he would gain nothing by being revengeful, and, mindful of his quest, accepted the Wolf's offer to be his steed.

"Tell me where you wish to go, dear master!" said the Gray Wolf, "and it shall be as you will." And, true enough, when he heard the object of Prince Ivan's journey, he galloped even more swiftly than the horse had done, till toward nightfall he came to a standstill behind a thick stone wall.

"On the other side of this wall," he said, "is a terraced garden, and there, in a golden cage, is the Magic Bird. The garden is empty now, so no one will stay you if you capture her; but if you touch her cage there will be trouble."

Dismounting from the Gray Wolf's back, Prince Ivan climbed the wall without much difficulty, and quickly seized the Magic Bird. She fluttered so wildly, however, as he tried to hold her, though without uttering a sound, that he quite forgot the Gray Wolf's warning, and hastened back for the cage. As he touched it, the stillness of the garden was broken by the pealing of bells and the clanking of armor, for the cage was connected with the palace courtyard by invisible wires. Before he could escape, Prince Ivan was surrounded by excited soldiers, who quickly carried him before the king.

"Are you not ashamed?" the monarch thundered, noting the young man's rich attire, "to be caught in my garden like a common thief? Where do you come from, and what is your name?"

"I am the son of a great tsar," the young prince answered, "and they call me Ivan. My father has a very beautiful garden, in which grows a tree of golden apples that is the pride of his heart. Night after night your Magic Bird rifled this precious fruit, until I all but succeeded in capturing her. She was too quick for me, however, and flew away, leaving one feather in my hand. This feather I took to my father, who admired it greatly, and ever since has longed to possess the Magic Bird."

Tsar Dolmat looked less angry, though he still frowned.

"If you had come to me," he said, "and told me what you wanted, I would have made your father a present of the Magic Bird. As it is, I feel inclined to let all nations know how dishonorably you have acted."

Prince Ivan bowed his head in shame, and after a searching glance at him the tsar continued his speech.

"You shall go forth free, young prince," he said, "if you will do me a service. In the realm of Tsar Afron, beyond the thrice-ninth kingdom, there is a gold-maned horse which belongs to him, and this I greatly covet. If you will procure it, and bring it here to me, I will forgive your theft of the Magic Bird, and present her to you as a mark of honor."

Prince Ivan promised to do his best, but he did not feel very hopeful as he rejoined the Gray Wolf, who was patiently waiting for him outside the wall. When Ivan had confessed the reason that led to his capture, the Gray Wolf patted his shoulder with one rough paw.

"It takes a wise man," he remarked, "to own himself in the wrong, so we will say no more about it. Jump on my back again, and I will take you to the far-famed realm of Tsar Afron, beyond the thrice-ninth kingdom."

The Gray Wolf ran so swiftly that Ivan could scarcely see the country through which they passed, and after traveling for many nights and days, they reached, at last, their journey's end. The marble stables of the tsar shone fair and stately in the morning light, and through a door which a careless groom had left half open, Prince Ivan made his way. The horse with the golden mane was feeding on the yellow pollen collected by the bees from the tall white lilies that edged the rose garden, and stared at Prince Ivan haughtily as he approached. Firmly grasping his golden mane, Prince Ivan led him out of the stall. The Gray Wolf had cautioned him more than once not to attempt to bring the golden bridle that hung above the door, but as he was leaving the stable the prince suddenly thought how useful this would be, and turning back, stretched out his hand and touched it. Immediately he did so, bells pealed all over the palace, for, like the cage of the Magic Bird, the bridle was fastened to invisible wires.

The stable guards came hurrying in, full of alarm, and when they saw Prince Ivan they seized him angrily, and took him before their master. Tsar Afron was even more indignant than Tsar Dolmat had been at the prince's attempt to rob him. When he had questioned him as to his birth and station his face became sterner still.

"Is this the deed of a gallant knight?" he asked with withering scorn. "I have a great regard for your father's name, and if you had come to me openly and in good faith, I would gladly have given you my gold-maned horse. But now all nations shall know of your dishonor, for such acts of yours must not go unpunished."

This was more than Prince Ivan could bear, and with eager haste he protested his willingness to atone for his fault.

"Very well, then," said Tsar Afron, "I will take you at your word. Go forth and bring me Queen Helen the Beautiful, whom I have long loved with all my heart and soul. I have seen a picture of her in my seer's white crystal, and she is more fair to look upon than any other maid. I cannot reach her, try as I may, since her kingdom is guarded by elves and goblins. If you can capture her for me and bring her here, in return I will give you anything you ask."

Prince Ivan hurried away to the Gray Wolf, fearing that since he had disregarded his advice for a second time, he might refuse to help him in this new enterprise. Once more he humbly confessed that he had been at fault, and once more the Gray Wolf consoled him.

"One must buy wit," he growled. "Well, jump on my back, and I will see what I can do for you."

Then he ran so swiftly that it seemed as though his feet were winged, and the elves and goblins that guarded the kingdom of Helen the Beautiful scattered before him in all directions, thinking him to be a specter. When he came to the golden streamlet that bordered the queen's magic garden, he told Prince Ivan that he must now dismount.

"Go back by the road we came," he commanded, "and wait for me in the shade of that spreading oak tree we passed just now."

Prince Ivan did as he was told, and the Gray Wolf crouched under a bush of juniper, and waited until evening fell. As the light faded out of the sunset sky and the pale little moon rose slowly over the mountain-tops, Queen Helen walked in her garden. She was so fair and sweet to look upon that even the heart of the Gray Wolf was moved to admiration, and he wished her a worthier mate than the stern Tsar Afron, who knew not how to be gentle even in his love. After a while she approached the streamlet, winding round her dainty throat a cloud of milk-white gossamer, that she might not feel the touch of the evening breeze.

"Do not fear, sweet lady! I will not harm you!" the Gray Wolf cried, as he sprang from his hiding place and crossed the stream. Holding her tenderly by her flowing draperies, he leaped back to the other side, and galloped with her to the prince, who waited under the spreading oak.

When the queen and prince beheld each other, it was as if a veil had fallen from their eyes. Never had the world appeared so beautiful, and as they gazed at each other in the soft twilight, the queen's fears fled. As for Prince Ivan, he knew from that moment that she was intended for his wife, and when they rode away together on the Gray Wolf's back, he already felt that she belonged to him.

The journey was all too short, and soon Tsar Afron's palace loomed before them.

"Why are you weeping?" the Gray Wolf inquired, as their tears splashed on his head. Queen Helen could make no answer, but Prince Ivan's words poured forth like a raging flood.

"How can we help it, Gray Wolf," he cried, "since we love each other, and I must resign my beautiful queen to the stern Tsar Afron, or else be branded before all nations as a robber and a thief?"

"I have kept my promise, Prince Ivan," said the Gray Wolf, "and served you well, but I will do more for you still. By means of magic known to myself alone, I, the Gray Wolf, will take the form of beautiful Queen Helen. You shall leave the real queen here, in the shade of this grove of pine trees, and when you have taken Tsar Afron his 'strange wolf bride, who will appear to him as a lovely woman with golden hair, he will give you the gold-maned horse. Bid him farewell as quickly as you can, and, taking your queen behind you, ride swiftly toward the west. When I have given you time to journey far, I will ask Tsar Afron to let me walk with my maidens in the woods. Then, if you call me to your mind, I shall disappear from their midst even as they watch me, and join you and your queen."

Prince Ivan once more did as the Gray Wolf said, and great was the delight of the Tsar Afron as he beheld the tall and gracious woman whom the prince presented to him. She was even more beautiful than he had imagined from her picture, and he would have given not only his gold-maned horse, but his crown as well, to her captor had he desired it. Prince Ivan, however, asked nothing but the gold-maned horse, and was soon speeding across the plains with the real Queen Helen nestling against his side. He rode toward the west, where lay the kingdom of Tsar Dolmat.

Tsar Afron was more than content with his wolfish bride, who was not alarmed by his fierce caresses, and only smiled when he threatened to kill her if her love for him should waver for a single instant. On the fourth day after their marriage feast she complained of feeling stifled in the royal palace.

"If I might walk in the meadows," she said, "the breath of the cool fresh air would refresh my spirit, and I could once more laugh with my lord."

So the tsar allowed her to walk with her maidens.

Just at this time the thought of the Gray Wolf flashed into Prince Ivan's head.

"I had forgotten him," he exclaimed remorsefully to his dear wife. "What is he doing, I wonder? I wish we had him here."

He had no sooner spoken than there came a clap of thunder from the distant hills, and the Gray Wolf suddenly appeared.

"You must let the queen ride the gold-maned horse alone," he told the prince, "and I will be your steed."

Somewhat reluctantly, the prince accepted his suggestion, and in this manner they rode to the verge of Tsar Dolmat's capital. The kindly looks of the Gray Wolf emboldened the prince to ask him another favor.

"Since you can change yourself into a beautiful woman, and then back again into a Gray Wolf, could you not become for a time a gold-maned horse, so that I might give you to Tsar Dolmat, and keep the real one for my dear queen?"

The Gray Wolf readily assented, and striking his right paw three times in succession on a patch of bare earth, became the exact image of the gold-maned horse who bore the fair Queen Helen. Leaving the real horse with his bride in a flower-strewn meadow outside the city, Prince Ivan rode on to the tsar. He was greeted by that monarch with every sign of joy, for the mane of the Gray Wolf-horse shone in the sunshine like purest gold. The tsar kissed Prince Ivan on either cheek, and leading him to his palace, gave him a royal feast. For three whole days they reveled in the choicest wines and the richest viands the kingdom could supply, and on the third, Tsar Dolmat rewarded the prince with many thanks, and the gift of the Magic Bird in her golden cage.

Prince Ivan felt now that his quest was over, and quickly regaining Queen Helen's side, he fastened the cage of the Magic Bird round the neck of the gold-maned horse, and rode with her toward his father's kingdom. Early the next afternoon they were joined by the Gray Wolf; Tsar Dolmat had ridden his newly acquired treasure in an open field, and had been heavily thrown for his pains by the false horse, which had then galloped away.

As the Gray Wolf had been so good a friend to him, Prince Ivan could not refuse his request when he asked to be allowed to carry him, so once more the queen alone sat on the gold-maned horse.

Thus they rode on until they came to the place where the Gray Wolf had slain the horse which Prince Ivan had brought from his father's stable. Here the strange creature came to a sudden stop.

"I have done all that I said, and more," he told the prince. "Now I am your servant no longer. Farewell!" And he galloped back to the gloomy wood from which he had first come.

Prince Ivan's sorrow at parting with him was very real, but in the pleasure afforded by the queen's company he soon forgot his loss. When he came within sight of his father's realm, he stopped by the shade of a belt of fir trees, and placing the cage of the Magic Bird and the golden bridle beneath their shade, he lifted down his beautiful queen, and rested with her on a bank of fern. They were weary after their long journey, and soon, talking together softly as ring-doves coo in their nests, both fell asleep.

Now Prince Dimitri and Prince Vasili had fared badly on their travels, and were returning to the palace, empty-handed, and sadly out of temper, when they caught sight of the reclining forms of the two sleepers, with the gold-maned horse browsing close beside them. As they stared in amazement, an evil spirit of envy took possession of them, and there presently entered into their minds the thought of killing their brother. Each looked at the other, and then Prince Dimitri drew his sword, and ran it through Prince Ivan as he slept; he died without a murmur, and when the queen awoke, she found him lifeless.

"What is this you have done?" she sobbed to the guilty princes. "If you had met him in fair fight, and slain him thus, he might at least have struck a blow in self-defense. But you are cowards and dastards, fit only for ravens' food!"

In vain she wept and protested, as the princes drew lots for their dead brother's possessions. The queen fell to the keeping of Prince Vasili, and the gold-maned horse was adjudged to Prince Dimitri. In a passion of tears, the queen hid her face in her golden hair, as her would-be lord spoke roughly to her.

"You are in our power, fair Helen," he said. "We shall tell our father that it was we who found you, the Magic Bird, and the gold-maned horse. If you deny our words, we will instantly put you to death, so look to it that you hold your tongue, and keep our counsel."

The poor queen was so terrified by his cruel threat that speech forsook her, and when they arrived at the palace she was mute as some marble statue, and could not contradict the wicked statements which she heard them boldly utter.

Prince Ivan lay dead with his face to the sky, but the wood elves guarded his body, so that neither beast nor bird came near to devour it until the end of thirty days. Then, as the sun was sinking, a raven seeking food for her young, hopped on his breast, and would have pecked at his eyes had not the Gray Wolf galloped up in the nick of time. He knew at once that the dead man must be Ivan, and pouncing upon one of the young birds, would have torn it asunder in his rage.

"Do not touch my little birdling, O fierce Gray Wolf!" entreated the mother piteously. "It has done you no harm, and deserves no ill from you."

"Then listen," the Gray Wolf replied. "I will spare the life of your birdling, if you will fly away beyond the thrice-ninth lands, and bring me back the Water of Death and the Water of Life from the crystal stream whence they flow to the great Forever."

"I will do what you wish," cried the raven, "only do not touch my little son." And as she spoke she sped away.

Three days and three nights had passed before she returned to the Gray Wolf, carrying two small vials. One held the Water of Life, the other the Water of Death, and as the Gray Wolf took them from her, he gave a cry of triumph. With a snap of his teeth, he bit the young raven in two, tearing

it to pieces before its mother's frantic eyes. This
done, he broke one of the vials, and when he had
sprinkled three drops of the Water of Death on
the slain birdling, immediately its torn body grew
together again. Then he touched it with a few
drops from the second vial, and the little thing
spread its wings, and flew off rejoicing.

Thus the Gray Wolf knew that the raven had
served him well, and he poured what was left of the
Waters of Life and Death over the body of the
dead prince. In a few moments, life came back to
him, and stumbling to his feet, he smiled at the
Gray Wolf.

"Have I slept long?" he asked dreamily.

"You would have slept forever had it not been
for me," was the reply. And the prince listened
with grieved surprise as the Gray Wolf told him all
that had happened.

"Your brother is going to marry your bride
to-day," he ended by saying. "We must hasten
to the palace with all possible speed. Mount on my
back, and I will carry you once more."

So they galloped to the palace of the old tsar,
and the Gray Wolf bade Prince Ivan farewell for
the last time as he dismounted at the great gates.
The prince hurried into the banquet-hall, and there,
looking like some fair statue that had been moulded
from frozen snow, sat beautiful Queen Helen by
Prince Vasili's side. They had just returned from
the wedding ceremony, and all the nobles were
gathered round.

When Queen Helen saw who had entered the
hall, her speech came back to her, and she flew to

her lover with a cry of rapture and kissed him on the lips.

"This is my own dear husband," she cried. "I belong to him, and not to the wicked prince I have married to-day. From the shelter of Ivan's breast she told the old tsar all that had happened, and how it was to his youngest son that he owed the gold-maned horse and the Magic Bird.

The joy of the tsar at his favorite son's return was tempered by his grief and amazement at the conduct of the elder princes. They were cast into prison, where they languish still: but Prince Ivan and the beautiful Queen Helen are as happy as the days are long, and the Magic Bird was allowed to **return to her home in the golden West.**

KING ROBERT OF SICILY

Retold from the poem by Henry W. Longfellow

KING ROBERT of Sicily was at church one evening attended as usual by a great train of gallant knights and trusty squires and ladies of the court. As he sat proudly in his high place, dressed in rich and beautiful robes, he thought not so much of the service as of his own importance and state. Not only was he a king himself, but he was brother to the Pope and to Valmond, Emperor of Germany.

Presently his attention was attracted by the chant that the priests were singing. It was the Magnificat. Over and over again they repeated the words,

"Deposuit potentes de sede, et exaltavit humiles."

King Robert had heard the chant many times before, but now he found himself wondering what this particular phrase meant. A learned man was at his side, and the king spoke to him.

"What do those words mean?" he asked.

"He has put down the mighty from their seat,
And has exalted them of low degree,"

replied the scholar.

"It is well that such words are sung in Latin and only by the priests," muttered King Robert, scornfully. "Be it known to both priests and people that there is no power that can push me from my throne."

He leaned back in his seat yawning and soon fell asleep, lulled by the monotonous chant.

Now, it was St. John's eve and on that day strange and unlooked for things happen. When King Robert awoke from his nap it was night and he was alone in the church. The service was over and the priests and every one else except himself had gone. The great building was dark but for the little lamps which were kept burning constantly before the images of the saints.

King Robert started from his seat and looked around in amazement. All was still. He groped his way down the long aisle to the door; he took hold of the handle and tried to turn it; the door was locked. He called and listened for an answer but none came. He knocked and he shouted, but to no purpose. Growing angrier every minute, he cried out threats and complaints and the sound of his own voice came back to him echoing from the roofs and the walls. It was as though he were being mocked by unseen hearers.

After what seemed a long time, the knocking and the shouting brought the sexton to the church door. He came with his lantern suspecting that thieves were in the church.

"Who is there?" he called.

"Open the door at once," commanded the king, who was almost beside himself with rage. "It is I, the king."

The sexton trembled and waited to hear more.

before putting the great key in the lock. He thought that there must be a madman within.

"Art thou afraid?" cried the king.

"It is a drunken vagabond," muttered the old man and, turning the key, he flung the door wide open.

A figure leaped past him in the darkness. It was King Robert, but the sexton did not dream of that for the figure was half-naked and forlorn. The king's gorgeous robes had disappeared, his hat and his cloak were gone and he did not look like himself at all. Without a word or a look at the sexton he sped down the street.

Bare-headed and breathless and splashed with mud, Robert of Sicily, brother of Pope Urbane and of Valmond, Emperor of Germany, reached his palace gate—the gate that he had entered in triumph so many times.

He thundered for admittance, boiling with rage and half-mad with an overpowering sense of his wrongs. Through the gate he rushed and across the court-yard, thrusting aside every one who stood in his way, upsetting pages, and overwhelming guards. Past them all and up the broad stairway he hurried and then sped through the long halls. He paid no attention to the calls and the cries which pursued him, and did not pause until he reached the banquet room.

There on a dais sat another king wearing Robert's robes, his crown and his signet-ring. His features were like Robert's and so was his form, but he possessed a majesty and an exalted look which the real king lacked. The room, always well lighted, shone with an unusual brilliancy and the atmosphere was full of fragrance.

An Angel had taken the place of the king, and although no one was conscious of the change every one present vaguely felt the improvement.

Robert stood speechless before the miracle. Then his surprise gave way to anger at seeing another in his place. The Angel spoke first.

"Who art thou, and why comest thou here?" he asked benignly, meeting Robert's threatening look with one of almost divine compassion.

"I am the king," answered Robert indignantly, "and I have come to claim my throne from the impostor who is on it."

As he stood before the Angel, Robert did not look at all royal, and his clothing made such a difference in his appearance that the courtiers did not notice even a resemblance to their king, and took him for a stranger. At his bold words they sprang angrily from their seats and drew their swords to put him to death for his insolence.

The Angel was unmoved. He signed to the courtiers to sheath the weapons that they had drawn in his defense.

"No, thou art not the king," he said to Robert. "Thou art the king's jester and henceforth thou shalt wear bells and cap and a scalloped cape and lead a monkey about by a string. Thou shalt obey my servants and wait on my men."

In those days every king kept a jester or a fool whose duty it was to amuse his master and the court. Often the jester was not quite right in his mind and for that reason said odd things which would not have occurred to entirely sane people, and he was allowed to make speeches which would have been rebuked if they had come from others. Thus the Angel treated Robert's claim as a jest.

The attendants were delighted with the new joke. Paying no attention except laughter to Robert's cries and explanations, they thrust him from the banquet hall and down the stairs. A crowd of pages ran before him throwing the doors wide open with mock ceremony, while the boisterous men-at-arms shouted "Long live the King" with noisy glee.

How he got through the evening King Robert hardly knew. He was so tired when he was shown at last to his comfortless straw bed that he slept better than he had done many a night on his royal couch.

The next morning he awoke with the day.

"What a curious dream I have had," he exclaimed sleepily.

But it was no dream. Straw rustled as he turned his head and by his side were the cap and bells which he was to put on. His room was bare, its walls were discolored, and presently he heard horses stamping in their near-by stalls. He was in a stable. The monkey was there, too; King Robert saw the horrid thing grinning and chattering in a corner. His past life seemed far away. He had to begin to live again, this time the butt and the jest of the palace.

Days came and went, and the Angel still sat on the throne. The island of Sicily prospered under his reign. The crops were good, the vintage was abundant and the people were happy.

King Robert yielded to fate, but he did not yield willingly. He became sullen and silent and was a sorry jester in spite of his gay dress and his jingling bells and the chattering monkey. The courtiers mocked him in innumerable ways and the nimble pages played pranks on him; he had to be content with scraps from the tables of his masters, and the monkey was his only friend.

Sometimes the Angel asked him, as though in jest, "Art thou the king?" and Robert, still defiant, replied haughtily, "I am, I am the king!"

Almost three years passed. Then messengers came from Valmond, Emperor of Germany to tell King Robert that their brother, Pope Urbane, summoned him to come on Holy Thursday to his city, Rome. The Angel welcomed the ambassadors with fitting ceremony, and gave them magnificent presents, embroidered vests, velvet mantles, rare jewels and costly rings. Not only were his guests messengers from the great Valmond but they were mighty nobles.

As soon as he could get ready the Angel went with the ambassadors and a mighty train of followers over the sea to Italy. As the procession travelled along crowds gathered to watch its progress. Never had there been seen a more gorgeous assembly. The Angel and his courtiers and the ambassadors were dressed in splendid garments with gold and gems and laces and embroideries and velvets and satins and nodding plumes, each one according to his state, and their horses were

resplendent with gold and silver and jeweled
bridles. After them rode the servants, less fine
but equally gay, and among the lowliest of these
was poor Robert riding in mock state on an awk-
ward piebald pony. As the ridiculous steed
shambled along, his rider's cloak of fox-tails
flapped in the wind and his bells jingled. The king
was very unhappy and his face showed it, but it
was only a joke for a jester to look disconsolate
and people were no more sorry for him than for
the solemn monkey who perched demurely by his
side and aped his ways. In all the country towns
through which they went the gaping crowds stared
at them and laughed.

The Pope received the Angel and the emperor
with pomp. Trumpets sounded a welcome and
banners waved joyously, as they met on St. Peter's
square. The Pope embraced and blessed his
brothers, as he thought, for even he did not
know that he was entertaining an Angel. While
prayers and rejoicing were at their height
Robert the Jester burst through the crowd
and rushed into the presence of the Pope and his
guests.

"I am the king," he cried, addressing the Pope,
"look and behold in me Robert, your brother, King
of Sicily. That man who looks like me and wears
my robes and my crown is an impostor. Do you
not know me? Does nothing tell you that we are
akin?"

Robert was desperate. This seemed his last
chance of regaining his rights. He was appealing
to the highest authority in the world.

The Pope looked troubled. He turned silently from Robert to the Angel with searching glances. The Angel met his scrutiny with perfect serenity. Valmond only laughed.

"It is strange sport to have a madman for thy jester," he said to the Angel, whom he believed to be his brother.

The baffled jester was hustled back into the crowd. He was in disgrace and suffered punishment for his untimely joke.

Holy Week went by in solemn state, and Easter Sunday came. On that blessed morning the city was radiant with light even before the sun rose. The Angel's presence made Rome bright, and filled men's hearts with love and goodness. They felt as though Christ had indeed risen from the dead and were ready to devote themselves to him with fresh zeal. Even the jester, as he opened his eyes to the marvelous light felt within his heart a power that he had never felt before. What mattered it that his bed was straw? He fell on his knees beside it and prayed to the risen Christ.

When the visit was ended Valmond returned to Germany and the Angel and his train once more flashed along the towns of Italy and then set sail for Sicily. When they reached home the Angel occupied the throne as before. Robert could not understand it but he was humbled and no longer felt angry and bitter.

One evening when the convent bells were ringing for prayer the Angel beckoned to Robert to draw near and signed to the attendants to leave the room. When they were alone the Angel turned to Robert and asked with less sternness than ever before, "Art thou the king?"

King Robert bowed his head meekly and crossed his hands upon his breast.

"Thou knowest best," he said. "I have sinned. Let me go away from here and spend the rest of my days in a convent cell. There, kneeling on stones, I will beg heaven to forgive my pride."

The Angel smiled and the place was filled with a heavenly light. At the same moment through the open windows came the chant of the monks:

"He has put down the mighty from their seat
And has exalted them of low degree."

King Robert understood it at last. Then above the measured tones of the singers rose another voice, one of heavenly sweetness. It said:

"I am an Angel, thou art the king."

The king lifted his eyes. He was alone. No longer was he dressed in the motley attire of a jester, but he was in royal robes such as he used to wear, in velvet and ermine and cloth of gold.

When the courtiers came back to the room they found their king on his knees, absorbed in silent prayer.

THE RIDDLE OF THE SPHINX

By Elsie Finnimore Buckley

LONG ago, in the city of Thebes, there ruled a king named Laius and his queen Iocasta. They were children of the gods, and Thebes itself, men said, had been built by hands more than mortal; for Apollo had led Cadmus the Phœnician, the son of Zeus, to the sacred spot where he was to raise the citadel of Thebes, and Pallas Athene had helped him to slay the monstrous dragon that guarded the sacred spring of Ares. The teeth of the dragon Cadmus took and planted in the plain of Thebes, and from this seed there sprang up a great host of armed men, who would have slain him; but he took a stone and cast it in their midst, whereupon the serpent men turned their arms one against another, fighting up and down the plain till only five were left. With the help of these five, Cadmus built the citadel of Thebes, and round it made a wall so wide that a dozen men and more might walk upon it, and so huge were the stones and so strong was the masonry that parts of it are standing to this day.

As for the city itself, the tale goes that Amphion, the mightiest of all musicians, came with his lyre, and so sweetly did he play that the hearts of the very stones were stirred within them, so that of their own free will they fell into their places, and the town of Thebes rose up beneath the shadow of the citadel.

For many a long day did Laius and Iocasta rule over the people of Thebes, and all that time they had no children; for a dreadful curse lay on the head of Laius that, if ever he had a son, by that son's hand he should die. At last a boy was born to them, and Laius, remembering the curse, swore that the child should never grow to manhood, and he bade Iocasta slay him forthwith. But she, being his mother, was filled with a great love and pity for the helpless child. When it nestled in her arms and clung to her breast she could not find it in her heart to slay it, and she wept over it many a bitter salt tear, and pressed it closer to her bosom.

So she called a trusty house slave, who knew the king's decree, and placing the child in his arms, she said: "Go, take it away, and hide it in the hills. Perchance the gods will have pity on it, and put it in the heart of some shepherd, who feeds his flocks on distant pastures, to take the child home to his cot and rear it. Farewell, my pretty babe. The green grass must be thy cradle, and the mountain breezes must lull thee to sleep. May the gods in their mercy bless thy childhood's hours, and make thy name famous among men; for thou art a king's son, and a child of the Immortals, and the Immortals forget not those that are born of their blood."

So the man took the child from Iocasta; but, because he feared the king's decree, he pierced its ankles and bound them together, for he thought: "Surely, even if some shepherd wandering on the mountainside should light upon the child, he will never rear one so maimed; and if the king should ask, I will say that he is dead."

But because the child wept for the pain in its ankles, he took it home first to his wife to be fed and comforted, and when she gave it back into his arms, it smiled up into his face. Then all the hardness died out of his heart, for the gods had shed about it a grace to kindle love in the coldest breast.

Now Cithæron lies midway between Thebes and Corinth, and in winter-time the snow lies deep upon the summit, and the wild winds shriek through the rocks and clefts, and the pine trees pitch and bend beneath the fury of the blast, so that men called it the home of the Furies, the awful goddesses, who track out sin and murder. And there, too, in the streams and caverns, dwell the naiads and the nymphs, wild spirits of the rocks and waters; and if any mortal trespass on their haunts, they drive him to madness in their echoing grottoes and gloomy caves. Yet, for all that, though men called it dark Cithæron, the grass about its feet grew fine and green, so that the shepherds came from all the neighboring towns to pasture their flocks on its well-watered slopes. Here it was that Laius's herdsman fell in with a herdsman of Polybus, King of Corinth, and, seeing that he was a kindly man, and likely to have compassion on the child, he gave it to him to rear.

Now, it had not pleased the gods to grant any children to Polybus, King of Corinth, and Merope, his wife, though they wreathed their altars with garlands and burnt sweet savor of incense; and at last all hope died out of their hearts, and they said: "The gods are angry, and will destroy our race, and the kingdom shall pass into the hands of a stranger."

But one day it chanced that the queen saw in the arms of one of her women a child she had not seen before, and she questioned her, and asked if it were hers. And the woman confessed that her husband, the king's herdsman, had found it on dim Cithæron, and had taken pity on it, and brought it home.

Then the queen looked at the child, and seeing that it was passing fair, she said: "Surely this is no common babe, but a child of the Immortals. His hair is golden as the summer corn, and his eyes like the stars in heaven. What if the gods have sent him to comfort our old age, and rule the kingdom when we are dead? I will rear him in the palace as my own son, and he shall be a prince in the land of Corinth."

So the child lived in the palace, and became a son to Polybus and Merope, and heir to the kingdom. For want of a name they called him Œdipus, because his ankles, when they found him, were all swollen by the pin that the herdsman had put through them. As he grew up, he found favor in all men's eyes, for he was tall and comely and cunning withal.

"The gods are gracious," men said, "to grant the king such a son, and the people of Corinth so mighty a prince, to rule over them in days to come." For as yet they knew not that he was a foundling, and no true heir to the throne.

THE RIDDLE OF THE SPHINX

Now, while the child was still young, he played about the courts of the palace, and in running and leaping and in feats of strength and hardihood of heart there was none to beat him among his playmates, or even to stand up against him, save one. But so well matched were these two that the other children would gather round them in a ring to watch them box and wrestle, and the victor they would carry on their shoulders round the echoing galleries with shouting and clapping of hands; and sometimes it was Œdipus, and sometimes the other lad. But at length there came a time when again and again Œdipus was proved the stronger, and again and again the other slunk home beaten, like a dog that has been whipped: and he brooded over his defeat, and nourished hatred in his heart against Œdipus, and vowed that one day he would have his revenge by fair means or by foul.

But when Merope the queen saw Œdipus growing tall and fair, and surpassing all his comrades in strength, she took him up one day on to the citadel, and showed him all the lovely land of Hellas lying at his feet. Below them spread the shining city, with its colonnades and fountains and stately temples of the gods, like some jewel of the golden sands, and far away to the westward stretched the blue Corinthian Gulf. And she showed him the hills of Arcadia, the land of song and shepherds, where Pan plays his pipe beneath the oak trees, and nymphs and satyrs dance all the day long. Away to the bleak northwest stood out the snowy peaks of Mount Parnassus and Helicon, the home of the Muses, who fill men's minds with wisdom and their hearts with the love of all things beautiful. Then Merope turned him to the eastward and the land of the Dawning Day, and showed him the purple peaks of Ægina and the gleaming Attic shore. And she said to him: "Œdipus, my son, seest thou how Corinth lies midway 'twixt north and south and east and west, a link to join the lands together and a barrier to separate the seas?"

And Œdipus answered: "Of a truth, mother, he who rules in Corinth hath need of a lion's heart, for he must stand ever sword in hand and guard the passage from north to south."

"Courage is a mighty thing, my son, but wisdom is mightier. The sword layeth low, but wisdom buildeth up. Seest thou the harbors on either side, facing east and west, and the masts of the ships, like a forest in winter, and the traffic of sailors and merchants on the shore? From all lands they come and bring their wares and merchandise, and men of every nation meet together. Think not, my son, that a lion's heart and a fool's head therewith can ever be a match for the wisdom of Egypt or the cunning of Phœnicia."

Then Œdipus understood and said: "Till now I have wrestled and boxed and run races with my fellows on the sands the livelong day, and none can beat me. Henceforth I will sit in the market-place and discourse with foreigners and learned men, so that, when I come to rule in my father's place, I may be the wisest in all the land."

And Merope was pleased at his answer, but in her heart she was sad that his simple childish days

were past; and she prayed that if the gods granted
him wisdom they would keep his heart pure and
free from all uncleanness.

So Œdipus sat in the market-place and talked
with merchants and travelers, and he went down
to the ships in the harbor and learned many strange
things of strange lands—the wisdom of the Egyp-
tians, who were the wisest of all men in the south,
and the cunning of the Phœnicians, who were the
greatest merchants and sailors in all the world.
But in the evening, when the sun was low in the
west, and the hills all turned to amethyst and
sapphire, and the snow mountains blushed ruby
red beneath his parting kiss, then along the smooth,
gold sands of the Isthmus, by the side of the sounding sea, he would box and wrestle and run, till all
the ways were darkened and the stars stood out in
the sky. For he was a true son of Hellas, and
knew that nine times out of every ten a slack body
and a slack mind go together.

So he grew up in his beauty, a very god for wisdom and might, and there was no question he could
not answer nor riddle he could not solve, so that all
the land looked up to him, and the king and queen
loved him as their own son.

Now one day there was a great banquet in the
palace, to which all the noblest of the land were
bidden, and the minstrels played and the tumblers
danced and the wine flowed freely round the board,
so that men's hearts were opened, and they talked
of great deeds and heroes, and boasted what they
themselves could do. And Œdipus boasted as loud
as any, and challenged one and all to meet him in

fair fight. But the youth who had grown up with him in rivalry, and nourished jealousy and hatred in his heart, taunted him to his face, and said: "Base born that thou art, and son of slave, thinkest thou that free men will fight with thee? Lions fight not with curs, and though thou clothe thyself with purple and gold, all men know that thou art no true son to him thou callest thy sire."

And this he said being flushed with wine, and because myriad-mouthed Rumor had spread abroad the tale that Œdipus was a foundling, though he himself knew nought thereof.

Then Œdipus flushed red with rage, and swift as a gale that sweeps down from the mountains he fell upon the other, and seizing him by the throat, he shook him till he had not breath to beg for mercy. "What sayest thou now, thou whelp? Begone with thy lying taunt, now that thou hast licked the dust for thy falsehood."

And he flung him out from the hall. But Merope leant pale and sad against a pillar, and veiled her face in her mantle to hide her tears. And when they were alone, Œdipus took her hand and stroked it, and said: "Grieve not for my fiery spirit, mother, but call me thine own son, and say that I was right to silence the liar who would cast dishonor upon my father's name and upon thee."

But she looked at him sadly and longingly through her tears, and spoke in riddling words: "The gods, my child, sent thee to thy father and to me in answer to our prayers. A gift of God thou art, and a gift of God thou shalt be, living and dead, to them that love thee. The flesh groweth old and withereth away as a leaf, but the spirit liveth on forever, and those are the truest of kin who are kin in the spirit of goodness and of love."

But Œdipus was troubled, for she would say no more, but only held his hand, and when he drew it away it was wet with her tears. Then he thought in his heart: "Verily my mother would not weep for nought. What if, after all, there be something in the tale? I will go to the central shrine of Hellas and ask the god of Truth, golden-haired Apollo. If he say it is a lie, verily I will thrust it back down that coward's throat, and the whole land shall ring with his infamy. And if it be true —the gods will guide me how to act."

So he set forth alone upon his pilgrimage. He drew near to the sacred place and made due sacrifice, and washed in the great stone basin, and put away all uncleanness from his heart, and went through the portals of rock to the awful shrine within, where the undying fire burns night and day and the sacred laurel stands. And he put his question to the god and waited for an answer.

Through the dim darkness of the shrine he saw the priestess on her tripod, veiled in a mist of incense and vapor, and as the power of the god came upon her she beheld the things of the future and the hidden secrets of Fate. And she raised her hand toward Œdipus, and with pale lips spoke the words of doom: "Œdipus ill-fated, thine own sire shalt thou slay."

As she spoke the words his head swam round like a whirlpool, and his heart seemed turned to stone; then, with a loud and bitter cry, he rushed from the temple, through the thronging crowd of pilgrims down into the Sacred Way, and the people moved out of his path like shadows. Blindly he sped along the stony road, down through the pass to a place where three roads meet, and he shuddered as he crossed them; for Fear laid her cold hand upon his heart and filled it with a wild, unreasoning dread, and branded the image of that awful spot upon his brain so that he could never forget it. On every side the mountains frowned down upon him, and seemed to echo to and fro the doom which the priestess had spoken. Straight forward he went like some hunted thing, turning neither to right nor left, till he came to a narrow path, where he met an old man in a chariot drawn by mules, with his trusty servants round him.

"Ho! there, thou madman!" they shouted; "stand by and let the chariot pass."

"Madmen yourselves," he cried, for his sore heart could not brook the taunt. "I am a king's son, and will stand aside for no man."

So he tried to push past them by force, though he was one against many. And the old man stretched out his hand as though to stop him, but as well might a child hope to stand up against a wild bull. For he thrust him aside and felled him from his seat, and turned upon his followers, and, striking out to right and left, he stunned one and slew another, and forced his way through in blind fury. But the old man lay stiff and still upon the road. The fall from the chariot had quenched the feeble spark of life within him, and his spirit fled away to the house of Hades and the Kingdom of the Dead. One trusty servant lay slain by his side, and the other senseless and stunned, and when he awoke, to find his master and his comrades slain, Œdipus was far upon his way.

On and on he went, over hill and dale and mountain stream, till at length his strength gave way, and he sank down exhausted. And black despair laid hold of his heart, and he said within himself: "Better to die here on the bare hillside and be food for the kites and crows than return to my father's house to bring death to him and sorrow to my mother's heart."

But sweet sleep fell upon him, and when he awoke hope and the love of life put other thoughts in his breast. And he remembered the words which Merope the queen had spoken to him one day when he was boasting of his strength and skill.

"Strength and skill, my son, are the gifts of the gods, as the rain which falleth from heaven and giveth life and increase to the fruits of the earth. But man's pride is an angry flood that bringeth destruction on field and city. Remember that great gifts may work great good or great evil, and he who has them must answer to the gods if he use them well or ill."

And he thought within himself: "'Twere ill to die if, even in the uttermost parts of the earth, men need a strong man's arm and a wise man's cunning. Nevermore will I return to far-famed Corinth and my home by the sounding sea, but to far-distant lands will I go and bring blessing to those who are not of my kin, since to mine own folk I must be a curse if ever I return."

THE RIDDLE OF THE SPHINX

So he went along the road from Delphi till he came to seven-gated Thebes. There he found all the people in deep distress and mourning, for their king Laius was dead, slain by robbers on the high road, and they had buried him far from his native land at a place where three roads meet. And, worse still, their city was beset by a terrible monster, the Sphinx, part eagle and part lion, with the face of a woman, who every day devoured a man because they could not answer the riddle she set them.

All this Œdipus heard as he stood in the market place and talked with the people.

"What is this famous riddle that none can solve?" he asked.

"Alas! young man, that none can say. For he that would solve the riddle must go up alone to the rock where she sits. Then and there she chants the riddle, and if he answer it not forthwith she tears him limb from limb. And if none go up to try the riddle, then she swoops down upon the city and carries off her victims, and spares not woman or child. Our wisest and bravest have gone up, and our eyes have seen them no more. Now there is no man left who dare face the terrible beast."

Then Œdipus said: "I will go up and face this monster. It must be a hard riddle indeed if I cannot answer it."

"Oh, overbold and rash," they cried, "thinkest thou to succeed where so many have failed?"

"Better to try, and fail, than never to try at all."

"Yet, where failure is death, surely a man should think twice?"

THE RIDDLE OF THE SPHINX

"A man can die but once, and how better than in trying to save his fellows?"

As they looked at his strong young limbs and his fair young face they pitied him. "Stranger," they said, "who art thou to throw away thy life thus heedlessly? Are there none at home to mourn thee and no kingdom thou shouldst rule? For, of a truth, thou art a king's son and no common man."

"Nay, were I to return, my home would be plunged in mourning and woe, and the people would drive me from my father's house."

They marveled at his answer, but dared question him no further; and, seeing that nothing would turn him from his purpose, they showed him the path to the Sphinx's rock, and all the people went out with him to the gate with prayers and blessings. At the gate they left him, for he who goes up to face the Sphinx must go alone, and none can stand by and help him. So he went through the Crenean gate and across the stream of Dirce into the wide plain, and the mountain of the Sphinx stood out dark and clear on the other side. Then he prayed to Pallas Athene, the gray-eyed goddess of Wisdom, and she took all fear from his heart. So he went up boldly to the rock, where the monster sat waiting to spring upon her prey; yet for all his courage his heart beat fast as he looked on her. For at first she appeared like a mighty bird, with great wings of bronze and gold, and the glancing sunbeams played about them, casting a halo of light around, and in the midst of the halo her face shone out pale and beautiful as a star at dawn. But when she saw him coming near, a greedy fire lit up her eyes, and she put out her cruel claws and lashed her tail from side to side like an angry lion waiting for his prey. Nevertheless, Œdipus spoke to her fair and softly: "Oh, lady, I am come to hear thy famous riddle and answer it or die."

"Foolhardy manling, a dainty morsel the gods have sent this day, with thy fair young face and fresh young limbs." And she licked her cruel lips.

Then Œdipus felt his blood boil within him, and he wished to slay her then and there; for she who had been the fairest of women was now the foulest of beasts, and he saw that by her cruelty she had killed the woman's soul within her, and the soul of a beast had taken its place.

"Come, tell me thy famous riddle, foul Fury that thou art, that I may answer it and rid the land of this curse."

"At dawn it creeps on four legs; at noon it strides on two; at sunset and evening it totters on three. What is this thing, never the same, yet not many, but one?" So she chanted slowly, and her eyes gleamed cruel and cold.

Then thought Œdipus within himself: "Now or never must my learning and wit stand me in good stead, or in vain have I talked with the wisest of men and learnt the secrets of Phœnicia and Egypt."

And the gods who had given him understanding sent light into his heart, and boldly he answered: "What can this creature be but man, O Sphinx? For, a helpless babe at the dawn of life, he crawls on his hands and feet; at noontide he walks erect in the strength of his manhood; and at evening he supports his tottering limbs with a staff, the prop and stay of old age. Have I not answered aright and guessed thy famous riddle?"

Then with a loud cry of despair, and answering him never a word, the great beast sprang up from her seat on the rock and hurled herself over the precipice into the yawning gulf beneath. Far away across the plain the people heard her cry, and they saw the flash of the sun on her brazen wings like a gleam of lightning in the summer sky. Thereupon they sent up a great shout of joy to heaven, and poured out from every gate into the open plain, and some raised Œdipus upon their shoulders, and with shouts and songs of triumph bore him to the city. Then and there they made him king with one accord, for the old king had left no son behind him, and who more fitted to rule over them than the slayer of the Sphinx and the savior of their city?

So Œdipus became King of Thebes, and wisely and well did he rule, and for many a long year the land prospered both in peace and war.

But the day came when a terrible pestilence broke out, and the people died by hundreds, so that at last Œdipus sent messengers to Delphi to ask why the gods were angry and had sent a plague upon the land. And this was the answer they brought back: "There is an unclean thing in Thebes. Never has the murderer of Laius been found, and he dwells a pollution in the land. Though the vengeance of the gods is slow, yet it cometh without fail, and the shedding of blood shall not pass unpunished."

Then Œdipus made proclamation through the land that if any man knew who the murderer was,

they should give him up to his doom and appease
the anger of Heaven. And he laid a terrible curse
on any who dared to give so much as a crust of
bread or a draft of water to him who had brought
such suffering on the land. So throughout the
country far and wide a search was made to track
out the stain of blood and cleanse the city from
pollution, but day after day the quest was fruitless, and the pestilence raged unceasingly, and
darkness fell upon the soul of the people, as their
prayers remained unanswered and their burnt-
offerings smoked in vain upon the altars of the
gods. Then at last Œdipus sent for the blind
seer Teiresias, who had lived through six generations of mortal men, and was the wisest of all
prophets on earth. He knew the language of the
birds, and, though his eyes were closed in darkness, his ears were opened to hear the secrets of
the universe, and he knew the hidden things of the
past and of the future. But at first when he came
before the king he would tell him nothing, but
begged him to question no further. "For the
things of the future will come of themselves," he
cried, "though I shroud them in silence, and evil
will it be for thee, O king, and evil for thine house
if I speak out the knowledge that is hidden in my
heart."

At last Œdipus grew angry at his silence, and
taunted him: "Verily, methinks thou thyself didst
aid in the plotting of this deed, seeing that thou
carest nought for the people bowed down beneath
the pestilence and the dark days that are fallen
on the land, so be it thou canst shield the mur-

derer and escape thyself from the curse of the gods."

Then Teiresias was stung past bearing, and would hold his tongue no longer. "By thine own doom shalt thou be judged, O king," he said. "Thou thyself art the murderer, thyself the pollution that staineth the land with the blood of innocent men."

Then Œdipus laughed aloud: "Verily, old man, thou pratest. What rival hath urged thee to this lie, hoping to drive me from the throne of Thebes? Of a truth, not thine eyes only, but thy heart, is shrouded in a mist of darkness."

"Woe to thee, Œdipus, woe to thee! Thou hast sight, yet seest not who thou art, nor knowest the deed of thine hand. Soon shalt thou wander sightless and blind, a stranger in a strange land, feeling the ground with a staff, and men shall shrink back from thee in horror when they hear thy name and the deed that thou hast done."

And the people were hushed by the words of the old man, and knew not what to think. But the wife of Œdipus, who stood by his side, said: "Hearken not to him, my lord. For verily no mortal can search the secrets of Fate, as I can prove full well by the words of this same man that he spoke in prophecy. For he it was who said that Laius, the king who is dead, should be slain by the hand of his own son. However, that poor innocent never grew to manhood, but was exposed on the trackless mountainside to die of cold and hunger; and Laius, men say, was slain by robber bands at a place where three roads meet. So hearken not to seer-craft, ye people, nor trust in the words of one who is proved a false prophet."

But her words brought no comfort to Œdipus, and a dreadful fear came into his heart, like a cold, creeping snake, as he listened. For he thought of his journey from Delphi, and of how in his frenzy he had struck down an old man and his followers at a place where three roads meet. When he questioned her further, the time and the place and the company all tallied, save only that rumor had it that Laius had been slain by robber bands, while he had been single-handed against many.

"Was there none left," he asked, "who saw the deed and lived to tell the tale?"

"Yea, one faithful follower returned to bear the news, but so soon as the Sphinx was slain and the people had made thee king he went into distant pastures with his flocks, for he could not brook to see a stranger in his master's place, albeit he had saved the land from woe."

"Go, summon him," said Œdipus. "If the murderers were many, as rumor saith, with his aid we may track them out; but if he was one man single-handed—yea, though that man were myself—of a truth he shall be an outcast from the land, that the plague may be stayed from the people. Verily, my queen, my heart misgives me when I remember my wrath and the deed that I wrought at the cross-roads."

In vain she tried to comfort him, for a nameless fear had laid hold of his heart.

Now, while they were waiting for the herdsman to come, a messenger arrived in haste from Corinth to say that Polybus was dead, and that Œdipus was chosen king of the land, for his fame had gone out far and wide as the slayer of the Sphinx and the wisest of the kings of Hellas.

When Œdipus heard the news, he bowed his head in sorrow to hear of the death of the father he had loved, and turning to the messenger, he said, "For many a long year my heart hath yearned toward him who is dead, and verily my soul is grieved that I shall see him no more in the pleasant light of the sun. But for the oracle's sake I stayed in exile, that my hand might not be red with a father's blood. And now I thank the gods that he has passed away in a green old age, in the fullness of years and of honor." But the messenger wondered at his words. "Knewest thou not, then, that Polybus was no father to thee in the flesh, but that for thy beauty and thy strength he chose thee out of all the land to be a son to him and heir to the kingdom of Corinth?"

"What sayest thou, bearer of ill news that thou art?" cried Œdipus. "To prove that same tale of thine a slanderous lie I went to Delphi, and there the priestess prophesied that I should slay mine own sire. Wherefore I went not back to my native land, but have lived in exile all my days."

"Then in darkness of soul hast thou lived, O king. For with mine own hands I received thee as a babe from a shepherd on dim Cithæron, from one of the herdsmen of Laius, who was king before thee in this land."

"Woe is me, then! The curse of the gods is over me yet. I know not my sire, and unwittingly I may slay him and rue the evil day. And a cloud of darkness hangeth over me for the slaying of King Laius. But lo! they bring the herdsman who saw the deed done, and pray Heaven he may clear me from all guilt. Bring him forward that I may question him."

Then they brought the man forward before the king, though he shrank back and tried to hide himsel . When the messenger from Corinth saw him he ꜱtarted back in surprise, for it was the very man from whose hands he had taken Œdipus on the mountain-side. And he said to the king, "Behold the man who will tell thee the secret of thy birth. From his hands did I take thee as a babe on dim Cithæron."

Then Œdipus questioned the man, and at first he denied it from fear, but at last he was fain to confess. "And who gave me to thee to slay on the barren mountain-side?"

"I pray thee, my king, ask no more. Some things there are that are better unsaid."

"Nay, tell me, and fear not. I care not if I am a child of shame and slavery stains my birth. A son of Fortune the gods have made me, and have given me good days with evil. Speak out, I pray thee. Though I be the son of a slave, I can bear it."

"No son of a slave art thou, but seed of a royal house. Ask no more, my king."

"Speak, speak, man. Thou drivest me to anger, and I will make thee tell, though it be by force."

"Ah! lay not cruel hands upon me. For thine own sake I would hide it. From the queen thy mother I had thee, and thy father was—Laius the

king. At the cross-roads from Delphi didst thou
meet him in his chariot, and slew him unwittingly
in thy wrath. Ah, woe is me! For the gods have
chosen me out to be an unwilling witness to the
truth of their oracles."

Then a great hush fell upon all the people like
the lull before a storm. For the words of the herdsman were so strange and terrible that at first they
could scarce take in their meaning. But when they
understood that Œdipus was Laius's own son, and
that he had fulfilled the dreadful prophecy and
slain his sire, a great tumult arose, some saying one
thing and some another; but the voice of Œdipus
was heard above the uproar, "Ah, woe is me, woe
is me! The curse of the gods is upon me, and none
can escape their wrath. Blindly have I done this
evil, and when I was striving to escape Fate caught
me in her hidden meshes. Oh, foolish hearts of
men, to think that ye can flee from the doom of
the gods; for lo! ye strive in the dark, and your
very struggles bind you but closer in the snare of
your fate. Cast me from the land, ye people; do
with me what ye will. For the gods have made me
a curse and a pollution, and by my death alone
will the land have rest from pestilence."

And the people would have taken him at his
word; for fickle is the heart of the multitude, and
swayed this way and that by every breath of
calamity.

They were sore stricken, too, by the pestilence,
and in their wrath against the cause of it they
forgot the slaying of the Sphinx and the long
days of peace and prosperity. But the blind

seer Teiresias rose up in their midst, and at his voice the people were silent.

"Citizens of Cadmus, foolish and blind of heart! Will ye slay the savior of your city? Have ye forgotten the man-devouring Sphinx and the days of darkness? Verily prosperity blunteth the edge of gratitude. And thou, Œdipus, curse not the gods for thine evil fate. He that putteth his finger in the fire is burnt, whether he do it knowingly or not. As to thy sire, him indeed didst thou slay in ignorance but the shedding of man's blood be upon thine own head, for that was the fruit of thy wrathful spirit, which, through lack of curbing, broke forth like an angry beast. Hadst thou never slain a man, never wouldst thou have slain thy sire. But now thou art a pollution to the land of thy birth, and by long exile and wandering must thou expiate thy sin and die a stranger in a strange land. Yet methinks that in the dark mirror of prophecy I see thy form, as it were, a guardian to the land of thy last resting-place, and in a grove of sacred trees thy spirit's lasting habitation, when thy feet have accomplished the ways of expiation and the days of thy wandering are done."

So the people were silenced. But Œdipus would not be comforted, and in his shame and misery he put out his own eyes because they had looked on unspeakable things. Then he clothed himself in rags and took a pilgrim's staff, to go forth alone upon his wanderings. And the people were glad at his going, because the plague had hardened their hearts, and they cared nothing for his gray hairs and sightless eyes, nor remembered all he had done for them, but thought only how the plague might be stayed. Even Eteocles and Polynices, his own sons, showed no pity, but would have let him go forth alone, that they might live on the fatness of the land. For their hardness of heart they were punished long after, when they quarreled as to which should be king, and brought down the flood of war upon Thebes, and fell each by the other's hand in deadly strife. Of all his children, Antigone alone refused to let him go forth a solitary wanderer, and would listen to none of his entreaties when he spoke of the hardness of the way that would lie before them.

"Nay, father," she cried; "thinkest thou that I could suffer thee to wander sightless and blind in thine old age with none to stay thy feeble steps or lend thee the light of their eyes?"

"The road before us is hard and long, my child, and no man can say when my soul shall find rest. The ways of the world are cruel, and men love not the cursed of the gods. As for thee, Heaven bless thee for thy love; but thou art too frail and tender a thing to eat of the bread and drink of the waters of sorrow."

"Ah, father, thinkest thou that aught could be more bitter than to sit in the seat of kings while thou wanderest a beggar on the face of the earth? Nay, suffer me to go with thee, and stay thy steps in the days of thy trial."

Nothing he could say would dissuade her. So they two set out alone upon their wanderings, the old man bowed down beneath the weight of sorrow, and the young girl in the freshness of youth and beauty, with a great love in her heart—a bright, burning love which was the light by which she lived, and a light which never led her astray.

At first Œdipus was filled with shame and bitterness, and cursed the day of his birth and his evil fate; but as time went on he remembered the words of Teiresias—how at his death he should be a blessing to the land of his last resting-place; and the hope sprang up in his heart that the gods had not forsaken him, but would wipe out the stain of his sin, and make his name once more glorious among men. Daily this hope grew stronger and brighter, and he felt that the days of wandering and expiation were drawing to a close, and a mysterious power guided his steps he knew not whither, except that it was toward the goal of his release. And many a hero's grave did they pass and many a sacred shrine, for all along that road men of old raised monuments to the undying glory of the dead and the heritage of honor which they left to unborn generations. And always Antigone tended the old man's feeble steps, and lent him the light of her young eyes, till at length they came to white Colonus and the grove of the Eumenides. There she set him on a rock to rest his weary limbs. And the soft spring breezes played about them, and the clear waters of Cephisus flowed sparkling at their feet to the fertile plain below. In the dark coverts and green glades the nightingale trilled her sweet song, and the grass was bright with many a golden crocus and white narcissus bloom. As he sat there a great calm filled the old man's heart, for he felt that the days of his wandering were done.

But while they were resting a man from the village happened to pass, and when he saw them he shouted out, "Ho! there, impious wanderers, know ye not that ye sit on sacred land and trespass on hallowed ground?"

Then Œdipus knew more surely than ever that the day of his release had come. "Oh, stranger!" he cried, "welcome is that which thou sayest. For here shall the words of the prophet be fulfilled, when he said that in a grove of sacred trees my spirit should find rest."

But the man was not satisfied, and he called to a band of his countrymen who were in the fields close by. And they came up and spoke roughly to Œdipus, and asked his name and business. When he told them they were filled with horror, for all men had heard of the slaying of Laius, and they would have turned him out by force.

But Œdipus raised himself from the rock on which he was seated, and in spite of his beggar's rags and sightless eyes, there was a majesty about his face and form that marked him as no common man. "Men of Colonus," he said, "ye judge by the evil I have done, and not by the good. Have ye forgotten the days when the name of Œdipus was honored throughout the land? Of a truth the days of darkness came, and the stain of my sin found me out. But now is my wrathful spirit curbed, and the gods will make me once more a blessing to men. Go, tell your king Theseus, who rules in Athena's sacred citadel, that Œdipus is here, and bid him come with all speed if he would win a guardian for this land, an everlasting safeguard for his city in the days of storm and stress."

So they sent off a messenger in hot haste, for there was a mysterious power about the aged wanderer that none could withstand. And soon Theseus arrived, himself a mighty hero, who had made Athens a great city and rid the country of many a foul pestilence. And he greeted Œdipus courteously and kindly, as befitted a great prince, and offered him hospitality.

But Œdipus said, "The hospitality I crave, O king, is for no brief sojourn in this land. Nay, 'tis an everlasting home I ask. For the hand of Heaven is upon me, and full well I know that this day my soul shall leave this frail and broken body. And to thee alone is it given to know where my bones shall rest—to thee and thy seed after thee. As long as my bones shall remain in the land, so long shall my spirit watch over it, and men shall call upon my name to turn the tide of battle and stay the flood of pestilence and war. Wilt thou come with me, O king, whither the gods shall lead, and learn the secret of my grave?"

Then Theseus bowed his head, and answered, "Show thou the way, and I will come."

So Œdipus turned and led the way into the grove, and Theseus and Antigone followed after. For a mysterious power seemed to guide him, and he walked as one who could see, and his steps were strong and firm as those of a man in his prime. Straight into the grove did he go till they came to the heart of the wood, where there was a sacred well beneath a hollow pear-tree. Close by was a great chasm going deep down into the bowels of the earth, and men called it the Gate of Hades, the Kingdom of the Dead.

When they reached the well, Œdipus sat down upon a rock and called his daughter to his side, and said, "Antigone, my child, thy hand hath ministered to me in exile, and smoothed the path for the wanderer's feet. Go now, fetch water, and pour libation and drink-offering to the gods below. It is the last thing thou canst do for me on earth."

So Antigone fetched water from the well, and dressed and tended him, and poured libation to the gods.

And when she had finished, Œdipus drew her to him and kissed her tenderly, and said, "Grieve not for me, my child. Well I know that thy heart will ache, for love hath made light the burden of toil. But for me life's day is done, and I go to my rest. Do thou seek thy brethren, and be to them as thou hast been to me. My child, my child, hard is the way that lies before thee, and my soul yearneth over thee for the evil day that shall come. But look thou to thine own pure heart, on which the gods have set the seal of truth that changeth not with passing years, and heed not the counsels of men."

And he held her closely to him, and she clung weeping about his neck. As they sat a hush fell upon the grove, and the nightingales ceased their song, and from the depths of the grove a voice was heard like the voice of distant thunder. "Œdipus, Œdipus, why dost thou tarry?"

When they heard it they were afraid. But Œdipus rose up and gently put his daughter from him, saying, "Lo! the voice of Zeus, who calleth me. Fare thee well, my child; thou canst go no further with me. For Theseus only is it meet to see the manner of my death, and he and I must go forward alone into the wood."

With firm, unfaltering steps he led the way once more, and Theseus followed after. And what happened there none can tell, for Theseus kept the secret to his dying day. But men say that when he came out of the wood his face was as the face of one who had seen things passing mortal speech.

As for Œdipus, the great twin Brethren Sleep and Death carried his bones to Athens, where the people built him a shrine, and for many a long year they honored him as a hero in the land of Attica. For though the sin that he sinned in his wrath and ignorance was great and terrible, yet his life had brought joy to many men and prosperity to more lands than one. For with wisdom and love he guided his days, and with sorrow and tears he wiped out the stain of his sin, so that, in spite of all he suffered, men love to tell of the glory and wisdom of Œdipus, and of how he solved the riddle of the Sphinx.

THE GIFT OF ATHÊNÊ[1]

By Sir George W. Cox

NEAR the banks of the stream Cephisus, Erechtheus had built a city in a rocky and thin-soiled land. He was the father of a free and brave people; and though his city was proud and humble, yet Zeus by his wisdom foresaw that one day it would become the noblest of all cities throughout the wide earth, and there was a quarrel between Poseidon the lord of the sea and Athênê the child of Zeus, to see by whose name the city of Erechtheus should be called. So Zeus appointed a day in the which he would judge between them in presence of the great gods who dwell on high Olympus.

When the day was come, the gods sat each on his golden throne on the banks of the stream Kephisos. High above all was the throne of Zeus, the great father of gods and men, and by his side sat Hërê the queen. This day even the sons of men might gaze upon them, for Zeus had laid aside his lightnings, and all the gods had come down in peace to listen to his judgment between Poseidon and Athênê. There sat Phœbus Apollo with his golden harp in his hand. His face glistened for the brightness of his beauty; but there was no anger in his gleaming eyes, and idle by his side lay the unerring spear with which he smites all who deal

---

[1] In this Greek tale, the Greek names are preserved. In the Latin mythology Zeus is Jupiter, Poseidon is Neptune, Athênê is Minerva, Artemis is Diana, Hermes is Mercury, Hephaistos is Vulcan, Dionysos is Bacchus, Hestia is Vesta, Ares is Mars, and Aphrodite is Venus.

falsely and speak lies. There beside him sat Artemis, his sister, whose days were spent in chasing the beasts of the earth and in sporting with the nymphs on the reedy banks of Eurotas. There by the side of Zeus sat Hermes ever bright and youthful, the spokesman of the gods, with staff in hand to do the will of the great father. There sat Hephaistos the lord of fire, and Hestia who guards the hearth. There, too, was Ares, who delights in war; and Dionysos, who loves the banquet and the wine-cup, and Aphrodite, who rose from the sea-foam to fill the earth with laughter and woe.

Before them all stood the great rivals, awaiting the judgment of Zeus. High in her left hand, Athênê held the invincible spear; and on her shield, hidden from mortal sight, was the face on which no man may gaze and live. Close beside her, proud in the greatness of his power, Poseidon waited the issue of the contest. In his right hand gleamed the trident with which he shakes the earth and cleaves the waters of the sea.

Then from his golden seat rose the spokesman Hermes, and his clear voice sounded over all the great council. "Listen," he said, "to the will of Zeus, who judges now between Poseidon and Athênê. The city of Erechtheus shall bear the name of that god who shall bring forth out of the earth the best gift for the sons of men. If Poseidon do this, the city shall be called Poseidonia; but if Athênê brings the higher gift, it shall be called Athens."

Then King Poseidon rose up in the greatness of his majesty, and with his trident he smote the earth where he stood. Straightway the hill was shaken to its depths, and the earth split asunder, and forth from the chasm leaped a horse, such as never shall be seen again for strength and beauty. His body shone white all over as the driven snow; his mane streamed proudly in the wind as he stamped on the ground and scoured in very wantonness over hill and valley. "Behold my gift," said Poseidon, "and call the city after my name. Who shall give ought better than the horse to the sons of man?"

But Athênê looked steadfastly at the gods with her keen gray eye; and she stooped slowly down to the ground, and planted in it a little seed which she held in her right hand. She spake no word, but still gazed calmly on that great council. Presently they saw springing from the earth a little germ, which grew up and threw out its boughs and leaves. Higher and higher it rose, with all its thick green foliage, and put forth fruit on its clustering branches. "My gift is better, O Zeus," she said, "than that of King Poseidon. The horse which he has given shall bring war and strife and anguish to the children of men; my olive tree is the sign of peace and plenty, of health and strength, and the pledge of happiness and freedom. Shall not, then, the city of Erechtheus be called after my name?" Then with one accord rose the voices of the gods in the air, as they cried out, "the gift of Athênê is the best which may be given to the sons of men; it is the token that the city of Erechtheus shall be greater in peace than in war, and nobler in its freedom than its power. Let the city be called Athens."

Then Zeus, the mighty son of Kronos, bowed his head in sign of judgment that the city should be called by the name of Athênê. From his head the immortal locks streamed down, and the earth trembled beneath his feet as he rose from his golden throne to return to the halls of Olympus. But still Athênê stood gazing over the land which was now her own; and she stretched out her spear toward the city of Erechtheus, and said: "I have won the victory and here shall be my home. Here shall my children grow up in happiness and freedom; and hither shall the sons of men come to learn of law and order. Here shall they see what great things may be done by mortal hands when aided by the gods who dwell on Olympus; and when the torch of freedom has gone out at Athens, its light shall be handed on to other lands, and men shall learn that my gift is still the best, and they shall say that reverence for law and the freedom of thought and deed has come to them from the city of Erechtheus, which bears the name of Athênê."

DAPHNÊ, CHILD OF THE MORNING

By Sir George W. Cox

IN the vale of Tempê, where the stream of Peneios flows beneath the heights of Olympus towards the sea, the beautiful Daphnê passed the days of her happy childhood. She climbed the crags to greet the first rays of the rising sun, and when he had driven his fiery horses over the sky, she watched his chariot sink behind the western mountains. Over hill and dale she roamed, free and light as the breeze of spring. Other maidens round her spoke each of her love, but Daphnê cared not to listen to the voice of man, though many a one sought her to be his wife.

One day, as she stood on the slopes of Ossa in the glow of early morning, she saw before her a glorious form. The light of the new-risen sun fell on his face with a golden splendour, and she knew that it was Phœbus Apollo. Hastily he ran towards her, and said, "I have found thee, Child of the Morning. Others thou hast cast aside, but from me thou canst not escape. I have sought thee long, and now will I make thee mine." But the heart of Daphnê was bold and strong; and her cheek flushed and her eye sparkled with anger, as she said, "I know neither love nor bondage. I live free among the streams and hills; and to none will I yield my freedom." Then the face of Apollo grew dark with anger, and he drew near to seize the maiden; but swift as the wind she fled away. Over hill and dale, over crag and river, the feet of Daphnê fell lightly as falling leaves in autumn; but nearer yet came Phœbus Apollo, till at last the strength of the maiden began to fail. Then she stretched out her hands, and cried for help to the goddess Ceres; but she came not to her aid. Her head was dizzy, and her limbs trembled in utter feebleness as she drew near to the broad river which gladdens the plains of Thessaly. She almost felt the breath of Phœbus, and her robe was almost in his grasp. With a wild cry, she said, "Father

Peneios, receive thy child," and she rushed into the stream, whose waters closed gently over her.

She was gone; and Apollo mourned for his madness in chasing thus the free maiden. And he said, "I have punished myself by my folly; the light of the morning is taken out of the day. I must go on alone till my journey shall draw towards its end." Then he spake the word, and a laurel came up on the bank where Daphnê had plunged into the stream; and the green bush with its thick clustering leaves keeps her name forever.

THE VENGEANCE OF APOLLO

By Sir George W. Cox

IN the cool evening time King Darius walked in his royal garden, and the noblest of the Persians were around him. Then came there a messenger from the western land in haste and said, "O king, the men of Athens with the sons of Javan have taken the city of Sardes, and the temple of the great goddess Kybêlê has been burnt." And King Darius answered quickly and said, "What sayest thou, O messenger, that men of whom I have never heard the name, have come with my slaves against the land of the great king?" Then he bade them bring a bow and arrows; and while some one went for them, the Persians stood round him in silence, for they feared to speak while the king was angry. He took the bow, fitted an arrow to it and shot it up into the sky, and prayed, "O Jupiter, that dwellest in the high heavens, suffer me to be avenged upon the men of Athens. The sons of Javan are my slaves, and sorely shall they be smitten for the deeds which they have done." Then he gave command, and each day, when the banquet was spread in the gilded hall and the king sat down to meat, there stood forth one who said with a loud voice, "O king, forget not the men of Athens."

But Jupiter hearkened not to the prayer of the great king, for the ships were made ready, and his chieftains and warriors hastened away to the Athenian land and fought in Marathon. They fared not well in the battle, for the men of Athens strove mightily for their country. So in great fear the Persians fled to the sea-shore, while the men of Athens slew them on the land and in the water as they struggled to reach the ships. And when the fight was over, they spoiled the Persians who lay dead on the sea-shore and took rich plunder, for scattered about they found embroidered turbans and bright swords and daggers, and golden bits and bridles, and silken robes and jewels.

Thus sped the hosts of King Darius; and the messenger came again in haste, as he sat on his golden throne in Susa, while the nobles of Persia did obeisance before him. Then the king said, "Speak, O man, hast thou brought good tidings that my slaves have chastised the people of the strange city?" And the messenger answered, saying, "O king, the men of Athens have slain thy mighty men with the sword, and burned thy ships; and few have come back of all the great army which thou didst send against them."

VENGEANCE OF APOLLO

Great and fierce was the wrath of King Darius when he heard the tidings, and he hastened to make ready ships and men and horses, that he might go forth himself against the men of Athens. Then in every city of the Persian land was heard the noise as of men who have a great work to do; and the armourers wrought spears and swords and shields, and in the harbours they built countless ships to sail over the dark sea. But Jupiter hearkened not yet to the prayer of the king; so Darius died, and Xerxes his son sat upon his throne, and the chief men of the Persians were gathered round him. Then the king spake and said, "Be ready, O Persians, every one of you, for I will go forth with all my great power, and make slaves of the men of Athens; and so may the gods do to me, and more also, if I burn not the temples of their gods with fire, and bring not hither the golden treasures which lie in the house of Phœbus Apollo at Delphi."

Then, with all his great hosts, King Xerxes set forth from Susa, and his governors and warriors and slaves followed him, with a great multitude of every nation and people; and they crossed over from the land of Asia by a bridge which was built over the sea of Hellê. Thus they journeyed on in pomp and glory, and King Xerxes thought that they had done great things when his host slew Leonidas and three hundred men of Sparta who guarded the passes of Thermopylæ. So his heart was filled with pride, and he chose out the bravest of his warriors, and charged the men of Thessaly to lead them to Delphi and the temple of Phœbus Apollo.

VENGEANCE OF APOLLO

There was great fear and terror in Delphi. A messenger came and said, "The hosts of King Xerxes are coming to slay the men of this land and take away the treasures which lie in the house of King Apollo." So the Delphians went in great sorrow to the temple, and bowed their heads to the earth and prayed, saying, "Child of the light, who dwellest here in thy holy temple, thieves and robbers are coming against us, and they are purposed to take away thy sacred treasures; tell us, then, what we shall do, for at thy bidding we are ready to bury them deep in the earth till the storm of war be overpast." Then came there a voice from the inmost shrine, but it was not the voice of the priestess, for Phœbus Apollo himself came down to speak his will, and said, "Move them not, men of Delphi. I will guard my holy place, and none shall lay hand on my sacred things."

So they went away in gladness of heart, and made ready for the coming of the Persians. All the men of Delphi left the city, saving only sixty men and the prophet Acêratos, and these sat down before the steps of the temple. In silence they waited till the Persians should come, and they marvelled at the great stillness on the earth and in the heaven. There was not a cloud in the sky, and the two peaks of Parnassus glistened in the blazing sunshine. Not a breath lifted the green leaves of the sacred laurels, not a bird sang in the breathless air. Presently, as he turned round to look, the prophet saw the sacred weapons of Phœbus, which no mortal man might touch, lying on the temple steps; and he said to the sixty men who tarried with him, "Lo, now will Phœbus fight for his holy temple, for his own hand hath made ready the weapons for the battle."

Soon in the deep valley and along the bank of the Castalian stream were seen the hosts of the Persians, as they came on with their long spears flashing in the bright sunshine. Far away the men of Delphi saw the blaze of their burnished armour, and heard the tramp of their warhorses. Onward they came, and they said one to another, "The gods have fought for us, and the prize is won already. See, yonder is the home of Phœbus, and none remain of the men of Delphi to do battle for his holy temple."

Still the sun shone without a cloud in the sky, and no breeze broke the stillness of the laurel groves. Still glistened the sacred arms as they lay on the steps of the temple, and the opened doors showed the golden treasures which were stored up within. There lay the throne of Midas, and the golden lion of Crœsus. There lay the mighty mixing bowl, all of pure gold, which at the bidding of Crœsus was wrought by the Samian Theodoros. There lay all the rich gifts which the men of Hellas had offered up to win the favour of the lord Apollo.

Then the leaders of the Persians stretched forth their hands, as though all these things were given up to them by the god who had forsaken his people; but even as they came near his holy ground, the lightning flashed forth, and the crash of the thunder was heard in the blue heaven, and the dark cloud fell on the peaks of Parnassus. Like the roar of a raging torrent, the mighty wind burst forth.

VENGEANCE OF APOLLO

Down from the steeps of the Delphian hill thundered the huge rocks, and trees uptorn from their roots were hurled on the hosts of the barbarians. Louder and fiercer grew the din. Cries and shoutings were heard from the Alean chapel, for the virgin Minerva fought against the men of Xerxes. Smitten by the fiery lightnings, they fell on the quaking earth. Suddenly there was heard a sound more fierce and terrible, and two cliffs were hurled down from the mountain-top. Underneath this huge mass the mightiest of the Persians lay still in the sleep of death; and all who yet lived fled with quaking hearts and trembling steps from the great wrath of the lord Apollo.

So fought the god for his holy temple. When from their hiding places the men of Delphi saw that the Persians fled they poured forth from the caves and thickets to slay them. They smote them as sheep are slain before the altar of sacrifice, for even the bravest of their warriors lifted not their arms against them. Long time they followed after them in hot haste; and among them were seen two giant forms, clothed in bright armour, smiting down the hosts of the enemy. Then they knew that Phylacos and Autonoös, the heroes of the place, had come forth to aid them, and they smote the Persians more fiercely till the going down of the sun.

So the fight was ended; and the stars came forth in the cloudless sky, and the laurel groves were stirred by the soft evening breeze. With songs of high thanksgiving the men of Delphi drew near to the temple, and saw that Phœbus had placed again within his shrine the sacred arms which no mortal man may handle. Then was there rich spoil gathered, and the holy place of Apollo shone with gifts of gold and silver, which the men of Delphi offered in gladness of heart for all the great things which he had done for them. And in every house of the Delphians were seen robes and turbans rich with gold and silver and embroidery. On their walls hung spears and shields and swords and daggers which the Persians bore when they came to Delphi.

In after days they told their children the wondrous tale how Phœbus Apollo smote down the hosts of Xerxes; and they showed them the spoils which they took by the aid of the bright heroes, and the two rocks, lying on the holy ground before his shrine, which Phœbus tore from the peaks of Parnassus in the day of his great vengeance.

THE STORY OF ARION

By Sir George W. Cox

A LONG time ago, in the great city of Corinth, there lived a man whose name was Arîon, and he made beautiful music on a golden harp, which all the people flocked to listen to. Men and women, boys and girls, all came to hear Arîon play and sing; and when his songs were ended they gave him money, and Arîon became a rich man. When he had lived for a long time in the house of Periandros, who was called the tyrant of Corinth, he thought that he would like to see some new places which he had never seen before. So he went into a ship and asked the sailors to take him to Sicily and Italy. They sailed over the blue sea a long way for many days and weeks, and came to many towns, where Arîon played and sang and got more money, till at last he came to Taras. There he stayed a long time, because it was a rich and beautiful city, and all the people who came to hear him gave him plenty of money.

By and by Arîon thought that he had enough and he began to wish to see Corinth and his friend Periandros once more. He went down to the beach and said that he wanted a ship to take him back to Corinth, and that he would only go with Corinthians, because he thought the men of Corinth better than the men of any other place. Just then there was drawn up on the beach a ship which had come from Corinth, and the sailors told him that they were Corinthians, and would take him home again. So Arîon promised to go with them, and he sent down his harp and all his boxes full of fine clothes and gold and silver, to be put on board the ship. When the sailors saw the boxes, and felt how heavy they were, they said to each other, "What a rich man he must be! would it not be pleasant to have only a little of all this money which has been given to Arîon for playing on a harp?"

The next day Arîon came down to the shore and went into the ship. It was a beautiful day; there was scarcely a cloud in the sky, and there was a fresh breeze just strong enough to fill the sails and move the ship gently through the water. The waves danced and shone like gold in the bright sunshine, while the ship tossed up the white foam as she sailed merrily on towards Corinth. So they went on many days, for Arîon sat at the head of the ship to see how it cut through the water, and as they passed one place after another, he thought that they would soon reach Corinth. But the sailors in the ship were wicked men. They had seen the large boxes full of money which Arîon had brought with him into the ship, and now they made up their mind to kill him and take his gold and silver. So one day while he was sitting at the bow of the ship, and looking down on the dark blue sea, three or four of the sailors came up to him and said that they were going to kill him. Now Arîon knew that they said this because they wanted his money; so he promised to give them all that he had if they would spare his life. But they would not. Then he asked them to let him play once more on his harp, and sing one of the songs which he loved the best, and he said that when it was finished he would leap into the sea. When they had given him leave to do this, Arîon put on a beautiful dress, took his harp in his hand, and stood up to sing. And as he sang, the sailors began to feel sorry that they were going to kill him, because they would have no more of his sweet music when he was dead. But when they thought of all the gold and silver which Arîon was taking to Corinth, they made up their minds that they would not let him live; and Arîon took one last look at the bright and sunny sky, and then leaped into the sea, and the sailors saw him no more.

The ship sailed on merrily over the dark water, just as though it were not carrying so many wicked men to Corinth. But Arîon was not drowned. A

great fish called a dolphin was swimming by the
ship when Arîon leaped over; and it caught him on
its back and swam away with him towards Corinth
much faster than the ship could sail. On and on
the great fish swam, cutting through the foam of
the sea which was tossed up over Arîon; and by
and by he saw at a distance the high cliffs and
peaks which he knew were the cliffs and peaks
above Corinth. So presently the fish came close to
the shore and left Arîon on the beach, and swam
away again into the deep sea.

Arîon was cold and tired with being so long in
the water, and he could hardly crawl up into the
city as far as the house where Periandros the tyrant
lived. At last he reached the house, and was taken
into the great hall where Periandros was sitting. And when he saw Arîon, Periandros rose up,
and came to meet him, and said, "Why, Arîon,
what is all this? Your clothes are dripping with
water; I thought you were coming to Corinth from
Sicily in a ship, but you look more as if you had
been in the sea than in a ship: did you swim here
through the water?" Then Arîon told him all the
story; how he had left Taras in a ship with Corinthian men whom he had hired to bring him home,
how they had tried to kill him that they might take
his money, and how the dolphin had brought him to
the shore when they made him leap from the ship
into the sea. But Periandros did not believe the
story, and said to Arîon, "You cannot make me
think that this strange tale is true: who ever swam
on a dolphin's back before?" So he told his servants to give Arîon all that he wanted, but not to

let him go until the ship in which he had left Taras came to Corinth.

Two days afterwards, Arîon was standing by the side of Periandros, and looking out over the sea. Presently he saw the white sails of a ship which was sailing into the harbour with a gentle breeze from the west. As it came nearer and nearer, Arîon thought that it looked very like his own ship, until at last he was able to see from the colours on its prow that it was the very ship in which he had been sailing. Then he said to Periandros, "See, they are come at last, and now go and send for these sailors, and see whether I have not told you the truth." So Periandros sent down fifty soldiers with swords and spears and shields, to bring up all the sailors from the ship.

The ship was sailing in merrily towards the shore, and the soft west wind filled out its white sails as it cut through the water. As they looked on the beautiful land to which they were coming, they thought of all the things which they should be able to buy with Arîon's gold and silver; and how they would do nothing but eat and drink and be merry, as soon as they got out of the ship. So when they came to the beach, they let down the sails, lowered the masts, and threw out ropes from the stern to fasten the ship to the shore. They never thought that the fifty soldiers whose spears and shields were shining gaily in the sunshine had been sent on purpose to take them; and they could not make out why it was that, as soon as they came out from the ship upon the dry land, the soldiers said that they must all go as quickly as they could

to the house of Periandros. Ten of the soldiers
stayed behind to guard the ship, while the rest led
the sailors to the palace. When they were brought
before him, Periandros spoke to them kindly, and
asked them from what place they had come; and
the sailors said that they had come from Italy, from
the great city of Taras. Then Periandros said, "If
you have come from Italy, perhaps you can tell me
something about my friend Arîon. A long time
ago he left Corinth, and said that he was going to
Sicily and Italy; and I cannot think why he should
be away so long, for if the people have given him
as much money for his music as they did here, he
must now be a very rich man." Then the sailors
said, "Yes, we can tell you all about Arîon. We
left him quite safe at Taras, where every one
wanted to hear him sing; but he said that he should
not come to Corinth, until they had given him
more gold and silver and made him a richer man."
Just as they were telling this lie, the door of the
room was opened, and Arîon himself walked in;
and Periandros turned round to the sailors, and
said, "See, here is the man whom you left quite safe
and well at Taras. How dare you tell me so great
a lie? Now I know that Arîon has told me the truth,
and that you wished to kill him, and made him leap
into the sea; but the dolphin caught him as he fell,
and brought him here on its back. And now listen
to me. Of all Arîon's gold and silver you shall have
none; everything that was his you shall give back
to him; and I shall take away your ship, and everything in it which belongs to you, because you wished
to rob and kill Arîon." Then the soldiers came,

and turned these wicked sailors into the street, and drove them on, calling to the people to come and see the men who had sought to murder Arîon. And all came out of their houses, and hooted at the sailors as they passed by, until they were ready to sink down with fear and shame.

So Periandros took their ship, and gave back to Arîon all his gold and silver, and what he loved better than his riches—his golden harp. And every one came to hear the wonderful tale of Arîon and the dolphin; and Arîon made a large statue out of stone to look like a man on a dolphin's back, and placed it on Cape Tainaron, that the people might never forget how the dolphin saved Arîon when he leaped into the sea.

THE BATTLE OF THE FROGS AND THE MICE

By Sir George W. Cox

A THIRSTY mouse, who had just escaped from a weasel, was drinking from a pool of water, when a croaking frog saw him, and said, "Stranger, whence hast thou come to our shore, and who is thy father? Tell me the truth, and deceive me not, for if thou deservest it, I will lead thee to my house and give thee rich and beautiful gifts. My name is Puffcheek, and I rule over the frogs who dwell in this lake, and I see that thou, too, art an excellent prince and a brave warrior. So make haste, and tell me to what race thou dost belong."

The mouse answered him and said, "Friend, why dost thou ask me of my race? It is known to all the gods, and to men, and to all the birds of heaven. My name is Crumbfilcher, and I am the son of the great-hearted Breadgnawer, and my mother is Lickmill, the daughter of King Hamnibbler. I was born in a hovel, and fed on figs and nuts and on all manner of good things. But how can we be friends? We are not at all like each other. You frogs live in the water; we feed on whatever is eaten by man. No dainty escapes my eye, whether it be bread, or cake, or ham, or new-made cheese, or rich dishes prepared for feasts. As to war, I have never dreaded its noise, but, going straight into it, have taken my place among the foremost warriors. Nor do I fear men, although they have large bodies; for at night I can bite a finger or nibble a heel without waking the sleeper from his pleasant slumber. But there are two things which I dread greatly—a mouse-trap and a hawk; but worse than these are the weasels, for they can catch us in our holes. What then am I to do? for I cannot eat the cabbages, radishes, and pumpkins, which furnish food to the race of frogs."

Then Puffcheek answered with a smile, "My friend, thou art dainty enough, but we have fine things to show on the dry land and in the marsh, for the son of Cronos has given us the power to dwell on land or in the water as it may please us. If thou wouldest see these things, it is soon done. Get on my back and hold on well, so that thou mayest reach my house with a cheerful heart." So he turned his back to the mouse, who sprang lightly on it and put his arms round his soft neck. Much pleased he was at first to swim on the back of Puff-cheek, while the haven was near; but when he got out into midwater, he began to weep and to curse his useless sorrow. He tore his hair, and drew his feet tightly round the frog's stomach. His heart beat wildly, and he wished himself well on shore, as he uttered a pitiful cry and spread out his tail on the water, moving it about like an oar. Then in the bitterness of his grief he said, "Surely it was not thus the bull carried the beautiful Europa on his back over the sea to Crete; surely——" But before he could say more, a snake, of which frogs and mice alike are afraid, lifted up his head straight above the water. Down dived Puffcheek, when he saw the snake, never thinking that he had left the mouse to die. The frog was safe at the bottom of the marsh, but the mouse fell on his back and screamed terribly. Many times he sank and many times he came up again, kicking hard; but there was no hope. The hair on his skin was soaked and weighed him down, and with his last breath he cried, "Puffcheek, thou shalt not escape for thy treachery. On the land I could have beaten thee in boxing, wrestling, or running; but thou hast beguiled me into the water, where I can do nothing. The eye of justice sees thee, and thou shalt pay a fearful penalty to the great army of the mice."

So the Crumbfilcher died; but Lickplatter saw him as he sat on the soft bank, and uttering a sharp cry, went to tell the mice. Then was there great wrath among them, and messengers were sent to bid all come in the morning to the house of Breadgnawer, the father of the luckless Crumbfilcher, whose body could not even be buried, because it was floating in the middle of the pond. They came at dawn, and Breadgnawer, rising in grief and rage, said, "Friends, I may be the only one whom the frogs have sorely injured; but we all live a poor life, and I am in sad plight, for I have lost three sons. The first was slain by a hateful weasel who caught him outside his hole. The next one cruel men brought to his death by a newfangled device of wood, which they call a trap; and now my darling Crumbfilcher has been drowned. Come and let us arm ourselves for war and go forth to battle."

So they each put on his armour. For greaves around their legs they used the beans on which they fed at night, and their breastplates they made cunningly out of the skin of a dead weasel. For spears they carried skewers, and the shell of a nut for a helmet. So they stood in battle array, and the frogs, when they came to hear of it, rose from the water and summoned a council in a corner of the pond. As they wondered what might be the cause of these things, there came a messenger from the mice, who declared war against them and said, "Ye frogs, the mice bid you arm yourselves and come forth to battle, for they have seen Crumbfilcher, whom your king Puffcheek drowned, floating dead on the water." Then the valiant frogs feared exceedingly, and blamed the deed of Puffcheek; but the king said, "Friends, I did not kill the mouse or see him die; of course he was drowned while he amused himself in the pond by trying to swim like a frog, and the wretches now bring a charge against me who am wholly guiltless. But come, let us take counsel how we may destroy these mice and this, I think, is the best plan. Let us arm ourselves and take our stand where the bank is steepest, and when they come charging against us, let us seize their helmets and drag them down into the pond. Thus we shall drown them all and set up a trophy for our victory." So they each put on his armour. They covered their legs with mallow leaves, and carried radish leaves for shields, rushes for spears, snail-shells for helmets. Thus they stood in array on the high bank, brandishing their spears and shouting for battle.

But Jupiter summoned the gods to the starry heaven, and, pointing to the hosts of the frogs and mice, mighty as the armies of the Centaurs or the giants, he asked who would aid each side as it might be hard pressed in the strife; and he said to Minerva, "Daughter, thou wilt go surely to the aid of the mice, for they are always running about thy shrine, and delight in the fat and the morsels which they pick from the sacrifices."

But Minerva said to the son of Cronos, "Father, I go not to help the mice, for they have done me grievous mischief, spoiling the garlands and the lamps for the sake of the oil. Nay, I have greater cause for anger, for they have eaten the robe which I wove from fine thread, and made holes in it; and the man who mended it charges a high price, and, worse still, I borrowed the stuff of which I wove it, and now I cannot pay it back. Yet neither will I aid the frogs, for they are not in their right senses. A little while ago, I came back tired from war and wanting sleep; but they never let me close my eyes with their clatter, and I lay sleepless with a headache till the cock crew in the morning. But, O ye gods, let us aid neither side, lest we be wounded with their swords or spears, for they are sharp and strong, even against gods; let us take our sport by watching the strife in safety."

The gods did as Minerva bade them, and went all to one place. The gnats, with their great trumpets, gave the signal for battle, and Jupiter thundered out of the sky because of the woes that were coming. Mighty were the deeds that were done on both sides, and the earth and the pond were reddened with the blood of the slain. As the fight went on, Crumbstealer slew Garliceater before he came to land; and Mudwalker, seeing it, threw at him a clod of earth, and, hitting him on the forehead, almost blinded him. In his fury, Crumbstealer seized a great stone, and crushed the leg of the frog, so that he fell on his back in the dust. Then Breadgnawer wounded Puffcheek in the foot, and made him limp into the water.

But among the mice was a young hero, with whom none could be matched for boldness and strength, and his name was Bitstealer. On the bank of the pond he stood alone, and vowed a vow to destroy the whole race of frogs. And the vow would have been accomplished, for his might was great indeed, had not the son of Cronos pitied the frogs in their misery, and charged Minerva and Mars to drive Bitstealer from the battle. But Mars made answer and said, "O Jupiter, neither Minerva nor Mars alone can save the frogs from death.

Let us all go and help them; and do thou, son of Cronos, wield thy mighty weapon with which thou didst slay the Titans, and the wild race of giants, for thus only can the bravest of them be slain." So spake Mars; and Jupiter hurled his scathing thunderbolts, and the lightnings flashed from the sky, and Olympus shook with the earthquake. The frogs and mice heard and trembled; but the mice ceased not yet from the battle, and strove only the more to slay their enemies, until Jupiter, in his pity, sent a new army to aid the frogs.

Suddenly they came on the mice, with mailed backs and crooked claws, with limping gait, and mouths like shears. Their backs were hard and horny, their arms were long and lean, and their eyes were in their breasts. They had eight feet and two heads, and no hands. Men call them crabs. With their mouths they bit the tails and feet and hands of the mice, and broke their spears, and great terror came on all the mice, so that they turned and fled. Thus the battle was ended, and the sun went down.

ORPHEUS THE SWEET SINGER

By Sir George W. Cox

IN the pleasant valleys of a country which was called Thessaly, there lived a man whose name was Orpheus. Every day he made soft music with his golden harp, and sang beautiful songs such as no one had ever heard before. And whenever

Orpheus sang, then everything came to listen to him, and the trees bowed down their heads to hear; even the clouds sailed along more gently and brightly in the sky when he sang, and the stream which ran close to his feet made a softer noise, to show how glad his music made it.

Now Orpheus had a wife who was called Eurydicê, whom he loved very dearly. All through the winter when the snow was on the hills, and all through the summer when the sunshine made everything beautiful, Orpheus used to sing to her; and Eurydicê sat on the grass by his side while the beasts came round to listen, and the trees bowed down their heads to hear him.

But one day when Eurydicê was playing with some children on the banks of the river, she trod upon a snake in the long grass, and the snake bit her. And by and by she began to be very sick, and Eurydicê knew that she must die. So she told the children to go to Orpheus (for he was far away) and say how sorry she was to leave him, and that she loved him always very dearly; and then she put her head down upon the soft grass, and fell asleep and died. Sad indeed was Orpheus when the children came to tell him that Eurydicê was dead. He felt so wretched that he never played upon his golden harp, and he never opened his lips to sing; and the beasts that used to listen to him wondered why Orpheus sat all alone on the green bank where Eurydicê used to sit with him, and why it was that he never made any more beautiful music. All day long he sat there, and his cheeks were often wet with tears. At last he said,

"I cannot stay here any more; I must go and look for Eurydicê. I cannot bear to be without her, and perhaps the king of the land where people go after they are dead will let her come back and live with me again."

So he took his harp in his hand, and went to look for Eurydicê in the land where the sun goes down into his golden cup before the night comes on. He went on and on a very long way, till at last he came to a high and dark gateway. It was barred across with iron bars, and was bolted and locked so that nobody could open it. It was a wretched and gloomy place, because the sunshine never came there, and it was covered with clouds and mist. In front of this great gateway there sat a monstrous dog, with three heads, six eyes, and three tongues; and everything was dark around, except his eyes, which shone like fire, and which saw every one that dared to come near. Now when Orpheus came looking for Eurydicê, the dog raised his three heads, opened his three mouths, and gnashed his teeth at him, and roared terribly; but when Orpheus came nearer, the dog jumped up on his feet ready to fly at him and tear him to pieces. Then Orpheus took down his harp and began to play upon its golden strings. And the dog Cerberus (for that was his name) growled and snarled and showed the great white teeth in his three mouths; but he could not help hearing the sweet music, and he wondered why it was that he no longer wished to tear Orpheus in pieces. Soon the music made him quiet and still, and at last it lulled him to sleep. Then Orpheus passed by him and came up to the gate, and found it wide open, for it had come open of its own accord while he was singing. He was glad when he saw this, for he thought that now he should see Eurydicê.

So he went on and on a long way, until he came to the palace of the king; and there were guards placed before the door who tried to keep him from going in; but Orpheus played upon his harp, and they could not help letting him pass.

So he went into the great hall, where he saw the king and queen sitting on a throne; and as he came near, the king called out to him with a loud and terrible voice, "Who are you, and how dare you to come here? Do you not know that no one is allowed to come here till after he is dead? I will have you chained and placed in a dungeon, from which you will never be able to get out." Orpheus said nothing; but took his golden harp in his hand and began to sing more sweetly and gently than ever. And as he sang, the face of the king began to look almost glad, and his anger passed away. Then the king said, "You have made me feel happy with your sweet music, although I have never felt happy before; and now tell me why you have come, because you must want something, for, otherwise, no one would come, before he was dead, to this sad and gloomy land of which I am the king." Then Orpheus said, "O king, give me back my dear Eurydicê, and let her go from this gloomy place and live with me on the bright earth again." So the king said that she could go. And the king said to Orpheus, "I have given you what you wanted, because you sang so sweetly; and when you go back to the earth from this place, your wife whom you love shall go up after you: but remember that you must never look back until she has reached the earth, for if you do, Eurydicê will be brought back here, and I shall not be able to give her to you again, even if you should sing more sweetly and gently than ever."

Now Orpheus was longing to see Eurydicê, and he hoped that the king would let him see her at once; but when the king said that he must not try to see her till she had reached the earth, he was quite content, for he said, "Shall I not wait patiently a little while, that Eurydicê may come and live with me again?" So he promised the king that he would go up to the earth without stopping to look behind and see whether Eurydicê was coming after him.

Then Orpheus left the palace of the king, and he passed through the dark gateway, and the dog Cerberus did not bark or growl, for he knew that Orpheus would not have been allowed to come back, if the king had not wished it. So he went on and on a long way; and he became impatient, and longed more and more to see Eurydicê. At last he came near to the land of living men, and he saw just a little streak of light, where the sun was going to rise from the sea; and presently the sky became brighter, and he saw everything before him so clearly that he could not help turning round to look at Eurydicê. But, ah! she had not yet quite reached the earth, and so he lost her again. He saw something pale and white, which looked like his own dear wife; and he just heard a soft and gentle voice, which sounded like the voice of Eurydicê, and then it all melted away. And still he thought that he saw that pale white face, and heard that soft voice, which said, "O Orpheus, Orpheus, why did you look back? How dearly I love you, and how glad I should have been to live with you again; but now I must go back, because you have broken your promise to the king, and I must not even kiss you, and say how much I love you."

Orpheus sat down at the place where Eurydicê was taken from him; he could go no further. There he stayed day after day, and his cheeks became paler, and his body weaker and weaker, till at last he knew that he must die. And Orpheus was not sorry; for although he loved the bright earth, with all its flowers and grass and sunny streams, he knew that he could not be with Eurydicê again until he had left it. So at last he laid his head upon the earth, and fell asleep, and died: and then he and Eurydicê saw each other in the land which is far away, where the sun goes down at night into his golden cup, and were never parted again.

NIOBE, A VICTIM OF LATONA'S JEALOUSY

By Thomas Bulfinch

NIOBE, the Queen of Thebes, had much to be proud of; but it was not her husband's fame, nor her own beauty, nor their great descent, nor the power of their kingdom that elated her. It was her children; and truly the happiest of mothers would Niobe have been if only she had not claimed to be so.

It was on occasion of the annual celebration in honor of Latona and her offspring, Apollo and Diana,—when the people of Thebes were assembled, their brows crowned with laurel, bearing frankincense to the altars and paying their vows,—that Niobe appeared among the crowd. Her attire was splendid with gold and gems, and her aspect beautiful as the face of an angry woman can be. She stood and surveyed the people with haughty looks. "What folly," said she, "is this!—to prefer beings whom you never saw to those who stand before your eyes! Why should Latona be honored with worship, and none be paid to me? My father was Tantalus, who was received as a guest at the table of the gods; my mother was a goddess. My husband built and rules this city, Thebes, and Phrygia is my paternal inheritance. Wherever I turn my eyes I survey the elements of my power; nor is my form and presence unworthy of a goddess. To all this let me add I have seven sons and seven daughters, and look for sons-in-law and daughters-in-law of pretensions worthy of my alliance. Have I not cause for pride? Will you prefer to me this Latona, the Titan's daughter, with her two children? I have seven times as many. Fortunate indeed am I, and fortunate I shall remain! Will any one deny this? My abundance is my security. I feel myself too strong for Fortune to subdue. She may take from me much; I shall still have much left. Were I to lose some of my children, I should hardly be left as poor as Latona with her two only. Away with you from these solemnities, —put off the laurel from your brows,—have done with this worship!" The people obeyed, and left the sacred services uncompleted.

The goddess was indignant. On the Cynthian mountain top where she dwelt she thus addressed her son and daughter: "My children, I who have been so proud of you both, and have been used to hold myself second to none of the goddesses except Juno alone, begin now to doubt whether I am indeed a goddess. I shall be deprived of my worship altogether unless you protect me."

She was proceeding in this strain, but Apollo interrupted her. "Say no more," said he; "speech only delays punishment."

So said Diana also. Darting through the air, veiled in clouds, they alighted on the towers of the city. Spread out before the gates was a broad plain, where the youth of the city pursued their warlike sports. The sons of Niobe were there with the rest,—some mounted on spirited horses richly caparisoned, some driving gay chariots.

Ismenos, the first-born, as he guided his foaming steeds, struck with an arrow from above, cried out, "Ah me!" dropped the reins, and fell lifeless. Another, hearing the sound of the bow,—like a boatman who sees the storm gathering and makes all sail for the port,—gave the reins to his horses and attempted to escape. The arrow overtook him as he fled. Two younger boys, just from their tasks, had gone to the playground to have a game of wrestling. As they stood breast to breast, one arrow pierced them both. They uttered a cry together, cast a parting look around them, and together breathed their last. Alphenor, an elder brother, seeing them fall, hastened to the spot to render assistance, and fell stricken in the act.

One only was left, Ilioneus. He raised his arms to heaven to try whether prayer might not avail. "Spare me, ye gods!" he cried, addressing all; and Apollo would have spared him, but the arrow had already left the string, and it was too late.

The terror of the people and grief of the attendants soon made Niobe acquainted with what had taken place. She could hardly think it possible; she was indignant that the gods had dared, and amazed that they had been able, to do it. Her husband, Amphion, overwhelmed with the blow, destroyed himself.

Alas! how different was this Niobe from her who had so lately driven away the people from the sacred rites, and held her stately course through the city, the envy of her friends, now the pity even of her foes! She knelt over the lifeless bodies, and kissed now one, now another of her dead sons. Raising her pallid arms to heaven, "Cruel Latona," said she, "feed full your rage with my anguish! Satiate your hard heart, while I follow to the grave my seven sons. Yet where is your triumph? Bereaved as I am, I am still richer than you, my conqueror."

Scarce had she spoken, when the bow sounded and struck terror into all hearts except Niobe's alone. She was brave from excess of grief. The sisters stood in garments of mourning over the biers of their dead brothers. One fell, struck by an arrow, and died on the corpse she was bewailing. Another, attempting to console her mother, suddenly ceased to speak, and sank lifeless to the earth. A third tried to escape by flight, a fourth by concealment, another stood trembling, uncertain what course to take. Six were now dead, and only one remained, whom the mother held clasped in her arms, and covered as it were with her whole body. "Spare me one, and that the youngest! O spare me one of so many!" she cried; and while she spoke, that one fell dead. Desolate she sat, among sons, daughters, husband, all dead, stunned with grief. The breeze moved not her hair, no color was on her cheek, her eyes glared fixed and immovable, there was no sign of life about her. Her very tongue cleaved to the roof of her mouth. She was changed to stone. Yet tears continued to flow; and borne on a whirlwind to her native mountain, she still remains, a mass of rock, from which a trickling stream flows, the tribute of her never-ending grief.

THE SAD STORY OF PYRAMUS AND THISBE

By Thomas Bulfinch

PYRAMUS was the handsomest youth, and Thisbe the fairest maiden, in all Babylon, where Semiramis reigned. Their parents occupied adjoining houses, and acquaintance ripened into love. They would gladly have married, but their parents forbade. One thing, however, they could not forbid—that love should glow with equal ardor in the hearts of both. They conversed by signs and glances, and the fire burned more intensely for being covered up. In the wall that separated the two houses there was a crack. No one had remarked it before, but the lovers discovered it. It afforded a passage to the voice, and messages used to pass backward and forward through the gap. "Cruel wall," they said, "why do you keep us apart? But we will not be ungrateful. We owe you the privilege of transmitting loving words to willing ears." Such words they uttered on different sides of the wall; and when night came and they must say farewell, they pressed their lips upon the wall, she on her side, he on his, as they could come no nearer.

Next morning, when the sun had melted the frost from the grass, they met at the accustomed spot. Then, after lamenting their hard fate, they agreed that next night, when all was still, they would slip away from watchful eyes, leave their dwellings and walk out into the fields; and to insure a meeting, repair to a well-known edifice standing without the city's bounds, called the Tomb of Ninus, and that the one who came first should await the other at the foot of a certain tree. It was a white mulberry tree, and stood near a cool spring. All was agreed on, and they waited impatiently for the sun to go down beneath the waters and night to rise up from them. Then cautiously Thisbe stole forth, unobserved by the family, her head covered with a veil, made her way to the monument and sat down under the tree. As she sat alone in the dim light of the evening she descried a lioness, her jaws stained with recent slaughter, approaching the fountain to slake her thirst. Thisbe fled at the sight, and sought refuge in the hollow of a rock. As she fled she dropped her veil. The lioness after drinking at the spring turned to retreat to the woods, and seeing the veil on the ground, tossed and rent it with her bloody mouth.

Pyramus, having been delayed, now approached the place of meeting. He saw in the sand the footsteps of the lion, and the color fled from his cheeks at the sight. Presently he found the veil all rent and bloody. "O hapless girl," said he, "I have been the cause of thy death! Thou, more worthy of life than I, hast fallen the first victim. I will follow. I am the guilty cause, in tempting thee forth to a place of such peril, and not being myself on the spot to guard thee. Come forth, ye lions, from the rocks, and tear this guilty body with your teeth." He took up the veil, carried it with him to the appointed tree, and covered it with kisses and with tears. "My blood also shall stain your texture," said he, and drawing his sword plunged it into his heart. The blood spurted from the wound, and tinged the white mulberries of the tree all red; and sinking into the earth reached the roots, so that the red color mounted through the trunk to the fruit.

By this time Thisbe, still trembling with fear, yet wishing not to disappoint her lover, stepped cautiously forth, looking anxiously for the youth, eager to tell him the danger she had escaped. When she came to the spot and saw the changed color of the mulberries she doubted whether it was the same place. While she hesitated she saw the form of one struggling in the agonies of death. She started back, a shudder ran through her frame as a ripple on the face of the still water when a sudden breeze sweeps over it. But as soon as she recognized her lover, she screamed, beat her breast, and embraced the lifeless body. "O Pyramus," she cried, "what has done this? Answer me, Pyramus; it is Thisbe that speaks. Hear me, dearest, and lift that drooping head!" At the name of Thisbe Pyramus opened his eyes, then closed them again. She saw her veil stained with blood and the scabbard empty of its sword. "Thy own hand has slain thee, and for my sake," she said. "I too can be brave for once, and my love is as strong as thine. I will follow thee in death, for I have been the cause; and death which alone could part us shall not prevent my joining thee. And ye, unhappy parents of us both, deny us not our united request. As love and death have joined us, let one tomb contain us. And thou, tree, retain the marks of slaughter. Let thy berries still serve for memorials of our blood." So saying she plunged the sword into her breast. Her parents ratified her wish, the gods also ratified it. The two bodies were buried in one sepulchre, and the tree ever after brought forth purple berries, as it does to this day.

THE TWELVE LABORS OF HERCULES

By Thomas Bulfinch

HERCULES was the son of Jupiter and Alcmena. As Juno was always hostile to the offspring of her husband by mortal mothers, she declared war against Hercules from his birth. She sent two serpents to destroy him as he lay in his cradle, but the brave infant strangled them with his own hands.

He was, however, by the arts of Juno rendered subject to Eurystheus and compelled to perform all his commands. Eurystheus gave him a succession of desperate tasks, which are called the "Twelve Labors of Hercules." The first was the fight with the Nemean lion.

The valley of Nemea was infested by a terrible lion. Eurystheus ordered Hercules to bring him the skin of this monster. After using in vain his club and arrows against the lion, Hercules strangled the animal with his hands. He returned carrying the dead lion on his shoulders; but Eurystheus was so frightened at the sight of it and at this proof of the prodigious strength of the hero, that he ordered him to deliver the account of his exploits in future outside the town.

His next labor was the slaughter of the Hydra. This monster ravaged the country of Argos, and dwelt in a swamp near the well of Amymone. This well had been discovered by Amymone when the country was suffering from drought, and the story was that Neptune, who loved her, had permitted her to touch the rock with his trident, and a spring of three outlets burst forth. Here the Hydra took up his position, and Hercules was sent to destroy him. The Hydra had nine heads, of which the middle one was immortal.

Hercules struck off its heads with his club, but in the place of the head knocked off, two new ones grew forth each time. At length with the assistance of his faithful servant Iolaus, he burned away the heads of the Hydra, and buried the ninth or immortal one under a huge rock.

Another labor was the cleaning of the Augean stables. Augeas, King of Elis, had a herd of three thousand oxen, whose stalls had not been cleansed for thirty years. Hercules brought the rivers Alpheus and Peneus through them, and cleansed them thoroughly in one day.

His next labor was of a more delicate kind. Admeta, the daughter of Eurystheus, longed to obtain the girdle of the Queen of the Amazons, and Eurystheus ordered Hercules to go and get it. The Amazons were a nation of women. They were very warlike and held several flourishing cities. It was their custom to bring up only the female children; the boys were either sent away to the neighboring nations or put to death. Hercules was accompanied by a number of volunteers, and after various adventures at last reached the country of the Amazons. Hippolyta, the queen, received him kindly, and consented to yield him her girdle, but Juno, taking the form of an Amazon, went and persuaded the rest that the strangers were carrying off their queen. They instantly armed and came in great numbers down to the ship. Hercules, thinking that Hippolyta had acted treacherously, slew her, and taking her girdle made sail homeward.

Another task enjoined him was to bring to Eurystheus the oxen of Geryon, a monster with three bodies, who dwelt in the island Erytheia (the red), so called because it lay at the west, under the rays of the setting sun. This description is thought to apply to Spain, of which Geryon was king. After traversing various countries, Hercules reached at length the frontiers of Libya and Europe, where he raised the two mountains of Calpe and Abyla, as monuments of his progress, or, according to another account, rent one mountain into two and left half on each side, forming the straits of Gibraltar, the two mountains being called the Pillars of Hercules. The oxen were guarded by the giant Eurytion and his two-headed dog, but Hercules killed the giant and his dog and brought away the oxen in safety to Eurystheus.

The most difficult labor of all was getting the golden apples of the Hesperides, for Hercules did not know where to find them. These were the apples which Juno had received at her wedding from the goddess of the Earth, and which she had intrusted to the keeping of the daughters of Hesperus, assisted by a watchful dragon.

A celebrated exploit of Hercules was his victory over Antæus. Antæus, the son of Terra, the Earth, was a mighty giant and wrestler, whose strength was invincible so long as he remained in contact with his mother Earth. He compelled all strangers who came to his country to wrestle with him, on condition that if conquered (as they all were) they should be put to death. Hercules encountered him, and finding that it was of no avail to throw him, for he always rose with renewed strength from every fall, he lifted him up from the earth and strangled him in the air.

Cacus was a huge giant, who inhabited a cave on Mount Aventine, and plundered the surrounding country. When Hercules was driving home the oxen of Geryon, Cacus stole part of the cattle, while the hero slept. That their footprints might not serve to show where they had been driven, he dragged them backward by their tails to his cave; so their tracks all seemed to show that they had gone in the opposite direction. Hercules was deceived by this stratagem, and would have failed to find his oxen, if it had not happened that in driving the remainder of the herd past the cave where the stolen ones were concealed, those within began to low, and were thus discovered. Cacus was slain by Hercules.

The last exploit we shall record was bringing Cerberus from the lower world. Cerberus was the three-headed dog that guarded the entrance to Hades. Hercules descended into Hades, accompanied by Mercury and Minerva. He obtained permission from Pluto to carry Cerberus to the upper air, provided he could do it without the use of weapons; and in spite of the monster's struggling, he seized him, held him fast, and carried him to Eurystheus, and afterward brought him back again. When he was in Hades he obtained the liberty of Theseus, his admirer and imitator, who had been detained a prisoner there for an unsuccessful attempt to carry off Proserpine.

Hercules in a fit of madness killed his friend Iphitus, and was condemned for this offence to become the slave of Queen Omphale for three years. While in this service the hero's nature seemed changed. He lived effeminately, wearing at times the dress of a woman, spinning wool with the handmaidens of Omphale, while the queen wore his lion's skin. When this service was ended he married Dejanira and lived in peace with her three years. On one occasion as he was travelling with his wife, they came to a river, across which the Centaur Nessus carried travellers for a stated fee. Hercules himself forded the river, but gave Dejanira to Nessus to be carried across. Nessus attempted to run away with her, but Hercules heard her cries and shot an arrow into the heart of Nessus. The dying Centaur told Dejanira to take a portion of his blood and keep it, as it might be used as a charm to preserve the love of her husband.

Dejanira did so and before long fancied she had occasion to use it. Hercules in one of his conquests had taken prisoner a fair maiden, named Iole, of whom he seemed more fond than Dejanira approved. When Hercules was about to offer sacrifices to the gods in honor of his victory, he sent to his wife for a white robe to use on the occasion. Dejanira, thinking it a good opportunity to try her love-spell, steeped the garment in the blood of Nessus. As soon as the garment became warm on the body of Hercules the poison penetrated into all his limbs and caused him the most intense agony.

In his frenzy he seized Lichas, who had brought him the fatal robe, and hurled him into the sea. He wrenched off the garment, but it stuck to his flesh, and with it he tore away whole pieces of his body. In this state he embarked on board a ship and was conveyed home. Dejanira, on seeing what she had unwittingly done, hung herself. Hercules, prepared to die, ascended Mount Œta, where he built a funeral pile of trees, gave his bow and arrows to Philoctetes, and laid himself down on the pile, his head resting on his club, and his lion's skin spread over him. With a countenance as serene as if he were taking his place at a festal board he commanded Philoctetes to apply the torch. The flames spread apace and soon invested the whole mass.

The gods themselves felt troubled at seeing the champion of the earth so brought to his end. But Jupiter with cheerful countenance thus addressed them: "Fear not. He who conquered all else is not to be conquered by those flames which you see blazing on Mount Œta. Only his mother's share in him can perish; what he derived from me is immortal. I shall take him, dead to earth, to the heavenly shores, and I require of you all to receive him kindly." Jupiter enveloped him in a cloud, and took him up in a four-horse chariot to dwell among the stars.

HERCULES'S SEARCH FOR THE APPLES OF HESPERIDES

By Nathaniel Hawthorne

D ID you ever hear of the golden apples, that grew in the garden of the Hesperides? Ah, those were such apples as would bring a great price, by the bushel, if any of them could be found growing in the orchards of nowadays! But there is not, I suppose, a graft of that wonderful fruit on a single tree in the wide world. Not so much as a seed of those apples exists any longer.

And, even in the old, old, half-forgotten times, before the garden of the Hesperides was overrun with weeds, a great many people doubted whether they could be real trees that bore apples of solid gold upon their branches. All had heard of them, but nobody remembered to have seen any. Children, nevertheless, used to listen, open-mouthed, to stories of the golden apple-tree, and resolved to discover it, when they should be big enough. Adventurous young men, who desired to do a braver thing than any of their fellows, set out in quest of this fruit. Many of them returned no more; none of them brought back the apples. No wonder that they found it impossible to gather them! It is said that there was a dragon beneath the tree, with a hundred terrible heads, fifty of which were always on the watch, while the other fifty slept.

In my opinion it was hardly worth running so much risk for the sake of a solid golden apple.

Had the apples been sweet, mellow, and juicy, indeed that would be another matter. There might then have been some sense in trying to get at them, in spite of the hundred-headed dragon.

But, as I have already told you, it was quite a common thing with young persons, when tired of too much peace and rest, to go in search of the garden of the Hesperides. And once the adventure was undertaken by a hero who had enjoyed very little peace or rest since he came into the world. At the time of which I am going to speak, he was wandering through the pleasant land of Italy, with a mighty club in his hand, and a bow and quiver slung across his shoulders. He was wrapt in the skin of the biggest and fiercest lion that ever had been seen, and which he himself had killed; and though, on the whole, he was kind, and generous, and noble, there was a good deal of the lion's fierceness in his heart. As he went on his way, he continually inquired whether that were the right road to the famous garden. But none of the country people knew anything about the matter, and many looked as if they would have laughed at the question, if the stranger had not carried so very big a club.

So he journeyed on and on, still making the same inquiry, until, at last, he came to the brink of a river where some beautiful young women sat twining wreaths of flowers.

"Can you tell me, pretty maidens," asked the stranger, "whether this is the right way to the garden of the Hesperides?"

The young women had been having a fine time

together, weaving the flowers into wreaths, and crowning one another's heads. And there seemed to be a kind of magic in the touch of their fingers, that made the flowers more fresh and dewy, and of brighter hues, and sweeter fragrance, while they played with them, than even when they had been growing on their native stems. But, on hearing the stranger's question, they dropped all their flowers on the grass, and gazed at him with astonishment.

"The garden of the Hesperides!" cried one. "We thought mortals had been weary of seeking it, after so many disappointments. And pray, adventurous traveller, what do you want there?"

"A certain king, who is my cousin," replied he, "has ordered me to get him three of the golden apples."

"Most of the young men who go in quest of these apples," observed another of the damsels, "desire to obtain them for themselves, or to present them to some fair maiden whom they love. Do you, then, love this king, your cousin, so very much?"

"Perhaps not," replied the stranger, sighing. "He has often been severe and cruel to me. But it is my destiny to obey him."

"And do you know," asked the damsel who had first spoken, "that a terrible dragon, with a hundred heads, keeps watch under the golden apple-tree?"

"I know it well," answered the stranger, calmly. "But from my cradle upwards, it has been my business, and almost my pastime, to deal with serpents and dragons."

The young women looked at his massive club, and at the shaggy lion's skin which he wore, and likewise at his heroic limbs and figure; and they whispered to each other that the stranger appeared to be one who might reasonably expect to perform deeds far beyond the might of other men. But, then, the dragon with a hundred heads! What mortal, even if he possessed a hundred lives, could hope to escape the fangs of such a monster? So kind-hearted were the maidens, that they could not bear to see this brave and handsome traveller attempt what was so very dangerous, and devote himself, most probably, to become a meal for the dragon's hundred ravenous mouths.

"Go back," cried they all,—"go back to your own home! Your mother, beholding you safe and sound, will shed tears of joy; and what can she do more, should you win ever so great a victory? No matter for the golden apples! No matter for the king, your cruel cousin! We do not wish the dragon with the hundred heads to eat you up!"

The stranger seemed to grow impatient at these remonstrances. He carelessly lifted his mighty club, and let it fall upon a rock that lay half buried in the earth, near by. With the force of that idle blow, the great rock was shattered all to pieces. It cost the stranger no more effort to achieve this feat of a giant's strength than for one of the young maidens to touch her sister's rosy cheek with a flower.

"Do you not believe," said he, looking at the damsels with a smile, "that such a blow would have crushed one of the dragon's hundred heads?"

Then he sat down on the grass, and told them the story of his life, or as much of it as he could remember, from the day when he was first cradled in a warrior's brazen shield. While he lay there, two immense serpents came gliding over the floor, and opened their hideous jaws to devour him; and he, a baby of a few months old, had gripped one of the fierce snakes in each of his little fists, and strangled them to death. When he was but a stripling, he had killed a huge lion, almost as big as the one whose vast and shaggy hide he now wore upon his shoulders. The next thing that he had done was to fight a battle with an ugly sort of monster, called a hydra, which had no less than nine heads, and exceedingly sharp teeth in every one.

"But the dragon of the Hesperides, you know," observed one of the damsels, "has a hundred heads!"

"Nevertheless," replied the stranger, "I would rather fight two such dragons than a single hydra. For, as fast as I cut off a head, two others grew in its place; and, besides, there was one of the heads that could not possibly be killed, but kept biting as fiercely as ever, long after it was cut off. So I was forced to bury it under a stone, where it is doubtless alive to this very day. But the hydra's body, and its eight other heads, will never do any further mischief."

The damsels, judging that the story was likely to last a good while, had been preparing a repast of bread and grapes, that the stranger might refresh himself in the intervals of his talk. They took pleasure in helping him to this simple food; and, now and then, one of them would put a sweet grape between her rosy lips, lest it should make him bashful to eat alone.

The traveller proceeded to tell how he had chased a very swift stag, for a twelvemonth together, without ever stopping to take breath, and had at last caught it by the antlers, and carried it home alive. And he had fought with a very odd race of people, half horses and half men, and had put them all to death, from a sense of duty, in order that their ugly figures might never be seen any more. Besides all this, he took to himself great credit for having cleaned out a stable.

"Do you call that a wonderful exploit?" asked one of the young maidens, with a smile. "Any clown in the country has done as much!"

"Had it been an ordinary stable," replied the stranger, "I should not have mentioned it. But this was so gigantic a task that it would have taken me all my life to perform it, if I had not luckily thought of turning the channel of a river through the stable-door. That did the business in a very short time!"

Seeing how earnestly his fair auditors listened, he next told them how he had shot some monstrous birds, and had caught a wild bull alive and let him go again, and had tamed a number of very wild horses, and had conquered Hippolyta, the warlike Queen of the Amazons. He mentioned, likewise, that he had taken off Hippolyta's enchanted girdle, and had given it to the daughter of his cousin, the king.

"Was it the girdle of Venus," inquired the prettiest of the damsels, "which makes women beautiful?"

"No," answered the stranger. "It had formerly been the sword-belt of Mars; and it can only make the wearer valiant and courageous."

"An old sword-belt!" cried the damsel, tossing her head. "Then I should not care about having it!"

"You are right," said the stranger.

Going on with his wonderful narrative, he informed the maidens that as strange an adventure as ever happened was when he fought with Geryon, the six-legged man. This was a very odd and frightful sort of figure, as you may well believe. Any person, looking at his tracks in the sand or snow, would suppose that three sociable companions had been walking along together. On hearing his footsteps at a little distance, it was no more than reasonable to judge that several people must be coming. But it was only the strange man Geryon clattering onward, with his six legs!

Six legs, and one gigantic body! Certainly, he must have been a very queer monster to look at; and, my stars, what a waste of shoe-leather!

When the stranger had finished the story of his adventures, he looked around at the attentive faces of the maidens.

"Perhaps you may have heard of me before," said he, modestly. "My name is Hercules!"

"We had already guessed it," replied the maidens; "for your wonderful deeds are known all over the world. We do not think it strange, any longer, that you should set out in quest of the golden apples of the Hesperides. Come, sisters, let us crown the hero with flowers!"

Then they flung beautiful wreaths over his stately head and mighty shoulders, so that the lion's skin was almost entirely covered with roses. They took possession of his ponderous club, and so entwined it about with the brightest, softest, and most fragrant blossoms, that not a finger's breadth of its oaken substance could be seen. It looked all like a huge bunch of flowers. Lastly, they joined hands, and danced around him, chanting words which became poetry of their own accord, and grew into a choral song, in honor of the illustrious Hercules.

And Hercules was rejoiced, as any other hero would have been, to know that these fair young girls had heard of the valiant deeds which it had cost him so much toil and danger to achieve. But, still, he was not satisfied. He could not think that what he had already done was worthy of so much honor, while there remained any bold or difficult adventure to be undertaken.

"Dear maidens," said he, when they paused to take breath, "now that you know my name, will you not tell me how I am to reach the garden of the Hesperides?"

"Ah! must you go so soon?" they exclaimed. "You—that have performed so many wonders, and spent such a toilsome life—cannot you content yourself to repose a little while on the margin of this peaceful river?"

Hercules shook his head.

"I must depart now," said he.

"We will then give you the best directions we can," replied the damsels. "You must go to the sea-shore, and find out the Old One, and compel him to inform you where the golden apples are to be found."

"The Old One!" repeated Hercules, laughing at this odd name. "And, pray, who may the Old One be?"

"Why, the Old Man of the Sea, to be sure!" answered one of the damsels. "He has fifty daughters, whom some people call very beautiful; but we do not think it proper to be acquainted with them, because they have sea-green hair, and taper away like fishes. You must talk with this Old Man of the Sea. He is a sea-faring person, and knows all about the garden of the Hesperides; for it is situated in an island which he is often in the habit of visiting."

Hercules then asked whereabouts the Old One was most likely to be met with. When the damsels had informed him, he thanked them for all their kindness,—for the bread and grapes with which they had fed him, the lovely flowers with which they had crowned him, and the songs and dances wherewith they had done him honor,—and he thanked them, most of all, for telling him the right way,—and immediately set forth upon his journey.

But, before he was out of hearing, one of the maidens called after him.

"Keep fast hold of the Old One, when you catch him!" cried she, smiling, and lifting her finger to make the caution more impressive. "Do not be astonished at anything that may happen. Only hold him fast, and he will tell you what you wish to know."

Hercules again thanked her, and pursued his way, while the maidens resumed their pleasant labor of making flower-wreaths. They talked about the hero, long after he was gone.

"We will crown him with the loveliest of our garlands," said they, "when he returns hither with the three golden apples, after slaying the dragon with a hundred heads."

Meanwhile, Hercules travelled constantly onward, over hill and dale, and through the solitary woods. Sometimes he swung his club aloft, and splintered a mighty oak with a downright blow. His mind was so full of the giants and monsters with whom it was the business of his life to fight, that perhaps he mistook the great tree for a giant or a monster. And so eager was Hercules to achieve what he had undertaken, that he almost regretted to have spent so much time with the damsels, wasting idle breath upon the story of his adventures.

But thus it always is with persons who are destined to perform great things. What they have already done seems less than nothing. What they have taken in hand to do seems worth toil, danger, and life itself.

Persons who happened to be passing through the forest must have been affrighted to see him smite the trees with his great club. With but a single blow, the trunk was riven as by the stroke of lightning, and the broad boughs came rustling and crashing down.

Hastening forward, without ever pausing or looking behind, he by and by heard the sea roaring at a distance. At this sound, he increased his speed, and soon came to a beach, where the great surf-waves tumbled themselves upon the hard sand, in a long line of snowy foam. At one end of the beach, however, there was a pleasant spot, where some green shrubbery clambered up a cliff, making its rocky face look soft and beautiful. A carpet of verdant grass, largely intermixed with sweet-smelling clover, covered the narrow space between the bottom of the cliff and the sea. And what should Hercules espy there, but an old man, fast asleep!

But was it really and truly an old man? Certainly, at first sight, it looked very like one; but on closer inspection, it rather seemed to be some kind of a creature that lived in the sea. For, on his legs and arms there were scales, such as fishes have; he was web-footed and web-fingered, after the fashion of a duck; and his long beard, being of a greenish tinge, had more the appearance of a tuft of sea-weed than of an ordinary beard. Have you never seen a stick of timber, that has been long tossed about by the waves, and has got all overgrown with barnacles, and, at last drifting ashore, seems to have been thrown up from the very deepest bottom of the sea? Well, the old man would have put you in mind of just such a wave-tost spar! But Hercules, the instant he set eyes on this strange figure, was convinced that it could be no other than the Old One, who was to direct him on his way.

Yes, it was the selfsame Old Man of the Sea whom the hospitable maidens had talked to him about. Thanking his stars for the lucky accident of finding the old fellow asleep, Hercules stole on tiptoe towards him, and caught him by the arm and leg.

"Tell me," cried he, before the Old One was well awake, "which is the way to the garden of the Hesperides?"

As you may easily imagine, the Old Man of the Sea awoke in a fright. But his astonishment could hardly have been greater than was that of Hercules, the next moment. For, all of a sudden, the Old One seemed to disappear out of his grasp, and he found himself holding a stag by the fore and hind leg! But still he kept fast hold. Then the stag disappeared, and in its stead there was a sea-bird, fluttering and screaming, while Hercules clutched it by the wing and claw! But the bird could not get away. Immediately afterwards, there was an ugly three-headed dog, which growled and barked at Hercules, and snapped fiercely at the hands by which he held him! But Hercules would not let him go. In another minute, instead of the three-headed dog, what should appear but Geryon, the six-legged man-monster, kicking at Hercules with five of his legs, in order to get the remaining one at liberty! But Hercules held on. By and by, no Geryon was there, but a huge snake, like one of those which Hercules had strangled in his babyhood, only a hundred times as big; and it twisted and twined about the hero's neck and body, and threw its tail high into the air, and opened its deadly jaws as if to devour him outright; so that it was really a very terrible spectacle! But Hercules was no whit disheartened, and squeezed the great snake so tightly that he soon began to hiss with pain.

You must understand that the Old Man of the Sea, though he generally looked so much like the wave-beaten figure-head of a vessel, had the power of assuming any shape he pleased. When he found himself so roughly seized by Hercules, he had been in hopes of putting him into such surprise and terror, by these magical transformations, that the hero would be glad to let him go. If Hercules had relaxed his grasp, the Old One would certainly have plunged down to the very bottom of the sea, whence he would not soon have given himself the trouble of coming up, in order to answer any impertinent questions. Ninety-nine people out of a hundred, I suppose, would have been frightened out of their wits by the very first of his ugly shapes, and would have taken to their heels at once. For one of the hardest things in this world is to see the difference between real dangers and imaginary ones.

But, as Hercules held on so stubbornly, and only squeezed the Old One so much the tighter at every change of shape, and really put him to no small torture, he finally thought it best to reappear in his own figure. So there he was again, a fishy, scaly, web-footed sort of personage, with something like a tuft of sea-weed at his chin.

"Pray, what do you want with me?" cried the Old One as soon as he could take breath; for it is quite a tiresome affair to go through so many false shapes. "Why do you squeeze me so hard? Let me go, this moment, or I shall begin to consider you an extremely uncivil person!"

"My name is Hercules!" roared the mighty stranger. "And you will never get out of my clutch, until you tell me the nearest way to the garden of the Hesperides!"

When the old fellow heard who it was that had caught him, he saw, with half an eye, that it would be necessary to tell him everything that he wanted to know. The Old One was an inhabitant of the sea, you must recollect, and roamed about everywhere, like other sea-faring people. Of course, he had often heard of the fame of Hercules, and of the wonderful things that he was constantly performing, in various parts of the earth, and how determined he always was to accomplish whatever he undertook. He therefore made no more attempts to escape, but told the hero how to find the garden of the Hesperides, and likewise warned him of many difficulties which must be overcome, before he could arrive thither.

"You must go on, thus and thus," said the Old Man of the Sea, after taking the points of the compass, "till you come in sight of a very tall giant, who holds the sky on his shoulders. And the giant, if he happens to be in the humor, will tell you exactly where the garden of the Hesperides lies."

"And if the giant happens not to be in the humor," remarked Hercules, balancing his club on the tip of his finger, "perhaps I shall find means to persuade him!"

Thanking the Old Man of the Sea, and begging his pardon for having squeezed him so roughly, the hero resumed his journey. He met with a great many strange adventures, which would be well worth your hearing, if I had leisure to narrate them as minutely as they deserve.

It was in this journey, if I mistake not, that he encountered a prodigious giant, who was so wonderfully contrived by nature, that every time he touched the earth, he became ten times as strong as ever he had been before. His name was Antæus. You may see, plainly enough, that it was a very difficult business to fight with such a fellow; for, as often as he got a knock-down blow, up he started again, stronger, fiercer, and abler to use his weapons, than if his enemy had let him alone. Thus, the harder Hercules pounded the giant with his club, the further he seemed from winning the victory. I have sometimes argued with such people, but never fought with one. The only way in which Hercules found it possible to finish the battle, was by lifting Antæus off his feet into the air, and squeezing, and squeezing, and squeezing him, until, finally, the strength was quite squeezed out of his enormous body.

When this affair was finished, Hercules continued his travels, and went to the land of Egypt, where he was taken prisoner, and would have been put to death, if he had not slain the king of the country, and made his escape. Passing through the deserts of Africa, and going as fast as he could, he arrived at last on the shore of the great ocean. And here, unless he could walk on the crests of the billows, it seemed as if his journey must needs be at an end.

Nothing was before him, save the foaming, dashing, measureless ocean. But, suddenly, as he looked towards the horizon, he saw something, a great way off, which he had not seen the moment before. It gleamed very brightly, almost as you may have beheld the round, golden disk of the sun, when it rises or sets over the edge of the world. It evidently drew nearer; for, at every instant, this wonderful object became larger and more lustrous. At length, it had come so nigh that Hercules discovered it to be an immense cup or bowl, made either of gold or burnished brass. How it had got afloat upon the sea is more than I can tell you. There it was, at all events, rolling on the tumultuous billows, which tossed it up and down, and heaved their foamy tops against its sides, but without ever throwing their spray over the brim.

"I have seen many giants, in my time," thought Hercules, "but never one that would need to drink his wine out of a cup like this!"

And, true enough, what a cup it must have been! It was as large—as large—but, in short, I am afraid to say how immeasurably large it was. To speak within bounds, it was ten times larger than a great mill-wheel; and, all of metal as it was, it floated over the heaving surges more lightly than an acorn-cup adown the brook. The waves tumbled it onward, until it grazed against the shore, within a short distance of the spot where Hercules was standing.

As soon as this happened, he knew what was to be done; for he had not gone through so many remarkable adventures without learning pretty well how to conduct himself, whenever anything came to pass a little out of the common rule. It was just as clear as daylight that this marvellous cup had been set adrift by some unseen power, and guided hitherward, in order to carry Hercules across the sea, on his way to the garden of the Hesperides. Accordingly, without a moment's delay, he clambered over the brim, and slid down on the inside, where, spreading out his lion's skin, he proceeded to take a little repose. He had scarcely rested, until now, since he bade farewell to the damsels on the margin of the river. The waves dashed, with a pleasant and ringing sound, against the circumference of the hollow cup; it rocked lightly to and fro, and the motion was so soothing that it speedily rocked Hercules into an agreeable slumber.

His nap had probably lasted a good while, when the cup chanced to graze against a rock, and, in consequence, immediately resounded and reverberated through its golden or brazen substance, a hundred times as loudly as ever you heard a church-bell. The noise awoke Hercules, who instantly started up and gazed around him, wondering whereabouts he was. He was not long in discovering that the cup had floated across a great part of the sea, and was approaching the shore of what seemed to be an island. And, on that island, what do you think he saw?

No; you will never guess it, not if you were to try fifty thousand times! It positively appears to me that this was the most marvellous spectacle that had ever been seen by Hercules, in the whole course of his wonderful travels and adventures. It was a greater marvel than the hydra with nine heads, which kept growing twice as fast as they were cut off; greater than the six-legged man-monster; greater than Antæus; greater than anything that was ever beheld by anybody, before or since the days of Hercules, or than anything that remains to be beheld, by travellers in all time to come. It was a giant!

But such an intolerably big giant. A giant as tall as a mountain; so vast a giant, that the clouds rested about his midst, like a girdle, and hung like a hoary beard from his chin, and flitted before his huge eyes, so that he could neither see Hercules nor the golden cup in which he was voyaging. And, most wonderful of all, the giant held up his great hands and appeared to support the sky, which, so far as Hercules could discern through the clouds, was resting upon his head! This does really seem almost too much to believe.

Meanwhile, the bright cup continued to float onward, and finally touch the strand. Just then a breeze wafted away the clouds from before the giant's visage, and Hercules beheld it, with all its enormous features; eyes each of them as big as yonder lake, a nose a mile long, and a mouth of the same width. It was a countenance terrible from its enormity of size, but disconsolate and weary, even as you may see the faces of many people, nowadays, who are compelled to sustain burdens above their strength. What the sky was to the giant, such are the cares of earth to those who let themselves be weighed down by them. And whenever men undertake what is beyond the just measure of their abilities, they encounter precisely such a doom as had befallen this poor giant.

Poor fellow! He had evidently stood there a long while. An ancient forest had been growing and decaying around his feet; and oak-trees, of six or seven centuries old, had sprung from the acorn, and forced themselves between his toes.

The giant now looked down from the far height of his great eyes, and, perceiving Hercules, roared out, in a voice that resembled thunder, proceeding out of the cloud that had just flitted away from his face.

"Who are you, down at my feet there? And whence do you come, in that little cup?"

"I am Hercules!" thundered back the hero, in a voice pretty nearly or quite as loud as the giant's own. "And I am seeking for the garden of the Hesperides!"

"Ho! ho! ho!" roared the giant, in a fit of immense laughter. "That is a wise adventure truly!"

"And why not?" cried Hercules, getting a little angry at the giant's mirth. "Do you think I am afraid of the dragon with a hundred heads!"

Just at this time, while they were talking together, some black clouds gathered about the giant's middle, and burst into a tremendous storm of thunder and lightning, causing such a pother that Hercules found it impossible to distinguish a word. Only the giant's immeasurable legs were to be seen, standing up into the obscurity of the tempest; and, now and then, a momentary glimpse of his whole figure, mantled in a volume of mist. He seemed to be speaking, most of the time; but his big, deep, rough voice chimed in with the reverberations of the thunder-claps, and rolled away over the hills, like them. Thus, by talking out of season, the foolish giant expended an incalculable quantity of breath, to no purpose; for the thunder spoke quite as intelligibly as he.

At last, the storm swept over, as suddenly as it had come. And there again was the clear sky, and the weary giant holding it up, and the pleasant sunshine beaming over his vast height, and illuminating it against the background of the sullen thunder-clouds. So far above the shower had been his head, that not a hair of it was moistened by the rain-drops!

When the giant could see Hercules still standing on the sea-shore, he roared out to him anew.

"I am Atlas, the mightiest giant in the world! And I hold the sky upon my head!"

"So I see," answered Hercules. "But, can you show me the way to the garden of the Hesperides?"

"What do you want there?" asked the giant.

"I want three of the golden apples," shouted Hercules, "for my cousin, the king."

"There is nobody but myself," quoth the giant, "that can go to the garden of the Hesperides, and gather the golden apples. If it were not for this little business of holding up the sky, I would make half a dozen steps across the sea, and get them for you."

"You are very kind," replied Hercules. "And cannot you rest the sky upon a mountain?"

"None of them are quite high enough," said Atlas, shaking his head. "But, if you were to take your stand on the summit of that nearest one, your head would be pretty nearly on a level with mine. You seem to be a fellow of some strength. What if you should take my burden on your shoulders, while I do your errand for you?"

Hercules, as you must be careful to remember, was a remarkably strong man; and though it certainly requires a great deal of muscular power to uphold the sky, yet, if any mortal could be supposed capable of such an exploit, he was the one. Nevertheless, it seemed so difficult an undertaking, that, for the first time in his life, he hesitated.

"Is the sky very heavy?" he inquired.

"Why, not particularly so, at first," answered the giant, shrugging his shoulders. "But it gets to be a little burdensome, after a thousand years!"

"And how long a time," asked the hero, "will it take you to get the golden apples?"

"Oh, that will be done in a few moments," cried Atlas. "I shall take ten or fifteen miles at a stride, and be at the garden and back again before your shoulders begin to ache."

"Well, then," answered Hercules, "I will climb

the mountain behind you there, and relieve you of your burden."

The truth is, Hercules had a kind heart of his own, and considered that he should be doing the giant a favor, by allowing him this opportunity for a ramble. And, besides, he thought that it would be still more for his own glory, if he could boast of upholding the sky, than merely to do so ordinary a thing as to conquer a dragon with a hundred heads. Accordingly, without more words, the sky was shifted from the shoulders of Atlas, and placed upon those of Hercules.

When this was safely accomplished, the first thing that the giant did was to stretch himself; and you may imagine what a prodigious spectacle he was then. Next, he slowly lifted one of his feet out of the forest that had grown up around it; then, the other. Then, all at once, he began to caper, and leap, and dance, for joy at his freedom; flinging himself nobody knows how high into the air, and floundering down again with a shock that made the earth tremble. Then he laughed—Ho! ho! ho! —with a thunderous roar that was echoed from the mountains, far and near, as if they and the giant had been so many rejoicing brothers. When his joy had a little subsided, he stepped into the sea; ten miles at the first stride, which brought him mid-leg deep; and ten miles at the second, when the water came just above his knees; and ten miles more at the third, by which he was immersed nearly to his waist. This was the greatest depth of the sea.

Hercules watched the giant, as he still went on-ward; for it was really a wonderful sight, this im-

mense human form, more than thirty miles off, half
hidden in the ocean, but with his upper half as tall,
and misty, and blue, as a distant mountain. At
last the gigantic shape faded entirely out of view.
And now Hercules began to consider what he
should do, in case Atlas should be drowned in the
sea, or if he were to be stung to death by the dragon
with the hundred heads, which guarded the golden
apples of the Hesperides. If any such misfortune
were to happen, how could he ever get rid of the
sky? And, by the by, its weight began already to
be a little irksome to his head and shoulders.

"I really pity the poor giant," thought Hercules.
"If it wearies me so much in ten minutes, how must
it have wearied him in a thousand years!"

O my sweet little people, you have no idea what
a weight there was in that same blue sky, which
looks so soft and aerial above our heads! And
there, too, was the bluster of the wind, and the
chill and watery clouds, and the blazing sun, all
taking their turns to make Hercules uncomfort-
able! He began to be afraid that the giant would
never come back. He gazed wistfully at the
world beneath him, and acknowledged to himself
that it was a far happier kind of life to be a shepherd at the foot of a mountain, than to stand on
its dizzy summit, and bear up the firmament with
his might and main. For, of course, as you will
easily understand, Hercules had an immense re-
sponsibility on his mind, as well as a weight on his
head and shoulders. Why, if he did not stand perfectly still, and keep the sky immovable, the sun
would perhaps be put ajar! Or, after nightfall, a

great many of the stars might be loosened from their places, and shower down, like fiery rain, upon the people's heads! And how ashamed would the hero be, if, owing to his unsteadiness beneath its weight, the sky should crack, and show a great fissure quite across it!

I know not how long it was before, to his unspeakable joy, he beheld the huge shape of the giant, like a cloud, on the far-off edge of the sea. At his nearer approach, Atlas held up his hand, in which Hercules could perceive three magnificent golden apples, as big as pumpkins, all hanging from one branch.

"I am glad to see you again," shouted Hercules, when the giant was within hearing. "So you have got the golden apples?"

"Certainly, certainly," answered Atlas; "and very fair apples they are. I took the finest that grew on the tree, I assure you. Ah! it is a beautiful spot, that garden of the Hesperides. Yes; and the dragon with a hundred heads is a sight worth any man's seeing. After all, you had better have gone for the apples yourself."

"No matter," replied Hercules. "You have had a pleasant ramble, and have done the business as well as I could. I heartily thank you for your trouble. And now, as I have a long way to go, and am rather in haste,—and as the king, my cousin, is anxious to receive the golden apples,— will you be kind enough to take the sky off my shoulders again?"

"Why, as to that," said the giant, chucking the golden apples into the air twenty miles high, or

thereabouts and catching them as they came down,
—"as to that, my good friend, I consider you a
little unreasonable. Cannot I carry the golden
apples to the king, your cousin, much quicker than
you could? As his majesty is in such a hurry to
get them, I promise you to take my longest strides.
And besides, I have no fancy for burdening myself
with the sky, just now."

Here Hercules grew impatient, and gave a great
shrug of his shoulders. It being now twilight, you
might have seen two or three stars tumble out of
their places. Everybody on earth looked upward
in affright, thinking that the sky might be going to
fall next.

"Oh, that will never do!" cried Giant Atlas, with
a great roar of laughter. "I have not let fall so
many stars within the last five centuries. By the
time you have stood there as long as I did, you will
begin to learn patience!"

"What!" shouted Hercules, very wrathfully, "do
you intend to make me bear this burden forever?"

"We will see about that, one of these days,"
answered the giant. "At all events, you ought
not to complain, if you have to bear it the next
hundred years, or perhaps the next thousand. I
bore it a good while longer, in spite of the back-
ache. Well, then, after a thousand years, if I
happen to feel in the mood, we may possibly shift
about again. You are certainly a very strong man,
and can never have a better opportunity to prove it.
Posterity will talk of you, I warrant it!"

"Pish! a fig for its talk!" cried Hercules, with
another hitch of his shoulders. "Just take the

sky upon your head one instant, will you? I want to make a cushion of my lion's skin, for the weight to rest upon. It really chafes me, and will cause unnecessary inconvenience in so many centuries as I am to stand here."

"That's no more than fair, and I'll do it!" quoth the giant; for he had no unkind feeling towards Hercules, and was merely acting with a too selfish consideration of his own ease. "For just five minutes, then, I'll take back the sky. Only for five minutes, recollect! I have no idea of spending another thousand years as I spent the last. Variety is the spice of life, say I."

Ah, the thick-witted old rogue of a giant! He threw down the golden apples, and received back the sky, from the head and shoulders of Hercules, upon his own, where it rightly belonged. And Hercules picked up the three golden apples, that were as big or bigger than pumpkins, and straightway set out on his journey homeward, without paying the slightest heed to the thundering tones of the giant, who bellowed after him to come back. Another forest sprang up around his feet, and grew ancient there; and again might be seen oak-trees, of six or seven centuries old, that had waxed thus aged betwixt his enormous toes.

And there stands the giant to this day; or, at any rate, there stands a mountain as tall as he, and which bears his name; and when the thunder rumbles about its summit, we may imagine it to be the voice of Giant Atlas, bellowing after Hercules!

THE STORY OF CUPID AND PSYCHE

By Thomas Bulfinch

A CERTAIN king and queen had three daughters. The charms of the two elder were more than common, but the beauty of the youngest was so wonderful that the poverty of language is unable to express its due praise. The fame of her beauty was so great that strangers from neighboring countries came in crowds to enjoy the sight, and looked on her with amazement, paying her that homage which is due only to Venus herself. In fact Venus found her altars deserted, while men turned their devotion to this young virgin. As she passed along, the people sang her praises, and strewed her way with chaplets and flowers.

This gave great offense to the real Venus. Shaking her locks with indignation, she exclaimed, "Am I then to be eclipsed in my honors by a mortal girl? She shall not so quietly usurp my honors. I will give her cause to repent of so unlawful a beauty."

Thereupon she calls her winged son Cupid, mischievous enough in his own nature, and rouses and provokes him yet more by her complaints. She points out Psyche to him and says, "My dear son, punish that obstinate beauty; give thy mother a revenge as sweet as her injuries are great; infuse into the bosom of that haughty girl a passion for some low, mean, unworthy being, so that she may reap a mortification as great as her present exultation and triumph."

Cupid prepared to obey the commands of his mother. There are two fountains in Venus's garden, one of sweet waters, the other of bitter. Cupid filled two amber vases, one from each fountain, and suspending them from the top of his quiver, hastened to the chamber of Psyche, whom he found asleep. He shed a few drops from the bitter fountain over her lips, though the sight of her almost moved him to pity; then touched her side with the point of his arrow. At the touch she awoke, and opened eyes upon Cupid (himself invisible), which so startled him that in his confusion he wounded himself with his own arrow. Heedless of his wound, his whole thought now was to repair the mischief he had done, and he poured the balmy drops of joy over all her silken ringlets.

Psyche, henceforth frowned upon by Venus, derived no benefit from all her charms. True, all eyes were cast eagerly upon her, and every mouth spoke her praises; but neither king, royal youth, nor plebeian presented himself to demand her in marriage. Her two elder sisters of moderate charms, had now long been married to two royal princes; but Psyche, in her lonely apartment, deplored her solitude, sick of that beauty which, while it procured abundance of flattery, had failed to awaken love.

Her parents, afraid they had incurred the anger of the gods, consulted the oracle of Apollo, and received this answer: "The virgin is destined for

the bride of no mortal lover. Her future husband
awaits her on the top of the mountain. He is a
monster whom neither gods nor men can resist."

This dreadful decree of the oracle filled all the
people with dismay, and her parents abandoned
themselves to grief. But Psyche said, "Why, my
dear parents, do you now lament me? You should
rather have grieved when the people showered
upon me undeserved honors, and with one voice
called me a Venus. I now perceive that I am a
victim to that name. I submit. Lead me to that
rock to which my unhappy fate has destined me."
Accordingly, all things being prepared, the royal
maid took her place in the procession, which more
resembled a funeral than a nuptial pomp, and with
her parents, amid the lamentations of the people,
ascended the mountain, on the summit of which
they left her alone, and with sorrowful hearts
returned home.

While Psyche stood on the ridge of the mountain, panting with fear and with eyes full of tears,
the gentle Zephyr raised her from the earth and
bore her with an easy motion into a flowery dale.
By degrees her mind became composed, and she
laid herself down on the grassy bank to sleep.
When she awoke refreshed with sleep, she looked
round and beheld near by a pleasant grove of tall
and stately trees. She entered it, and in the midst
discovered a fountain, sending forth clear and
crystal waters, and fast by, a magnificent palace
whose august front impressed the spectator that it
was not the work of mortal hands, but the happy
retreat of some god. Drawn by admiration and

wonder, she approached the building and ventured to enter. Every object she met filled her with pleasure and amazement. Golden pillars supported the vaulted roof, and the walls were enriched with carvings and paintings representing beasts of the chase and rural scenes. Proceeding onward, she perceived that besides the apartments of state there were others filled with all manner of treasures, and beautiful and precious productions of nature and art.

While her eyes were thus occupied, a voice addressed her, though she saw no one, uttering these words: "Sovereign lady, all that you see is yours. We whose voices you hear are your servants and shall obey all your commands with our utmost care and diligence. Retire, therefore, to your chamber and repose on your bed of down, and when you see fit repair to the bath. Supper awaits you in the adjoining alcove when it pleases you to take your seat there."

Psyche gave ear to the admonitions of her vocal attendants, and after repose and the refreshment of the bath, seated herself in the alcove, where a table immediately presented itself, without any visible aid from waiters or servants, and covered with the greatest delicacies of food. Her ears too were feasted with music from invisible performers; of whom one sang, another played on the lute, and all closed in the wonderful harmony of a full chorus.

She had not yet seen her destined husband. He came only in the hours of darkness and fled before the dawn of morning, but his accents were full of love, and inspired a like passion in her. She often begged him to stay and let her behold him, but he would not consent. On the contrary he charged her to make no attempt to see him, for it was his pleasure, for the best of reasons, to keep concealed. "Why should you wish to behold me?" he said; "have you any doubt of my love? have you any wish ungratified? If you saw me, perhaps you would fear me, perhaps adore me, but all I ask of you is to love me. I would rather you would love me as an equal than adore me as a god."

This reasoning somewhat quieted Psyche for a time, and while the novelty lasted she felt quite happy. But at length the thought of her parents, left in ignorance of her fate, and of her sisters, preyed on her mind and made her begin to feel her palace as but a splendid prison. When her husband came one night, she told him her distress, and at last drew from him an unwilling consent that her sisters should be brought to see her.

So, calling Zephyr, she acquainted him with her husband's commands, and he, promptly obedient, soon brought them across the mountain down to their sister's valley. They embraced her and she returned their caresses. "Come," said Psyche, "enter with me my house and refresh yourselves with whatever your sister has to offer." Then taking their hands she led them into her golden palace, and committed them to the care of her numerous train of attendant voices, to refresh them in her baths and at her table, and to show them all her treasures. The view of these celestial delights caused envy to enter their bosoms, at seeing their young sister possessed of such state and splendor, so much exceeding their own.

They asked her numberless questions, among others what sort of a person her husband was. Psyche replied that he was a beautiful youth, who generally spent the daytime in hunting upon the mountains. The sisters, not satisfied with this reply, soon made her confess that she had never seen him. Then they proceeded to fill her mind with dark suspicions. "Call to mind," they said, "the Pythian oracle that declared you destined to marry a direful and tremendous monster. The inhabitants of this valley say that your husband is a terrible and monstrous serpent, who nourishes you for a while with dainties that he may by and by devour you. Take our advice. Provide yourself with a lamp and a sharp knife; put them in concealment that your husband may not discover them, and when he is sound asleep, slip out of bed, bring forth your lamp, and see for yourself whether what they say is true or not. If it is, hesitate not to cut off the monster's head, and thereby recover your liberty."

Psyche resisted these persuasions as well as she could, but they did not fail to have their effect on her mind, and when her sisters were gone, their words and her own curiosity were too strong for her to resist. So she prepared her lamp and a sharp knife, and hid them out of sight of her husband. When he had fallen asleep, she silently rose and uncovering her lamp beheld not a hideous monster, but the most beautiful and charming of the gods, with golden ringlets wandering over his snowy neck and crimson cheek, with two wings on his shoulders, whiter than snow, and with shining feathers like the tender blossoms of spring. As she leaned over to have a nearer view of his face a drop of burning oil fell on the shoulder of the god, startled with which he opened his eyes and fixed them full upon her; then, without saying one word, he spread his white wings and flew out of the window. Psyche, in vain endeavoring to follow him, fell from the window to the ground. Cupid, beholding her as she lay in the dust, stopped his flight for an instant and said, "O foolish Psyche, is it thus you repay my love? After having disobeyed my mother's commands and made you my wife, will you think me a monster and cut off my head? But go; return to your sisters, whose advice you seem to think preferable to mine. I inflict no other punishment on you than to leave you forever. Love cannot dwell with suspicion." So saying, he fled away, leaving poor Psyche prostrate on the ground, filling the place with mournful lamentations.

When she had recovered some degree of composure she looked around her, but the palace and gardens had vanished, and she found herself in the open field not far from the city where her sisters dwelt. She repaired thither and told them the story of her misfortunes, at which, pretending to grieve, those spiteful creatures inwardly rejoiced. "For now," said they, "he will perhaps choose one of us." With this idea, without saying a word of her intentions, each of them rose early the next morning and ascended the mountain, and having reached the top, called upon Zephyr to recive her and bear her to his lord; then leaping up, and not being sustained by Zephyr, fell down the precipice and was dashed to pieces.

Psyche meanwhile wandered day and night, without food or repose, in search of her husband. Casting her eyes on a lofty mountain having on its brow a magnificent temple, she sighed and said to herself, "Perhaps my lord inhabits there," and directed her steps thither.

She had no sooner entered than she saw heaps of corn, some in loose ears and some in sheaves, with mingled ears of barley. Scattered about, lay sickles and rakes, and all the instruments of harvest, without order, as if thrown carelessly out of the weary reapers' hands in the sultry hours of the day.

This unseemly confusion Psyche put an end to, by separating and sorting everything to its proper place and kind, believing that she ought neglect none of the gods, but endeavor by her piety to engage them all in her behalf. The holy Ceres, whose temple it was, finding her so religiously employed, thus spoke to her: "O Psyche, truly worthy of our pity, though I cannot shield you from the frowns of Venus, yet I can teach you how best to allay her displeasure. Go, then, and voluntarily surrender yourself to your lady and sovereign, and try by modesty and submission to win her forgiveness, and perhaps her favor will restore you the husband you have lost."

Psyche obeyed the commands of Ceres and took her way to the temple of Venus, endeavoring to fortify her mind and ruminating on what she should say and how best propitiate the angry goddess, feeling that the issue was doubtful and perhaps fatal.

Venus received her with angry countenance. "Most undutiful and faithless of servants," said she, "do you at last remember that you really have a mistress? Or have you rather come to see your sick husband, yet laid up of the wound given him by his loving wife? You are so ill-favored and disagreeable that the only way you can merit your lover must be by dint of industry and diligence. I will make trial of your housewifery." Then she ordered Psyche to be led to the storehouse of her temple, where was laid up a great quantity of wheat, barley, millet, vetches, beans, and lentils prepared for food for her pigeons, and said, "Take and separate all these grains, putting all of the same kind in a parcel by themselves, and see that you get it done before evening." Then Venus departed and left her to her task.

But Psyche, in a perfect consternation at the enormous work, sat stupid and silent, without moving a finger to the inextricable heap.

While she sat despairing, Cupid stirred up the little ant, a native of the fields, to take compassion on her. The leader of the ant hill, followed by whole hosts of his six-legged subjects, approached the heap, and with the utmost diligence taking grain by grain, they separated the pile, sorting each kind to its parcel; and when it was all done, they vanished out of sight in a moment.

Venus at the approach of twilight returned from the banquet of the gods, breathing odors and crowned with roses. Seeing the task done, she exclaimed, "This is no work of yours, wicked one, but his, whom to your own and his misfortune you have enticed." So saying, she threw her a piece of black bread for her supper and went away.

Next morning Venus ordered Psyche to be called and said to her, "Behold yonder grove which stretches along the margin of the water. There you will find sheep feeding without a shepherd, with golden-shining fleeces on their backs. Go fetch me a sample of that precious wool gathered from every one of their fleeces."

Psyche obediently went to the riverside, prepared to do her best to execute the command. But the river god inspired the reeds with harmonious murmurs, which seemed to say, "O maiden, severely tried, tempt not the dangerous flood, nor venture among the formidable rams on the other side, for as long as they are under the influence of the rising sun, they burn with a cruel rage to destroy mortals with their sharp horns or rude teeth. But when the noontide sun has driven the cattle to the shade, and the serene spirit of the flood has lulled them to rest, you may then cross in safety, and you will find the woolly gold sticking to the bushes and the trunks of the trees."

Thus the compassionate river god gave Psyche instructions how to accomplish her task, and by observing his directions she soon returned to Venus with her arms full of the golden fleece; but she received not the approbation of her implacable mistress, who said, "I know very well that it is by none of your own doings that you have succeeded in this task, and I am not satisfied yet that you have any capacity to make yourself useful. But I have another task for you. Here, take this box and go your way to the infernal shades, and give this box to Proserpine and say, 'My mistress Venus desires you to send her a little of your beauty, for in tending her sick son she has lost some of her own.' Be not too long on your errand, for I must paint myself with it to appear at the circle of the gods and goddesses this evening."

Psyche was now satisfied that her destruction was at hand, being obliged to go with her own feet directly down to Erebus. Wherefore, to make no delay of what was not to be avoided, she goes to the top of a high tower to precipitate herself headlong, thus to descend the shortest way to the shades below. But a voice from the tower said to her, "Why, poor unlucky girl, dost thou design to put an end to thy days in so dreadful a manner? And what cowardice makes thee sink under this last danger who hast been so miraculously supported in all thy former?" Then the voice told her how by a certain cave she might reach the realms of Pluto, and how to avoid all the dangers of the road, to pass by Cerberus, the three-headed dog, and prevail on Charon, the ferryman, to take her across the black river and bring her back again. But the voice added, "When Proserpine has given you the box filled with her beauty, of all things this is chiefly to be observed by you, that you never once open or look into the box nor allow your curiosity to pry into the treasure of the beauty of the goddesses."

Psyche, encouraged by this advice, obeyed it in all things, and taking heed to her ways travelled

safely to the kingdom of Pluto. She was admitted
to the palace of Proserpine, and without accepting
the seat or delicious banquet that was offered her,
but contented with coarse bread for her food, she
delivered her message from Venus. Presently the
box was returned to her, shut and filled with the
precious commodity. Then she returned the way
she came, and glad was she to come out once more
into the light of day.

But having got so far successfully through her
dangerous task, a longing desire seized her to
examine the contents of the box. "What," said
she, "shall I, the carrier of this divine beauty, not
take the least bit to put on my cheeks to appear to
more advantage in the eyes of my beloved husband!" So she carefully opened the box, but found
nothing there of any beauty at all, but an infernal
and truly Stygian sleep, which being thus set free
from its prison, took possession of her, and she
fell down in the midst of the road, without sense
or motion.

But Cupid, being now recovered from his wound,
and not able longer to bear the absence of his
beloved Psyche, slipping through the smallest crack
of the window of his chamber which happened to
be left open, flew to the spot where Psyche lay, and
gathering up the sleep from her body closed it again
in the box, and waked Psyche with a light touch of
one of his arrows. "Again," said he, "hast thou
almost perished by the same curiosity. But now
perform exactly the task imposed on you by my
mother, and I will take care of the rest."

Then Cupid, as swift as lightning penetrating

the heights of heaven, presented himself before
Jupiter with his supplication. Jupiter lent a
favoring ear, and pleaded the cause of the lovers
so earnestly with Venus that he won her consent.
On this he sent Mercury to bring Psyche up to the
heavenly assembly, and when she arrived, handing
her a cup of ambrosia, he said, "Drink this, Psyche,
and be immortal; nor shall Cupid ever break away
from the knot in which he is tied, but these nuptials
shall be perpetual."

HOW PHAËTON DROVE THE SUN

By Thomas Bulfinch

PHAËTON was the son of Apollo and the
nymph Clymene. One day a schoolfellow
laughed at the idea of his being the son of the god,
and Phaëton went in rage and shame and reported
it to his mother. "If," said he, "I am indeed of
heavenly birth, give me, mother, some proof of it,
and establish my claim to the honor." Clymene
stretched forth her hands towards the skies, and
said, "I call to witness the Sun which looks down
upon us, that I have told you the truth. If I
speak falsely, let this be the last time I behold his
light. But it needs not much labor to go and
inquire for yourself; the land whence the Sun rises
lies next to ours. Go and demand of him whether
he will own you as a son." Phaëton heard with
delight. He travelled to India, which lies directly
in the regions of sunrise; and, full of hope and

pride, approached the goal whence his parent
begins his course.

The palace of the Sun stood reared aloft on
columns, glittering with gold and precious stones,
while polished ivory formed the ceilings, and silver
the doors. Upon the walls Vulcan had represented
earth, sea, and skies, with their inhabitants. In the
sea were the nymphs, some sporting in the waves,
some riding on the backs of fishes, while others sat
upon the rocks and dried their sea-green hair.
The earth had its towns and forests and rivers.
Over all was carved the likeness of the glorious
heaven; and on the silver doors the twelve signs of
the zodiac, six on each side.

Clymene's son advanced up the steep ascent, and
entered the halls of his father. He approached the
paternal presence, but stopped at a distance, for
the light was more than he could bear. Phœbus,
arrayed in a purple vesture, sat on a throne, which
glittered as with diamonds. On his right hand and
his left stood the Day, the Month, and the Year,
and, at regular intervals, the Hours. Spring stood
with her head crowned with flowers, and Summer,
with a garland formed of spears of ripened grain,
and Autumn, with his feet stained with grape-
juice, and icy Winter, with his hair stiffened with
hoar frost.

Surrounded by these attendants, the Sun, with
the eye that sees everything, beheld the youth
dazzled with the novelty and splendor of the
scene, and inquired the purpose of his errand.
The youth replied, "O light of the boundless world,
Phœbus, my father,—if you permit me to use that

name,—give me some proof, I beseech you, by which I may be known as yours." He ceased; and his father, laying aside the beams that shone all around his head, bade him approach, and embracing him, said, "My son, you deserve not to be disowned, and I confirm what your mother has told you. To put an end to your doubts, ask what you will, the gift shall be yours. I call to witness that dreadful lake, which I never saw, but which we gods swear by in our most solemn engagements." Phaëton immediately asked to be permitted for one day to drive the chariot of the Sun. The father repented of his promise; thrice and four times he shook his radiant head in warning. "I have spoken rashly," said he; "this request only I would deny. I beg you to withdraw it. It is not a safe boon, nor one, my Phaëton, suited to your youth and strength. Your lot is mortal, and you ask what is beyond a mortal's power. In your ignorance you aspire to do that which not even the gods themselves may do. None but myself may drive the flaming car of day. Not even Jupiter, whose terrible right arm hurls the thunderbolts. The first part of the way is steep, and such as the horses when fresh in the morning can hardly climb; the middle is high up in the heavens, whence I myself can scarcely, without alarm, look down and behold the earth and sea stretched beneath me. The last part of the road descends rapidly, and requires most careful driving. Tethys, who is waiting to receive me, often trembles for me lest I should fall headlong. Add to all this, the heaven is all the time turning round and carrying the stars with it.

PHAETON

I have to be perpetually on my guard lest that movement, which sweeps everything else along, should hurry me also away. Suppose I should lend you the chariot, what would you do? Could you keep your course while the earth was revolving under you? Perhaps you think that there are forests and cities, the abodes of gods, and palaces and temples on the way. On the contrary, the road is through the midst of frightful monsters. You pass by the horns of the Bull, in front of the Archer, and near the Lion's jaws, and where the Scorpion stretches its arms in one direction and the Crab in another. Nor will you find it easy to guide those horses, with their breasts full of fire that they breathe forth from their mouths and nostrils. I can scarcely govern them myself, when they are unruly and resist the reins. Beware, my son, lest I be the donor of a fatal gift, recall your request while yet you may. Do you ask me for a proof that you are sprung from my blood? I give you a proof in my fears for you. Look at my face—I would that you could look into my heart, you would there see all a father's anxiety. Finally," he continued, "look round the world and choose whatever you will of what earth or sea contains most precious—ask it and fear no refusal. This only I pray you not to urge. It is not honor, but destruction you seek. Why do you hang round my neck and still entreat me? You shall have it if you persist,—the oath is sworn and must be kept,—but I beg you to choose more wisely."

He ended; but the youth rejected all admonition and held to his demand. So, having resisted as long as he could, Phœbus at last led the way to where stood the lofty chariot.

It was of gold, the gift of Vulcan; the axle was of gold, the pole and wheels of gold, the spokes of silver. Along the seat were rows of chrysolites and diamonds which reflected the brightness of the sun. While the daring youth gazed in admiration, the early Dawn threw open the purple doors of the east, and showed the pathway strewn with roses. The stars withdrew, marshalled by the Day-star, which last of all retired also. The father, when he saw the earth beginning to glow, and the Moon preparing to retire, ordered the Hours to harness up the horses. They obeyed, and led forth the steeds from the lofty stalls, and attached the reins. Then the father bathed the face of his son with a powerful ointment, and made him capable of enduring the brightness of the flame. He set the rays on his head, and, with a foreboding sigh, said, "If, my son, you will in this at least heed my advice, spare the whip and hold tight the reins. They go fast enough of their own accord; the labor is to hold them in. You are not to take the straight road directly between the five circles, but turn off to the left. Keep within the limit of the middle zone, and avoid the northern and the southern alike. You will see the marks of the wheels, and they will serve to guide you. And, that the skies and the earth may each receive their due share of heat, go not too high, or you will burn the heavenly dwellings, nor too low, or you will set the earth on fire; the middle course is safest and best. And now I leave you to your chance, which I hope will plan better for you than you have done for yourself. Night is passing out of the western gates and we can delay no longer. Take the reins; but if at last your heart fails you, and you will benefit by my advice, stay where you are in safety, and suffer me to light and warm the earth." The agile youth sprang into the chariot, stood erect, and grasped the reins with delight, pouring out thanks to his reluctant parent.

Meanwhile the horses fill the air with their snortings and fiery breath, and stamp the ground impatiently. Now the bars are let down, and the boundless plain of the universe lies open before them. They dart forward and cleave the opposing clouds, and outrun the morning breezes which started from the same eastern goal. The steeds soon perceived that the load they drew was lighter than usual; and as a ship without ballast is tossed hither and thither on the sea, so the chariot, without its accustomed weight, was dashed about as if empty. They rush headlong and leave the travelled road. Phaëton is alarmed, and knows not how to guide them; nor, if he knew, has he the power. Then, for the first time, the Great and Little Bear were scorched with heat, and would fain, if it were possible, have plunged into the water; and the Serpent which lies coiled up round the north pole, torpid and harmless, grew warm, and with warmth felt its rage revive.

When Phaëton looked down upon the earth, now spreading in vast extent beneath him, he grew pale and his knees shook with terror. In spite of the glare all around him, the sight of his eyes

grew dim. He wished he had never touched his
father's horses, never learned his parentage,
never prevailed in his request. He is borne along
like a vessel that flies before a tempest, when the
pilot can do no more. What shall he do? Much
of the heavenly road is left behind, but more
remains before. He turns his eyes from one direction to the other; now to the goal whence he
began his course, now to the realms of sunset which
he is not destined to reach. He loses his self-
command, and knows not what to do,—whether to
draw tight the reins or throw them loose; he forgets
the names of the horses. He sees with terror the
monstrous forms scattered over the surface of
heaven. Here the Scorpion extended his two great
arms, with his tail and crooked claws stretching
over two signs of the zodiac. When the boy beheld
him, reeking with poison and menacing with his
fangs, his courage failed, and the reins fell from his
hands. The horses, when they felt them loose on
their backs, dashed headlong, and unrestrained
went off into unknown regions of the sky, in
among the stars, hurling the chariot over pathless
places, now up in high heaven, now down almost
to the earth. The Moon saw with astonishment her
brother's chariot running beneath her own. The
clouds begin to smoke, and the mountain tops take
fire; the fields are parched with heat, the plants
wither, the trees with their leafy branches burn,
the harvest is ablaze! But these are small things.
Great cities perished, with their walls and towers;
whole nations with their people were consumed to
ashes! Then Phaëton beheld the world on fire,

and felt the heat intolerable. The air he breathed
was like the air of a furnace and full of burning
ashes, and the smoke was of a pitchy darkness. He
dashed forward he knew not whither. Then, it is
believed, the people of Æthiopia became black by
the blood being forced so suddenly to the surface,
and the Libyan desert was dried up to the condition
in which it remains to this day. The Nymphs of
the fountains, with dishevelled hair, mourned their
waters, nor were the rivers safe beneath their banks.
The Nile fled away and hid his head in the desert,
and there it still remains concealed. Where he
used to discharge his waters through seven mouths
into the sea, there seven dry channels alone remained. The earth cracked open, and through the
chinks light broke into Tartarus, and frightened
the King of Shadows and his queen. The sea
shrank up. Where before was water, it became a
dry plain; and the mountains that lie beneath the
waves lifted up their heads and became islands.
The fishes sought the lowest depths, and the
dolphins no longer ventured as usual to sport on
the surface. Thrice Neptune essayed to raise his
head above the surface, and thrice was driven back
by the heat. Earth, surrounded as she was by
waters, yet with head and shoulders bare, screening
her face with her hand, looked up to heaven, and
with a husky voice called on Jupiter:

"O ruler of the gods, if I have deserved this
treatment, and it is your will that I perish with fire,
why withhold your thunderbolts? Let me at least
fall by your hand. Is this the reward of my
fertility, of my obedient service? Is it for this that

PHAETON

I have supplied herbage for cattle, and fruits for men, and frankincense for your altars? But if I am unworthy of regard, what has my brother Ocean done to deserve such a fate? If neither of us can excite your pity, think, I pray you, of your own heaven, and behold how both the poles are smoking which sustain your palace, which must fall if they be destroyed. Atlas faints, and scarce holds up his burden. If sea, earth, and heaven perish, we fall into ancient Chaos. Save what yet remains to us from the devouring flame. Oh, take thought for our deliverance in this awful moment!".

Thus spoke Earth, and overcome with heat and thirst, could say no more. Then Jupiter omnipotent, calling to witness all the gods, including him who had lent the chariot, and showing them that all was lost unless some speedy remedy were applied, mounted the lofty tower from whence he diffuses clouds over the earth, and hurls the forked lightnings. But at that time not a cloud was to be found to interpose for a screen to earth, nor was a shower remaining unexhausted. He thundered, and brandishing a lightning bolt in his right hand launched it against the charioteer, and struck him at the same moment from his seat and from existence! Phaëton, with his hair on fire, fell headlong, like a shooting star which marks the heavens with its brightness as it falls, and Eridanus, the great river, received him and cooled his burning frame.

BAUCIS AND PHILEMON, WHO WERE CHANGED INTO TWO TREES

By Thomas Bulfinch

ON a certain hill in Phrygia stands a linden tree and an oak, enclosed by a low wall. Not far from the spot is a marsh, formerly good habitable land, but now indented with pools, the resort of fen-birds and cormorants. Once on a time Jupiter, in human shape, visited this country, and with him his son Mercury, without his wings.

They presented themselves, as weary travellers, at many a door, seeking rest and shelter, but found all closed, for it was late, and the inhospitable inhabitants would not rouse themselves to open for their reception.

At last a humble mansion received them, a small thatched cottage, where Baucis, a pious old dame, and her husband Philemon had grown old together. Not ashamed of their poverty, they made it endurable by moderate desires and kind dispositions. One need not look there for master or for servant; they two were the whole household, master and servant alike.

When the two heavenly guests crossed the humble threshold, and bowed their heads to pass under the low door, the old man placed a seat, on which Baucis, bustling and attentive, spread a cloth, and begged them to sit down. Then she raked out the coals from the ashes and kindled up a fire, fed it with leaves and dry bark, and with her scanty breath blew it into a flame. She brought out of a corner split sticks and dry branches, broke them up, and placed them under the small kettle. Her husband collected some pot-herbs in the garden and she shred them from the stalks and prepared them for the pot. He reached down with a forked stick a flitch of bacon hanging in the chimney, cut a small piece, and put it in the pot to boil with the herbs, setting away the rest for another time. A beechen bowl was filled with warm water, that their guests might wash. While all was doing, they beguiled the time with conversation.

On the bench designed for the guests was laid a cushion stuffed with sea-weed; and a cloth, only produced on great occasions, but ancient and coarse enough, was spread over that. The old lady, with her apron on, with trembling hand set the table. One leg was shorter than the rest, but a piece of slate put under restored the level. When fixed, she rubbed the table down with some sweet-smelling herbs. Upon it she set some olives, some berries preserved in vinegar, and added radishes and cheese, with eggs lightly cooked in the ashes. All were served in earthen dishes, and an earthenware pitcher, with wooden cups, stood beside them. When all was ready, the stew, smoking hot, was set on the table. Some wine, not of the oldest, was added; and for dessert, apples and wild honey; and over and above all, friendly faces, and simple but hearty welcome.

Now while the repast proceeded, the old folks were astonished to see that the wine, as fast as it was poured out, renewed itself in the pitcher, of its own accord.

Struck with terror, Baucis and Philemon recognized their heavenly guests, fell on their knees, and with clasped hands implored forgiveness for their poor entertainment.

There was an old goose, which they kept as the guardian of their humble cottage; and they bethought them to make this a sacrifice in honor of their guests. But the goose, too nimble, with the aid of feet and wings, for the old folks, eluded their pursuit, and at last took shelter between the gods themselves.

They forbade it to be slain; and spoke in these words: "We are gods. This inhospitable village shall pay the penalty of its impiety; you alone shall go free from the chastisement. Quit your house, and come with us to the top of yonder hill."

They hastened to obey, and, staff in hand, labored up the steep ascent. They had reached to within an arrow's flight of the top, when turning their eyes below, they beheld all the country sunk in a lake, only their own house left standing.

While they gazed with wonder at the sight, and lamented the fate of their neighbors, that old house of theirs was changed into a *temple*. Columns took the place of the corner posts, the thatch grew yellow and appeared a gilded roof, the floors became marble, the doors were enriched with carving and ornaments of gold.

Then spoke Jupiter in benignant accents: "Excellent old man, and woman worthy of such a husband, speak, tell us your wishes; what favor have you to ask of us?"

Philemon took counsel with Baucis a few moments; then declared to the gods their united wish. "We ask to be priests and guardians of this your temple; and since here we have passed our lives in love and concord, we wish that one and the same hour may take us both from life, that I may not live to see her grave, nor be laid in my own by her." Their prayer was granted. They were the keepers of the temple as long as they lived.

When grown very old, as they stood one day before the steps of the sacred edifice, and were telling the story of the place, Baucis saw Philemon begin to put forth leaves, and old Philemon saw Baucis changing in like manner. And now a leafy crown had grown over their heads while exchanging parting words, as long as they could speak. "Farewell, dear spouse," they said, together, and at the same moment the bark closed over their mouths. The Tyanean shepherd still shows the two trees, standing side by side, made out of the two good old people.

THE PARADISE OF CHILDREN

By Nathaniel Hawthorne

LONG, long ago, when this old world was in its tender infancy, there was a child, named Epimetheus, who never had either father or mother; and, that he might not be lonely, another child, fatherless and motherless like himself, was sent from a far country to live with him, and be his playfellow and helpmate. Her name was Pandora.

The first thing that Pandora saw when she entered the cottage where Epimetheus dwelt was a great box. And almost the first question which she put to him after crossing the threshold was this: "Epimetheus, what have you in that box?"

"My dear little Pandora," answered Epimetheus, "that is a secret, and you must be kind enough not to ask any questions about it. The box was left here to be kept safely, and I do not myself know what it contains."

"But who gave it to you?" asked Pandora. "And where did it come from?"

"That is a secret, too," replied Epimetheus.

"How provoking!" exclaimed Pandora, pouting her lip. "I wish the great ugly box were out of the way!"

"Oh, come, don't think of it any more," cried Epimetheus. "Let us run out of doors and have some nice play with the other children."

It is thousands of years since Epimetheus and Pandora were alive; and the world nowadays is a very different sort of thing from what it was in their time. Then everybody was a child. There needed no fathers and mothers to take care of the children, because there was no danger nor trouble of any kind, and no clothes to be mended, and there was always plenty to eat and drink. Whenever a child wanted his dinner he found it growing on a tree; and, if he looked at the tree in the morning, he could see the expanding blossom of that night's supper; or, at eventide, he saw the tender bud of to-morrow's breakfast. It was a very pleasant life indeed. No labor to be done, no tasks to be studied; nothing but sports and dances, and sweet voices of children talking, or carolling like birds, or gushing out in merry laughter throughout the livelong day.

What was most wonderful of all, the children never quarrelled among themselves; neither had they any crying fits; nor, since time first began, had a single one of these little mortals ever gone apart into a corner, and sulked. Oh, what a good time was that to be alive in? The truth is, those ugly little winged monsters, called Troubles, which are now almost as numerous as mosquitoes, had never yet been seen on the earth. It is probable that the very greatest disquietude which a child had ever experienced was Pandora's vexation at not being able to discover the secret of the mysterious box.

This was at first only the faint shadow of a Trouble; but, every day, it grew more and more substantial, until, before a great while, the cottage of Epimetheus and Pandora was less sunshiny than those of the other children.

"Whence can the box have come?" Pandora continually kept saying to herself and to Epimetheus. "And what in the world can be inside of it?"

"Always talking about this box!" said Epimetheus, at last; for he had grown extremely tired of the subject. "I wish, dear Pandora, you would try to talk of something else. Come, let us go and gather some ripe figs, and eat them under the trees, for our supper. And I know a vine that has the sweetest and juiciest grapes you ever tasted."

"Always talking about grapes and figs!" cried Pandora, pettishly.

"Well, then," said Epimetheus, who was a very good-tempered child, like a multitude of children in those days, "let us run out and have a merry time with our playmates."

"I am tired of merry times, and don't care if I never have any more!" answered our pettish little Pandora. "And, besides, I never do have any. This ugly box! I am so taken up with thinking about it all the time. I insist upon your telling me what is inside of it."

"As I have already said, fifty times over, I do not know!" replied Epimetheus, getting a little vexed. "How, then, can I tell you what is inside?"

"You might open it," said Pandora, looking sideways at Epimetheus, "and then we could see for ourselves."

"Pandora, what are you thinking of?" exclaimed Epimetheus.

And his face expressed so much horror at the idea of looking into a box, which had been confided to him on the condition of his never opening it, that Pandora thought it best not to suggest it any more. Still, however, she could not help thinking and talking about the box. "At least," said she, "you can tell me how it came here."

"It was left at the door," replied Epimetheus, "just before you came, by a person who looked very smiling and intelligent, and who could hardly forbear laughing as he put it down. He was

dressed in an odd kind of a cloak, and had on a cap
that seemed to be made partly of feathers, so that
it looked almost as if it had wings."

"What sort of a staff had he?" asked Pandora.

"Oh, the most curious staff you ever saw!" cried
Epimetheus. "It was like two serpents twisting
around a stick, and was carved so naturally that I,
at first, thought the serpents were alive."

"I know him," said Pandora, thoughtfully.
"Nobody else has such a staff. It was Quicksilver;[1] and he brought me hither, as well as the
box. No doubt he intended it for me; and, most
probably, it contains pretty dresses for me to wear,
or toys for you and me to play with, or something
very nice for us both to eat!"

"Perhaps so," answered Epimetheus, turning
away. "But until Quicksilver comes back and
tells us so, we have neither of us any right to lift
the lid of the box."

"What a dull boy he is!" muttered Pandora, as
Epimetheus left the cottage. "I do wish he had a
little more enterprise!"

For the first time since her arrival, Epimetheus
had gone out without asking Pandora to accompany
him. He went to gather figs and grapes by himself, or to seek whatever amusement he could find,
in other society than his little playfellow's. He
was tired to death of hearing about the box, and
heartily wished that Quicksilver, or whatever was
the messenger's name, had left it at some other
child's door, where Pandora would never have set
eyes on it. So perseveringly as she did babble

[1] Hawthorne's name for Mercury

about this one thing! The box, the box, and nothing but the box! It seemed as if the box were bewitched, and as if the cottage were not big enough
to hold it, without Pandora's continually stumbling
over it, and making Epimetheus stumble over it
likewise, and bruising all four of their shins.

Well, it was really hard that poor Epimetheus
should have a box in his ears from morning till
night; especially as the little people of the earth
were so unaccustomed to vexations, in those happy
days, that they knew not how to deal with them.
Thus, a small vexation made as much disturbance
then, as a far bigger one would in our own times.

After Epimetheus was gone, Pandora stood
gazing at the box. She had called it ugly, above
a hundred times; but, in spite of all that she had
said against it, it was positively a very handsome
article of furniture, and would have been quite an
ornament to any room in which it should be placed.
It was made of a beautiful kind of wood, with dark
and rich veins spreading over its surface, which
was so highly polished that little Pandora could
see her face in it. As the child had no other looking-glass, it is odd that she did not value the box,
merely on this account.

The edges and corners of the box were carved
with most wonderful skill. Around the margin
there were figures of graceful men and women, and
the prettiest children ever seen, reclining or sporting amid a profusion of flowers and foliage; and
these various objects were so exquisitely represented, and were wrought together in such harmony, that flowers, foliage, and human beings

seemed to combine into a wreath of mingled beauty. But here and there, peeping forth from behind the carved foliage, Pandora once or twice fancied that she saw a face not so lovely, or something or other that was disagreeable, and which stole the beauty out of all the rest. Nevertheless on looking more closely, and touching the spot with her finger, she could discover nothing of the kind. Some face, that was really beautiful, had been made to look ugly by her catching a sideway glimpse at it.

The most beautiful face of all was done in what is called high relief, in the centre of the lid. There was nothing else, save the dark, smooth richness of the polished wood, and this one face in the centre with a garland of flowers about its brow. Pandora had looked at this face a great many times, and imagined that the mouth could smile if it liked, or be grave when it chose, the same as any living mouth. The features, indeed, all wore a very lively and rather mischievous expression, which looked almost as if it needs must burst out of the carved lips, and utter itself in words.

Had the mouth spoken, it would probably have been something like this: "Do not be afraid, Pandora! What harm can there be in opening the box? Never mind that poor, simple Epimetheus! You are wiser than he, and have ten times as much spirit. Open the box, and see if you do not find something very pretty!"

The box, I had almost forgotten to say, was fastened; not by a lock, nor by any other such contrivance, but by a very intricate knot of gold cord. There appeared to be no end to this knot, and no beginning. Never was a knot so cunningly twisted, nor with so many ins and outs, which roguishly defied the skilfullest fingers to disentangle them. And yet, by the very difficulty that there was in it, Pandora was the more tempted to examine the knot, and just see how it was made. Two or three times, already, she had stooped over the box, and taken the knot between her thumb and forefinger, but without positively trying to undo it.

"I really believe," said she to herself, "that I begin to see how it was done. Nay, perhaps I could tie it up again, after undoing it. There would be no harm in that, surely. Even Epimetheus would not blame me for that. I need not open the box, and should not, of course, without the foolish boy's consent, even if the knot were untied."

It might have been better for Pandora if she had had a little work to do, or anything to employ her mind upon, so as not to be so constantly thinking of this one subject. But children led so easy a life, before any Troubles came into the world, that they had really a great deal too much leisure. They could not be forever playing at hide-and-seek among the flower-shrubs, or at blind-man's-buff with garlands over their eyes, or at whatever other games had been found out, while Mother Earth was in her babyhood. When life is all sport, toil is the real play. There was absolutely nothing to do. A little sweeping and dusting about the cottage, I suppose, and the gathering of fresh flowers (which were only too abundant everywhere), and arranging them in vases,—and poor little Pandora's day's work was over. And then, for the rest of the day, there was the box!

After all, I am not quite sure that the box was not a blessing to her in its way. It supplied her with such a variety of ideas to think of, and to talk about, whenever she had anybody to listen! When she was in good-humor, she could admire the bright polish of its sides, and the rich border of beautiful faces and foliage that ran all around it. Or, if she chanced to be ill-tempered, she could give it a push, or kick it with her naughty little foot. And many a kick did the box—(but it was a mischievous box, as we shall see, and deserved all it got)—many a kick did it receive. But, certain it is, if it had not been for the box, our active-minded little Pandora would not have known half so well how to spend her time as she now did.

For it was really an endless employment to guess what was inside. What could it be, indeed? Just imagine, my little hearers, how busy your wits would be, if there were a great box in the house, which, as you might have reason to suppose, contained something new and pretty for your Christmas or New Year's gifts. Do you think that you should be less curious than Pandora? If you were left alone with the box, might you not feel a little tempted to lift the lid? But you would not do it. Oh, fie! No, no! Only, if you thought there were toys in it, it would be so very hard to let slip an opportunity of taking just one peep! I know not whether Pandora expected any toys; for none had yet begun to be made, probably, in those days, when the world itself was one great plaything for the

children that dwelt upon it. But Pandora was convinced that there was something very beautiful and
valuable in the box; and therefore she felt just as
anxious to take a peep as any of these little girls,
here around me, would have felt. And, possibly,
a little more so; but of that I am not quite so
certain.

On this particular day, however, which we have
so long been talking about, her curiosity grew so
much greater than it usually was, that, at last, she
approached the box. She was more than half determined to open it, if she could. Ah, naughty Pandora!

First, however, she tried to lift it. It was heavy;
quite too heavy for the slender strength of a child,
like Pandora. She raised one end of the box a few
inches from the floor, and let it fall again, with a
pretty loud thump. A moment afterwards, she
almost fancied that she heard something stir inside
of the box. She applied her ear as closely as possible, and listened. Positively, there did seem to be
a kind of stifled murmur, within! Or was it merely
the singing in Pandora's ears? Or could it be the
beating of her heart? The child could not quite
satisfy herself whether she had heard anything or
no. But, at all events, her curiosity was stronger
than ever.

As she drew back her head, her eyes fell upon the
knot of gold cord.

"It must have been a very ingenious person who
tied this knot," said Pandora to herself. "But I
think I could untie it nevertheless. I am resolved,
at least, to find the two ends of the cord."

So she took the golden knot in her fingers, and pried into its intricacies as sharply as she could. Almost without intending it, or quite knowing what she was about, she was soon busily engaged in attempting to undo it. Meanwhile, the bright sunshine came through the open window; as did likewise the merry voices of the children, playing at a distance, and perhaps the voice of Epimetheus among them. Pandora stopped to listen. What a beautiful day it was! Would it not be wiser, if she were to let the troublesome knot alone, and think no more about the box, but run and join her little playfellows, and be happy?

All this time, however, her fingers were half unconsciously busy with the knot; and happening to glance at the flower-wreathed face on the lid of the enchanted box, she seemed to perceive it slyly grinning at her.

"That face looks very mischievous," thought Pandora. "I wonder whether it smiles because I am doing wrong! I have the greatest mind in the world to run away!"

But just then, by the merest accident, she gave the knot a kind of a twist, which produced a wonderful result. The gold cord untwined itself as if by magic, and left the box without a fastening.

"This is the strangest thing I ever knew!" said Pandora. "What will Epimetheus say? And how can I possibly tie it up again?"

She made one or two attempts to restore the knot, but soon found it quite beyond her skill. It had disentangled itself so suddenly that she could not in the least remember how the strings had been doubled into one another; and when she tried to recollect the shape and appearance of the knot, it seemed to have gone entirely out of her mind. Nothing was to be done, therefore, but to let the box remain as it was until Epimetheus should come in.

"But," said Pandora, "when he finds the knot untied, he will know that I have done it. How shall I make him believe that I have not looked into the box?"

And then the thought came into her naughty little heart, that, since she would be suspected of having looked into the box, she might just as well do so at once. Oh, very naughty and very foolish Pandora! You should have thought only of doing what was right, and of leaving undone what was wrong, and not of what your playfellow Epimetheus would have said or believed. And so perhaps she might, if the enchanted face on the lid of the box had not looked so bewitchingly persuasive at her, and if she had not seemed to hear, more distinctly than before, the murmur of small voices within. She could not tell whether it was fancy or no; but there was quite a little tumult of whispers in her ear,—or else it was her curiosity that whispered,—"Let us out, dear Pandora,—pray let us out! We will be such nice pretty playfellows for you! Only let us out!"

"What can it be?" thought Pandora. "Is there something alive in the box? Well!—yes!—I am resolved to take just one peep! Only one peep; and then the lid shall be shut down as safely as

ever! There cannot possibly be any harm in just
one little peep!"

But it is now time for us to see what Epimetheus
was doing.

This was the first time, since his little playmate
had come to dwell with him, that he had attempted
to enjoy any pleasure in which she did not partake.
But nothing went right; nor was he nearly so happy
as on other days. He could not find a sweet grape
or a ripe fig (if Epimetheus had a fault, it was a
little too much fondness for figs) ; or, if ripe at all,
they were overripe, and so sweet as to be cloying.
There was no mirth in his heart, such as usually
made his voice gush out, of its own accord, and
swell the merriment of his companions. In short,
he grew so uneasy and discontented, that the other
children could not imagine what was the matter
with Epimetheus. Neither did he himself know
what ailed him, any better than they did. For you
must recollect that, at the time we are speaking of,
it was everybody's nature, and constant habit, to be
happy. The world had not yet learned to be otherwise. Not a single soul or body, since these children
were first sent to enjoy themselves on the beautiful
earth, had ever been sick or out of sorts.

At length, discovering that, somehow or other, he
put a stop to all the play, Epimetheus judged it
best to go back to Pandora, who was in a humor
better suited to his own. But, with a hope of giving
her pleasure, he gathered some flowers, and made
them into a wreath, which he meant to put upon
her head. The flowers were very lovely,—roses,
and lilies, and orange-blossoms, and a great many

more, which left a trail of fragrance behind, as Epimetheus carried them along; and the wreath was put together with as much skill as could reasonably be expected of a boy. The fingers of little girls, it has always appeared to me, are the fittest to twine flower-wreaths; but boys could do it, in those days, rather better than they can now.

And here I must mention that a great black cloud had been gathering in the sky, for some time past, although it had not yet overspread the sun. But, just as Epimetheus reached the cottage door, this cloud began to intercept the sunshine, and thus to make a sudden and sad obscurity.

He entered softly; for he meant, if possible, to steal behind Pandora, and fling the wreath of flowers over her head, before she should be aware of his approach. But, as it happened, there was no need of his treading so very lightly. He might have trod as heavily as he pleased,—as heavily as a grown man,—as heavily, I was going to say, as an elephant,—without much probability of Pandora's hearing his footsteps. She was too intent upon her purpose. At the moment of his entering the cottage, the naughty child had put her hand to the lid, and was on the point of opening the mysterious box. Epimetheus beheld her. If he had cried out, Pandora would probably have withdrawn her hand, and the fatal mystery of the box might never have been known.

But Epimetheus himself, although he said very little about it, had his own share of curiosity to know what was inside. Perceiving that Pandora was resolved to find out the secret, he determined that his playfellow should not be the only wise person in the cottage. And if there were anything pretty or valuable in the box, he meant to take half of it to himself. Thus, after all his sage speeches to Pandora about restraining her curiosity, Epimetheus turned out to be quite as foolish, and nearly as much in fault, as she. So, whenever we blame Pandora for what happened, we must not forget to shake our heads at Epimetheus likewise.

As Pandora raised the lid, the cottage grew very dark and dismal; for the black cloud had now swept quite over the sun, and seemed to have buried it alive. There had, for a little while past, been a low growling and muttering, which all at once broke into a heavy peal of thunder. But Pandora, heeding nothing of all this, lifted the lid nearly upright, and looked inside. It seemed as if a sudden swarm of winged creatures brushed past her, taking flight out of the box, while, at the same instant, she heard the voice of Epimetheus, with a lamentable tone, as if he were in pain.

"Oh, I am stung!" cried he. "I am stung! Naughty Pandora! why have you opened this wicked box?"

Pandora let fall the lid, and, starting up, looked about her, to see what had befallen Epimetheus. The thunder-cloud had so darkened the room that she could not very clearly discern what was in it. But she heard a disagreeable buzzing, as if a great many huge flies, or gigantic mosquitoes, or those insects which we call dor-bugs, and pinching-dogs, were darting about. And, as her eyes grew more accustomed to the imperfect light, she saw a crowd of ugly little shapes, with bats' wings, looking abominably spiteful, and armed with terribly long stings in their tails. It was one of these that had stung Epimetheus. Nor was it a great while before Pandora herself began to scream, in no less pain and affright than her playfellow, and making a vast deal more hubbub about it. An odious little monster had settled on her forehead, and would have stung her I know not how deeply, if Epimetheus had not run and brushed it away.

Now, if you wish to know what these ugly things might be, which had made their escape out of the box, I must tell you that they were the whole family of earthly Troubles. There were evil Passions; there were a great many species of Cares; there were more than a hundred and fifty Sorrows; there were Diseases, in a vast number of miserable and painful shapes; there were more kinds of Naughtiness than it would be of any use to talk about. In short, everything that has since afflicted the souls and bodies of mankind had been shut up in the mysterious box, and given to Epimetheus and Pandora to be kept safely, in order that the happy children of the world might never be molested by them. Had they been faithful to their trust, all would have gone well. No grown person would ever have been sad, nor any child have had cause to shed a single tear, from that hour until this moment.

But—and you may see by this how a wrong act of any one mortal is a calamity to the whole world —by Pandora's lifting the lid of that miserable box, and by the fault of Epimetheus, too, in not preventing her, these Troubles have obtained a foothold among us, and do not seem very likely to be driven away in a hurry. For it was impossible, as you will easily guess, that the two children should keep the ugly swarm in their own little cottage. On the contrary, the first thing that they did was to fling open the doors and windows, in hopes of get-- ting rid of them; and, sure enough, away flew the winged Troubles all abroad, and so pestered and tormented the small people, everywhere about, that none of them so much as smiled for many days afterwards. And, what was very singular, all the flowers and dewy blossoms on earth, not one of which had hitherto faded, now began to droop and shed their leaves, after a day or two. The children, moreover, who before seemed immortal in the child- hood, now grew older, day by day, and came soon to be youths and maidens, and men and women by and by, and aged people, before they dreamed of such a thing.

Meanwhile, the naughty Pandora, and hardly less naughty Epimetheus, remained in their cottage. Both of them had been grievously stung, and were in a good deal of pain, which seemed the more intol- erable to them, because it was the very first pain that had ever been felt since the world began. Of course, they were entirely unaccustomed to it, and could have no idea what it meant. Besides all this, they were in exceedingly bad humor, both with themselves and with one another. In order to in- dulge it to the utmost, Epimetheus sat down sul- lenly in a corner with his back towards Pandora; while Pandora flung herself upon the floor and rested her head on the fatal and abominable box. She was crying bitterly, and sobbing as if her heart would break.

Suddenly there was a gentle little tap on the inside of the lid.

"What can that be?" cried Pandora, lifting her head.

But either Epimetheus had not heard the tap, or was too much out of humor to notice it. At any rate, he made no answer.

"You are very unkind," said Pandora, sobbing anew, "not to speak to me!"

Again the tap! It sounded like the tiny knuckles of a fairy's hand, knocking lightly and playfully on the inside of the box.

"Who are you?" asked Pandora, with a little of her former curiosity. "Who are you, inside of this naughty box?"

A sweet little voice spoke from within,—

"Only lift the lid, and you shall see."

"No, no," answered Pandora, again beginning to sob, "I have had enough of lifting the lid! You are inside of the box, naughty creature, and there you shall stay! There are plenty of your ugly brothers and sisters already flying about the world. You need never think that I shall be so foolish as to let you out!"

She looked towards Epimetheus, as she spoke, perhaps expecting that he would commend her for her wisdom. But the sullen boy only muttered that she was wise a little too late.

"Ah," said the sweet little voice again, "you had much better let me out. I am not like those naughty

359

creatures that have stings in their tails. They are
no brothers and sisters of mine, as you would see
at once, if you were only to get a glimpse of me.
Come, come, my pretty Pandora! I am sure you
will let me out!"

And, indeed, there was a kind of cheerful
witchery in the tone, that made it almost impossible
to refuse anything which this little voice asked.
Pandora's heart had insensibly grown lighter, at
every word that came from within the box. Epimetheus, too, though still in the corner, had turned half
round, and seemed to be in rather better spirits
than before.

"My dear Epimetheus," cried Pandora, "have
you heard this little voice?"

"Yes, to be sure I have," answered he, but in
no very good-humor as yet. "And what of it?"

"Shall I lift the lid again?" asked Pandora.

"Just as you please," said Epimetheus. "You
have done so much mischief already, that perhaps
you may as well do a little more. One other
Trouble, in such a swarm as you have set
adrift about the world, can make no very great
difference."

"You might speak a little more kindly!" murmured Pandora, wiping her eyes.

"Ah, naughty boy!" cried the little voice within
the box, in an arch and laughing tone. "He knows
he is longing to see me. Come, my dear Pandora,
lift up the lid. I am in a great hurry to comfort
you. Only let me have some fresh air, and you
shall soon see that matters are not quite so dismal
as you think them!"

THE PARADISE OF CHILDREN

"Epimetheus," exclaimed Pandora, "come what may, I am resolved to open the box!"

"And, as the lid seems very heavy," cried Epimetheus, running across the room, "I will help you!"

So, with one consent, the two children again lifted the lid. Out flew a sunny and smiling little personage, and hovered about the room, throwing a light wherever she went. Have you never made the sunshine dance into dark corners, by reflecting it from a bit of looking-glass? Well, so looked the winged cheerfulness of this fairy-like stranger, amid the gloom of the cottage. She flew to Epimetheus, and laid the least touch of her finger on the inflamed spot where the Trouble had stung him, and immediately the anguish of it was gone. Then she kissed Pandora on the forehead, and her hurt was cured likewise.

After performing these good offices, the bright stranger fluttered sportively over the children's heads, and looked so sweetly at them, that they both began to think it not so very much amiss to have opened the box, since, otherwise, their cheery guest must have been kept a prisoner among those naughty imps with stings in their tails.

"Pray, who are you, beautiful creature?" inquired Pandora.

"I am to be called Hope!" answered the sunshiny figure. "And because I am such a cheery little body, I was packed into the box, to make amends to the human race for that swarm of ugly Troubles, which was destined to be let loose among them. Never fear! we shall do pretty well in spite of them all."

"Your wings are colored like the rainbow!"
exclaimed Pandora. "How very beautiful!"

"Yes, they are like the rainbow," said Hope,
"because, glad as my nature is, I am partly made
of tears as well as smiles."

"And will you stay with us," asked Epimetheus,
"forever and ever?"

"As long as you need me," said Hope, with her
pleasant smile,—"and that will be as long as you
live in the world,—I promise never to desert you.
There may come times and seasons, now and then,
when you will think that I have utterly vanished.
But again, and again, and again, when perhaps
you least dream of it, you shall see the glimmer of
my wings on the ceiling of your cottage. Yes, my
dear children, and I know something very good
and beautiful that is to be given you hereafter!"

"Oh tell us," they exclaimed,—"tell us what
it is!"

"Do not ask me," replied Hope, putting her
finger on her rosy mouth. "But do not despair,
even if it should never happen while you live on
this earth. Trust in my promise, for it is true."

"We do trust you!" cried Epimetheus and Pandora, both in one breath.

And so they did; and not only they, but so has
everybody trusted Hope, that has since been alive.
And to tell you the truth, I cannot help being glad
—(though, to be sure, it was an uncommonly
naughty thing for her to do)—but I cannot help
being glad that our foolish Pandora peeped into
the box. No doubt—no doubt—the Troubles
are still flying about the world, and have increased

in multitude, rather than lessened, and are a very ugly set of imps, and carry most venomous stings in their tails. I have felt them already, and expect to feel them more, as I grow older. But then that lovely and lightsome little figure of Hope! What in the world could we do without her? Hope spiritualizes the earth; Hope makes it always new; and, even in the earth's best and brightest aspect, Hope shows it to be only the shadow of an infinite bliss hereafter!

RIP VAN WINKLE

By Washington Irving

WHOEVER has made a voyage up the Hudson must remember the Kaatskill mountains. They are a dismembered branch of the great Appalachian family, and are seen away to the west of the river, swelling up to a noble height, and lording it over the surrounding country. Every change of season, every change of weather, indeed, every hour of the day, produces some change in the magical hues and shapes of these mountains, and they are regarded by all the good wives, far and near, as perfect barometers. When the weather is fair and settled, they are clothed in blue and purple, and print their bold outlines on the clear evening sky; but, sometimes, when the rest of the landscape is cloudless, they will gather a hood of gray vapors about their summits, which, in the last rays of the setting sun, will glow and light up like a crown of glory.

At the foot of these fairy mountains, the voyager may have descried the light smoke curling up from a village, whose shingle-roofs gleam among the trees, just where the blue tints of the upland melt away into the fresh green of the nearer landscape. It is a little village of great antiquity, having been founded by some of the Dutch colonists, in the early times of the province, just about the beginning of the government of the good Peter Stuyvesant (may he rest in peace!), and there were some of the houses of the original settlers standing within a few years, built of small yellow bricks brought from Holland, having latticed windows and gable fronts, surmounted with weather-cocks.

In that same village, and in one of these very houses (which, to tell the precise truth, was sadly time-worn and weather-beaten), there lived many years since, while the country was yet a province of Great Britain, a simple good-natured fellow of the name of Rip Van Winkle. He was a descendant of the Van Winkles who figured so gallantly in the chivalrous days of Peter Stuyvesant, and accompanied him to the siege of Fort Christina. He inherited, however, but little of the martial character of his ancestors. I have observed that he was a simple, good-natured man; he was, moreover, a kind neighbor, and an obedient, hen-pecked husband. Indeed, to the latter circumstance might be owing that meekness of spirit which gained him such universal popularity; for those men are most apt to be obsequious and conciliating abroad, who are under the discipline of shrews at home. Their tempers, doubtless, are rendered pliant and malleable in the fiery furnace of domestic tribulation; and a curtain lecture is worth all the sermons in the world for teaching the virtues of patience and long-suffering. A termagant wife may, therefore, in some respects, be considered a tolerable blessing; and if so, Rip Van Winkle was thrice blessed.

Certain it is, that he was a great favorite among

all the good wives of the village, who, as usual, with the amiable sex, took his part in all family squabbles; and never failed, whenever they talked those matters over in their evening gossipings, to lay all the blame on Dame Van Winkle. The children of the village, too, would shout with joy whenever he approached. He assisted at their sports, made their playthings, taught them to fly kites and shoot marbles, and told them long stories of ghosts, witches, and Indians. Whenever he went dodging about the village, he was surrounded by a troop of them, hanging on his skirts, clambering on his back, and playing a thousand tricks on him with impunity; and not a dog would bark at him throughout the neighborhood.

The great error in Rip's composition was an insuperable aversion to all kinds of profitable labor. It could not be from the want of assiduity or perseverance; for he would sit on a wet rock, with a rod as long and heavy as a Tartar's lance, and fish all day without a murmur, even though he should not be encouraged by a single nibble. He would carry a fowling-piece on his shoulder for hours together, trudging through woods and swamps, and up hill and down dale, to shoot a few squirrels or wild pigeons. He would never refuse to assist a neighbor even in the roughest toil, and was a foremost man at all country frolics for husking Indian corn, or building stone fences; the women of the village, too, used to employ him to run their errands, and to do such little odd jobs as their less obliging husbands would not do for them. In a word Rip was ready to attend to anybody's business but his own; but as to doing family duty, and keeping his farm in order, he found it impossible.

In fact, he declared it was of no use to work on his farm, it was the most pestilent little piece of ground in the whole country; everything about it went wrong, and would go wrong, in spite of him. His fences were continually falling to pieces; his cow would either go astray, or get among the cabbages; weeds were sure to grow quicker in his fields than anywhere else; the rain always made a point of setting in just as he had some out-door work to do; so that though his patrimonial estate had dwindled away under his management, acre by acre, until there was little more left than a mere patch of Indian corn and potatoes, yet it was the worst conditioned farm in the neighborhood.

His children, too, were as ragged and wild as if they belonged to nobody. His son Rip, an urchin begotten in his own likeness, promised to inherit the habits, with the old clothes of his father. He was generally seen trooping like a colt at his mother's heels, equipped in a pair of his father's cast-off galligaskins, which he had much ado to hold up with one hand, as a fine lady does her train in bad weather.

Rip Van Winkle, however, was one of those happy mortals, of foolish, well-oiled dispositions, who take the world easy, eat white bread or brown, whichever can be got with least thought or trouble, and would rather starve on a penny than work for a pound. If left to himself, he would have whistled life away in perfect contentment; but his wife kept continually dinning in his ears about his idleness, his carelessness, and the ruin he was bringing on his family. Morning, noon, and night, her tongue was incessantly going, and everything he said or did was sure to produce a torrent of household eloquence. Rip had but one way of replying to all lectures of the kind, and that, by frequent use, had grown into a habit. He shrugged his shoulders, shook his head, cast up his eyes, but said nothing. This, however, always provoked a fresh volley from his wife; so that he was fain to draw off his forces, and take to the outside of the house—the only side which, in truth, belongs to a hen-pecked husband.

Rip's sole domestic adherent was his dog Wolf, who was as much hen-pecked as his master; for Dame Van Winkle regarded them as companions in idleness, and even looked upon Wolf with an evil eye, as the cause of his master's going so often astray. True it is, in all points of spirit befitting an honorable dog, he was as courageous an animal as ever scoured the woods—but what courage can withstand the ever-during and all-besetting terrors of a woman's tongue? The moment Wolf entered the house his crest fell, his tail drooped to the ground, or curled between his legs, he sneaked about with a gallows air, casting many a sidelong glance at Dame Van Winkle, and at the least flourish of a broomstick or ladle, he would fly to the door with yelping precipitation.

Times grew worse and worse with Rip Van Winkle as years of matrimony rolled on; a tart temper never mellows with age, and a sharp tongue is the only edged tool that grows keener with constant use. For a long while he used to console himself, when driven from home, by frequenting a kind of perpetual club of the sages, philosophers, and other idle personages of the village, which held its sessions on a bench before a small inn, designated by a rubicund portrait of his Majesty George the Third. Here they used to sit in the shade through a long lazy summer's day, talking listlessly over village gossip, or telling endless sleepy stories about nothing. But it would have been worth any statesman's money to have heard the profound discussions that sometimes took place, when by chance an old newspaper fell into their hands from some passing traveller. How solemnly they would listen to the contents, as drawled out by Derrick Van Bummel, the schoolmaster, a dapper, learned little man, who was not to be daunted by the most gigantic word in the dictionary; and how sagely they would deliberate upon the public events some months after they had taken place.

The opinions of this junto were completely controlled by Nicholas Vedder, a patriarch of the village, and landlord of the inn, at the door of which he took his seat from morning till night, just moving sufficiently to avoid the sun and keep in the shade of a large tree; so that the neighbors could tell the hour by his movements as accurately as by a sun-dial. It is true he was rarely heard to speak, but smoked his pipe incessantly. His adherents, however (for every great man has his adherents), perfectly understood him, and knew how to gather his opinions. When any thing that was read or related displeased him, he was observed to smoke his pipe vehemently, and to send forth short, frequent and angry puffs; but when pleased, he would inhale the smoke slowly and tranquilly, and emit it in light and placid clouds; and sometimes, taking the pipe from his mouth, and letting the fragrant vapor curl about his nose, would gravely nod his head in token of perfect approbation.

From even this stronghold the unlucky Rip was at length routed by his termagant wife, who would suddenly break in upon the tranquillity of the assemblage and call the members all to naught; nor was that august personage, Nicholas Vedder himself, sacred from the daring tongue of this terrible virago, who charged him outright with encouraging her husband in habits of idleness.

Poor Rip was at last reduced almost to despair; and his only alternative, to escape from the labor of the farm and clamor of his wife, was to take gun in hand and stroll away into the woods. Here he would sometimes seat himself at the foot of a tree, and share the contents of his wallet with Wolf, with whom he sympathized as a fellow-sufferer in persecution. "Poor Wolf," he would say, "thy mistress leads thee a dog's life of it; but never mind, my lad, whilst I live thou shalt never want a friend to stand by thee!" Wolf would wag his tail, look wistfully in his master's face, and if dogs can feel pity I verily believe he reciprocated the sentiment with all his heart.

In a long ramble of the kind on a fine autumnal day, Rip had unconsciously scrambled to one of the highest parts of the Kaatskill mountains. He was after his favorite sport of squirrel shooting, and the still solitudes had echoed and re-echoed with the reports of his gun. Panting and fatigued he threw himself, late in the afternoon, on a green knoll, covered with mountain herbage, that crowned the brow of a precipice. From an opening between the trees he could overlook all the lower country for many a mile of rich woodland. He saw at a distance the lordly Hudson, far, far below him, moving on its silent but majestic course, with the reflection of a purple cloud, or the sail of a lagging bark, here and there sleeping on its glassy bosom, and at last losing itself in the blue highlands.

On the other side he looked down into a deep mountain glen, wild, lonely, and shagged, the bottom filled with fragments from the impending cliffs, and scarcely lighted by the reflected rays of the setting sun. For some time Rip lay musing on this scene; evening was gradually advancing; the mountains began to throw their long blue shadows over the valleys; he saw that it would be dark long before he could reach the village, and he heaved a heavy sigh when he thought of encountering the terrors of Dame Van Winkle.

As he was about to descend, he heard a voice from a distance, hallooing, "Rip Van Winkle! Rip Van Winkle!" He looked round, but could see nothing but a crow winging its solitary flight across the mountain. He thought his fancy must have deceived him, and turned again to descend, when he heard the same cry ring through the still evening air: "Rip Van Winkle! Rip Van Winkle!"—at the same time Wolf bristled up his back, and giving a low growl, skulked to his master's side, looking fearfully down into the glen. Rip now felt a vague apprehension stealing over him; he looked anxiously in the same direction, and perceived a strange figure slowly toiling up the rocks, and bending under the weight of something he carried on his back. He was surprised to see any human being in this lonely and unfrequented place, but supposing it to be some one of the neighborhood in need of his assistance, he hastened down to yield it.

On nearer approach he was still more surprised at the singularity of the stranger's appearance. He was a short square-built old fellow, with thick bushy hair, and a grizzled beard. His dress was of the antique Dutch fashion—a cloth jerkin strapped round the waist—several pair of breeches, the outer one of ample volume, decorated with rows of buttons down the sides, and bunches at the knees. He bore on his shoulder a stout keg, that seemed full of liquor, and made signs for Rip to approach and assist him with the load. Though rather shy and distrustful of this new acquaintance, Rip complied with his usual alacrity; and mutually relieving one another, they clambered up a narrow gully, apparently the dry bed of a mountain torrent. As they ascended, Rip every now and then heard long rolling peals, like distant thunder, that seemed to issue out of a deep ravine, or rather cleft, between lofty rocks, toward which their rugged path conducted. He paused for an instant, but supposing it to be the muttering of one of those transient thunder-showers which often take place in mountain heights, he proceeded. Passing through the ravine, they came to a hollow, like a small amphitheatre, surrounded by perpendicular precipices, over the brinks of which impending trees shot their branches, so that you only caught glimpses of the azure sky and the bright evening cloud. During the whole time Rip and his companion had labored on in silence; for though the former marvelled greatly what could be the object of carrying a keg of liquor up this wild mountain, yet there was something strange and incomprehensible about the unknown, that inspired awe and checked familiarity.

On entering the amphitheatre, new objects of wonder presented themselves. On a level spot in the centre was a company of odd-looking personages playing at ninepins. They were dressed in a quaint outlandish fashion; some wore short doublets, others jerkins, with long knives in their belts, and most of them had enormous breeches, of similar style with that of the guide's. Their visages, too, were peculiar: one had a large beard, broad face, and small piggish eyes; the face of another seemed to consist entirely of nose, and was surmounted by a white sugar-loaf hat set off with a little red cock's tail. They all had beards, of various shapes and colors. There was one who seemed to be the commander. He was a stout old gentleman, with a weather-beaten countenance; he wore a laced doublet, broad belt and hanger, high-crowned hat and feather, red stockings, and high-heeled shoes, with roses in them. The whole group reminded Rip of the figures in an old Flemish painting, in the parlor of Dominie Van Shaick, the village parson, and which had been brought over from Holland at the time of the settlement.

What seemed particularly odd to Rip was, that though these folks were evidently amusing themselves, yet they maintained the gravest faces, the most mysterious silence, and were, withal, the most melancholy party of pleasure he had ever witnessed. Nothing interrupted the stillness of the scene but the noise of the balls, which, whenever they were rolled, echoed along the mountains like rumbling peals of thunder.

As Rip and his companion approached them, they suddenly desisted from their play, and stared at him with such fixed statue-like gaze, and such strange, uncouth, lack-lustre countenances, that his heart turned within him, and his knees smote together. His companion now emptied the contents of the keg into large flagons, and made signs to him to wait upon the company. He obeyed with fear and trembling; they quaffed the liquor in profound silence, and then returned to their game.

By degrees Rip's awe and apprehension subsided. He even ventured, when no eye was fixed upon him, to taste the beverage, which he found had much of the flavor of excellent Hollands. He was naturally a thirsty soul, and was soon tempted to repeat the draught. One taste provoked another; and he reiterated his visits to the flagon so often that at length his senses were overpowered, his eyes swam in his head, his head gradually declined, and he fell into a deep sleep.

On waking, he found himself on the green knoll

whence he had first seen the old man of the glen. He rubbed his eyes—it was a bright sunny morning. The birds were hopping and twittering among the bushes, and the eagle was wheeling aloft, and breasting the pure mountain breeze. "Surely," thought Rip, "I have not slept here all night." He recalled the occurrences before he fell asleep. The strange man with a keg of liquor—the mountain ravine—the wild retreat among the rocks—the woebegone party at ninepins—the flagon—"Oh! that flagon! that wicked flagon!" thought Rip—"what excuse shall I make to Dame Van Winkle!"

He looked round for his gun, but in place of the clean well-oiled fowling-piece, he found an old firelock lying by him, the barrel incrusted with rust, the lock falling off, and the stock worm-eaten. He now suspected that the grave roysters of the mountain had put a trick upon him, and, having dosed him with liquor, had robbed him of his gun. Wolf, too, had disappeared, but he might have strayed away after a squirrel or partridge. He whistled after him and shouted his name, but all in vain; the echoes repeated his whistle and shout, but no dog was to be seen.

He determined to revisit the scene of the last evening's gambol, and if he met with any of the party, to demand his dog and gun. As he rose to walk, he found himself stiff in the joints, and wanting in his usual activity. "These mountain beds do not agree with me," thought Rip, "and if this frolic should lay me up with a fit of the rheumatism, I shall have a blessed time with Dame Van Winkle." With some difficulty he got down into the glen: he found the gully up which he and his companion had ascended the preceding evening; but to his astonishment a mountain stream was now foaming down it, leaping from rock to rock, and filling the glen with babbling murmurs. He, however, made shift to scramble up its sides, working his toilsome way through thickets of birch, sassafras, and witch-hazel, and sometimes tripped up or entangled by the wild grapevines that twisted their coils or tendrils from tree to tree, and spread a kind of network in his path.

At length he reached to where the ravine had opened through the cliffs to the amphitheatre; but no traces of such opening remained. The rocks presented a high impenetrable wall, over which the torrent came tumbling in a sheet of feathery foam, and fell into a broad deep basin, black from the shadows of the surrounding forest. Here, then, poor Rip was brought to a stand. He again called and whistled after his dog; he was only answered by the cawing of a flock of idle crows, sporting high in air about a dry tree that overhung a sunny precipice; and who, secure in their elevation, seemed to look down and scoff at the poor man's perplexities. What was to be done? The morning was passing away, and Rip felt famished for want of his breakfast. He grieved to give up his dog and gun; he dreaded to meet his wife; but it would not do to starve among the mountains. He shook his head, shouldered the rusty firelock, and, with a heart full of trouble and anxiety, turned his steps homeward.

As he approached the village he met a number

of people, but none whom he knew, which somewhat surprised him, for he had thought himself
acquainted with every one in the country round.
Their dress, too, was of a different fashion from
that to which he was accustomed. They all stared
at him with equal marks of surprise, and whenever
they cast their eyes upon him, invariably stroked
their chins. The constant recurrence of this gesture induced Rip, involuntarily, to do the same,
when, to his astonishment, he found his beard had
grown a foot long!

He had now entered the skirts of the village. A
troop of strange children ran at his heels, hooting
after him, and pointing at his gray beard. The
dogs, too, not one of which he recognized for an
old acquaintance, barked at him as he passed. The
very village was altered; it was larger and more
populous. There were rows of houses which he
had never seen before, and those which had been
his familiar haunts had disappeared. Strange
names were over the doors—strange faces at the
windows—everything was strange. His mind now
misgave him; he began to doubt whether both he
and the world around him were not bewitched.
Surely this was his native village, which he had left
but the day before. There stood the Kaatskill
mountains—there ran the silver Hudson at a distance—there was every hill and dale precisely as
it had always been. Rip was sorely perplexed—
"That flagon last night," thought he, "has addled
my poor head sadly!"

It was with some difficulty that he found the way
to his own house, which he approached with silent

awe, expecting every moment to hear the shrill voice of Dame Van Winkle. He found the house gone to decay—the roof fallen in, the windows shattered, and the doors off the hinges. A half-starved dog that looked like Wolf was skulking about it. Rip called him by name, but the cur snarled, showed his teeth, and passed on. This was an unkind cut indeed—"My very dog," sighed poor Rip, "has forgotten me!"

He entered the house, which, to tell the truth, Dame Van Winkle had always kept in neat order. It was empty, forlorn, and apparently abandoned. This desolateness overcame all his connubial fears —he called loudly for his wife and children—the lonely chambers rang for a moment with his voice, and then all again was silence.

He now hurried forth, and hastened to his old resort, the village inn—but it too was gone. A large rickety wooden building stood in its place, with great gaping windows, some of them broken and mended with old hats and petticoats, and over the door was painted, "the Union Hotel, by Jonathan Doolittle." Instead of the great tree that used to shelter the quiet little Dutch inn of yore, there now was reared a tall naked pole, with something on the top that looked like a red night-cap, and from it was fluttering a flag, on which was a singular assemblage of stars and stripes—all this was strange and incomprehensible. He recognized on the sign, however, the ruby face of King George, under which he had smoked so many a peaceful pipe; but even this was singularly metamorphosed. The red coat was changed for one of blue and buff, a sword was held in the hand instead of a sceptre, the head was decorated with a cocked hat, and underneath was painted in large characters, GENERAL WASHINGTON.

There was, as usual, a crowd of folk about the door, but none that Rip recollected. The very character of the people seemed changed. There was a busy, bustling, disputatious tone about it, instead of the accustomed phlegm and drowsy tranquillity. He looked in vain for the sage Nicholas Vedder, with his broad face, double chin, and fair long pipe, uttering clouds of tobacco-smoke instead of idle speeches; or Van Bummel, the schoolmaster, doling forth the contents of an ancient newspaper. In place of these, a lean, bilious-looking fellow, with his pockets full of handbills, was haranguing vehemently about rights of citizens—elections—members of Congress—liberty—Bunker's Hill—heroes of seventy-six—and other words, which were a perfect Babylonish jargon to the bewildered Van Winkle.

The appearance of Rip, with his long, grizzled beard, his rusty fowling-piece, his uncouth dress, and an army of women and children at his heels, soon attracted the attention of the tavern politicians. They crowded round him, eyeing him from head to foot with great curiosity. The orator bustled up to him, and, drawing him partly aside, inquired "on which side he voted?" Rip stared in vacant stupidity. Another short but busy little fellow pulled him by the arm, and, rising on tiptoe, inquired in his ear, "whether he was Federal or Democrat?" Rip was equally at a loss to comprehend the question; when a knowing, self-important old gentleman, in a sharp cocked hat, made his way through the crowd, putting them to the right and left with his elbows as he passed, and planting himself before Van Winkle, with one arm akimbo, the other resting on his cane, his keen eyes and sharp hat penetrating, as it were, into his very soul, demanded in an austere tone, "what brought him to the election with a gun on his shoulder, and a mob at his heels, and whether he meant to breed a riot in the village?"—"Alas! gentlemen," cried Rip, somewhat dismayed, "I am a poor quiet man, a native of the place, and a loyal subject of the king, God bless him!"

Here a general shout burst from the bystanders— "A tory! a tory! a spy! a refugee! hustle him! away with him!" It was with great difficulty that the self-important man in the cocked hat restored order; and, having assumed a tenfold austerity of brow, demanded again of the unknown culprit, what he came there for, and whom he was seeking? The poor man humbly assured him that he meant no harm, but merely came there in search of some of his neighbors, who used to keep about the tavern.

"Well—who are they?—name them."

Rip bethought himself a moment, and inquired, "Where's Nicholas Vedder?"

There was a silence for a little while, when an old man replied in a thin piping voice, "Nicholas Vedder! why, he is dead and gone these eighteen years! There was a wooden tombstone in the church-yard that used to tell all about him, but that's rotten and gone too."

"Where's Brom Dutcher?"

"Oh, he went off to the army in the beginning of the war; some say he was killed at the storming of Stony Point—others say he was drowned in a squall at the foot of Anthony Nose. I don't know—he never came back again."

"Where's Van Bummel, the schoolmaster?"

"He went off to the wars too, was a great militia general, and is now in Congress."

Rip's heart died away at hearing of these sad changes in his home and friends, and finding himself thus alone in the world. Every answer puzzled him too, by treating of such enormous lapses of time, and of matters which he could not understand: war—congress—Stony Point;—he had no courage to ask after any more friends, but cried out in despair, "Does nobody here know Rip Van Winkle?"

"Oh, Rip Van Winkle!" exclaimed two or three, "Oh, to be sure! that's Rip Van Winkle yonder, leaning against the tree."

Rip looked, and beheld a precise counterpart of himself, as he went up the mountain: apparently as lazy, and certainly as ragged. The poor fellow was now completely confounded. He doubted his own identity, and whether he was himself or another man. In the midst of his bewilderment, the man in the cocked hat demanded who he was, and what was his name?

"God knows," exclaimed he, at his wit's end; "I'm not myself—I'm somebody else—that's me yonder—no—that's somebody else got into my shoes—I was myself last night, but I fell asleep on the mountain, and they've changed my gun, and everything's changed, and I'm changed and I can't tell my name, or who I am!"

The bystanders began now to look at each other, nod, wink significantly, and tap their fingers against their foreheads. There was a whisper, also, about securing the gun, and keeping the old fellow from doing mischief, at the very suggestion of which the self-important man in the cocked hat retired with some precipitation. At this critical moment a fresh, comely woman pressed through the throng to get a peep at the gray-bearded man. She had a chubby child in her arms, which, frightened at his looks, began to cry. "Hush, Rip," cried she, "hush, you little fool; the old man won't hurt you." The name of the child, the air of the mother, the tone of her voice, all awakened a train of recollections in his mind. "What's your name, my good woman?" asked he.

"Judith Gardenier."

"And your father's name?"

"Ah, poor man, Rip Van Winkle was his name, but it's twenty years since he went away from home with his gun, and never has been heard of since— his dog came home without him; but whether he shot himself, or was carried away by the Indians, nobody can tell. I was then but a little girl."

Rip had but one question more to ask; but he put it with a faltering voice:

"Where's your mother?"

"Oh, she too had died but a short time since; she broke a blood-vessel in a fit of passion at a New England peddler."

RIP VAN WINKLE

There was a drop of comfort, at least, in this intelligence. The honest man could contain himself no longer. He caught his daughter and her child in his arms. "I am your father!" cried he—"Young Rip Van Winkle once—old Rip Van Winkle now! —Does nobody know poor Rip Van Winkle?"

All stood amazed, until an old woman, tottering out from among the crowd, put her hand to her brow, and peering under it in his face for a moment, exclaimed, "Sure enough; it is Rip Van Winkle— it is himself! Welcome home again, old neighbor —Why, where have you been these twenty long years?"

Rip's story was soon told, for the whole twenty years had been to him but as one night. The neighbors stared when they heard it; some were seen to wink at each other, and put their tongues in their cheeks; and the self-important man in the cocked hat, who, when the alarm was over, had returned to the field, screwed down the corners of his mouth, and shook his head—upon which there was a general shaking of the head throughout the assemblage.

It was determined, however, to take the opinion of old Peter Vanderdonk, who was seen slowly advancing up the road. He was a descendant of the historian of that name, who wrote one of the earliest accounts of the province. Peter was the most ancient inhabitant of the village, and well versed in all the wonderful events and traditions of the neighborhood. He recollected Rip at once and corroborated his story in the most satisfactory manner. He assured the company that it was a fact, handed down from his ancestor the historian, that

the Kaatskill mountains had always been haunted
by strange beings. That it was affirmed that the
great Hendrick Hudson, the first discoverer of the
river and country, kept a kind of vigil there every
twenty years, with his crew of the *Half-Moon;*
being permitted in this way to revisit the scenes of
his enterprise, and keep a guardian eye upon the
river, and the great city called by his name. That
his father had once seen them in their old Dutch
dresses playing at ninepins in a hollow of the
mountain; and that he himself had heard, one summer afternoon, the sound of their balls like distant
peals of thunder.

To make a long story short, the company broke
up, and returned to the more important concerns
of the election. Rip's daughter took him home to
live with her; she had a snug, well-furnished house,
and a stout cheery farmer for a husband, whom
Rip recollected for one of the urchins that used to
climb upon his back. As to Rip's son and heir, who
was the ditto of himself, seen leaning against the
tree, he was employed to work on the farm; but
evinced an hereditary disposition to attend to anything else but his business.

Rip now resumed his old walks and habits; he
soon found many of his former cronies, though all
rather the worse for the wear and tear of time, and
preferred making friends among the rising genera-
tion, with whom he soon grew into great favor.

Having nothing to do at home, and being arrived
at that happy age when a man can be idle with
impunity, he took his place once more on the bench
at the inn door, and was reverenced as one of the

patriarchs of the village, and a chronicle of the old times "before the war." It was some time before he could get into the regular track of gossip, or could be made to comprehend the strange events that had taken place during his torpor. How that there had been a revolutionary war—that the country had thrown off the yoke of old England—and that, instead of being a subject of his Majesty George the Third, he was now a free citizen of the United States. Rip, in fact, was no politician; the changes of states and empires made but little impression on him; but there was one species of despotism under which he had long groaned, and that was—petticoat government. Happily that was at an end; he had got his neck out of the yoke of matrimony, and could go in and out whenever he pleased, without dreading the tyranny of Dame Van Winkle. Whenever her name was mentioned, however, he shook his head, shrugged his shoulders, and cast up his eyes; which might pass either for an expression of resignation to his fate, or joy at his deliverance.

He used to tell his story to every stranger that arrived at Mr. Doolittle's hotel. He was observed, at first, to vary on some points every time he told it, which was, doubtless, owing to his having so recently awakened. It at last settled down precisely to the tale I have related, and not a man, woman or child in the neighborhood but knew it by heart. Some always pretended to doubt the reality of it, and insisted that Rip had been out of his head, and that this was one point on which he always remained flighty. The old Dutch inhabitants,

however, almost universally gave it full credit.
Even to this day they never hear a thunderstorm
of a summer afternoon about the Kaatskill, but
they say Hendrick Hudson and his crew are at their
game of ninepins; and it is a common wish of all
hen-pecked husbands in the neighborhood, when life
hangs heavy on their hands, that they might have
a quieting draught out of Rip Van Winkle's
flagon.

THE LEGEND OF SLEEPY HOLLOW

By Washington Irving

IN the bosom of one of those spacious coves
which indent the eastern shore of the Hudson,
at that broad expansion of the river denominated
by the ancient Dutch navigators the Tappan Zee,
and where they always prudently shortened sail,
and implored the protection of St. Nicholas when
they crossed, there lies a small market-town or
rural port, which by some is called Greensburgh,
but which is more generally and properly known
by the name of Tarrytown. This name was given,
we are told, in former days, by the good housewives of the adjacent country, from the inveterate
propensity of their husbands to linger about the
tavern on market days. Be that as it may, I do
not vouch for the fact, but merely advert to it, for
the sake of being precise and authentic. Not far
from this village, perhaps about two miles, there
is a little valley, or rather lap of land, among high
hills, which is one of the quietest places in the

A TROOP OF STRANGE CHILDREN RAN AT HIS HEELS
— page 377
From the painting by Arthur Rackham

whole world. A small brook glides through it, with just murmur enough to lull one to repose; and the occasional whistle of a quail, or tapping of a woodpecker, is almost the only sound that ever breaks in upon the uniform tranquillity.

I recollect that, when a stripling, my first exploit in squirrel-shooting was in a grove of tall walnut-trees that shades one side of the valley. I had wandered into it at noon time, when all nature is peculiarly quiet, and was startled by the roar of my own gun, as it broke the Sabbath stillness around, and was prolonged and reverberated by the angry echoes. If ever I should wish for a retreat, whither I might steal from the world and its distractions, and dream quietly away the remnant of a troubled life, I know of none more promising than this little valley.

From the listless repose of the place, and the peculiar character of its inhabitants, who are descendants from the original Dutch settlers, this sequestered glen has long been known by the name of SLEEPY HOLLOW, and its rustic lads are called the Sleepy Hollow Boys throughout all the neighboring country. A drowsy, dreamy influence seems to hang over the land, and to pervade the very atmosphere. Some say that the place was bewitched by a high German doctor, during the early days of the settlement; others, that an old Indian chief, the prophet or wizard of his tribe, held his pow-wows there before the country was discovered by Master Hendrick Hudson. Certain it is, the place still continues under the sway of some witching power, that holds a spell over the minds of the good people, causing them to walk in a continual reverie. They are given to all kinds of marvellous beliefs; are subject to trances and visions; and frequently see strange sights, and hear music and voices in the air. The whole neighborhood abounds with local tales, haunted spots, and twilight superstitions; stars shoot and meteors glare oftener across the valley than in any other part of the country, and the nightmare, with her whole nine-fold, seems to make it the favorite scene of her gambols.

The dominant spirit, however, that haunts this enchanted region, and seems to be commander-in-chief of all the powers of the air, is the apparition of a figure on horseback without a head. It is said by some to be the ghost of a Hessian trooper, whose head had been carried away by a cannon-ball, in some nameless battle during the revolutionary war; and who is ever and anon seen by the country folk, hurrying along in the gloom of night as if on the wings of the wind. His haunts are not confined to the valley, but extend at times to the adjacent roads, and especially to the vicinity of a church at no great distance. Indeed, certain of the most authentic historians of those parts, who have been careful in collecting and collating the floating facts concerning this spectre, allege that the body of the trooper, having been buried in the churchyard, the ghost rides forth to the scene of battle in nightly quest of his head; and that the rushing speed with which he sometimes passes along the Hollow, like a midnight blast, is owing to his being belated, and in a hurry to get back to the churchyard before daybreak.

Such is the general purport of this legendary superstition, which has furnished materials for many a wild story in that region of shadows; and the spectre is known, at all the country firesides, by the name of the Headless Horseman of Sleepy Hollow.

It is remarkable that the visionary propensity I have mentioned is not confined to the native inhabitants of the valley, but is unconsciously imbibed by every one who resides there for a time. However wide awake they may have been before they entered that sleepy region, they are sure, in a little time, to inhale the witching influence of the air, and begin to grow imaginative—to dream dreams, and see apparitions.

I mention this peaceful spot with all possible laud; for it is in such little retired Dutch valleys, found here and there embosomed in the great State of New York, that population, manners, and customs, remain fixed; while the great torrent of migration and improvement, which is making such incessant changes in other parts of this restless country, sweeps by them unobserved. They are like those little nooks of still water which border a rapid stream; where we may see the straw and bubble riding quietly at anchor, or slowly revolving in their mimic harbor, undisturbed by the rush of the passing current.

Though many years have elapsed since I trod the drowsy shades of Sleepy Hollow, yet I question whether I should not still find the same trees and the same families vegetating in its sheltered bosom.

In this by-place of nature, there abode, in a remote period of American history, that is to say, some thirty years since, a worthy wight of the name of Ichabod Crane; who sojourned, or, as he expressed it, "tarried," in Sleepy Hollow, for the purpose of instructing the children of the vicinity. He was a native of Connecticut; a State which supplies the Union with pioneers for the mind as well as for the forest, and sends forth yearly its legions of frontier woodsmen and country school-masters. The cognomen of Crane was not inapplicable to his person. He was tall, but exceedingly lank, with narrow shoulders, long arms and legs, hands that dangled a mile out of his sleeves, feet that might have served for shovels, and his whole frame most loosely hung together. His head was small, and flat at top, with huge ears, large green glassy eyes, and a long snipe nose, so that it looked like a weathercock, perched upon his spindle neck, to tell which way the wind blew. To see him striding along the profile of a hill on a windy day, with his clothes bagging and fluttering about him, one might have mistaken him for the genius of famine descending upon the earth, or some scare-crow eloped from a cornfield.

His school-house was a low building of one large room, rudely constructed of logs; the windows partly glazed, and partly patched with leaves of old copy-books. It was most ingeniously secured at vacant hours, by a withe twisted in the handle of the door, and stakes set against the window shutters; so that, though a thief might get in with perfect ease, he would find some embarrassment in getting out; an idea most probably borrowed by the architect, Yost Van Houten, from the mystery of an eel-pot. The school-house stood in a rather lonely but pleasant situation, just at the foot of a woody hill, with a brook running close by, and a formidable birch tree growing at one end of it. From hence the low murmur of his pupils' voices, conning over their lessons, might be heard in a drowsy summer's day, like the hum of a bee-hive; interrupted now and then by the authoritative voice of the master, in the tone of menace or command; or, peradventure, by the appalling sound of the birch, as he urged some tardy loiterer along the flowery path of knowledge. Truth to say, he was a conscientious man, and ever bore in mind the golden maxim, "Spare the rod and spoil the child." —Ichabod Crane's scholars certainly were not spoiled.

I would not have it imagined, however, that he was one of those cruel potentates of the school, who joy in the smart of their subjects; on the contrary, he administered justice with discrimination rather than severity; taking the burthen off the backs of the weak, and laying it on those of the strong. Your mere puny stripling, that winced at the least flourish of the rod, was passed by with indulgence; but the claims of justice were satisfied by inflicting a double portion on some little, tough, wrong-headed, broad-skirted Dutch urchin, who sulked and swelled and grew dogged and sullen beneath the birch. All this he called "doing his duty by their parents"; and he never inflicted a chastisement without following it by the assurance, so consolatory to the smarting urchin, that "he would remember it, and thank him for it the longest day he had to live."

When school hours were over, he was even the companion and playmate of the larger boys; and on holiday afternoons would convoy some of the smaller ones home, who happened to have pretty sisters, or good housewives for mothers, noted for the comforts of the cupboard. Indeed, it behooved him to keep on good terms with his pupils. The revenue arising from his school was small, and would have been scarcely sufficient to furnish him with daily bread, for he was a huge feeder, and though lank, had the dilating powers of an anaconda; but to help out his maintenance, he was, according to country custom in those parts, boarded and lodged at the houses of the farmers, whose children he instructed. With these he lived successively a week at a time; thus going the rounds of the neighborhood, with all his worldly effects tied up in a cotton handkerchief.

That all this might not be too onerous on the purses of his rustic patrons, who are apt to consider the costs of schooling a grievous burden, and schoolmasters as mere drones, he had various ways of rendering himself both useful and agreeable. He assisted the farmers occasionally in the lighter labors of their farms; helped to make hay; mended the fences; took the horses to water; drove the cows from pasture; and cut wood for the winter fire. He laid aside, too, all the dominant dignity and absolute sway with which he lorded it in his little empire, the school, and became wonderfully gentle and ingratiating. He found favor in the eyes of the mothers, by petting the children, particularly the youngest; and like the lion bold, which whilom so magnanimously the lamb did hold, he would sit with a child on one knee, and rock a cradle with his foot for whole hours together.

In addition to his other vocations, he was the singing-master of the neighborhood, and picked up many bright shillings by instructing the young folks in psalmody. It was a matter of no little vanity to him, on Sundays, to take his station in front of the church gallery, with a band of chosen singers; where, in his own mind, he completely carried away the palm from the parson. Certain it is, his voice resounded far above all the rest of the congregation; and there are peculiar quavers still to be heard in that church, and which may be heard half a mile off, quite to the opposite side of the mill-pond, on a still Sunday morning, which are said to be legitimately descended from the nose of Ichabod Crane. Thus, by divers little make-shifts in that ingenious way which is commonly denominated "by hook and by crook," the worthy pedagogue got on tolerably enough, and was thought, by all who understood nothing of the labor of headwork, to have a wonderfully easy life of it.

The schoolmaster is generally a man of some importance in the female circle of a rural neighborhood; being considered a kind of idle gentlemanlike personage, of vastly superior taste and accomplishments to the rough country swains, and indeed, inferior in learning only to the parson. His appearance, therefore, is apt to occasion some little stir at the tea-table of a farmhouse, and the addition of a supernumerary dish of cakes or sweetmeats, or, peradventure, the parade of a silver teapot. Our man of letters, therefore, was peculiarly happy in the smiles of all the country damsels. How he would figure among them in the churchyard, between services on Sundays! gathering grapes for them from the wild vines that overran the surrounding trees; reciting for their amusement all the epitaphs on the tombstones; or sauntering, with a whole bevy of them, along the banks of the adjacent mill-pond; while the more bashful country bumpkins hung sheepishly back, envying his superior elegance and address.

From his half itinerant life, also, he was a kind of travelling gazette, carrying the whole budget of local gossip from house to house; so that his appearance was always greeted with satisfaction. He was, moreover, esteemed by the women as a man of great erudition, for he had read several books quite through, and was a perfect master of Cotton Mather's History of New England Witchcraft, in which, by the way, he most firmly and potently believed.

He was, in fact, an odd mixture of small shrewdness and simple credulity. His appetite for the marvellous, and his powers of digesting it, were equally extraordinary; and both had been increased by his residence in this spellbound region. No tale was too gross or monstrous for his capacious swallow. It was often his delight, after his school was dismissed in the afternoon, to stretch himself on the rich bed of clover bordering the little brook that whimpered by his school-house, and there con over old Mather's direful tales, until the gathering dusk of the evening made the printed page a mere mist before his eyes. Then, as he wended his way, by swamp and stream and awful woodland, to the farmhouse where he happened to be quartered, every sound of nature, at that witching hour, fluttered his excited imagination: the moan of the whip-poor-will[1] from the hillside; the boding cry of the tree-toad, that harbinger of storm; the dreary hooting of the screech-owl, or the sudden rustling in the thicket of birds frightened from their roost. The fireflies, too, which sparkled most vividly in the darkest places, now and then startled him, as one of uncommon brightness would stream across his path; and if, by chance, a huge blockhead of a beetle came winging his blundering flight against him, the poor varlet was ready to give up the ghost, with the idea that he was struck with a witch's token. His only resource on such occasions, either to drown thought, or drive away evil spirits, was to sing psalm tunes;—and the good people of Sleepy Hollow, as they sat by their doors of an evening, were often filled with awe at hearing his nasal melody, "in linked sweetness long drawn

[1] The whip-poor-will is a bird which is only heard at night. It receives its name from its note, which is thought to resemble those words.

out," floating from the distant hill, or along the dusky road.

Another of his sources of fearful pleasure was, to pass long winter evenings with the old Dutch wives, as they sat spinning by the fire, with a row of apples roasting and spluttering along the hearth, and listen to their marvellous tales of ghosts and goblins, and haunted fields, and haunted brooks, and haunted bridges, and haunted houses, and particularly of the headless horseman, or galloping Hessian of the Hollow, as they sometimes called him. He would delight them equally by his anecdotes of witchcraft, and of the direful omens and portentous sights and sounds in the air, which prevailed in the earlier times of Connecticut; and would frighten them wofully with speculations upon comets and shooting stars; and with the alarming fact that the world did absolutely turn round, and that they were half the time topsy-turvy!

But if there was a pleasure in all this, while snugly cuddling in the chimney-corner of a chamber that was all of a ruddy glow from the crackling wood fire, and where, of course, no spectre dared to show his face, it was dearly purchased by the terrors of his subsequent walk homewards. What fearful shapes and shadows beset his path amidst the dim and ghastly glare of a snowy night!—With what wistful look did he eye every trembling ray of light streaming across the waste fields from some distant window!—How often was he appalled by some shrub covered with snow, which, like a sheeted spectre, beset his very path!—How often did he shrink with curdling awe at the sound of his own steps on the frosty crust beneath his feet; and dreaded to look over his shoulder, lest he should behold some uncouth being tramping close behind him!—and how often was he thrown into complete dismay by some rushing blast, howling among the trees, in the idea that it was the Galloping Hessian on one of his nightly scourings!

All these, however, were mere terrors of the night, phantoms of the mind that walked in darkness; and though he had seen many spectres in his time, and been more than once beset by Satan in divers shapes, in his lonely perambulations, yet daylight put an end to all these evils; and he would have passed a pleasant life of it, in despite of the devil and all his works, if his path had not been crossed by a being that causes more perplexity to mortal man than ghosts, goblins, and the whole race of witches put together, and that was—a woman.

Among the musical disciples who assembled, one evening in each week, to receive his instructions in psalmody, was Katrina Van Tassel, the daughter and only child of a substantial Dutch farmer. She was a blooming lass of fresh eighteen; plump as a partridge; ripe and melting and rosy-cheeked as one of her father's peaches, and universally famed, not merely for her beauty, but her vast expectations. She was withal a little of a coquette, as might be perceived even in her dress, which was a mixture of ancient and modern fashions, as most suited to set off her charms. She wore the ornaments of pure yellow gold, which her great-great-grandmother had brought over from Saardam; the tempting stomacher of the olden time; and withal a provokingly short petticoat, to display the prettiest foot and ankle in the country round.

Ichabod Crane had a soft and foolish heart towards the sex; and it is not to be wondered at that so tempting a morsel soon found favor in his eyes; more especially after he had visited her in her paternal mansion. Old Baltus Van Tassel was a perfect picture of a thriving, contented, liberal-hearted farmer. He seldom, it is true, sent either his eyes or his thoughts beyond the boundaries of his own farm; but within those everything was snug, happy, and well-conditioned. He was satisfied with his wealth, but not proud of it; and piqued himself upon the hearty abundance rather than the style in which he lived. His stronghold was situated on the banks of the Hudson, in one of those green, sheltered, fertile nooks, in which Dutch farmers are so fond of nestling. A great elm-tree spread its broad branches over it; at the foot of which bubbled up a spring of the softest and sweetest water, in a little well, formed of a barrel; and then stole sparkling away through the grass, to a neighboring brook, that bubbled along among alders and dwarf willows. Hard by the farmhouse was a vast barn, that might have served for a church; every window and crevice of which seemed bursting forth with the treasures of the farm. The flail was busily resounding within it from morning to night; swallows and martins skimmed twittering about the eaves; and rows of pigeons, some with one eye turned up, as if watching the weather, some with their heads under their wings, or buried in their bosoms, and others swelling, and cooing, and bowing about their dames, were enjoying the sunshine on the roof. Sleek unwieldy porkers were grunting in the repose and abundance of their pens; whence sallied forth, now and then, troops of sucking pigs, as if to snuff the air. A stately squadron of snowy geese were riding in an adjoining pond, convoying whole fleets of ducks; regiments of turkeys were gobbling through the farmyard, and guinea fowls fretting about it, like ill-tempered housewives, with their peevish, discontented cry. Before the barn door strutted the gallant cock, that pattern of a husband, a warrior, and a fine gentleman, clapping his burnished wings, and crowing in the pride and gladness of his heart—sometimes tearing up the earth with his feet, and then generously calling his ever-hungry family of wives and children to enjoy the rich morsel which he had discovered.

The pedagogue's mouth watered, as he looked upon this sumptuous promise of luxurious winter fare. In his devouring mind's eye, he pictured to himself every roasting-pig running about with a pudding in his belly, and an apple in his mouth; the pigeons were snugly put to bed in a comfortable pie, and tucked in with a coverlet of crust; the geese were swimming in their own gravy; and the ducks pairing cosily in dishes, like snug married couples, with a decent competency of onion sauce. In the porkers he saw carved out the future sleek side of bacon, and juicy relishing ham; not a turkey but he beheld daintily trussed up, with its gizzard

under its wing, and, peradventure, a necklace of
savory sausages; and even bright chanticleer himself lay sprawling on his back, in a side-dish, with
uplifted claws, as if craving that quarter which his
chivalrous spirit disdained to ask while living.

As the enraptured Ichabod fancied all this, and
as he rolled his great green eyes over the fat
meadow-lands, the rich fields of wheat, of rye, of
buckwheat, and Indian corn, and the orchards
burdened with ruddy fruit, which surrounded
the warm tenement of Van Tassel, his heart
yearned after the damsel who was to inherit these
domains, and his imagination expanded with the
idea, how they might be readily turned into cash,
and the money invested in immense tracts of wild
land, and shingle palaces in the wilderness. Nay,
his busy fancy already realized his hopes, and
presented to him the blooming Katrina, with a
whole family of children, mounted on the top of a
wagon loaded with household trumpery, with pots
and kettles dangling beneath; and he beheld himself bestriding a pacing mare, with a colt at her
heels, setting out for Kentucky, Tennessee, or the
Lord knows where.

When he entered the house the conquest of his
heart was complete. It was one of those spacious
farmhouses, with high-ridged, but lowly-sloping
roofs, built in the style handed down from the
first Dutch settlers, the low projecting eaves
forming a piazza along the front, capable of being
closed up in bad weather. Under this were hung
flails, harness, various utensils of husbandry, and
nets for fishing in the neighboring river. Benches

were built along the sides for summer use; and a great spinning-wheel at one end, and a churn at the other, showed the various uses to which this important porch might be devoted. From this piazza the wondering Ichabod entered the hall, which formed the centre of the mansion and the place of usual residence. Here, rows of resplendent pewter, ranged on a long dresser, dazzled his eyes. In one corner stood a huge bag of wool ready to be spun; in another a quantity of linsey-woolsey just from the loom; ears of Indian corn, and strings of dried apples and peaches, hung in gay festoons along the walls, mingled with the gaud of red peppers, and a door left ajar gave him a peep into the best parlor, where the claw-footed chairs, and dark mahogany tables, shone like mirrors. And irons, with their accompanying shovel and tongs, glistened from their covert of asparagus tops; mock-oranges and conch-shells decorated the mantel-piece; strings of various colored birds' eggs were suspended above it. A great ostrich egg was hung from the centre of the room, and a corner cupboard, knowingly left open, displayed immense treasures of old silver and well-mended china.

From the moment Ichabod laid his eyes upon these regions of delight, the peace of his mind was at an end, and his only study was how to gain the affections of the peerless daughter of Van Tassel. In this enterprise, however, he had more real difficulties than generally fell to the lot of a knight-errant of yore, who seldom had anything but giants, enchanters, fiery dragons, and such like easily conquered adversaries, to contend with; and had to make his way merely through gates of iron and brass, and walls of adamant, to the castle keep, where the lady of his heart was confined, all of which he achieved as easily as a man would carve his way to the centre of a Christmas pie, and then the lady gave him her hand as a matter of course. Ichabod, on the contrary, had to win his way to the heart of a country coquette, beset with a labyrinth of whims and caprices, which were forever presenting new difficulties and impediments; and he had to encounter a host of fearful adversaries of real flesh and blood, the numerous rustic admirers, who beset every portal to her heart, keeping a watchful and angry eye upon each other, but ready to fly out in the common cause against any new competitor.

Among these the most formidable was a burly, roaring, roystering blade, of the name of Abraham, or, according to the Dutch abbreviation, Brom Van Brunt, the hero of the country round, which rang with his feats of strength and hardihood. He was broad-shouldered and double-jointed, with short curly black hair, and a bluff, but not unpleasant countenance, having a mingled air of fun and arrogance. From his Herculean frame and great powers of limb, he had received the nickname of BROM BONES, by which he was universally known. He was famed for great knowledge and skill in horsemanship, being as dexterous on horseback as a Tartar. He was foremost at all races and cockfights; and, with the ascendency which bodily strength acquires in rustic life, was the umpire in all disputes, setting his hat on one side, and giving his decisions with an air and tone admitting of no gainsay or appeal. He was always ready for either a fight or a frolic; but had more mischief than ill-will in his composition; and, with all his overbearing roughness, there was a strong dash of waggish good-humor at bottom. He had three or four boon companions, who regarded him as their model, and at the head of whom he scoured the country, attending every scene of feud or merriment for miles round. In cold weather he was distinguished by a fur cap, surmounted with a flaunting fox's tail; and when the folks at a country gathering descried this well-known crest at a distance, whisking about among a squad of hard riders, they always stood by for a squall. Sometimes his crew would be heard dashing along past the farmhouses at midnight, with whoop and halloo, like a troop of Don Cossacks; and the old dames, startled out of their sleep, would listen for a moment till the hurry-scurry had clattered by, and then exclaim, "Ay, there goes Brom Bones and his gang!" The neighbors looked upon him with a mixture of awe, admiration, and good will; and when any madcap prank or rustic brawl occurred in the vicinity, always shook their heads, and warranted Brom Bones was at the bottom of it.

This rantipole hero had for some time singled out the blooming Katrina for the object of his uncouth gallantries, and though his amorous toyings were something like the gentle caresses and endearments of a bear, yet it was whispered that she did not altogether discourage his hopes.

Certain it is, his advances were signals for rival candidates to retire, who felt no inclination to cross a lion in his amours; insomuch, that when his horse was seen tied to Van Tassel's paling, on a Sunday night, a sure sign that his master was courting, or, as it is termed, "sparking," within, all other suitors passed by in despair, and carried the war into other quarters.

Such was the formidable rival with whom Ichabod Crane had to contend, and, considering all things, a stouter man than he would have shrunk from the competition, and a wiser man would have despaired. He had, however, a happy mixture of pliability and perseverance in his nature; he was in form and spirit like a supple-jack—yielding, but tough; though he bent, he never broke; and though he bowed beneath the slightest pressure, yet, the moment it was away—jerk! he was as erect, and carried his head as high as ever.

To have taken the field openly against his rival would have been madness; for he was not a man to be thwarted in his amours, any more than that stormy lover, Achilles. Ichabod, therefore, made his advances in a quiet and gently-insinuating manner. Under cover of his character of singing-master, he made frequent visits at the farmhouse; not that he had any thing to apprehend from the meddlesome interference of parents, which is so often a stumbling-block in the path of lovers. Balt Van Tassel was an easy, indulgent soul; he loved his daughter better even than his pipe, and like a reasonable man and an excellent father, let her have her way in every thing. His notable

little wife, too, had enough to do to attend to her
housekeeping and manage her poultry; for, as she
sagely observed, ducks and geese are foolish things,
and must be looked after, but girls can take care
of themselves. Thus while the busy dame bustled
about the house, or plied her spinning-wheel at one
end of the piazza, honest Balt would sit smoking
his evening pipe at the other, watching the achieve-
ments of a little wooden warrior, who, armed with a
sword in each hand, was most valiantly fighting the
wind on the pinnacle of the barn. In the meantime,
Ichabod would carry on his suit with the daughter
by the side of the spring under the great elm, or
sauntering along in the twilight, that hour so
favorable to the lover's eloquence.

I profess not to know how women's hearts are
wooed and won. To me they have always been
matters of riddle and admiration. Some seem to
have but one vulnerable point, or door of access;
while others have a thousand avenues, and may be
captured in a thousand different ways. It is a
great triumph of skill to gain the former, but a still
greater proof of generalship to maintain possession
of the latter, for the man must battle for his fortress at every door and window. He who wins a
thousand common hearts is therefore entitled to
some renown; but he who keeps undisputed sway
over the heart of a coquette, is indeed a hero.
Certain it is, this was not the case with the redoubt-
able Brom Bones; and from the moment Ichabod
Crane made his advances, the interests of the
former evidently declined; his horse was no longer
seen tied at the palings on Sunday nights, and a

deadly feud gradually arose between him and the preceptor of Sleepy Hollow.

Brom, who had a degree of rough chivalry in his nature, would fain have carried matters to open warfare, and have settled their pretensions to the lady, according to the mode of those most concise and simple reasoners, the knights-errant of yore—by single combat; but Ichabod was too conscious of the superior might of his adversary to enter the lists against him: he had overheard a boast of Bones, that he would "double the schoolmaster up, and lay him on a shelf of his own school-house"; and he was too wary to give him an opportunity. There was something extremely provoking in this obstinately pacific system; it left Brom no alternative but to draw upon the funds of rustic waggery in his disposition, and to play off boorish practical jokes upon his rival. Ichabod became the object of whimsical persecution to Bones, and his gang of rough riders. They harried his hitherto peaceful domains; smoked out his singing-school, by stopping up the chimney; broke into the school-house at night, in spite of its formidable fastenings of withe and window stakes, and turned every thing topsy-turvy: so that the poor schoolmaster began to think all the witches in the country held their meetings there. But what was still more annoying, Brom took all opportunities of turning him into ridicule in presence of his mistress, and had a scoundrel dog whom he taught to whine in the most ludicrous manner, and introduced as a rival of Ichabod's to instruct her in psalmody.

In this way matters went on for some time, without producing any material effect on the relative situation of the contending powers. On a fine autumnal afternoon, Ichabod, in pensive mood, sat enthroned on the lofty stool whence he usually watched all the concerns of his little literary realm. In his hand he swayed a ferule, that sceptre of despotic power; the birch of justice reposed on three nails, behind the throne, a constant terror to evil doers; while on the desk before him might be seen sundry contraband articles and prohibited weapons, detected upon the persons of idle urchins; such as half-munched apples, popguns, whirligigs, fly-cages, and whole legions of rampant little paper game-cocks. Apparently there had been some appalling act of justice recently inflicted, for his scholars were all busily intent upon their books, or slyly whispering behind them with one eye kept upon the master; and a kind of buzzing stillness reigned throughout the school-room. It was suddenly interrupted by the appearance of a negro, in tow-cloth jacket and trousers, a round-crowned fragment of a hat, like the cap of Mercury, and mounted on the back of a ragged, wild, half-broken colt, which he managed with a rope by way of halter. He came clattering up to the school door with an invitation to Ichabod to attend a merry-making or "quilting frolic," to be held that evening at Mynheer Van Tassel's; and having delivered his message with that air of importance, and effort at fine language, which a negro is apt to display on petty embassies of the kind, he dashed over the brook, and was seen scampering away up the hollow, full of the importance and hurry of his mission.

All was now bustle and hubbub in the late quiet school-room. The scholars were hurried through their lessons, without stopping at trifles; those who were nimble skipped over half with impunity, and those who were tardy, had a smart application now and then in the rear, to quicken their speed, or help them over a tall word. Books were flung aside without being put away on the shelves, ink-stands were overturned, benches thrown down, and the whole school was turned loose an hour before the usual time, bursting forth like a legion of young imps, yelping and racketing about the green, in joy at their early emancipation.

The gallant Ichabod now spent at least an extra half-hour at his toilet, brushing and furbishing up his best, and indeed only suit of rusty black, and arranging his locks by a bit of broken looking-glass, that hung up in the school-house. That he might make his appearance before his mistress in the true style of a cavalier, he borrowed a horse from the farmer with whom he was domiciliated, a choleric old Dutchman, of the name of Hans Van Ripper, and, thus gallantly mounted, issued forth, like a knight-errant in quest of adventures. But it is meet I should, in the true spirit of romantic story, give some account of the looks and equipments of my hero and his steed. The animal he bestrode was a broken-down plough-horse, that had outlived almost everything but his viciousness. He was gaunt and shagged, with a ewe neck and a head like a hammer; his rusty mane and tail were tangled and knotted with burrs; one eye had lost its pupil, and was glaring and spectral; but the other had the gleam of a genuine devil in it. Still he must have had fire and mettle in his day, if we may judge from the name he bore of Gunpowder, He had, in fact, been a favorite steed of his master's, the choleric Van Ripper, who was a furious rider, and had infused, very probably, some of his own spirit into the animal; for, old and broken-down as he looked, there was more of the lurking devil in him than in any young filly in the country.

Ichabod was a suitable figure for such a steed. He rode with short stirrups, which brought his knees nearly up to the pommel of the saddle; his sharp elbows stuck out like grasshoppers'; he carried his whip perpendicularly in his hand, like a sceptre, and, as his horse jogged on, the motion of his arms was not unlike the flapping of a pair of wings. A small wool hat rested on the top of his nose, for so his scanty strip of forehead might be called; and the skirts of his black coat fluttered out almost to the horse's tail. Such was the appearance of Ichabod and his steed, as they shambled out of the gate of Hans Van Ripper, and it was altogether such an apparition as is seldom to be met with in broad daylight.

It was, as I have said, a fine autumnal day, the sky was clear and serene, and nature wore that rich and golden livery which we always associate with the idea of abundance. The forests had put on their sober brown and yellow, while some trees of the tenderer kind had been nipped by the frosts into brilliant dyes of orange, purple, and scarlet. Streaming files of wild ducks began to make their appearance high in the air; the bark of the squirrel might be heard from the groves of beech and hickory nuts, and the pensive whistle of the quail at intervals from the neighboring stubble-field.

The small birds were taking their farewell banquets. In the fulness of their revelry, they fluttered, chirping and frolicking, from bush to bush, and tree to tree, capricious from the very profusion and variety around them. There was the honest cock-robin, the favorite game of stripling sportsmen, with its loud querulous note; and the twittering blackbirds flying in sable clouds; and the golden-winged woodpecker, with his crimson crest, his broad black gorget, and splendid plumage; and the cedar-bird, with its red-tipt wings and yellow-tipt tail, and its little montero cap of feathers; and the blue-jay, that noisy coxcomb, in his gay light-blue coat and white underclothes; screaming and chattering, nodding and bobbing and bowing, and pretending to be on good terms with every songster of the grove.

As Ichabod jogged slowly on his way, his eye, ever open to every symptom of culinary abundance, ranged with delight over the treasures of jolly autumn. On all sides he beheld vast store of apples; some hanging in oppressive opulence on the trees; some gathered into baskets and barrels for the market; others heaped up in rich piles for the cider-press. Farther on he beheld great fields of Indian corn, with its golden ears peeping from their leafy coverts, and holding out the promise of cakes and hasty-pudding; and the yellow pumpkins lying beneath them, turning up their fair round bellies to the sun, and giving ample prospects of

the most luxurious of pies; and anon he passed
the fragrant buckwheat fields, breathing the odor
of the bee-hive, and as he beheld them, soft antici-
pations stole over his mind of dainty slapjacks,
well buttered, and garnished with honey or treacle,
by the delicate little dimpled hand of Katrina Van
Tassel.

Thus feeding his mind with many sweet thoughts
and "sugared suppositions," he journeyed along
the sides of a range of hills which look out upon
some of the goodliest scenes of the mighty Hudson.
The sun gradually wheeled his broad disk down
into the west. The wide bosom of the Tappan
Zee lay motionless and glassy, excepting that here
and there a gentle undulation waved and prolonged the blue shadow of the distant mountain.
A few amber clouds floated in the sky, without a
breath of air to move them. The horizon was of
a fine golden tint, changing gradually into a pure
apple green, and from that into the deep blue of
the mid-heaven. A slanting ray lingered on the
woody crests of the precipices that overhung some
parts of the river, giving greater depth to the
dark-gray and purple of their rocky sides. A sloop
was loitering in the distance, dropping slowly down
with the tide, her sail hanging uselessly against
the mast; and as the reflection of the sky gleamed
along the still water, it seemed as if the vessel was
suspended in the air.

It was towards evening that Ichabod arrived at
the castle of the Heer Van Tassel, which he found
thronged with the pride and flower of the adjacent country. Old farmers, a spare leathern-

faced race, in homespun coats and breeches, blue
stockings, huge shoes, and magnificent pewter
buckles. Their brisk withered little dames, in
close crimped caps, long-waisted short gowns,
homespun petticoats, with scissors and pin-
cushions, and gay calico pockets hanging on the
outside. Buxom lasses, almost as antiquated as
their mothers, excepting where a straw hat, a fine
ribbon, or perhaps a white frock gave symptoms
of city innovation. The sons, in short square-
skirted coats with rows of stupendous brass
buttons, and their hair generally queued in the
fashion of the times, especially if they could procure an eel-skin for the purpose, it being esteemed,
throughout the country, as a potent nourisher and
strengthener of the hair.

Brom Bones, however, was the hero of the scene,
having come to the gathering on his favorite steed
Daredevil, a creature, like himself, full of mettle
and mischief, and which no one but himself could
manage. He was, in fact, noted for preferring
vicious animals, given to all kinds of tricks, which
kept the rider in constant risk of his neck, for he
held a tractable well-broken horse as unworthy of
a lad of spirit.

Fain would I pause to dwell upon the world of
charms that burst upon the enraptured gaze of
my hero, as he entered the state parlor of Van
Tassel's mansion. Not those of the bevy of
buxom lasses, with their luxurious display of red
and white; but the ample charms of a genuine
Dutch country tea-table, in the sumptuous time
of autumn. Such heaped-up platters of cakes of

various and almost indescribable kinds, known only to experienced Dutch housewives! There was the doughty doughnut, the tenderer oly-koek, and the crisp and crumbling cruller; sweet cakes and short cakes, ginger cakes and honey cakes, and the whole family of cakes. And then there were apple pies and peach pies and pumpkin pies; besides slices of ham and smoked beef; and moreover delectable dishes of preserved plums, and peaches, and pears, and quinces; not to mention broiled shad and roasted chickens; together with bowls of milk and cream, all mingled higgledy-piggledy, pretty much as I have enumerated them, with the motherly teapot sending up its clouds of vapor from the midst—Heaven bless the mark! I want breath and time to discuss this banquet as it deserves, and am too eager to get on with my story. Happily, Ichabod Crane was not in so great a hurry as his historian, but did ample justice to every dainty.

He was a kind and thankful creature, whose heart dilated in proportion as his skin was filled with good cheer; and whose spirits rose with eating as some men's do with drink. He could not help, too, rolling his large eyes round him as he ate, and chuckling with the possibility that he might one day be lord of all this scene of almost unimaginable luxury and splendor. Then, he thought, how soon he'd turn his back upon the old school-house, snap his fingers in the face of Hans Van Ripper, and every other niggardly patron, and kick any itinerant pedagogue out of doors that should dare to call him comrade!

Old Baltus Van Tassel moved about among his guests with a face dilated with content and good humor, round and jolly as the harvest moon. His hospitable attentions were brief, but expressive, being confined to a shake of the hand, a slap on the shoulder, a loud laugh, and a pressing invitation to "fall to, and help themselves."

And now the sound of the music from the common room, or hall, summoned to the dance. The musician was an old gray-headed negro, who had been the itinerant orchestra of the neighborhood for more than half a century. His instrument was as old and battered as himself. The greater part of the time he scraped on two or three strings, accompanying every movement of the bow with a motion of the head, bowing almost to the ground, and stamping with his foot whenever a fresh couple were to start.

Ichabod prided himself upon his dancing as much as upon his vocal powers. Not a limb, not a fibre about him was idle; and to have seen his loosely hung frame in full motion, and clattering about the room, you would have thought Saint Vitus himself, that blessed patron of the dance, was figuring before you in person. He was the admiration of all the negroes; who, having gathered, of all ages and sizes, from the farm and the neighborhood, stood forming a pyramid of shining black faces at every door and window, gazing with delight at the scene, rolling their white eyeballs, and showing grinning rows of ivory from ear to ear. How could the flogger of urchins be otherwise than animated and joyous? the lady of his heart was his partner in the dance, and smiling graciously in reply to all his amorous oglings; while Brom Bones, sorely smitten with love and jealously, sat brooding by himself in one corner.

When the dance was at end, Ichabod was attracted to a knot of the sager folks, who, with old Van Tassel, sat smoking at one end of the piazza, gossiping over former times, and drawing out long stories about the war.

This neighborhood, at the time of which I am speaking, was one of those highly-favored places which abound with chronicle and great men. The British and American line had run near it during the war; it had, therefore, been the scene of marauding, and infested with refugees, cow-boys, and all kinds of border chivalry. Just sufficient time had elapsed to enable each story-teller to dress up his tale with a little becoming fiction, and, in the indistinctness of his recollection, to make himself the hero of every exploit.

There was the story of Doffue Martling, a large, blue-bearded Dutchman, who had nearly taken a British frigate with an old iron nine-pounder from a mud breastwork, only that his gun burst at the sixth discharge. And there was an old gentleman who shall be nameless, being too rich a mynheer to be lightly mentioned, who, in the battle of Whiteplains, being an excellent master of defence, parried a musket ball with a small sword, insomuch that he absolutely felt it whiz round the blade, and glance off at the hilt; in proof of which, he was ready at any time to show the sword, with the hilt a little bent. There were several more

that had been equally great in the field, not one
of whom but was persuaded that he had a consid-
erable hand in bringing the war to a happy
termination.

But all these were nothing to the tales of ghosts
and apparitions that succeeded. The neighborhood is rich in legendary treasures of the kind.
Local tales and superstitions thrive best in these
sheltered, long-settled retreats; but are trampled
under foot by the shifting throng that forms the
population of most of our country places. Besides, there is no encouragement for ghosts in most
of our villages, for they have scarcely had time to
finish their first nap, and turn themselves in their
graves, before their surviving friends have travelled away from the neighborhood; so that when
they turn out at night to walk their rounds, they
have no acquaintance left to call upon. This
is perhaps the reason why we so seldom hear
of ghosts except in our long-established Dutch
communities.

The immediate cause, however, of the preva-
lence of supernatural stories in these parts, was
doubtless owing to the vicinity of Sleepy Hollow.
There was a contagion in the very air that blew
from that haunted region; it breathed forth an
atmosphere of dreams and fancies infecting all the
land. Several of the Sleepy Hollow people were
present at Van Tassel's, and, as usual, were doling
out their wild and wonderful legends. Many
dismal tales were told about funeral trains, and
mourning cries and wailings heard and seen above
the great tree where the unfortunate Major

André was taken, and which stood in the neighborhood. Some mention was made also of the woman in white, that haunted the dark glen at Raven Rock, and was often heard to shriek on winter nights before a storm, having perished there in the snow. The chief part of the stories, however, turned upon the favorite spectre of Sleepy Hollow, the headless horseman, who had been heard several times of late, patrolling the country; and, it was said, tethered his horse nightly among the graves in the churchyard.

The sequestered situation of this church seems always to have made it a favorite haunt of troubled spirits. It stands on a knoll, surrounded by locust-trees and lofty elms, from among which its decent whitewashed walls shine modestly forth, like Christian purity beaming through the shades of retirement. A gentle slope descends from it to a silver sheet of water, bordered by high trees, between which peeps may be caught at the blue hills of the Hudson. To look upon its grass-grown yard, where the sunbeams seem to sleep so quietly, one would think that there at least the dead might rest in peace. On one side of the church extends a wide woody dell, along which raves a large brook among broken rocks and trunks of fallen trees. Over a deep black part of the stream, not far from the church, was formerly thrown a wooden bridge; the road that led to it, and the bridge itself, were thickly shaded by overhanging trees, which cast a gloom about it, even in the daytime; but occasioned a fearful darkness at night. This was one of the favorite haunts of the headless horseman; and the place where he was most frequently encountered. The tale was told of old Brouwer, a most heretical disbeliever in ghosts, how he met the horseman returning from his foray into Sleepy Hollow, and was obliged to get up behind him; how they galloped over bush and brake, over hill and swamp, until they reached the bridge; when the horseman suddenly turned into a skeleton, threw old Brouwer into the brook, and sprang away over the tree-tops with a clap of thunder.

This story was immediately matched by a thrice marvellous adventure of Brom Bones, who made light of the galloping Hessian as an arrant jockey. He affirmed that, on returning one night from the neighboring village of Sing-Sing, he had been over-taken by this midnight trooper; that he had offered to race with him for a bowl of punch, and should have won it too, for Daredevil beat the goblin horse all hollow, but, just as they came to the church bridge, the Hessian bolted, and vanished in a flash of fire.

All these tales, told in that drowsy undertone with which men talk in the dark, the countenances of the listeners only now and then receiving a casual gleam from the glare of a pipe, sank deep in the mind of Ichabod. He repaid them in kind with large extracts from his invaluable author, Cotton Mather, and added many marvellous events that had taken place in his native State of Connecticut, and fearful sights which he had seen in his nightly walks about Sleepy Hollow.

The revel now gradually broke up. The old

farmers gathered together their families in their wagons, and were heard for some time rattling along the hollow roads, and over the distant hills. Some of the damsels mounted on pillions behind their favorite swains, and their light-hearted laughter, mingling with the clatter of hoofs, echoed along the silent woodlands, sounding fainter and fainter until they gradually died away—and the late scene of noise and frolic was all silent and deserted. Ichabod only lingered behind, according to the custom of country lovers, to have a tête-à-tête with the heiress, fully convinced that he was now on the highroad to success. What passed at this interview I will not pretend to say, for in fact I do not know. Something, however, I fear me, must have gone wrong, for he certainly sallied forth, after no great interval, with an air quite desolate and chopfallen.—Oh these women! these women! Could that girl have been playing off any of her coquettish tricks?—Was her encouragement of the poor pedagogue all a mere sham to secure her conquest of his rival?—Heaven only knows, not I!—Let it suffice to say, Ichabod stole forth with the air of one who had been sacking a hen-roost, rather than a fair lady's heart. Without looking to the right or left to notice the scene of rural wealth, on which he had so often gloated, he went straight to the stable, and with several hearty cuffs and kicks, roused his steed most uncourteously from the comfortable quarters in which he was soundly sleeping, dreaming of mountains of corn and oats, and whole valleys of timothy and clover.

It was the very witching time of night that Ichabod, heavy-hearted and crest-fallen, pursued his travel homewards, along the sides of the lofty hills which rise above Tarrytown, and which he had traversed so cheerily in the afternoon. The hour was as dismal as himself. Far below him, the Tappan Zee spread its dusky and indistinct waste of waters, with here and there the tall mast of a sloop, riding quietly at anchor under the land. In the dead hush of midnight, he could even hear the barking of the watch-dog from the opposite shore of the Hudson; but it was so vague and faint as only to give an idea of his distance from this faithful companion of man. Now and then, too, the long-drawn crowing of a cock, accidentally awakened, would sound far, far off, from some farmhouse away among the hills—but it was like a dreaming sound in his ear. No signs of life occurred near him, but occasionally the melancholy chirp of a cricket, or perhaps the guttural twang of a bull-frog, from a neighboring marsh, as if sleeping uncomfortably, and turning suddenly in his bed.

All the stories of ghosts and goblins that he had heard in the afternoon, now came crowding upon his recollection. The night grew darker and darker; the stars seemed to sink deeper in the sky, and driving clouds occasionally hid them from his sight. He had never felt so lonely and dismal. He was, moreover, approaching the very place where many of the scenes of the ghost stories had been laid. In the centre of the road stood an enormous tulip-tree, which towered like a giant above all the other trees of the neighborhood, and formed a kind of landmark. Its limbs were gnarled, and fantastic, large enough to form trunks for ordinary trees, twisting down almost to the earth, and rising again into the air. It was connected with the tragical story of the unfortunate André, who had been taken prisoner hard by; and was universally known by the name of Major André's tree. The common people regarded it with a mixture of respect and superstition, partly out of sympathy for the fate of its ill-starred namesake, and partly from the tales of strange sights and doleful lamentations told concerning it.

As Ichabod approached this fearful tree, he began to whistle: he thought his whistle was answered —it was but a blast sweeping sharply through the dry branches. As he approached a little nearer, he thought he saw something white hanging in the midst of the tree—he paused and ceased whistling, but on looking more narrowly, perceived that it was a place where the tree had been scathed by lightning; and the white wood laid bare. Suddenly he heard a groan—his teeth chattered and his knees smote against the saddle: it was but the rubbing of one huge bough upon another, as they were swayed about by the breeze. He passed the tree in safety, but new perils lay before him.

About two hundred yards from the tree a small brook crossed the road, and ran into a marshy and thickly-wooded glen, known by the name of Wiley's Swamp. A few rough logs, laid side by side, served for a bridge over this stream. On that side of the road where the brook entered the wood, a group of oaks and chestnuts, matted thick with wild grapevines, threw a cavernous gloom over it. To pass this bridge was the severest trial. It was at this identical spot that the unfortunate André was captured, and under the covert of those chestnuts and vines were the sturdy yeomen concealed who surprised him. This has ever since been considered a haunted stream, and fearful are the feelings of the schoolboy who has to pass it alone after dark.

As he approached the stream his heart began to thump; he summoned up, however, all his resolution, gave his horse half a score of kicks in the ribs, and attempted to dash briskly across the bridge; but instead of starting forward, the perverse old animal made a lateral movement, and ran broadside against the fence. Ichabod, whose fears increased with the delay, jerked the reins on the other side, and kicked lustily with the contrary foot: it was all in vain; his steed started, it is true, but it was only to plunge to the opposite side of the road into a thicket of brambles and alder bushes. The schoolmaster now bestowed both whip and heel upon the starveling ribs of old Gunpowder, who dashed forward, snuffling and snorting, but came to a stand just by the bridge, with a suddenness that had nearly sent his rider sprawling over his head. Just at this moment a plashy tramp by the side of the bridge caught the sensitive ear of Ichabod. In the dark shadow of the grove, on the margin of the brook, he beheld something huge, misshapen, black and towering. It stirred not, but seemed gathered up in the gloom, like some gigantic monster ready to spring upon the traveller.

The hair of the affrighted pedagogue rose upon his head with terror. What was to be done? To turn and fly was now too late; and besides, what chance was there of escaping ghost or goblin, if such it was, which could ride upon the wings of the wind? Summoning up, therefore, a show of courage, he demanded in stammering accents—"Who are you?" He received no reply. He repeated his demand in a still more agitated voice. Still there was no answer. Once more he cudgelled the sides of the inflexible Gunpowder, and, shutting his eyes, broke forth with involuntary fervor into a psalm tune. Just then the shadowy object of alarm put itself in motion, and, with a scramble and a bound, stood at once in the middle of the road. Though the night was dark and dismal, yet the form of the unknown might now in some degree be ascertained. He appeared to be a horseman of large dimensions, and mounted on a black horse of powerful frame. He made no offer of molestation or sociability, but kept aloof on one side of the road, jogging along on the blind side of old Gunpowder, who had now got over his fright and waywardness.

Ichabod, who had no relish for this strange midnight companion, and bethought himself of the adventure of Brom Bones with the Galloping Hessian, now quickened his steed, in hopes of leaving him behind. The stranger, however, quickened his horse to an equal pace. Ichabod pulled up, and fell into a walk, thinking to lag behind—the other did the same. His heart began to sink within him; he endeavored to resume his psalm tune, but his parched tongue clove to the roof of his mouth, and he could not utter a stave. There was something in the moody and dogged silence of this pertinacious companion, that was mysterious and appalling. It was soon fearfully accounted for. On mounting a rising ground, which brought the figure of his fellow-traveller in relief against the sky, gigantic in height, and muffled in a cloak, Ichabod was horror-struck, on perceiving that he was headless!—but his horror was still more increased, on observing that the head, which should have rested on his shoulders, was carried before him on the pommel of the saddle: his terror rose to desperation; he rained a shower of kicks and blows upon Gunpowder, hoping, by a sudden movement, to give his companion the slip—but the spectre started full jump with him. Away then they dashed, through thick and thin; stones flying, and sparks flashing at every bound. Ichabod's flimsy garments fluttered in the air, as he stretched his long lank body away over his horse's head, in the eagerness of his flight.

They had now reached the road which turns off to Sleepy Hollow; but Gunpowder, who seemed possessed with a demon, instead of keeping up it, made an opposite turn, and plunged headlong down hill to the left. This road leads through a sandy hollow, shaded by trees for about a quarter of a mile, where it crosses the bridge famous in goblin story, and just beyond swells the green knoll on which stands the whitewashed church.

As yet the panic of the steed had given his unskilful rider an apparent advantage in the chase; but just as he had got half way through the hollow, the girths of the saddle gave way, and he felt it slipping from under him. He seized it by the pommel, and endeavored to hold it firm, but in vain; and had just time to save himself by clasping old Gunpowder round the neck, when the saddle fell to the earth, and he heard it trampled under foot by his pursuer. For a moment the terror of Hans Van Ripper's wrath passed across his mind—for it was his Sunday saddle; but this was no time for petty fears; the goblin was hard on his haunches; and (unskilful rider that he was!) he had much ado to maintain his seat; sometimes slipping on one side, sometimes on another, and sometimes jolted on the high ridge of his horse's backbone, with a violence that he verily feared would cleave him asunder.

An opening in the trees now cheered him with the hopes that the church bridge was at hand. The wavering reflection of a silver star in the bosom of the brook told him that he was not mistaken. He saw the walls of the church dimly glaring under the trees beyond. He recollected the place where Brom Bone's ghostly competitor had disappeared. "If I can but reach that bridge," thought Ichabod, "I am safe." Just then he heard the black steed panting and blowing close behind him; he even fancied that he felt his hot breath. Another convulsive kick in the ribs, and old Gunpowder sprang upon the bridge; he thundered over the resounding planks; he gained the opposite side; and now Ichabod cast a look behind to see if his pursuer should vanish, according to rule, in a flash of fire and brimstone. Just then he saw the goblin rising in his stirrups, and in the very act of hurling his head at him. Ichabod endeavored to dodge the horrible missile, but too late. It encountered his cranium with a tremendous crash—he was tumbled headlong into the dust, and Gunpowder, the black steed, and the goblin rider, passed by like a whirlwind.

The next morning the old horse was found without his saddle, and with the bridle under his feet, soberly cropping the grass at his master's gate. Ichabod did not make his appearance at breakfast —dinner-hour came, but no Ichabod. The boys assembled at the school-house, and strolled idly about the banks of the brook; but no schoolmaster. Hans Van Ripper now began to feel some uneasiness about the fate of poor Ichabod, and his saddle. An inquiry was set on foot, and after diligent investigation they came upon his traces. In one part of the road leading to the church was found the saddle trampled in the dirt; the tracks of horses' hoofs deeply dented in the road, and evidently at furious speed, were traced to the bridge, beyond which, on the bank of a broad part of the brook, where the water ran deep and black, was found the hat of the unfortunate Ichabod, and close beside it a shattered pumpkin.

The brook was searched, but the body of the schoolmaster was not to be discovered. Hans Van Ripper, as executor of his estate, examined the bundle which contained all his worldly effects. They consisted of two shirts and a half; two stocks for the neck; a pair or two of worsted stockings; an old pair of corduroy smallclothes; a rusty razor;

a book of psalm tunes, full of dogs' ears; and a broken pitchpipe. As to the books and furniture of the school-house, they belonged to the community, excepting Cotton Mather's History of Witchcraft, a New England Almanac, and a book of dreams and fortune-telling; in which last was a sheet of foolscap much scribbled and blotted in several fruitless attempts to make a copy of verses in honor of the heiress of Van Tassel. These magic books and the poetic scrawl were forthwith consigned to the flames by Hans Van Ripper; who from that time forward determined to send his children no more to school; observing, that he never knew any good come of this same reading and writing. Whatever money the schoolmaster possessed, and he had received his quarter's pay but a day or two before, he must have had about his person at the time of his disappearance.

The mysterious event caused much speculation at the church on the following Sunday. Knots of gazers and gossips were collected in the churchyard, at the bridge, and at the spot where the hat and pumpkin had been found. The stories of Brouwer, of Bones, and a whole budget of others, were called to mind; and when they had diligently considered them all, and compared them with the symptoms of the present case, they shook their heads, and came to the conclusion that Ichabod had been carried off by the Galloping Hessian. As he was a bachelor, and in nobody's debt, nobody troubled his head any more about him. The school was removed to a different quarter of the hollow, and another pedagogue reigned in his stead.

It is true, an old farmer, who had been down to New York on a visit several years after, and from whom this account of the ghostly adventure was received, brought home the intelligence that Ichabod Crane was still alive; that he had left the neighborhood, partly through fear of the goblin and Hans Van Ripper, and partly in mortification at having been suddenly dismissed by the heiress; that he had changed his quarters to a distant part of the country; had kept school and studied law at the same time, had been admitted to the bar, turned politician, electioneered, written for the newspapers, and finally had been made a justice of the Ten Pound Court. Brom Bones, too, who shortly after his rival's disappearance conducted the blooming Katrina in triumph to the altar, was observed to look exceedingly knowing whenever the story of Ichabod was related, and always burst into a hearty laugh at the mention of the pumpkin; which led some to suspect that he knew more about the matter than he chose to tell.

The old country wives, however, who are the best judges of these matters, maintain to this day that Ichabod was spirited away by supernatural means; and it is a favorite story often told about the neighborhood round the winter evening fire. The bridge became more than ever an object of superstitious awe, and that may be the reason why the road has been altered of late years, so as to approach the church by the border of the mill-pond. The schoolhouse being deserted, soon fell to decay, and was reported to be haunted by the ghost of the unfortunate pedagogue; and the plough-boy, loitering homeward of a still summer evening, has often fancied his voice at a distance, chanting a melancholy psalm tune among the tranquil solitudes of Sleepy Hollow.

THE HARE WHO THOUGHT THE
WORLD HAD COME TO
AN END

Translated by H. N. Francis

ONCE upon a time there was near the Western Ocean a grove of palm and vilva trees. A certain Hare lived here beneath a palm sapling, at the foot of a vilva tree. One day this Hare after feeding came and lay down beneath a young palm tree, and the thought struck him: "If this earth should be destroyed, what would become of me?"

At this very moment a ripe vilva fruit fell on a palm leaf. At the sound of it the Hare suddenly thought, "This solid earth is collapsing," and starting up he fled without so much as looking behind him.

Another Hare saw him scampering off as if frightened to death, and asked the cause of his sudden flight. "Pray don't ask me," he said. The second Hare, followed, crying, "Pray, sir, what is it?" and kept running after him.

Then the Hare stopped a moment and, without looking back, he said, "The earth here is breaking up." And at this the second Hare ran after the first. And then first one and then another Hare caught sight of him running and joined in the chase, till one hundred thousand Hares all took their flight together. They were seen by a Deer, a Boar, an Elk, a Buffalo, a Wild Ox, a Rhinoceros, a Tiger, a Lion and an Elephant. And when they asked what it meant and were told that the earth was breaking up, they too took to flight. By degrees this host of animals was a league long.

A wise Brahmin who saw this headlong flight of animals, and was told that the cause of it was that the earth was coming to an end, thought: "The earth is nowhere coming to an end. Surely it must be some sound which was misunderstood by them. If I don't make a great effort they will all perish. I will save their lives." With the speed of a lion he got before them to the foot of a mountain, and roared three times like a lion. They were terribly frightened and stopped in their flight, standing all huddled together. The Brahmin, in the guise of a Lion, went amongst them and asked why they were running away.

"The earth is collapsing," they answered.

"Who saw it collapsing?" he said.

"The Elephants know all about it," they replied. He asked the Elephants, but they didn't know. They said the Lions knew. But the Lions said, "We don't know; the Tigers know." The Tigers said, "The Wild Oxen know." The Wild Oxen, "The Buffaloes." The Buffaloes, "The Elks." The Elks, "The Boars." The Boars, "The Deer." The Deer said, "We don't know; the Hares know." When the Hares were questioned they pointed to one particular Hare and said, "This one told us."

THE HARE AND THE WORLD

So the Brahmin went up to him and asked, "Is it true, sir, that the earth is breaking up?"

"Yes, sir, I saw it," said the Hare.

"Where," he asked, "were you living when you saw it?"

"Near the ocean, sir, in a grove of palm and vilva trees. As I was lying beneath the shade of a palm sapling at the foot of a vilva tree, I thought, 'If this earth should break up, where shall I go?' And at that very moment I heard the sound of the earth breaking up, and I fled."

The Lion thought to himself: "A ripe vilva fruit evidently must have fallen on a palm leaf and made a 'thud,' and this Hare jumped to the conclusion that the earth was coming to an end, and ran away. I will find out the exact truth about it." So he reassured the herd of animals and said: "I will take the Hare and go and find out exactly whether the earth is coming to an end or not, in the place pointed out by him. Until I return do you stay here." Then, placing the Hare on his back, he sprang forward with the speed of a lion, and putting the Hare down in a palm grove, he said, "Come, show us the place you meant."

"I dare not, my lord," said the Hare.

"Come, don't be afraid," said the Lion. The Hare, not daring to go near the vilva tree, stood afar off and cried, "Yonder, sir, is the place of dreadful sounds."

The Lion went to the foot of the vilva tree, and saw the spot where the Hare had been lying beneath the shade of the palm tree, and the ripe vilva fruit that fell on the palm leaf, and having ascer-

432

tained that the earth had not broken up, he placed the Hare on his back and with the speed of a lion soon came again to the herd of beasts.

He told them the whole story, and having thus reassured the herd of beasts he let them go.

THE WATERING OF THE SAPLINGS

Translated by Rev. W. H. D. Rouse

ONCE upon a time a king named Vissasena was reigning over the city of Benares, and proclamation was made of a holiday. The park-keeper thought he would take a holiday, so, calling the Monkeys that lived in the park, he said:

"This park is a great blessing to you. I want to take a week's holiday. Will you water the saplings on the seventh day?" "Oh, yes," they said. He gave them the watering skins, and went away.

The Monkeys drew water and began to water the roots, when the eldest Monkey cried out:

"Wait, now! It's hard to get water. We must not waste it. Let us pull up the plants, and notice the length of their roots; if they have long roots, they need plenty of water; but short ones need but a little."

"True, true," they agreed; so some of them pulled up the plants while others put them back and watered them.

HARE AND THE ELEPHANTS

"Who bids you do that?" asked a young gentleman living in Benares.

"Our chief," they replied.

To this the young gentleman answered:

> "If he was chosen as the best,
> What sort of creatures are the rest!"

Whereat the Monkeys repeated:

> "Brahmin, you know not what you say
> Blaming us in such a way!
> If the root we do not know,
> How can we tell the trees that grow?"

THE OLD HARE AND THE ELEPHANTS

Translated by Sir Edwin Arnold

ONCE on a time very little rain had fallen in the due season; and the Elephants, being oppressed with thirst, thus addressed their leader: "Master, how are we to live? The small creatures find something to wash in, but we cannot, and we are half dead in consequence; whither shall we go then, and what shall we do?"

Upon that the King of the Elephants led them away a little distance and showed them a beautiful pool of water clear as crystal, where they took their ease.

Now it chanced that a company of Hares resided on the banks of the pool and the going and coming of the Elephants trampled many of them to death, till one of their number grumbled out, "This troop will be coming here to water every day, and every one of our family will be crushed."

"Do not disquiet yourself," said an old Buck Hare named Good-speed; "I will manage to stop it," and so saying, he set off, bethinking himself on his way how he should approach and accost a herd of Elephants; for

Elephants destroy by touching, snakes with point of tooth
    beguile;
Kings by favor kill, and traitors murder with a fatal smile.

"I will get on the top of a hill," he thought, "and address the Elephants from there."

This being done, and the lord of the herd perceiving him, it was asked of the Hare, "Who art thou? and whence comest thou?"

"I am an ambassador from His Godship the Moon," replied Good-speed.

"State your business," said the Elephant King.

"Sire," began the Hare, "an ambassador speaks the truth safely by reason of his position. Thus saith the Moon then: 'These Hares were the guardians of my pool, and thine Elephants in coming here have scared them away. This is not well. Am I not "S'às'anka" whose banner bears a hare, and are not these Hares my followers?'" "Please your worship," said the Elephant King with much fear, "we knew nothing of this; we will go there no more."

"It were well," said the make-believe ambassador, "that you first made your apologies to the God, who is quaking with rage in his pool, and then went about your business."

"We will do so," replied the Elephant with meekness; and being led by night to the pool, in the ripples of which the image of the Moon was quivering, the herd made their prostrations; the Hare explaining to the Moon that their fault was committed in ignorance, and therefore they got their dismissal.

THE ELEPHANT HAS A BET WITH THE TIGER

By Walter Skeat, M.R.A.S., F.A.L.

IN the beginning Gajah the Elephant and Rimau the Tiger were sworn friends. But one day they came to a clearing and presently encountered Lobong, the long-tailed Spectacle-Monkey. And when he saw the Monkey the Elephant said, "Mr. Lobong yonder is far too noisy; let us try and shake him off; if he falls to me I am to eat you; and if he falls to you, you are to eat me—we will make a wager of it." The Tiger said, "Agreed?" and the Elephant replied, "Agreed." "Very well!" said the Tiger; "you shall try and menace him first." So the Elephant tried to menace the Monkey. *"Au! Au! Au!"* he trumpeted, and each time he trumpeted the Monkey was scared. But the Monkey went jumping head foremost through the branches and never fell to the ground at all.

Presently, therefore, the Tiger asked the Elephant, "Well, Friend Elephant, would you like to try your luck again?" But the Elephant said, "No, thank you. It shall be your turn now; and if he falls to you, you shall eat me—if you really can make him fall!"

Then the Tiger went and roared his longest and loudest, and shortened his body as for a spring and growled and menaced the Monkey thrice. And the Monkey leaped and fell at the Tiger's feet, for his feet and hands were paralyzed and would not grip the branches any more. Then the Tiger said, "Well, Friend Elephant, I suppose I may eat you now!" But the Elephant said, "You have, I admit, won the wager; but I beg you to grant me just seven days' respite, to enable me to visit my wife and children and to make my will." The Tiger granted the request, and the Elephant went home, bellowing and sobbing every foot of the way.

Now the Elephant's wife heard the sound of her husband's voice, and said to her children, "What can be the matter with your father that he keeps sobbing so?" And the children listened to make sure and said, "Yes, it really is father's voice, the sobbing, and not that of anybody else." Presently Father Elephant arrived, and Mother Elephant asked, "What were you sobbing for, father? What have you done to yourself?" Father Elephant replied, "I made a wager with Friend Tiger about shaking down a Monkey, and Friend Tiger beat me; I menaced the Monkey, but he did not fall; if he had fallen to me, I was to have eaten Friend Tiger, but if he fell to Friend Tiger, Friend Tiger was to eat me. I was beaten, and now Friend Tiger says he is going to eat me. So I begged leave to come home and see you, and he has given me just seven days' respite."

Now for the seven days Father Elephant kept sobbing aloud, and neither ate nor slept. And the thing came to the hearing of Friend Mouse-deer. "What can be the matter with Friend Elephant that he keeps bellowing and bellowing, neither does he sleep, so that night is turned into day, and day into night? What on earth is the matter with him? Suppose I go and see" (said the Mouse-deer). Then the Mouse-deer went to see what was wrong, and asked, "What is the matter with you, Friend Elephant, that we hear you bellowing and bellowing every single day and every single night, just now, too, when the Rams are upon us? You are far too noisy."

But the Elephant said, "It is no mere empty noise, Friend Mouse-deer, I have got into a dreadful scrape." "What sort of a scrape?" inquired the Mouse-deer. "I made a wager with Friend Tiger about shaking down a Monkey, and he beat me." "What was the stake?" asked the Mouse-deer. "The stake was that Friend Tiger might eat me if Friend Tiger frightened it down; and if I frightened it down, I might eat Friend Tiger. It fell to Friend Tiger, and now Friend Tiger wants to eat me. And my reason for not eating or sleeping any more is that I have got only just seven days' respite to go home and visit my wife and children and to make my will." Then the Mouse-deer said, "If it came to Friend Tiger's eating you, I should feel exceedingly sorrowful, exceedingly distressed; but things being only as you say, I feel neither." "If you will assist me, I will become your slave, and my descendants shall be your slaves forever." ".Very well, if that is the case, I will assist you," said the Mouse-deer. "Go and look for a jar full of molasses." Friend Elephant promised to do so, and went to look for it at the house of a maker of Palm-wine. The owner of the house fled for his life, and the jar fell into Friend Elephant's possession, who bore it back to the Mouse-deer.

Then Friend Mouse-deer said, "When does your promise expire?" and Friend Elephant replied, "To-morrow." So when next morning arrived they started, and the Mouse-deer said, "Now pour the molasses over your back and let it spread and spread and run down your legs." Friend Elephant did as he was ordered. Friend Mouse-deer then instructed the Elephant as follows: "As soon as I begin to lick up the molasses on your back, bellow as loud as you can and make believe to be hurt, and writhe and wriggle this way and that."

And presently Friend Mouse-deer commenced to lick hard, and Friend Elephant writhed and wriggled and made believe to be hurt, and made a prodigious noise of trumpeting. In this way they proceeded and Friend Mouse-deer got up and sat astride upon Friend Elephant's back. And the Elephant trumpeted and trumpeted all the way till they met with Friend Tiger. At this Friend Mouse-deer exclaimed, "A single Elephant is very short commons; if I could only catch that big and fat old Tiger there, it would be just enough to satisfy my hunger."

Now when Friend Tiger heard these words of

the Mouse-deer, he said to himself, "So I suppose if you catch me, you'll eat me into the bargain, will you?" And Friend Tiger stayed not a moment longer, but fled for his life, fetching very lofty bounds. And soon he met with the Black Ape, and Friend Ape asked, "Why running so hard, Friend Tiger? Why so much noise, and why, just when the Rams are upon us, too, do you go fetching such lofty bounds?" Friend Tiger replied, "What do you mean by 'So much noise'? What was the Thing that was got upon Friend Elephant's back, that had caught Friend Elephant and was devouring him so that he went writhing and wriggling for the pain of it, and the blood went streaming down in floods? Moreover the Thing that was on Friend Elephant's back said, to my hearing, that a single Elephant was very short commons; but if It could catch a fat old Tiger like myself that would be just enough to satisfy Its hunger." Friend Ape said, "What was that Thing, Friend Tiger?" "I don't know," said the Tiger. "Ah," mused the Ape, "I wonder if It *could* be Friend Mouse-deer!" "Certainly not," said the Tiger; "why, how in the world could Friend Mouse-deer swallow *Me?* To say nothing of his not being used to meat food" (said he). "Come and let us go back again."

Then they went back again to find the Elephant, and first the Ape went the faster, and then the Tiger went the faster, and then the Ape got in front again. But Friend Mouse-deer sitting on Friend Elephant's back saw them coming and shouted, "Hallo, Father Ape" (said he), "this is a dog's trick indeed; you promise to bring me two Tigers and you only bring me one. I refuse to accept it, Father Ape."

Now when the Tiger heard this, he ran off at first as fast as he could, but presently he slackened his pace and said, "It is too bad of you, Friend Ape, for trying to cozen me in order to pay your own debts. For shame! Father Ape! It was only through good luck that he refused to accept me; if he had accepted, I should have been dead and done with. So now, if you come down to the ground, you shall die the death yourself, just for your trying to cheat me."

Thus the Tiger and the Ape were set at enmity, and to this day the Tiger is very wroth with the Ape for trying to cheat him. And here the story ends.

HOW THE TORTOISE OUT-RAN THE DEER

By C. F. Hartt

A TORTOISE met a Deer out walking, one day, and asked him what he was looking for. The Deer answered, "I am out for a walk, to see if I cannot find something to eat; and pray where are you going, Tortoise?"

"Oh, out walking, looking for water to drink."

"How soon do you expect to reach the water?" asked the Deer.

"Why do you ask that question?" returned the Tortoise.

TORTOISE AND THE DEER

"Because your legs are so short."

"Well!" answered the Tortoise, "I can run faster than you can. If you are long-legged you cannot run so fast as I."

"Then let us run a race!" said the Deer.

"Well," answered the Tortoise, "when shall we run?"

"To-morrow."

"At what time?"

"Very early in the morning."

"All right," assented the Tortoise, who then went into the forest and called together his relations, the other Tortoises, saying, "Come on let's catch him!"

"But how are you going to catch him?" they inquired.

"I said to the Deer," answered the Tortoise, "'Let us run a race, to see who can run the faster.' Now I am going to cheat that Deer. You scatter yourselves along the edge of the campo, in the forest, keeping not very far from one another, and see that you keep perfectly still, each in his place! To-morrow, when we begin the race, the deer will run on the campo, but I will remain quietly in my place. When he calls out to me, if you are ahead of him, answer, but take care not to respond if he has passed you."

Early the next morning the Deer went out to meet the Tortoise.

"Come," said the former, "let us run!"

"Wait a bit!" said the Tortoise, "I am going to run in the woods."

"Why, how are you, a little, short-legged fellow,

442

going to run in the forest?" asked the Deer, surprised.

The Tortoise insisted that he could not run in the campo, but that he was accustomed to run in the forest, so the Deer assented, and the Tortoise went into the woods, saying: "When I take my position I will make a noise with a little stick, so that you may know I am ready."

When the Tortoise, having reached his place, gave the signal, the Deer started off leisurely, laughing to himself, not thinking it worth his while to run. After the Deer had gone quite a little distance, he turned round and called out, "Hullo, Tortoise!" When to his astonishment, a Tortoise a little way ahead cried out, "Hullo, Deer!"

"Well," said the Deer to himself, "that Tortoise does run fast!" Whereupon he hurried up for a bit and then called out again, but the voice of the Tortoise still seemed to be beyond him.

"Why, how's this?" exclaimed the Deer, and he ran briskly for a little ways till, thinking that he surely must have passed the Tortoise, he stopped, turned about, and called again. "Hullo, Deer!" the answer came from the edge of the forest just ahead.

On this the Deer set off at full speed, and, after a little, but without stopping this time, he called to the Tortoise. And still the cry, "Hullo, Deer!" came back to him from ahead. He then redoubled his forces, but with no better success, and at last, tired and bewildered, he ran against a tree and fell dead.

The noise made by the feet of the Deer having

ceased, the first Tortoise listened. Not a sound was heard. Then he called to the Deer, but received no response. So he went to see what was the matter and found the Deer lying at the foot of the tree.

This is an Amazonian myth of the Tupi-speaking population, as related in the Lingua Geral.—CHARLES F. HARTT.

A myth of the slow Tortoise (Sun) and the swift Deer (Moon), a race which the Sun always wins.

WHICH WAS THE STRONGER, THE TORTOISE, THE TAPIR, OR THE WHALE?

By C. F. Hartt

ONE day a Tortoise went down to the sea to drink. A Whale saw him and called out: "Here, what are you doing, Tortoise?"

"Why, I'm drinking, 'cause I'm thirsty."

Then the Whale began to make fun of the Tortoise's short legs, but the Tortoise indignantly replied: "Even if my legs are short, I am stronger than you, and I can pull you on shore."

The Whale laughed, "Come on let me see you do it!"

"Well," said the Tortoise, "just wait until I go into the forest and get a sipó!"[1]

Away went the Tortoise into the forest, and there he met a Tapir, who asked him what he was looking for.

[1] A sipó is a long root growing in the air, often used as a rope.

"I am looking for a sipó."

"And what are you going to do with a sipó?" asked the Tapir.

"I want it to pull you down to the sea."

"You!" exclaimed the Tapir, surprised. "I'll pull you into the forest, and, what's more—but never mind, let's try who may be the stronger! Go get your sipó!" The Tortoise went off, and presently came back with a very long sipó, one end of which he tied around the body of the Tapir.

"Now," said the Tortoise, "wait here until I go down to the sea. When I shake this sipó, run with all your might into the forest." Having attached one end to the Tapir, he dragged the other down to the sea and fastened it to the tail of the Whale. This accomplished, he said, "I will go up into the forest, and when I shake the sipó, pull as hard as you can, for I am going to draw you on shore."

The Tortoise then went into the wood, midway between the Whale and the Tapir, shook the sipó, and awaited the result. First the Whale, swimming vigorously, dragged the Tapir backward to the sea, but the latter, resisting with all his might, finally gained a firm foothold and began to get the better of the Whale, drawing him in toward the shore. Then the Whale made another effort, and in this manner they kept tugging against one another, each thinking the Tortoise at the other end of the sipó, until at last, both gave up the struggle from sheer exhaustion.

The Tortoise then walked down to the shore, and the Whale called out to him: "Well, you certainly are strong, Tortoise; I am very tired."

THE TURTLE

The Tortoise untied the sipó from the whale, and, having dipped himself in the water, went over to where the Tapir was puffing after his labors.

"Well, Tapir," he said, as he untied the sipó, "you see that I am the stronger."

"It is true, Tortoise, you are very, very strong."

The Tortoise (Sun) has a trial of strength with the Tapir (Moon) or perhaps this is the Tortoise (Sun) provoking the everlasting tidal contest between sea and land.—C. F. HARTT.

HOW THE TURTLE GOT HIS SHELL

By Annie Ker

LONG ago, our fathers have told us, the Turtle and the Wallaby were friends. Now on a certain day the Turtle was hungry, and asked his friend to go with him to the beach and from thence to the Hornbill's garden, where was much sugarcane and where bananas also were plentiful. This they did, and fed plentifully on all that was there. The Wallaby trod upon the stalks of the bananas and bowed them to the ground that his friend might eat. Thus did he also to the tall sugarcanes and the flowering rush. And they both did eat and their hunger was stayed.

Now while they were eating the Birds were at work in their gardens, tilling the ground. When the work was finished they dug up much taro and returned to the village to cook their food. They peeled the roots and cut them up and placed them

446

in the pots for cooking. Then said Binama the Hornbill, "Let one of you go down to the beach and bring sea water that our food may be salted."

But nothing came of it, for one by one the Birds made excuse, fearing lest an enemy lay in wait. At last the Wagtail arose, and ran into the house to make ready to go to the beach. He hung his shell breastplate round his neck, tied waving feathers round his head, and took his spear and went forth. As he went he leapt from side to side the better to avoid the foe, if foe there were. In a little while he came to Binama's garden and saw the Turtle and Wallaby feeding. Their hearts trembled; nevertheless the Turtle made bold and said to the Wagtail, "Thy master has bidden us eat of his bananas that our hunger may be stayed."

Now the Wagtail knew in his heart that they lied, but he answered never a word, but filled his bottles with sea water and ran back to the village by another way. When he reached the village he cried aloud, "Friends, the Turtle and the Wallaby are eating in our master's garden!" At this word all arose and ran for their spears, and surrounded the garden. The Wallaby lifted up his head, and seeing naught but enemies round about him, tarried not but leaped mightily, and escaped. The Turtle could not jump, as he well knew, so he crawled with haste into a yam patch and hid himself under the leaves.

The Birds knew he was still there, and they hunted for him diligently until they found him and dragged him forth. The Turtle feared greatly, and cried, "Take not vengeance on me, for truly the Wallaby bade me come hither and with his feet he broke the stalks, while I only ate of the fruit." The Birds cared little for his words, and tied him to a pole and thus carried him to Binama's house, where they laid him upon a shelf till the morrow.

The next day Binama called his servants together and all went to dig food to make a feast, when they should slay the Turtle. None were in the house but the children whom Binama had set to guard the captive. Then the Turtle made his voice soft, and called to the children, "Loosen my bonds, O children," quoth he, "that we may play together." Now the children knew not what was in the Turtle's mind, and they did as he bade them. He crawled down from the shelf, and stretched himself, for he was stiff and sore. Then he said to the children, "Where are your ornaments? Leave the poor ones in the basket, and bring forth only the good ones, that I may see them."

The children ran to the place where Binama kept his ornaments, and brought forth a long necklace of shell money, also two shell armlets and a wooden bowl, and laid them before the Turtle. He forthwith wound the necklace many times round his neck, and put on both the shell armlets. Moreover the bowl he fastened upon his back. Then he said to the children, "Ye behold me now richly attired. Watch while I run a little and back again, and tell me if the sight is a good one or no."

The children watched him crawl a few paces and called him to return. This the Turtle did and all sat together in the shade of a tree. Then the Turtle crawled once more, and the children laughed to watch his ungainly form decorated with their father's ornaments. Again the Turtle returned to the children, but this time he did not sit with them. For on a sudden he heard voices and knew the men were drawing near. Then he saw them as they came forth, and ran swiftly to the sea. The children cried aloud to their father, "Come, for the Turtle is running away!"

When Binama heard this cry, he and the Birds with him threw the sheaves of taro aside and gave chase to the runaway. But the Turtle had already reached the sea, and he hastened to dive. The Birds called, "Show thyself now. Lift up thy head." So the Turtle did so, and the angry Birds cast great stones into the sea, and the left armlet which the turtle wore was shattered. So he dived, but they called again, "Show thyself. Lift up thy head," and a stone fell upon the right armlet and broke it into small pieces. Again they called, and again the Turtle raised himself in the water, and this time the stones cut the string on which the necklace of shell money was threaded.

And now for the last time came the call, "Show thyself. Lift up thy head." The Turtle once more raised himself and the Birds flung after him all the great stones they could find. They fell in scores upon the wooden bowl which had been carried away from Binama's home, but it was not destroyed, nay, nor was it harmed at all. And the Turtle fled far over the sea, nor was he seen again of Binama or his followers.

But since that day even until now, so our fathers have told us, all turtles carry upon their backs the bowl which in the old days was in the house of Binama.

THE LEGEND OF RATA

By Sir George Grey

WAHIEROA had been treacherously slain by a chief named Matuku, so it became the duty of his young son Rata to revenge his father's death. By the time he had grown up he had devised a plan for doing this, and gave the necessary orders to his followers. He then started on a journey.

Arrived at the entrance to Matuku's place he found a Man sitting in the courtyard who had been left in charge.

"Where is the man who killed my father?" he asked.

"He lives down in the earth and I call to warn him when the new moon appears. That is when he comes upon earth to do battle."

"How can he know when the proper time comes?"

"I call to him in a loud voice."

"When will there be a new moon?"

"In two nights. Return to your village, but come here again on the morning of the second day."

On the morning appointed, Rata returned and found the Man sitting in the same place.

"Do you know any spot where I can conceal

myself from the enemy with whom I am about to
fight?" he inquired.

The Man replied, "Come with me and I will
show you the two fountains of clear water."

"This spot that we stand on," said the Man, when
they arrived at the place, "is the place where
Matuku rises up from the earth, and yonder fountain is the one in which he combs and washes his
dishevelled hair; but this fountain is the one he uses
to reflect his face in while he dresses it. You cannot kill him while he is at the fountain he uses
to reflect his face in, because your shadow would
also be reflected in it and he would see it; but at the
fountain in which he washes his hair you may smite
and slay him."

"Will he make his appearance this evening?"

"Yes."

They had not waited long when the moon became
visible and the Man told Rata to hide himself near
the brink of the fountain in which Matuku
would wash his hair. Then he shouted aloud,
"Ho, ho, the new moon is visible—a moon two
days old."

Matuku heard him and, seeing his two-handed
wooden sword, rose from the earth. He laid his
sword on the ground at the edge of the fountain
where he dressed his hair, and kneeling down on
both sides of it he loosened the strings which bound
up his long locks, shook them out, and plunged his
head into the clear cool water. Rata crept out
from where he lay hid, and rapidly moved up and
stood behind him. As Matuku raised his head
above the water Rata with one hand seized him by

the hair, while with the other he smote and slew him.

"Where shall I find the bones of my father?" he next asked the Keeper.

"They are not here; a strange people who live at a distance came and carried them off."

Upon hearing this reply Rata returned to his village to think matters over. He went to the forest and, having found a very tall tree that grew straight throughout its entire length, he felled it and cut its noble branching tops, intending to fashion the trunk into a canoe.

The Insects which inhabit trees and the Spirits of the Forest were very angry at this, and as soon as Rata had returned to the village, when his day's work was done, they took the tree and raised it up again. The multitude of Insects, Birds and Spirits worked away at replacing each little chip and shaving in its proper place, and sang as they worked:

> "Fly together, chips and shavings,
> Stick ye fast together,
> Hold ye fast together;
> Stand upright again, O tree."

Early the next morning Rata came back. When he got to the place where he had left the trunk lying on the ground, he could not at first find it. That fine tall straight tree which he saw standing whole and sound, was the same he thought he had cut down, and there it was now, erect again; however, he stepped up to it and, hewing away he felled it to the ground once more. Off he cut its fine branching top, and he began to hollow out the hold of the canoe, and round off the prow and the stern into their proper, gracefully curved forms. In the evening when it became too dark to work, he returned to his village.

As soon as he was gone the multitudes of Insects, Birds and Spirits raised up the tree upon its stump once more. They sang as they worked, and when they had ended the tree again stood as sound as ever in its former place in the forest.

Morning dawned, and Rata returned once more to work at his canoe. When he reached the place was not he amazed to see the tree standing, untouched, just as he had first found it? Nothing daunted, however, he hews away at it again and down it topples, crashing to the earth. As soon as he saw the tree on the ground Rata went off, as if going home, but turned back and hid himself in the underwood, in a spot whence he could peep out and see what took place. He had not been hidden long when he heard the innumerable multitude of the children of Tane approaching singing their incantations, and at last they arrived at the place where the tree was lying on the ground.

Rata rushed upon them. He seized some of them, shouting: "Ha, ha, it is you, is it, who have been exercising your magical arts upon my tree?"

Then the children of Tane all cried aloud in reply, "Who gave you authority to fell the forest god to the ground? You had no right to do so."

When Rata heard this he was overcome with shame at what he had done. The children of Tane called out to him: "Return, O Rata, to thy village, we will make a canoe for you," and Rata obeyed their orders without delay.

They were so numerous and each understood so well what to do that they had no sooner begun to adze out a canoe, than it was finished. When the canoe was afloat upon the sea, one hundred and forty warriors embarked on board it and they paddled off to seek their foe.

One night, just at nightfall, they reached the fortress of their enemy. Rata landed alone, leaving all his warriors on board. As he stole along the shore he saw that a fire was burning on the sacred place where the enemy sacrificed to their gods. Without stopping he crept directly towards the fire and hid behind some thick bushes. There were several priests, and to assist them in their magical arts they were using the bones of Wahieroa, knocking them together to beat time while repeating a powerful incantation known only to themselves.

Rata listened attentively to this incantation until he had learned it by heart, and when he was quite sure he knew it he rushed suddenly upon the priests. Being ignorant of the numbers of the enemy or whence they came, they made little resistance and were in a moment overcome. The bones of his father Wahieroa were then eagerly snatched up. He hastened with them back to the canoe, embarked on board it, and his warriors at once paddled away.

Rata's task of avenging his father's death being thus ended, his tribe hauled up his large canoe on the shore and roofed it over with thatch to protect it from the sun and weather.

WHY THE HIPPOPOTAMUS LIVES IN THE WATER

By Elphinstone Dayrell, F.R.G.S., F.R.A.I.

MANY years ago the Hippopotamus, whose name was Isantim, was one of the biggest kings on the land; he was second only to the Elephant. The Hippo had seven large fat Wives, of whom he was very fond. Now and then he used to give a big feast to the people, but a curious thing was that, although every one knew the Hippo, no one, except his seven Wives, knew his name.

At one of the feasts, just as the people were about to sit down, the Hippo said, "You have come to feed at my table, but none of you know my name. If you cannot tell my name you shall all of you go away without your dinner."

As they could not guess his name, they had to go away and leave all the good food behind them. Before they left, however, the Tortoise stood up and asked the Hippopotamus what he would do if he told him his name at the next feast? So the Hippo replied that he would be so ashamed of himself that he and his whole family would leave the land, and for the future would dwell in the water.

Now, it was the custom for the Hippo and his seven Wives to go down every morning and evening to the river to wash and have a drink. Of this custom the Tortoise was aware. The Hippo used to walk first, and the seven Wives followed. One day when they had gone down to the river to bathe, the Tortoise made a small hole in the middle

455

of the path, and then waited. When the Hippo and his Wives returned two of the Wives were some distance behind, so the Tortoise came out from where he had been hiding and half buried himself in the hole he had dug, leaving the greater part of his shell exposed. When the two Hippo Wives came along, the first one knocked her foot against the Tortoise's shell, and immediately called out to her husband, "Oh, Isantim, my husband, I have hurt my foot." At this the Tortoise was very glad, and went joyfully home.

When the next feast was given by the Hippo, he made the same condition about his name; so the Tortoise got up and said, "You promise you will not kill me if I tell you your name?" and the Hippo promised. The Tortoise then shouted as loud as he was able, "Your name is Isantim," at which a cheer went up from all the people, and then they sat down to dinner.

When the feast was over, the Hippo with his seven Wives, in accordance with his promise, went down to the river, and they have always lived in the water from that day till now. Although they come on shore to feed at night, you never find a Hippo on the land in the daytime.

WHY THE ELEPHANT HAS SMALL EYES

By Elphinstone Dayrell, F.R.G.S., F.R.A.I.

WHEN Ambo was King of Calabar, the Elephant was not only a very big animal, but he had eyes in proportion to his bulk. In those days men and animals were friends, and all mixed together quite freely. At regular intervals King Ambo used to give a feast, and the Elephant used to eat more than any one, though the Hippopotamus used to do his best; however, not being as big as the Elephant, although he was very fat, he was left a long way behind.

As the Elephant ate so much at these feasts, the Tortoise, who was small and very cunning, made up his mind to put a stop to the Elephant eating more than a fair share of the food provided. He therefore placed some dry kernels and shrimps, of which the Elephant was very fond, in his bag, and went to the Elephant's house to make an afternoon call.

When the Tortoise arrived the Elephant told him to sit down, so he made himself comfortable, and, having shut one eye, took one palm kernel and a shrimp out of his bag and commenced to eat them with relish.

When the Elephant saw the Tortoise eating, he said, as he was always hungry himself, "You seem to have some good food there; what are you eating?"

The Tortoise replied that the food was sweet but

was rather painful, as he was eating one of his eyes; and he lifted up his head, showing one eye closed.

The Elephant said, "If the food is so good, take out one of my eyes and give me the same food."

The Tortoise, who was waiting for this, knowing how greedy the Elephant was, said, "I cannot reach your eye, you are so big." So the Elephant took the Tortoise in his trunk and lifted him up, and with one quick scoop he had the Elephant's eye out. The Elephant trumpeted with pain, but the Tortoise gave him some of the dried kernels and shrimps, and they so pleased the Elephant that he soon forgot the pain.

Soon the Elephant said, "That food is so sweet I must have some more;" but the Tortoise told him that before he could have any the other eye must come out. To this the Elephant agreed, and soon the Elephant was quite blind. The Elephant then began to make a great noise, and started pulling trees down and doing much damage, calling out for the Tortoise. The Tortoise had slid down the Elephant's trunk to the ground, and hid himself.

The next morning when the Elephant heard the people passing, he asked them what the time was, and the Bush Buck, who was nearest, shouted out, "The sun is now up, and I am going to market to get some yams and fresh leaves for my food."

Then the Elephant perceived that the Tortoise had deceived him, and began to ask all the passers-by to lend him a pair of eyes, as he could not see, but every one refused, as they wanted their eyes themselves. At last the Worm grovelled past, and seeing the big Elephant, greeted him in his humble way. He was much surprised when the King of the Forest returned his salutation, and very much flattered also.

The Elephant said, "Look here, Worm, I have mislaid my eyes. Will you lend me yours for a few days? I will return them next market-day."

The Worm was so flattered at being noticed by the Elephant that he gladly consented, and took his eyes out—which, as every one knows, were very small—and gave them to the Elephant. When the Elephant had put the Worm's eyes into his own large eye-sockets, the flesh immediately closed round them so tightly that when the market-day arrived it was impossible for the Elephant to get them out again to return to the Worm; and although the Worm repeatedly made applications to the Elephant to return his eyes, the Elephant always pretended not to hear, and sometimes used to say in a very loud voice, "If there are any Worms about, they had better get out of my way, as they are so small I cannot see them, and if I tread on them they will be squashed."

Ever since then the Worms have been blind, and for the same reason Elephants have such small eyes, quite out of proportion to the size of their huge bodies!

THE BOY WHO SET A SNARE FOR THE SUN

By H. R. Schoolcraft

AT the time when the animals reigned on the earth, they had killed all the people but a Girl and her little brother; and these two were living in fear in an out-of-the-way place. The Boy was a perfect little pigmy, and never grew beyond the size of a mere infant; but the Girl increased with her years, so that the task of providing food and shelter fell wholly upon her. She went out daily to get wood for the lodge-fire, and she took her little brother with her that no mishap might befall them, for he was too little to leave alone. A big bird of a mischievous disposition might have flown away with him. She made him a bow and arrows, and one day she said to him: "My little brother, I will leave you behind where I have been gathering the wood; you must hide yourself, and you will soon see the snowbirds come and peck the worms out of the logs which I have piled up. Shoot one of them and bring it home."

He obeyed her, and tried his best to kill one, but he came home unsuccessful. His sister told him that he must not despair, but try again the next day.

She accordingly left him at the gathering place of the wood, and returned to the lodge. Toward nightfall she heard his little footsteps crackling through the snow, and he hurried in and threw down, with an air of triumph, one of the birds which he had killed. "My sister," said he, "I wish you to skin it, and stretch the skin, and when I have killed more I will have a coat made out of them."

"But what shall we do with the body?" said she; for they had always up to that time lived upon greens and berries.

"Cut it in two," he answered, "and season our stew with one half of it at a time."

It was their first dish of game, and they greatly relished it.

The Boy kept on in his efforts, and in the course of time he killed ten birds, out of the skins of which his sister made him a pretty little coat. As he was small, there was one bird skin to spare.

"Sister," said he, one day, as he marched up and down before the lodge, dressed in his new coat and fancying himself the Greatest Little Fellow in the World—as he was, for there was no other beside him—"My sister, are we really alone in the world, or are we making believe? Is there nobody else living? And tell me, was all this great broad earth and this huge big sky made for a little boy and girl like you and me?"

"By no means," she said. And then she explained to him that there were many folks very unlike a harmless girl and boy, such as they were, who lived in another part of the earth, and that if he would live blameless and not endanger his life, he must never go where they were. This only served to inflame the Boy's curiosity, and he soon took his bows and arrows and went in that direction. After walking a long while and meeting no one, he became tired and stretched himself upon a high, green knoll, where the day's warmth had melted off the snow.

It was a charming place to lie upon, and he fell asleep. While he slept the Sun beat so hot upon him that it singed his bird-skin coat and so shrivelled and shrunk it upon his body as to wake him up.

When he saw the mischief the Sun's fiery beams had played with the coat he was so proud of, he flew into a great rage and scolded the Sun in a terrible way for a little boy no higher than a man's knee. "Do not think you are too high for me to get you," said he; "I shall revenge myself, oh Sun. I will have you for a plaything yet."

When he reached home he told his sister how unfortunate he had been, and bitterly bewailed the spoiling of his new coat. He would not eat, not so much as a single berry. He lay down, like one who fasts, without changing his position for ten days, nor could his sister persuade him to get up. At the end of ten days he turned over on the other side and lay in that position for ten days.

When he got up he was very pale, but very determined. He ordered his sister to make him a snare, as he meant to catch the Sun. She said she had nothing, but presently she brought forward a deer's sinew, which their father had left, and made it into a string suitable for a noose. The moment she showed it to her brother he said it would not do, and angrily bade her find something else. She said she had nothing else, but presently remembered the bird's skin that had been left over when the coat was made, and this she made into a string. With this the Boy was more vexed than over the other. "The Sun has had enough of my bird skins," he said; "find something else."

She did not dare to say again that she had nothing, so she went out of the lodge murmuring to herself, "Was there ever so obstinate a boy?" Luckily she thought of her hair, and pulling out some of it here and there from among her beautiful black locks, she quickly braided it into a fine cord and handed it to her brother.

The moment his eye fell on it he was delighted, and immediately began to run it back and forth through his hands, trying its strength. Satisfied that the long, glossy coil was strong enough, he wound it around his shoulders and set out from the lodge a little after midnight, his object being to catch the Sun before he rose.

Having fixed his snare firmly at a place where the Sun must strike the land as it rose above the earth, he waited patiently. The instant it appeared he drew the cord tight, so that the Sun was held fast and could not rise.

Soon there was a great commotion among the animals who ruled the earth. They had no light, and ran to and fro, calling out to each other and asking what had happened. They called together a council to discuss the matter. An old Dormouse, suspecting what was the trouble, proposed that some one should be appointed to go out and cut the cord. This was a bold thing to do, as the rays of the Sun would surely burn whoever ventured near them. No one seemed willing to run the risk, so the Dormouse himself undertook to go. The Dormouse was, at this time, the largest animal in the world. When he stood up he looked like a mountain.

He made haste to the place where the Sun lay ensnared, and as it came nearer and nearer its back began to smoke and burn with the heat, and the whole top of its huge body was turned in a very short time to enormous heaps of ashes. The Dormouse did succeed, however, in cutting the cord with its teeth, and the Sun blazed up into the high, blue sky, as beautiful as ever.

The poor Dormouse paid the price of his bravery. So great was the heat of the Sun, that he found himself, when it was all over, shrunk to a little bit of a thing, and that is the reason why the Dormouse is one of the tiniest creatures on the earth.

The Little Boy returned home, when he discovered that the Sun had escaped his snare and devoted himself entirely to hunting. "If the beautiful hair of my sister would not hold the Sun fast, nothing in the world could," he said. "I was not born, a little fellow like me, to look after the Sun. It takes some one greater and wiser than I to do that."

Whereupon he went out and shot ten more snowbirds, for at that he was very expert, and had a new bird-skin coat made, which was prettier than the one he had worn before.

THE BIRD LOVER

By Cornelius Mathews

IN a region of country where the forest and the
prairie strived which should be the most beautiful—the open plain, with its free sunshine and
winds and flowers, or the closed wood, with its
delicious twilight-walks and enamored haunts—
there lived a wicked manito in the disguise of an
old Indian.

Although the country furnished an abundance
of game, and whatever else a good heart could wish
for, it was the study of this wicked genius to destroy such as fell into his hands. He made use of
all his arts to decoy men into his power, for the
purpose of killing them. The country had been
once thickly peopled, but the Mudjee Monedo had
so thinned it by his cruel practices, that he now
lived almost solitary in the wilderness.

The secret of his success lay in his great speed.
He had the power to assume the shape of any four-
footed creature, and it was his custom to challenge
such as he sought to destroy, to run with him. He
had a beaten path on which he ran, leading around
a large lake, and he always ran around this circle
so that the starting and the winning-post was the
same.

Whoever failed, as every one had, yielded up
his life at this post; and although he ran every
day, no man was ever known to beat this evil
genius; for whenever he was pressed hard, he
changed himself into a fox, wolf, deer, or other

swift-footed animal, and was thus able to leave his competitor behind.

The whole country was in dread of this same Mudjee Monedo, and yet the young men were constantly running with him; for if they refused, he called them cowards, which was a reproach they could not bear. They would rather die than be called cowards.

To keep up his sport, the manito made light of these deadly foot-matches, and instead of assuming a braggart air, and going about in a boastful way, with the blood of such as he had overcome upon his hands, he adopted very pleasing manners, and visited the lodges around the country as any other sweet-tempered and harmless old Indian might.

His secret object in these friendly visits was to learn whether the young boys were getting old enough to run with him; he kept a very sharp eye upon their growth, and the day he thought them ready, he did not fail to challenge them to a trial on his racing-ground.

There was not a family in all that beautiful region which had not in this way been visited and thinned out; and the manito had quite naturally come to be held in abhorrence by all the Indian mothers in the country.

It happened that there lived near him a poor widow woman, whose husband and seven sons he had made way with; and she was now living with an only daughter, and a son of ten or twelve years old.

This widow was very poor and feeble, and she

suffered so much for lack of food and other comforts of the lodge, that she would have been glad to die, but for her daughter and her little son. The Mudjee Monedo had already visited her lodge to observe whether the boy was sufficiently grown to be challenged to the race; and so crafty in his approaches and so soft in his manners was the Monedo, that the mother feared that he would yet decoy the son and make away with him as he had done with his father and his seven brothers, in spite of all her struggles to save him.

And yet she strove with all her might to strengthen her son in every good course. She taught him, as best she could, what was becoming for the wise hunter and the brave warrior. She remembered and set before him all that she could recall of the skill and the craft of his father and his brothers who were lost.

The widow woman also instructed her daughter in whatever should make her useful as a wife; and in the leisure-time of the lodge, she gave her lessons in the art of working with the quills of porcupine, and bestowed on her such other accomplishments as should make her an ornament and a blessing to her husband's household. The daughter, Minda by name, was kind and obedient to her mother, and never failed in her duty. Their lodge stood high up on the banks of a lake, which gave them a wide prospect of country, embellished with groves and open fields, which waved with the blue light of their long grass, and made, at all hours of sun and moon, a cheerful scene to look upon.

Across this beautiful prairie, Minda had one

morning made her way to gather dry limbs for their fire; for she disdained no labor of the lodge. And while enjoying the sweetness of the air and the green beauty of the woods, she strolled far away.

She had come to a bank, painted with flowers of every hue, and was reclining on its fragrant couch, when a bird, of red and deep-blue plumage softly blended, alighted on a branch near by, and began to pour forth its carol. It was a bird of strange character, such as she had never before seen. Its first note was so delicious to the ear of Minda, and it so pierced to her young heart, that she listened as she had never before to any mortal or heavenly sound. It seemed like the human voice, forbidden to speak, and uttering its language through this wild wood-chant with a mournful melody, as if it bewailed the lack of the power or the right to make itself more plainly intelligible.

The voice of the bird rose and fell, and circled round and round, but whithersoever floated or spread out its notes, they seemed ever to have their center where Minda sat; and she looked with sad eyes into the sad eyes of the mournful bird, that sat in his red and deep-blue plumage just opposite to the flowery bank.

The poor bird strove more and more with his voice, and seemed ever more and more anxiously to address his notes of lament to Minda's ears, till at last she could not refrain from saying: "What aileth thee, sad bird?"

As if he had but waited to be spoken to, the bird left his branch, and alighting upon the bank, smiled on Minda, and, shaking his shining plumage, answered:

"I am bound in this condition until a maiden shall accept me in marriage. I have wandered these groves and sung to many and many of the Indian girls, but none ever heeded my voice till you. Will you be mine?" he added, and poured forth a flood of melody which sparkled and spread itself with its sweet murmurs over all the scene, and fairly entranced the young Minda, who sat silent, as if she feared to break the charm by speech.

The bird, approaching nearer, asked her, if she loved him, to get her mother's consent to their marriage. "I shall be free then," said the bird, "and you shall know me as I am."

Minda lingered and listened to the sweet voice of the bird in its own forest notes, or filling each pause with gentle human discourse; questioning her as to her home, her family, and the little incidents of her daily life.

She returned to the lodge later than usual, but she was too timid to speak to her mother of that which the bird had charged her. She returned again and again to the fragrant haunt in the wood; and every day she listened to the song and the discourse of her bird admirer with more pleasure, and he every day besought her to speak to her mother of the marriage. This she could not, however, muster heart and courage to do.

At last the widow began herself to have a suspicion that her daughter's heart was in the wood, from her long delays in returning, and the little success she had in gathering the fire-branches for which she went in search.

In answer to her mother's questions, Minda revealed the truth, and made known her lover's request. The mother, considering the lonely and destitute condition of her little household, gave her consent.

The daughter, with light steps, hastened with the news to the wood. The bird lover of course heard it with delight, and fluttered through the air in happy circles, and poured forth a song of joy which thrilled Minda to the heart.

He said that he would come to the lodge at sunset, and immediately took wing, while Minda hung fondly upon his flight, till he was lost far away in the blue sky.

With the twilight the bird lover, whose name was Monedowa, appeared at the door of the lodge, as a hunter, with a red plume and a mantle of blue upon his shoulders.

He addressed the widow as his friend, and she directed him to sit down beside her daughter, and they were regarded as man and wife.

Early on the following morning, he asked for the bow and arrows of those who had been slain by the wicked manito, and went out a-hunting. As soon as he had got out of sight of the lodge, he changed himself into the wood-bird, as he had been before his marriage, and took his flight through the air.

Although game was scarce in the neighborhood of the widow's lodge, Monedowa returned at evening, in his character of a hunter, with two deer.

This was his daily practice, and the widow's family never more lacked for food.

It was noticed, however, that Monedowa himself ate but little, and that of a peculiar kind of meat, flavored with berries, which, with other circumstances, convinced them that he was not as the Indian people around him.

In a few days his mother-in-law told him that the manito would come to pay them a visit, to see how the young man, her son, prospered.

Monedowa answered that he should on that day be absent. When the time arrived, he flew upon a tall tree, overlooking the lodge, and took his station there, as the wicked manito passed in.

The Mudjee Monedo cast sharp glances at the scaffolds so well laden with meat, and as soon as he had entered, he said, "Why, who is it that is furnishing you with meat so plentifully?"

"No one," she answered, "but my son; he is just beginning to kill deer."

"No, no," he retorted; "some one is living with you."

"Kaween, no indeed," replied the widow; "you are only making sport of my hapless condition. Who do you think would come and trouble themselves about me?"

"Very well," answered the manito, "I will go; but on such a day I will again visit you, and see who it is that furnishes the meat, and whether it is your son or not."

He had no sooner left the lodge and got out of sight, than the son-in-law made his appearance with two more deer. On being made acquainted with the conduct of the manito, "Very well," he said, "I will be at home the next time, to see him."

Both the mother and the wife urged Monedowa to be aware of the manito. They made known to him all of his cruel courses, and assured him that no man could escape from his power.

"No matter," said Monedowa; "if he invites me to the race-ground, I will not be backward. What follows may teach him, my mother, to show pity on the vanquished, and not to trample on the widow and those who are without fathers."

When the day of the visit of the manito arrived, Monedowa told his wife to prepare certain pieces of meat, which he pointed out to her, together with two or three buds of the birch-tree, which he requested her to put in the pot. He directed also that the manito should be hospitably received, as if he had been just the kind-hearted old Indian he professed to be. Monedowa then dressed himself as a warrior, embellishing his visage with tints of red, to show that he was prepared for either war or peace.

As soon as the Mudjee Monedo arrived, he eyed this strange warrior whom he had never seen before; but he dissembled, as usual, and, with a gentle laugh, said to the widow, "Did I not tell you that some one was staying with you, for I knew your son was too young to hunt."

The widow excused herself by saying that she did not think it necessary to tell him, inasmuch as he was a manito, and must have known before he asked.

The manito was very pleasant with Monedowa,

and after much other discourse, in a gentle-spoken voice, he invited him to the racing-ground, saying it was a manly amusement, that he would have an excellent chance to meet there with other warriors, and that he should himself be pleased to run with him.

Monedowa would have excused himself, saying that he knew nothing of running.

"Why," replied the Mudjee Monedo, trembling in every limb as he spoke, "don't you see how old I look, while you are young and full of life. We must at least run a little to amuse others."

"Be it so, then," replied Monedowa. "I will oblige you. I will go in the morning."

Pleased with his crafty success, the manito would have now taken his leave, but he was pressed to remain and partake of their hospitality. The meal was immediately prepared. But one dish was used.

Monedowa partook of it first, to show his guest that he need not fear, saying at the same time, "It is a feast, and as we seldom meet, we must eat all that is placed on the dish, as a mark of gratitude to the Great Spirit for permitting me to kill animals, and for the pleasure of seeing you, and partaking of it with you."

They ate and talked, on this and that, until they had nearly dispatched the meal, when the manito took up the dish and drank off the broth at a breath. On setting it down he immediately turned his head and commenced coughing with great violence. The old body in which he had disguised himself was well nigh shaken in pieces, for he had, as Monedowa expected, swallowed a grain of the birch-bud, and this, which relished to himself as being of the bird nature, greatly distressed the old manito, who partook of the character of an animal, or four-footed thing.

He was at last put to such confusion of face by his constant coughing, that he was enforced to leave, saying, or rather hiccoughing as he left the lodge, that he should look for the young man at the racing-ground in the morning.

When the morning came, Monedowa was early astir, oiling his limbs and enameling his breast and arms with red and blue, resembling the plumage in which he had first appeared to Minda. Upon his brow he placed a tuft of feathers of the same shining tints.

By his invitation his wife, Minda, the mother and her young son, attended Monedowa to the manito's racing-ground.

The lodge of the manito stood upon a high ground, and near it stretched out a long row of other lodges, said to be possessed by wicked kindred of his, who shared in the spoils of his cruelty.

As soon as the young hunter and his party approached, the inmates appeared at their lodge-doors and cried out:

"We are visited."

At this cry, the Mudjee Monedo came forth and descended with his companions to the starting-post on the plain. From this the course could be seen, winding in a long girdle about the lake; and as they were now all assembled, the old manito began to speak of the race, belted himself up and pointed to the post, which was an upright pillar of stone.

"But before we start," said the manito, "I wish it to be understood that when men run with me I make a wager, and I expect them to abide by it—life against life."

"Very well—be it so," answered Monedowa. "We shall see whose head is to be dashed against the stone."

"We shall," rejoined the Mudjee Monedo. "I am very old, but I shall try and make a run."

"Very well," again rejoined Monedowa; "I hope we shall both stand to our bargain."

"Good!" said the old manito; and he at the same time cast a sly glance at the young hunter, and rolled his eyes toward where stood the pillar of stone.

"I am ready," said Monedowa.

The starting shout was given, and they set off at high speed, the manito leading, and Monedowa pressing closely after. As he closed upon him, the old manito began to show his power, and changing himself into a fox he passed the young hunter with ease, and went leisurely along.

Monedowa now, with a glance upward, took the shape of the strange bird of red and deep-blue plumage, and with one flight, lighting at some distance ahead of the manito, resumed his mortal shape.

When the Mudjee Monedo espied his competitor before him, "Whoa! whoa!" he exclaimed; "this is strange;" and he immediately changed himself into a wolf, and sped past Monedowa.

As he galloped by, Monedowa heard a noise from his throat, and he knew that he was still in distress from the birch-bud which he had swallowed at his mother-in-law's lodge.

Monedowa again took wing, and, shooting into the air, he descended suddenly with great swiftness, and took the path far ahead of the old manito.

As he passed the wolf he whispered in his ear:

"My friend, is this the extent of your speed?"

The manito began to be troubled with bad forebodings, for, on looking ahead, he saw the young hunter in his own manly form, running along at leisure. The Mudjee Monedo, seeing the necessity of more speed, now passed Monedowa in the shape of a deer.

They were now far around the circle of the lake, and fast closing in upon the starting-post, when Monedowa, putting on his red and blue plumage, glided along the air and alighted upon the track far in advance.

To overtake him, the old manito assumed the shape of a buffalo; and he pushed on with such long gallops that he was again the foremost on the course. The buffalo was the last change he could make, and it was in this form that he had most frequently conquered.

The young hunter, once more a bird, in the act of passing the manito, saw his tongue lolling from his mouth with fatigue.

"My friend," said Monedowa, "is this all your speed?"

The manito made no answer. Monedowa had resumed his character of a hunter, and was within a run of the winning-post, when the wicked manito had nearly overtaken him.

"Bakah! bakah! nejee!" he called out to Monedowa; "stop, my friend, I wish to talk to you."

Monedowa laughed aloud as he replied:

"I will speak to you at the starting-post. When men run with me I make a wager, and I expect them to abide by it—life against life."

One more flight as the blue bird with red wings, and Monedowa was so near to the goal that he could easily reach it in his mortal shape. Shining in beauty, his face lighted up like the sky, with tinted arms and bosom gleaming in the sun, and the parti-colored plume on his brow waving in the wind, Monedowa, cheered by a joyful shout from his own people, leaped to the post.

The manito came on with fear in his face.

"My friend," he said, "spare my life;" and then added, in a low voice, as if he would not that the others should hear it, "Give me to live." And he began to move off as if the request had been granted.

"As you have done to others," replied Monedowa, "so shall it be done to you."

And seizing the wicked manito, he dashed him against the pillar of stone. His kindred, who were looking on in horror, raised a cry of fear and fled away in a body to some distant land, whence they have never returned.

The widow's family left the scene, and when they had all come out into the open fields, they walked on together until they had reached the fragrant bank and the evergreen wood, where the daughter had first encountered her bird lover.

Monedowa, turning to the widow, said:

THE BIRD LOVER

"My mother, here we must part. Your daughter and myself must now leave you. The Good Spirit, moved with pity, has allowed me to be your friend. I have done that for which I was sent. I am permitted to take with me the one whom I love. I have found your daughter ever kind, gentle and just. She shall be my companion. The blessing of the Good Spirit be ever with you. Farewell, my mother—my brother, farewell."

While the widow woman was still lost in wonder at these words, Monedowa, and Minda, his wife, changed at the same moment, rose into the air, as beautiful birds, clothed in shining colors of red and blue.

They caroled together as they flew, and their songs were happy, and falling, falling, like clear drops. As they rose, and rose, and winged their way far upward, a delicious peace came into the mind of the poor widow woman, and she returned to her lodge deeply thankful at heart for all the goodness that had been shown to her by the Master of Life.

From that day forth she never knew want, and her young son proved a comfort to her lodge, and the tuneful carol of Monedowa and Minda, as it fell from heaven, was a music always, go whither she would, sounding peace and joy in her ear.

WUNZH, THE FATHER OF INDIAN CORN

By Cornelius Mathews

IN time past—we cannot tell exactly how many, many years ago—a poor Indian was living, with his wife and children, in a beautiful part of the country. He was not only poor, but he was not expert in procuring food for his family, and his children were too young to give him assistance.

Although of a lowly condition and straitened in his circumstances, he was a man of kind and contented disposition. He was always thankful to the Great Spirit for everything he received. He even stood in the door of his lodge to bless the birds that flew past in the summer evenings; although, if he had been of a complaining temper, he might have repined that they were not rather spread upon the table for his evening meal.

The same generous and sweet disposition was inherited by his eldest son, who had now arrived at the proper age to undertake the ceremony of the fast, to learn what kind of a spirit would be his guide and guardian through life.

Wunzh, for this was his name, had been an obedient boy from his infancy—pensive, thoughtful, and gentle—so that he was beloved by the whole family.

As soon as the first buds of spring appeared, and the delicious fragrance of the young year began to sweeten the air, his father, with the help of his younger brothers, built for Wunzh the customary

479

little lodge, at a retired spot at some distance from their own, where he would not be disturbed during the solemn rite.

To prepare himself, Wunzh sought to clear his heart of every evil thought, and to think of nothing that was not good, and beautiful, and kindly.

That he might store his mind with pleasant ideas for his dreams, for the first few days he amused himself by walking in the woods and over the mountains, examining the early plants and flowers.

As he rambled far and wide, through the wild country, he felt a strong desire to know how the plants and herbs and berries grew, without any aid from man, and why it was that some kinds were good to eat, and that others were possessed of medicinal or poisonous power.

After he had become too languid to walk about, and confined himself strictly to the lodge, he re- called these thoughts, and turning them in his mind, he wished he could dream of something that would prove a benefit to his father and family, and to all others of his fellow-creatures.

"True," thought Wunzh, "the Great Spirit made all things, and it is to him that we owe our lives. Could he not make it easier for us to get our food, than by hunting animals and taking fish? I must try to find this out in my visions."

On the third day Wunzh became weak and faint and kept to his bed. Suddenly he fancied, as he lay thus, that a bright light came in at the lodge door, and ere he was aware, he saw a handsome young man, with a complexion of the softest and purest white, coming down from the sky, and advancing toward him.

The beautiful stranger was richly and gayly dressed, having on a great many garments of green and yellow colors, but differing in their deeper or lighter shades. He had a plume of waving feathers on his head, and all his motions were graceful, and reminded Wunzh of the deep green of the summer grass, and the clear amber of the summer sky, and the gentle blowing of the summer wind. Beautiful as the stranger was, he paused on a little mound of earth, just before the door of the lodge.

"I am sent to you, my friend," said his celestial visitor, in a voice most soft and musical to listen to, "I am sent to you by that Great Spirit who made all things in the sky, and on the earth. He has seen and knows your motives in fasting. He sees that it is from a kind and benevolent wish to do good to your people, and to procure a benefit for them; that you do not seek for strength in war, or the praise of the men of the bloody hand. I am sent to instruct you and to show you how you can do your kindred good."

He then told the young man to arise, and to prepare to wrestle with him, as it was only by this means that he could hope to succeed in his wishes.

Wunzh knew how weak he was from fasting, but the voice of the stranger was cheery, and put such a courage in his heart, that he promptly sprang up, determined to die rather than fail. Brave Wunzh! if you ever accomplish anything, it will be through the power of the resolve that spake within you at that moment.

He began the trial, and after a long-sustained struggle he was almost overpowered, when the beautiful stranger said:

"My friend, it is enough for once, I will come again to try you;" and smiling on him, he returned through the air in the same direction in which he had come.

The next day, although he saw how sweetly the wild-flowers bloomed upon the slopes, and the birds warbled from the woodland, he longed to see the celestial visitor, and to hear his voice.

To his great joy he reappeared at the same hour, toward the going down of the sun, and re-challenged Wunzh to a trial of strength.

The brave Wunzh felt that his strength of body was even less than on the day before, but the courage of his mind seemed to grow. Observing this, and how Wunzh put his whole heart in the struggle, the stranger again spoke to him in the words he used before, adding:

"To-morrow will be your last trial. Be strong, my friend, for this is the only way in which you can overcome me and obtain the boon you seek."

The light which shone after him as he left Wunzh was brighter than before.

On the third day he came again and renewed the struggle. Very faint in body was poor Wunzh, but he was stronger at heart than ever, and determined to prevail now or perish.

He put forth his utmost powers, and after a contest more severe than either of the others, the stranger ceased his efforts, and declared himself conquered.

For the first time he entered Wunzh's little fasting lodge, and sitting down beside the youth, he began to deliver his instructions to inform him in what manner he should proceed to take advantage of his victory.

"You have won your desire of the Great Spirit," said the beautiful stranger. "You have wrestled manfully. To-morrow will be the seventh day of your fasting. Your father will give you food to strengthen you, and as it is the last day of trial you will prevail. I know this, and now tell you what you must do to benefit your family and your people. To-morrow," he repeated, "I shall meet you and wrestle with you for the last time. As soon as you have prevailed against me, you will strip off my garments and throw me down, clean the earth of roots and weeds, make it soft, and bury me in the spot. When you have done this, leave my body in the earth, and do not disturb it, but come at times to visit the place, to see whether I have come to life, and above all be careful to never let the grass or weeds grow upon my grave. Once a month cover me with fresh earth. If you follow these my instructions you will accomplish your object of doing good to your fellow-creatures by teaching them the knowledge I now teach you."

He then shook Wunzh by the hand and disappeared, but he was gone so soon that Wunzh could not tell what direction he took.

In the morning, Wunzh's father came to his lodge with some slight refreshments, saying:

"My son, you have fasted long enough. If the Great Spirit will favor you, he will do it now. It is seven days since you have tasted food, and you must not sacrifice your life. The Master of Life does not require that."

"My father," replied Wunzh, "wait till the sun goes down. I have a particular reason for extending my fast to that hour."

"Very well," said the old man, "I shall wait till the hour arrives, and you shall be inclined to eat."

At his usual hour of appearing, the beautiful sky-visitor returned, and the trial of strength was renewed. Although he had not availed himself of his father's offer of food, Wunzh felt that new strength had been given him. His heart was mighty within him to achieve some great purpose. Courage was like the eagle that spreads his wings within the treetop for a great flight, within the bosom of the brave Wunzh.

He grasped his angel challenger with supernatural strength, threw him down, and, mindful of his own instructions, tore from him his beautiful garments and plume, and finding him dead, immediately buried him on the spot, using all the precautions he had been told of, and very confident was Wunzh, all the time, that his friend would again come to life.

Wunzh now returned to his father's lodge, where he was warmly welcomed, for as it had been appointed to him during the days of his fasting to walk apart with Heaven, he was not permitted to see any human face save that of his father, the representative to the little household upon earth of the Good Father who is in Heaven.

Wunzh partook sparingly of the meal that had been prepared for him, and once more mingled in the cares and sports of the family. But he never for a moment forgot the grave of his friend. He carefully visited it throughout the spring, and weeded out the grass, and kept the ground in a soft and pliant state; and sometimes, when the brave Wunzh thought of his friend that was gone from his sight, he dropped a tear upon the earth where he lay.

Watching and tending, and moistening the earth with his tears, it was not long before Wunzh saw the tops of green plumes coming through the ground; and the more faithful he was in obeying his instructions in keeping the ground in order, and in cherishing the memory of his departed friend, the faster they grew. He was, however, careful to conceal the charge of the earth which he had from his father.

Days and weeks had passed in this way; the summer was drawing toward a close, when one day, after a long absence in hunting, Wunzh invited his father to follow him to the quiet and lonesome spot of his former fast.

The little fasting-lodge had been removed, and the weeds kept from growing on the circle where it had stood; but in its place rose a tall and graceful plant, surmounted with nodding plumes and stately leaves, and golden clusters.

There was in its aspect and bearing the deep green of the summer grass, the clear amber of the summer sky, and the gentle blowing of the summer wind.

"It is my friend!" shouted Wunzh, "it is the friend of all mankind. It is Mondawmin; it is our Indian Corn! We need no longer rely on hunting alone, for as long as this gift is cherished and taken care of, the ground itself will give us a living."

He then pulled an ear.

"See, my father," said he, "this is what I fasted for. The Great Spirit has listened to my voice, and sent us something new, and henceforth our people will not alone depend upon the chase or upon the waters."

Wunzh then communicated to his father the instructions given to him by the stranger. He told him that the broad husks must be torn away, as he had pulled off the garments in his wrestling, and having done this, he directed him how the ear must be held before the fire till the outer skin became brown—as the complexion of his angel friend had been tinted by the sun—while all the milk was retained in the grain.

The whole family, in high spirits, and deeply grateful to the Merciful Master who gave it, assisted in a feast on the newly-grown ears of corn.

So came that mighty blessing into the world, and we owe all of those beautiful fields of healthful grain to the dream of the brave boy Wunzh.

WHEN BRER WOLF HAVE HIS CORN SHUCKING

Anonymous

BRER WOLF he make a powerful crop of
corn one year, and he turn it over in his
mind how he going to get all that corn shucked,
'cause Brer Wolf mighty unpopular man with his
neighbors, and when Brer Wolf have a corn shucking the creeters don't turn out like they do when
Sis Coon have a corn shucking.

But Brer Wolf he have a powerful handsome
daughter on the carpet. All the chaps about the
county has had their heads set to step up to Brer
Wolf's daughter. So Brer Wolf he send out word
how the chap what shucks the most corn at his
shucking shall have his handsome daughter.

Well, the chaps they come from the fur end of
Columbia County, and some come from Richmond
County, and they set to work, and they make the
shucks fly, and each chap have a pile to hisself.
Brer Coon he mighty set on Brer Wolf's daughter,
and Brer Coon he know hisself are powerful likely
corn shucker, and Brer Coon he 'low to hisself how
he have a right smart chance to get the gal.

Brer Fox his head done plain turned when Miss
Wolf role her handsome eyes at hisself; and so
Brer Fox he get a pile to hisself and fall to
work.

Now old Brer Rabbit his heart set on the gal,
but Brer Rabbit he are a mighty poor corn shucker.
Brer Rabbit he jest naterally know he don' stand

487

no chance shucking a pile of corn and making time against Brer Coon.

So Brer Rabbit he don' waste hisself, Brer Rabbit don', but he take his hat off and he go up to Brer Wolf, and he make his bow, and he ask Brer Wolf, if he learn his daughter to dance, can he have her? But Brer Wolf he say, "What I said, I said."

Well, Brer Rabbit he feel terrible put down, but he fall to, and he act most survigorous. He sing and he dance, and he dance and he sing, and he amuse the company most 'greeable like; and he sing before the gals, and he dance before the gals, and he show them the new step and the new shuffle, Brer Rabbit do. Brer Coon he just turn his eye on Brer Rabbit 'casionally, but he don't pay no attention to his acting and his frolicking. Brer Coon he just make time with his corn shucking, twell Brer Coon's pile it make three times the pile of the other chaps.

When it come time for Brer Wolf to come round and count his piles, Brer Rabbit he set down long side Brer Coon, and he fall to shucking corn to beat all. When Brer Wolf come 'round, Brer Rabbit he certainly do make the shucks fly powerful 'cause the old rascal just been cutting up and acting all the evening, and he ain't tired like the other chaps.

When Brer Wolf see the great pile so much bigger than what all the other chaps got, Brer Wolf he say, "What for both you chaps shuck on one pile?" Brer Coon he 'low that all his pile. He 'low, Brer Coon do, how Brer Rabbit been cutting up and frolicking all the evening, and he just now come and set down 'longside his pile.

Brer Rabbit he say he swear and kiss the book, this my pile. Brer Coon he just been frolicking and going on all the evening to beat all; he make us laugh nigh 'bout fit to kill ourselves while I done work my hands plum to the bone. Now he set hisself down here and say it his pile.

Brer Wolf he say he leave it to the company. But the chaps they don't want Brer Rabbit to have the gal, and they don't want Brer Coon to have the gal, so they won't take sides; they 'low they been working so powerful hard, they don't take noticement of Brer Coon or Brer Rabbit. Then Brer Wolf he 'low he leave it to the gals.

Now Miss Wolf she been favoring Brer Rabbit all the evening. Brer Rabbit dancing and singing plum turned Miss Wolf's head, so Miss Wolf she say, "It most surely are Brer Rabbit's pile." Miss Wolf she say she "plum 'stonished how Brer Coon can story so."

Brer Rabbit he take the gal and go off home clipity, lipity. Poor old Brer Coon he take hisself off home, he so tired he can scarcely hold hisself together.

BRER RABBIT'S COOL AIR SWING

Anonymous

MR. MAN he had a fine garden.
Brer Rabbit he visit Mr. Man's garden every
day to destroy the latest thing in it, twell Mr. Man
plum wore out with old Brer Rabbit, Mr. Man he
set a trap for old Brer Rabbit down 'longside the
big road.

One day when Mr. Man going down to the cross-
roads, he look in his trap, and sure 'nough, there old
Brer Rabbit.

Mr. Man he say, "Oh, so old man, here you is.
Now I'll have you for my dinner."

Mr. Man he takes a cord from his pocket, and tie
Brer Rabbit high on a limb of a sweet gum tree, and
he leave Brer Rabbit swinging there twell he come
back from the cross-roads, when he aim to fotch
Brer Rabbit home and cook him for his dinner.

Brer Rabbit he swing this away in the wind and
that away, and he swing this away in the wind and
that away in the wind, and he think he time done
come. Poor old Brer Rabbit don't know where
he's at.

Presently here come Brer Wolf loping down the
big road. When Brer Wolf see old Brer Rabbit
swinging this away and that away in the wind, Brer
Wolf he stop short and he say, "Fore the Lord,
man! What you doing up there?" Brer Rabbit he
say, "This just my cool air swing. I just taking a
swing this morning."

But Brer Rabbit he just know Brer Wolf going

490

to make way with him. Brer Rabbit he just turn it over in his mind which way he going to get to. The wind it swing poor Brer Rabbit way out this away and way out that away. While Brer Rabbit swinging, he work his brain, too.

Brer Wolf he say, "Brer Rabbit, I got you fast; now I going eat you up." Brer Rabbit he say, "Brer Wolf, open your mouth and shut your eyes, and I'll jump plum in your mouth." So Brer Wolf turn his head up and shut his eyes. Brer Rabbit he feel in his pocket and take out some pepper, and Brer Rabbit he throw it plum down Brer Wolf's throat. Brer Wolf he nigh 'bout 'stracted with the misery. He cough and he roll in the dirt, and he get up and he strike out for home, coughing to beat all. And Brer Rabbit he swing this away and that away in the wind.

Presently here come Brer Squirrel. When Brer Squirrel he see the wind swing Brer Rabbit way out this away and way out that away, Brer Squirrel he that 'stonished he stop short. Brer Squirrel he say, "Fore the Lord, Brer Rabbit, what you done done to yourself this yer time?"

Brer Rabbit he say, "This yer my cool swing, Brer Squirrel. I taking a fine swing this morning." And the wind it swing Brer Rabbit way out this away and way back that away. Brer Rabbit he fold his hands and look mighty restful and happy, like he settin' back fanning hisself on his front porch.

Brer Squirrel he say, "Please sir, Brer Rabbit, let me try your swing one time."

Brer Rabbit he say, "Certainly, Brer Squirrel,

you do me proud," and Brer Rabbit he make like he make haste to turn hisself loose. Presently Brer Rabbit he say, "Come up here, Brer Squirrel, and give me a hand with this knot," and Brer Squirrel he make haste to go and turn Brer Rabbit loose, and Brer Rabbit he make Brer Squirrel fast to the cord. The wind it swing Brer Squirrel way out this a way and way out that a way, and Brer Squirrel he think it fine.

Brer Rabbit he say, "I go down to the spring to get a fresh drink. You can swing twell I come back."

Brer Squirrel he say, "Take your time, Brer Rabbit, take your time." Brer Rabbit he take his time, and scratch out for home fast he can go, and he ain't caring how long Brer Squirrel swing.

Brer Squirrel he swing this away and he swing that away, and he think it fine.

Presently here come Mr. Man. When Mr. Man he see Brer Squirrel, he plum 'stonished. He say, "Oh, so old man, I done hear of many and many of your fine tricks, but I never done hear yourself into a squirrel before. Powerful kind of you, Brer Rabbit, to give me a fine squirrel dinner."

Mr. Man he take Brer Squirrel home and cook him for dinner.

THE FOUR SEASONS

By Lillian M. Gask

THERE was not a prettier cottage on the borders of the forest than that which was the home of Clare and Laura. A beautiful rose-tree clambered all over the little house, thrusting its clusters of small pink blossoms through the open windows, and nodding to Clare as though to say: "You are as sweet as we are, and the sun shines on us all."

The roses did not nod their heads at Laura, for she was as ugly and wicked as Clare was lovely. Her face wore always a heavy frown, which her mother's reflected; for Laura was her favourite child, and she could not bear to see that her second daughter, for whom she had no spark of love, should be so much the more attractive of the two.

Dame Nature had been very kind to the little Clare. The roses had given their delicate colouring to her soft cheeks, and her pretty eyes were just the hue of a purple pansy. The red of the crimson berries that glinted among the evergreens when winter came, was not more vivid than that of her lips, and her hair had the sheen of yellow corn when the sun is smiling on it. Laura could not look at her without a pang of envy, and longed to drive her away from home.

One bitter day in winter, when a waste of snow surrounded the cottage, and frozen icicles hung from the roof, Laura asked her mother if Clare might pick some violets in the woods for her.

" 'Violets?' " exclaimed the mother, "at this time of the year? Why, you must be dreaming, child! There is not a single flower in all the forest!"

But Laura insisted that Clare should be sent to seek for the flowers, and, loath to refuse her anything, her mother did as she was asked.

"Do not come back without them, or it will be the worse for you," Laura called from the doorway, as she watched her little sister go shiveringly down the pathway that led to the forest. In its depths, she knew, there lurked gaunt grey wolves, and these were fierce with hunger.

Clare knew this too, and her heart was faint with fear as she passed through the grove of fir-trees. A cheery little robin hopped down from one of the branches, and sang a few bars of his winter song as if to comfort her; she had gone but a few paces further when she saw the red of his breast repeated in a glimmer of ruddy light in the distance. She hastened towards it, and found it came from a huge fire, round which were sitting twelve strange men. The faces of all were kindly, but while three had long white beards and snowy garments, three had golden beards and long green garments, three had auburn beards and yellow garments, and yet another triplet, with long black beards, were dressed in violet. One of the three whose hair was frosted looked up as she approached.

"May I warm myself at the fire, kind sir?" she asked him timidly, and making room for her at once, he asked her why she wandered in the forest in such bitter weather.

"I was sent to pluck violets for my sister," Clare

explained, "and I dare not go home without them, or she would be very angry."

At this her questioner turned to one of the three men who were robed in purple.

"Violets are your concern, Brother May. Cannot you help the poor little thing?" he asked. "She will be frozen to death otherwise, for to-night 'twill be colder than ever."

"To be sure I will," said Brother May, laying a gentle hand on Clare's fair hair; and taking the staff from the white-haired man, he poked the fire.

This was the signal for a most marvellous change in the forest. Ice and snow disappeared, and the air became soft and balmy. Birds sang in the branches overhead, and flowers sprang up as if by magic round the path which Clare had trodden. She filled her hands with fragrant violets, and thanked the brothers for their help.

"You are welcome, dear child," they cried; and the old man took back his staff again, and in his turn poked the fire. Once more it was winter, and Clare hastened home to the cottage as quickly as she could.

Both Laura and her mother were surprised to see her, for they had made sure that she would lose her way. Laura snatched at the violets, only to toss them aside, and was so unkind for the rest of the day that Clare sobbed herself to sleep.

Next morning she was again sent out in the snow. This time it was to seek wild strawberries in the forest, and her sister's look was so full of meaning as she said, "Do not come home without them!" that the poor little maiden trembled with fear as well as with cold as she entered the gloomy wood. The same friendly robin fluttered across her path, and following the direction in which he flew, to her great delight she saw again the ruddy glow of the fire. The twelve strange men were still seated round it, and Brother January took her by the hand.

"Why are you here again, poor child?" he asked her gently. "It would surely be wiser for you to stay at home while King Frost reigns over the land, for you are young and tender, and his grip is very cruel."

"I had to come, sir," Clare explained. "My sister said she must have strawberries. We gathered some in June last year."

Brother January turned to a companion dressed in flowing yellow.

"Strawberries are your concern, Brother June," he said. "It is for you now to come to the aid of our little friend."

"I will do so with pleasure," said Brother June, taking the staff held out to him, and giving the fire a vigorous poke. At this, the winter disappeared, the trees sprang into full leaf, and crimson berries were seen amidst the creeping tendrils of the strawberry plant.

Clare gathered as much of the sweet fruit as she could carry, and once more thanked her friends with a grateful smile.

"You are welcome," they cried in chorus, and as Brother January took back his staff the winter once more spread its mantle over the earth.

Instead of being grateful for the delicious fruit

that Clare had brought her, Laura was more vexed than ever to find she had not been eaten by wolves. Her mother, too, looked at the poor girl angrily, and sent her out to the barn, as if she could no longer bear the sight of her.

Clare was barely awake next morning when she was told that she must go to the forest and bring home some apples for her sister Laura, who had a fancy for them.

"But it's so dark, dear mother," cried Clare in terror.

"Make haste and go," was the only answer, and as quickly as her numbed fingers would allow her, Clare finished her simple toilet and started on her way.

The robin was still asleep with his head tucked under his wing, but a tiny wood-mouse poked out his head from his nest in the foot of a hollow tree, as he heard her footsteps upon the frozen snow.

"If you walk straight on, you will find your friends," he squeaked, and Clare thankfully followed his directions. Before long she was warming herself before the glowing fire, and the brothers were asking with much sympathy why she had again been sent to face the cold.

"'Apples'!" cried Brother January, when she had told them. "Ah! it's your concern now, Brother September."

Forthwith September poked the fire, and lo and behold! it was cheery autumn, and the ground was strewn with crimson and russet leaves. A tree of wild apples close beside her was laden with fruit.

Brother September turned to the child with a

kindly smile. "Gather two of them," he said. Clare picked two of the largest and finest, and when she had done so, September handed back his staff to January; he stirred the fire, and ice and snow reappeared.

Laura made no effort to disguise her disappointment when Clare brought her the two apples. She ate them, however, and finding their flavour most delicious, commanded her to fetch her hood and cloak. In spite of all that her mother could say to dissuade her, she declared that she would go to the forest and gather some for herself.

"I shall find much finer ones than those you brought me, you greedy creature!" she said to Clare as she flounced away, refusing her gentle offer to go with her.

The sun shone brightly on the sparkling snow, and she took the same path that her sister had done. The robin glanced at her from his bright dark eyes, but he did not attempt to sing. He was frightened by something he saw in her face; it was the spirit of greed and envy.

After wandering about for some time, and, to her great disgust, finding nothing whatever in the way of fruit, Laura at last caught sight of the fire, with the twelve little men sitting round. Without a word of greeting, she pushed her way into their midst, and held out her hands towards the glowing embers.

"What do you want?" asked Brother January, somewhat nettled by her rude manners.

"Nothing from you!" she answered roughly, scowling as she spoke. The old man poked the fire in silence, and the sky grew dark; a heavy snow-storm began to fall, and Laura tried in vain to make her way home again, for the great flakes, dropping silently one on another, made the path she had come by impossible to tread. She stumbled at last into a great drift, and soon was buried in its depths.

Her mother grew more and more anxious about her as the day wore on, and when afternoon came, set out to seek her in the forest. She also found her way to the glowing fire, and pushing aside Brother January just as her daughter had done, proceeded to warm her hands. When asked what she wanted, she gave the same rude answer, with the same result. The old man poked the fire, and the snow fell swiftly and silently. Very soon she too was buried in a glistening bank, and Clare had neither mother nor sister left.

With all their faults she had loved them fondly, and it would have been lonely for her in the cottage now, if it had not been for her friends of the forest. As each month of the year came round, one paid her a visit, bringing flowers or fruit, or glorious crimson leaves. The white-bearded men alone came empty-handed, but these sat with her beside the fire, and told her wonderful stories of winter in many lands. In the course of time she became a good and beautiful woman, and wedded a prince from a distant shore.

THE THREE LEMONS

By Lillian M. Gask

A CERTAIN Sultan had a son of whom he was justly proud, for the young man was handsome and gay of temper, and had never been known to do an unworthy action. In the circle of the court he was the brightest star, and very sweet were the glances thrown him by the high-born ladies who served the Sultan. The Prince was courteous to them all, but he favoured no one, and as years went on, and he showed no signs of taking to himself a wife, the Sultan became disturbed.

"My son," he said, "why do you not choose a bride? It is time you were married, for I should like to see you the father of children before I go to my rest. Surely it would be easy to find a mate amidst these fair women you see around you? I should experience no difficulty were I in your place."

The young Prince looked at him thoughtfully.

"I must have something more than any of them can give me, my father," he replied, "and if you really wish me to take a wife, I will go on a long journey, perhaps even round the world, and seek a princess whom I can love. She must be fair as the morning, white as the snow, and as pure as an angel."

"Well said, my son," replied the Sultan. "I wish you good fortune and a safe return." And without more ado the Prince departed.

THE THREE LEMONS

The air was crisp with frost, and the glittering crystals of the snow threw back the radiance of the sunlight from bank to meadow. The waves that tossed and tumbled on the distant shore seemed to beckon him towards them, so he hastened to the coast, where he found a splendid vessel resting at anchor. While he was yet wondering how it had come there, and whither it was bound, invisible hands drew him on board, and as his feet touched the deck, the anchor lifted, and the ship set sail.

For three days and three nights it glided swiftly over the sea, steered by a shadowy pilot who spoke no word. On the morning of the fourth day it came to a stop beside a little islet, and the Prince was amazed to see his favourite horse issue from the hold, ready saddled and bridled. Concluding that he was expected to land, he led the horse on shore, and when he turned round to take another look at the ship, it had completely vanished.

No sign of any habitation was to be seen, and the cold was so intense that he could scarcely hold the reins. In spite of this, he rode on and on, till at last he reached a small white house that stood by itself on the top of a hill, unsheltered from the wind. He knocked at the door with eager haste, hoping for the glimpse of a fire, and perhaps some food. His summons was answered by a venerable woman with scanty hair like wisps of snow, who stared at him inquiringly.

"I seek a wife, good mother," said the Prince. "She must be the most beautiful princess in the world, and as good as she is beautiful. Can you tell me where to find her?"

501

THE THREE LEMONS

The old woman half shut the door. "You will not find her here," she said, "for I am Winter, and this is my kingdom. My sister Autumn perhaps may help you, but I have no time for thoughts of love. You will find her if you go straight on."

The Prince thanked the old lady, and remounted his horse, hoping that Autumn would at least give him rest and refreshment. After a while he found that the snow had disappeared, and that luscious fruit now hung in clusters from the trees. The stubble of the corn tinted the fields with gold, and the squirrels were busily engaged in storing nuts for the winter. A little further on he came to a small brown house beside a wood, and, again dismounting, he knocked at the door. It was opened by a woman with abundant dark hair and eyes like sloes. Her cheeks were ruddy, and her look was kind; she did not, however, ask him in.

"What are you seeking, young man?" she inquired in a gentle voice.

"I seek a wife," he answered briefly.

"Ah," she exclaimed, "then I cannot help you. My name is Autumn, and I am far too busy gathering fruit to have time to spare for such things as love and marriage. My sister Summer is full of dreams, and she may find you what you want."

So saying, she shut the door, and as there was nothing else for him to do, the Prince resumed his journey.

He noticed ere long that the grass by the roadside was very tall, and that the fields were heavy with corn ready for harvest. The air was so warm that it touched his cheek caressingly, and the sun shone down so hotly that he was fain to unloose his coat. He was very glad when at last he saw a small yellow house shaded by a group of trees. As he knocked at the door, he heard the sound of a distant waterfall, and the hope of quenching his thirst was more in his mind just then than the fairest wife in Summer's kingdom. His summons was answered by a stately woman crowned with auburn tresses.

"I am sorry I cannot help you," she said, when he had told her the object of his journey, "for I too am very busy. Hasten you to my sister Spring; she is the friend of lovers, and will surely aid you."

So the Prince went on till he saw a little green house in a bower of lilac. Hyacinths and violets, jonquils, narcissi, and fragrant lilies-of-the-valley bloomed beneath the windows, and when he knocked at the door, a little lady with flaxen hair, and eyes of soft deep violet, appeared on the threshold.

"Won't you take pity on me?" he asked her eagerly. "Your sisters sent me on to you. I seek a wife, who must be fair as the morning, white as the snow, and pure as an angel from Heaven."

"You ask a great deal," Spring told him, smilingly, "but I will do my best for you. Come in and rest—you must be tired and hungry." And to his great delight she ushered him into a long, low room, filled with the scent of flowers.

When he had feasted on bread and honey, and quenched his thirst with sweet new milk, she brought him three fine lemons on a crystal tray.

Beside them was a handsome silver knife, and a quaint gold cup of rare design.

"These are magic gifts," she said, "so guard them carefully. Return at once to your own home, and make your way to the great fountains in the palace gardens. Having made quite sure that you are alone, take your silver knife and cut open the first lemon. As you do so, a lovely princess will instantly appear, and will ask you to give her water. If you at once offer her some in this golden cup, she will stay with you and be your wife, but should you hesitate, even for the space of a second, she will vanish into thin air, and you will never see her again."

"I am not likely to be so foolish," said the Prince, "but if I do, shall I have no wife at all?"

"You must then cut open the second lemon," Spring answered gravely, "and exactly the same thing will occur. If you hesitate this time also, and she too disappears, you will have one more chance with the third lemon. Should your wits fail you a third time, you will die without a mate."

The Prince would have thanked her for her kindness, but she waved him away with a smile and a sigh, telling him not to delay. Full of joyful anticipation, he rode once more through the kingdoms of Summer, Autumn, and Winter, and when he arrived at the coast found the same stately vessel awaiting his pleasure. The wind was favourable on his homeward voyage, and in a very short time he had once more gained the precincts of his father's palace. Giving his horse into the care of a groom, he hurried into the great gardens, and when he had filled Spring's gold cup with water from the splashing fountains, cut open the first lemon. He had no sooner done so, than a most exquisite Princess appeared before him, and with a timid glance asked him to give her water.

"I am thirsty," she murmured. "Will you not let me drink from your golden cup?"

The Prince was so lost in admiration that he could only gaze at her, and with a gesture of reproach the lovely maiden vanished. It was in vain that he lamented his stupidity. Do as he would, he could not call her back again, and with many regrets he cut the rind of the second lemon. Once more the gleaming spray of the dancing fountains took the form of a beautiful girl.

"Fair as the morning and white as snow!" cried the Prince in rapture, too delighted to heed her request for a cup of water. He did not regain his senses until she also had disappeared, when he again bewailed his neglect of Spring's injunctions. With trembling fingers he inserted the silver knife into the third lemon, and as the pungent odour of the golden fruit escaped into the air another Princess appeared before him. Closing his eyes, lest they might be dazzled by her exceeding beauty, he immediately offered the golden cup. The maiden raised it to her lips with a bewitching smile, and drained it to its dregs. The Prince laughed aloud for joy; now at last he had found the bride he sought.

No summer morning was fairer than she, for the whiteness of snow gleamed on chin and brow, and her expression was pure and gentle as an angel's.

Drawing her down beside him on to a flowery bank, he held her hand and looked into her eyes.

"Will you be my wife?" he whispered, and to his delight she answered, "Yes."

When his first raptures were over, he noticed, with some disappointment, the simplicity of his bride's gown. It was of some simple stuff the colour of running water, and hung in long flowing folds round her lissom form. No necklace broke the outline of her dainty throat, and she looked so different from the maidens of the court that the Prince, who, after all, was only a man, and not, perhaps, a very wise one, felt that something was lacking to complete her beauty.

"Your robe is not worthy of you, dear love," he cried. "If you wait for me here, I will fetch you one of rich white satin from my father's palace, and a rope of pearls to twine around your neck."

But the Princess knew that she needed no ornaments to enhance her beauty, and she did not wish him to leave her. Her lover, however, was so insistent that she consented to stay by the fountains while he went home, and, more in love with her than ever, he hurried away.

Now the Princess was very timid, and as the Prince tarried long she grew frightened of being alone. So she stretched out her arms to a tree above her, and swung herself up that she might nestle amidst its branches. The foliage hid her slender limbs in their flowing draperies, but her exquisite face gleamed like a flower from a setting of glossy leaves, and was mirrored in the deep basin of the fountains. An ugly negress who came to fill her pitcher caught sight of its loveliness, and, since she had never gazed into a mirror, believed it to be her own.

"Oh, how very handsome I am!" she murmured. "I am far too beautiful to do the bidding of any mistress. I will never draw water again." And flinging the pitcher from her, she strutted home with the air of a peacock.

"Why have you come back empty-handed, Deborah?" inquired her mistress.

"I have seen my face in the fountain," was the reply, "and I am much too lovely to fetch and carry like a poor slave."

"Why, you are as ugly as sin!" her mistress retorted sharply. "Go back at once, and do as you are told."

Deborah fetched another pitcher and went back to the fountains, grumbling the while. Again she caught sight of the Princess's face reflected in the water, and again her swarthy features became distorted with pride.

"It is true!" she cried. "I am lovely as a dream. I will marry a prince, and live in a palace." With this she threw down the second pitcher, and flounced into her mistress's presence with such an assumption of dignity that that lady burst out laughing.

"If you only knew how ugly you are," she cried, when she could speak, "you would never talk such ridiculous nonsense." And daring her to return again without the water, she handed the mortified woman a third pitcher, and sent her back to the fountain.

The flower-like face of the fair Princess smiled back at the angry negress as she bent over the pool, and the poor creature grinned and ogled.

"But I am handsome," she cried triumphantly. "As handsome as a queen."

She spoke so loudly that the Princess heard her, and her laugh rang out like a peal of bells. Looking hastily up, the negress saw her in the branches, and disappointed vanity rendered her almost speechless. * * * Her mistress was right then, after all, and the lovely vision she had seen in the water was not the reflection of herself. As she stared upward with dilated eyes, there came to her thoughts of revenge.

"I will make her suffer for this," she murmured, but wreathing her wide lips in a false smile, she bade the Princess "Good-morrow."

"Why do you hide in a tree, lovely lady?" she asked her gently.

"I am waiting for my Prince, who has gone to fetch me a satin robe, and a rope of pearls to twine round my neck," answered the Princess shyly.

"Your golden hair has been tossed by the wind," remarked the negress. "Let me come up beside you, and I will make it smooth. It will not do to look untidy when your Prince arrives!"

"How kind you are!" said the Princess, and as she bent her silken head towards the negress, the treacherous woman stabbed it with a long sharp pin.

The Princess fell back, faint with pain, but before her body could touch the ground she turned into a snow-white pigeon, and flew off uttering plaintive cries.

THE THREE LEMONS

The negress took her place in the tree, and when at last the Prince appeared, bearing a satin robe and a bridal veil, it was she whom he saw looking down on him.

"Where is my sweet Princess?" he asked. "She is fair as the morning, and white as snow. What have you done with her?"

"Alas! dear Prince," answered the negress sadly, "while you were away an enchantress came and changed me into my present form. When you have proved your love by making me your wife, I shall, in three days' time, once more become a fair and beautiful Princess; but if you desert me, I must remain for ever hideous."

Although the sight of her filled him with repulsion, the Prince was a man of honour, and would not break his word. Calling the ladies who were waiting in the carriage which he had brought to convey his bride to the palace, he bade them array her in the satin gown, and, pretending not to see their astonishment and disgust, drove back with her to his father, introducing her as his promised wife.

The Sultan was naturally horrified at her appearance, but when the Prince explained to him how matters stood, he agreed that he must marry her, and hope for the best.

While the father and son talked thus together, the negress wandered over the palace, giving unnecessary orders to the servants, and making herself hateful to all. She even ventured into the great kitchens, and commanded the chief cook to prepare rich viands for her wedding ceremonies.

THE THREE LEMONS

As she issued her orders in a loud, harsh voice, she passed by the window, and noticed a slim white pigeon sitting on the sill.

"Kill me that bird," she cried, "and cook it for my supper."

Not daring to disobey her, the chief cook killed it immediately, plunging a sharp knife into its snowy breast. Three drops of blood fell from the window-sill into the courtyard, and a tiny seedling sprang from each of these. As if a fairy had waved her wand, they grew into trees of fragrant blossom, and in less time than it takes to tell, the blossoms turned into golden lemons.

Meanwhile the Prince was seeking for his bride, for since he had set himself so distasteful a task, he wished to perform it well.

"She is in the kitchen, your Royal Highness," he was informed by one of his shocked courtiers, and in going to meet her, the Prince passed under the lemon-trees. The sight of their fruit brought him a ray of hope, and gathering three of the finest that he could find, he hastened with them to his own room, where, having filled the golden cup with water, he plunged the blade of the silver knife into the rind of the first lemon.

As before, a beautiful girl appeared, and stretched out her fair hands for the golden cup.

"Ah, no!" he cried. "You are very charming, but you are not my Princess."

He cut the rind of a second lemon, and as he did so the second Princess took form before him. He shook his head at her mute entreaty for a cup of water, and she too disappeared. Then he cut

510

the rind of the third lemon, and lo, his own Princess was once more in his arms!

Great was the joy and relief of the old Sultan when he heard from the Prince that this beautiful girl was his real bride, but he listened with a frown of anger as she told them all that had happened when her lover left her by the fountain. He ordered the negress to be immediately brought before him, and, regarding her very sternly, asked her what she would think a fitting punishment for an affront offered to the future wife of his dear son.

"Nothing less than death," declared the negress, "and death by burning. Let the offender be cast into your Majesty's oven, and the great door shut."

"Madam, you have passed sentence on yourself," replied the Sultan dryly, and, shrieking with terror, the negress was led away.

But the sweet Princess would not let her suffer.

"She is but a poor ignorant woman," she said, "and it must be sad to be so ugly. Set her free, I entreat you, and let her go. This is the boon I ask you for my wedding gift."

The Sultan could not refuse his new daughter's first request, and the Prince regarded her fondly.

"I saw you were fair as morning, and white as snow," he murmured, "and now I know that you are sweet as an angel."

And though the years to come brought him trouble and sorrow as well as joy, he was indeed blest. Beloved of all, his Princess wielded a gentle sway, and he never saw the fruit of a lemon without sending a grateful thought to Spring for the magic gifts by which he had fared so well.

THE WINTER-SPIRIT AND HIS VISITOR

By Cornelius Mathews

AN old man was sitting alone in his lodge by the side of a frozen stream. It was the close of winter, and his fire was almost out. He appeared very old and very desolate. His locks were white with age, and he trembled in every joint. Day after day passed in solitude, and he heard nothing but the sounds of the tempest, sweeping before it the new-fallen snow.

One day as his fire was just dying, a handsome young man approached and entered his dwelling. His cheeks were red with the blood of youth; his eyes sparkled with life, and a smile played upon his lips. He walked with a light and quick step. His forehead was bound with a wreath of sweet grass, in place of the warrior's frontlet, and he carried a bunch of flowers in his hand.

"Ah! my son," said the old man, "I am happy to see you. Come in. Come, tell me of your adventures, and what strange lands you have been to see. Let us pass the night together. I will tell you of my prowess and exploits, and what I can perform. You shall do the same, and we will amuse ourselves."

He then drew from his sack a curiously-wrought antique pipe, and having filled it with tobacco, rendered mild by an admixture of certain dried leaves, he handed it to his guest.

When this ceremony was attended to, they began to speak.

"I blow my breath," said the old man, "and the streams stand still. The water becomes stiff and hard as clear stone."

"I breathe," said the young man, "and flowers spring up all over the plains."

"I shake my locks," retorted the old man, "and snow covers the land. The leaves fall from the trees at my command, and my breath blows them away. The birds rise from the water and fly to a distant land. The animals hide themselves from the glance of my eye, and the very ground where I walk becomes as hard as flint."

"I shake my ringlets," rejoined the young man, "and warm showers of soft rain fall upon the earth. The plants lift up their heads out of the ground like the eyes of children glistening with delight. My voice recalls the birds. The warmth of my breath unlocks the streams. Music fills the groves wherever I walk, and all nature welcomes my approach."

At length the sun begun to rise. A gentle warmth came over the place. The tongue of the old man became silent. The robin and the blue-bird began to sing on the top of the lodge. The stream began to murmur by the door, and the fragrance of growing herbs and flowers came softly on the vernal breeze.

Daylight fully revealed to the young man the character of his entertainer. When he looked upon him he had the visage of Peboan, the icy old Winter-Spirit. Streams began to flow from his eyes. As the sun increased he grew less and less in stature, and presently he had melted completely away. Nothing remained on the place of his lodge-fire but the miskodeed, a small white flower with a pink border, which the young visitor, Seegwun, the Spirit of Spring, placed in the wreath upon his brow, as his first trophy in the North.